LAND *of* JOYS

A Novel

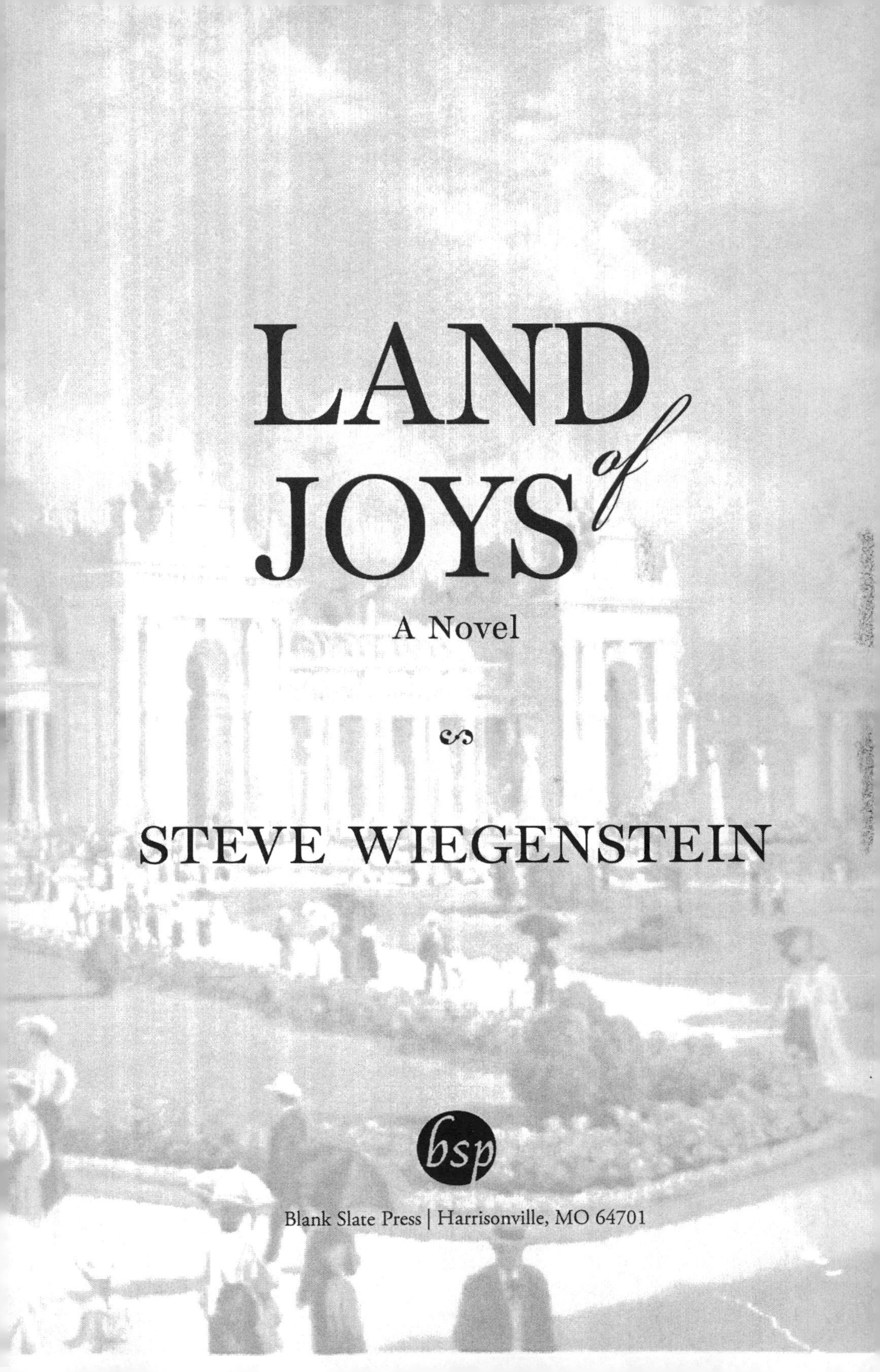

LAND *of* JOYS

A Novel

STEVE WIEGENSTEIN

bsp

Blank Slate Press | Harrisonville, MO 64701

Blank Slate Press
Blank Slate Press is an imprint of Amphorae Publishing Group, LLC
Harrisonville, MO 64701

Book 4 of the Daybreak Series

For information, contact
Blank Slate Press at 117 South Lexington St. Ste 100
Harrisonville, MO 64701

Publisher's Note: This book is a work of the imagination. Names, characters, places and incidents either are products of the author's imagination or are used fictitiously. While some of the characters and incidents portrayed here can be found in historical accounts, they have been altered and rearranged by the author to suit the strict purposes of storytelling. The book should be read solely as a work of fiction.

Manufactured in the United States of America
Cover Graphics: Shutterstock, iStock (Getty Images)
Set in Adobe Garamond Pro and Americanus Pro
Cover Design by Kristina Blank Makansi

Library of Congress Control Number: 2023939351
ISBN - 9781943075799

For history lovers everywhere

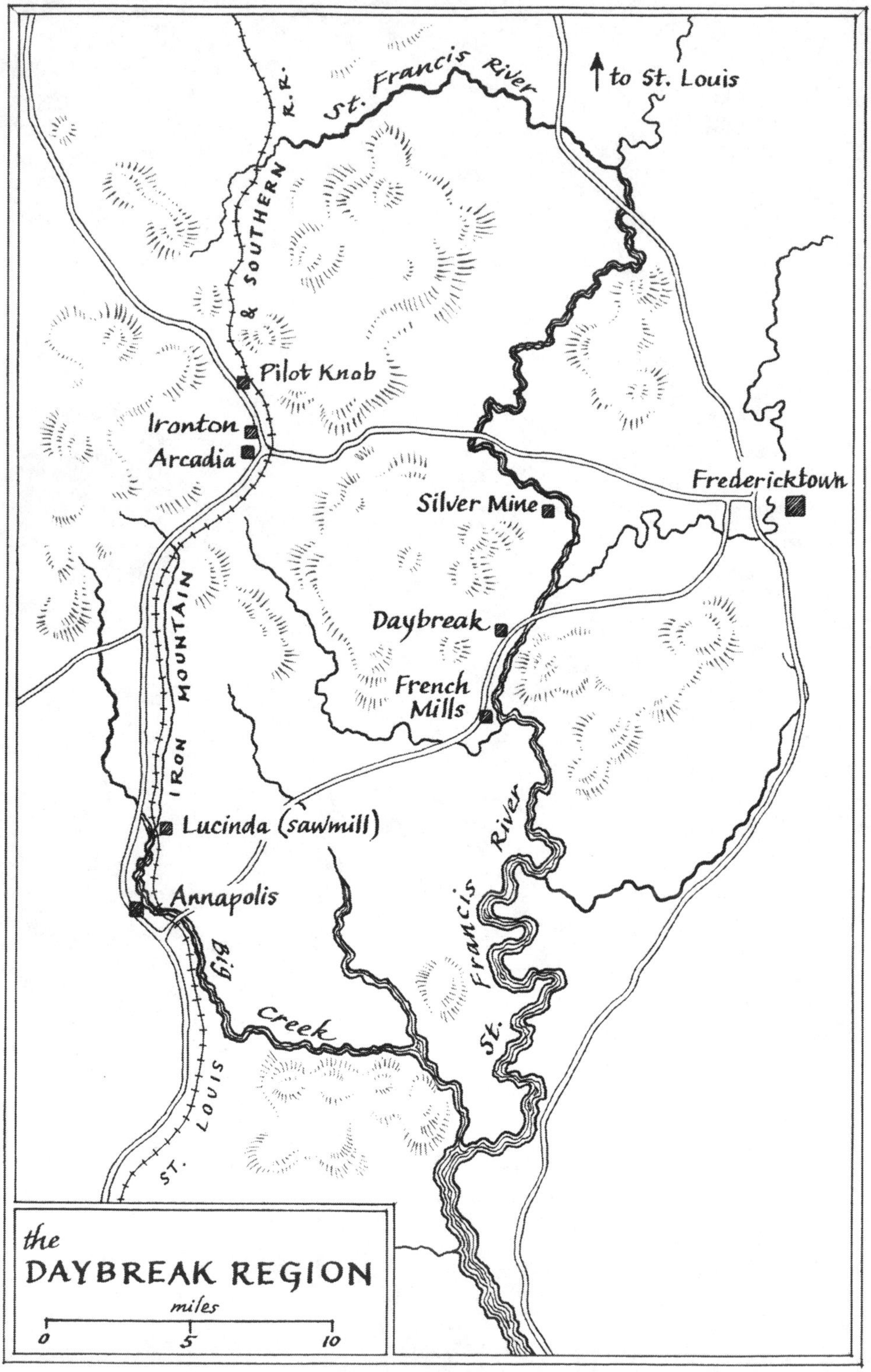

to St. Louis
St. Francis River
St. Louis & Southern R.R.
Pilot Knob
Ironton
Arcadia
Fredericktown
Silver Mine
Daybreak
French Mills
Iron Mountain
Lucinda (sawmill)
Annapolis
St. Francis River
Big Creek
St. Louis
the
DAYBREAK REGION
miles
0
5
10

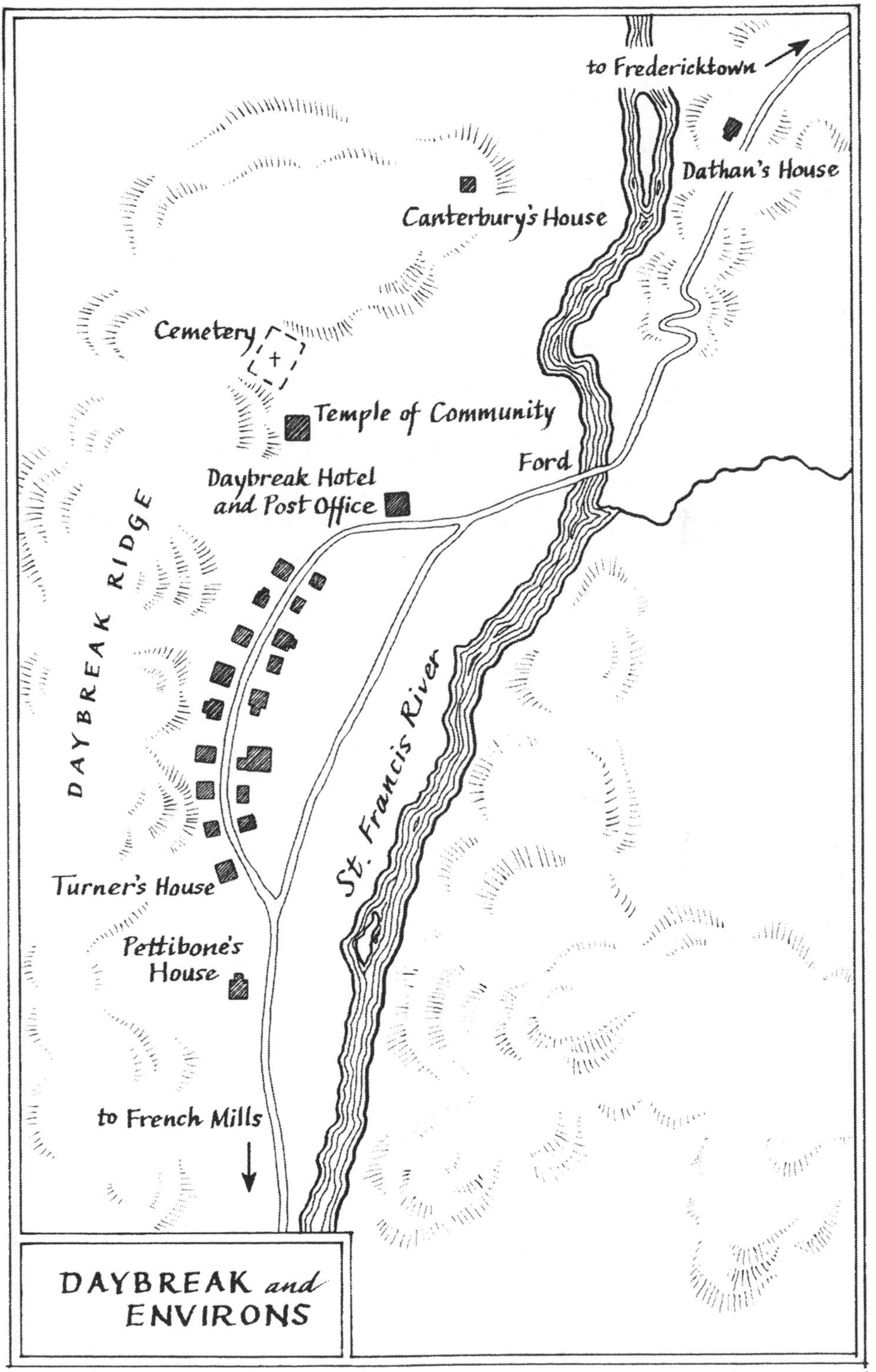
to Fredericktown
Dathan's House
Canterbury's House
Cemetery
Temple of Community
Ford
Daybreak Hotel
and Post Office
DAYBREAK RIDGE
St. Francis River
Turner's House
Pettibone's
House
to French Mills
DAYBREAK and
ENVIRONS

Just a few more weary days and then,
I'll fly away!
To a land where joys will never end,
I'll fly away!

—Albert E. Brumley

CHAPTER 1

1903

Charlotte and Petey were gathering greens along the riverbank when the horseless carriage came down the hill on the other side, in a stink of gasoline and a series of small explosions like the pops of a short-loaded revolver. Petey loped toward the ferry crossing for a better look, calling over her shoulder: "Grandma! Come see!" as if Charlotte hadn't spied it as well, the first one either of them had ever seen outside of a picture book, looking more like a prehistoric insect than a manmade thing. Charlotte clumped behind as best she could over the sprout-thick ground, but Petey, coltish, reached the ferry well before her.

Petey danced from foot to foot on the ferry, waiting for Charlotte to catch up, as the car reached the flat ground across the river and a man climbed out to inspect its tires. Charlotte finally arrived, and Petey cranked the wheel of the geared windlass that her Uncle Newton had devised so that anyone, even an eighty-pound fourteen-year-old like Petey, could cable the ferry across the St. Francis.

"Maybe you should wait to see if he wants to cross over," Charlotte said.

"He'll want to. Why else would he be here? Anyway, I want to see that thing close up," said Petey. "A little effort is a small price to pay."

That was just like Petey, headlong and inquisitive, with a vigor that delighted her grandmother as much as it scandalized the rest of Daybreak. A mechanically minded girl, more like her uncle than her dad, who could barely work a handsaw. But Adam drew from a different well of usefulness, and Charlotte had learned over the years the folly of comparison. Petey spun the wheel, and the ferry lurched from its rest into the current, inching its way along the cable stretched between two anchor trees. In higher water, Charlotte would have taken the matching wheel at the forward end of the ferry and added her strength, but winded from the dash across broken ground to get here, she held the handrail and let Petey take them across.

The young man stood beside the car, watching them approach, and as the ferry crunched to a stop in the gravel of the bank, he removed his derby and made a slight bow. "Good afternoon, ladies," he said. "You are quite a sight, out here in the deep woods."

"Not so deep," Charlotte said. "There are deeper farther on."

"I expect there are," he said. He took a calling card from the breast pocket of his overcoat and extended it to her.

WATSON KELLOGG
Kellogg Publishing Company
Bibles, Hymnals, Devotional Items of All Sorts
238 Market Street
St. Louis, Mo.

Charlotte ran her thumbnail along the edge of the card. "Well," she said. "I know this name."

"How so?" Kellogg's face showed his surprise. He was a slender man, dapper, with an aroma of Florida Water, a thin blond mustache and sandy blond hair in faint wisps that were slicked into place with great care. Fated to be bald by the time he was thirty, Charlotte suspected.

"My son's been talking about you. You must be here to see Adam. I'm Charlotte Turner, his mother, and this is his daughter Petey."

She didn't want to tell him the whole story, that Adam had been crowing all over Daybreak for the past half year about the great novel he'd been working on, about its imminent publication, about how it was going to change everyone's opinion about him. No more Adam the dilettante, the object of concealed laughter and condescending remarks. And here was the publisher in question, though from the look of him hardly a giant of the literary world.

"Petey? That's an unusual name."

Charlotte had to laugh. "Right you are. It's really Priscilla, Priscilla T., and along the way someone started calling her 'P.T.' And here we are."

Kellogg nodded and smiled, keeping one eye on Petey, who was circling the car like a cat around a grounded bird. "Look all you want, missy, but ask before touching anything," he said. Petey murmured assent but paid him little mind. He turned back to Charlotte. "Congratulations on your son's success. I've come to discuss our next venture." His tone was that of a man with big news he was itching to reveal, but Charlotte didn't indulge him. If Adam had something to tell, let him tell it in his own time.

"Success, eh? He'll be glad to hear that. You'll find him in our settlement over there."

She directed his gaze across the river, to the cluster of houses in the distance. Partway up the hillside above them sat the great gray stone building, combination schoolhouse and church, the village's landmark going on fifty years. "Daybreak," she said.

Kellogg looked appreciatively across the valley. "Then this must be Heaven Hollow." To her blank expression he added, "From your son's book."

"I'm sorry, but I don't know what you mean."

"You're not familiar with his book?"

"I'm afraid not."

Kellogg cleared his throat. "Several months ago, Mr. Turner sent us a novel. *The Hill-Billies of Heaven Hollow.* Not our usual fare. We specialize more in the directly devotional material, but it had a strong moral element and an inspirational story, so we added it to our list. Little did we know! The book has been flying out of our warehouse, and we can barely keep up with the demand."

She took another look at the man's card. "So this is your company?"

"My father's. Mr. Kellogg the elder didn't want to buy the book. But I hope to expand beyond our typical markets, so I persuaded him to give it a try." His face bore an alarmingly satisfied expression.

"Sounds like I should congratulate you, then. Come on across and we'll find Adam."

Kellogg hesitated, scrutinizing the ferry. "No offense, but will that thing hold me? And what's the road like farther down? I've already had to fix four punctures since I left St. Louis." He shuddered as he looked behind him. "This model has a gravity feed for the fuel, so I'd have to back my way up this hill."

"Help me roll this thing onto the ferry," Charlotte said, chuckling. "Mr. Kellogg, we carry two wagons at a time, loaded with grain, each with a team of oxen. This little conveyance will hardly bend the cable."

"And the roads on south?"

She shrugged. "They get worse. But there's a train stop at Lucinda, seven miles on, and you could load up there for the return."

Kellogg nodded. They rolled the auto on the ferry, and Kellogg set the brake.

"*The Hill-Billies of Heaven Hollow,* you say," said Charlotte. Petey raised the ramp, pushed them off, and spun the windlass, nudging them into the current with a grind of gravel.

"Yes, ma'am," Kellogg said. "But we changed it to 'holler' on publication. Seemed a little more down-home."

"I see," Charlotte said. She rested against the railing. Kellogg perched on the driver's seat of his automobile like a sparrow, ready to fly at the slightest disturbance, and placed his hat on the seat beside him.

"I should give her a hand," he murmured, watching Petey at the wheel.

"No, she likes to do it. Besides, it's how she earns her nickel. You do have a nickel, don't you?"

Kellogg stirred but settled himself again. "You all should post a sign that you charge."

Charlotte came near to telling him that most people had the sense to ask before boarding, but politeness restrained her. She gazed across the quiet water at Daybreak in the distance, where smoke from its chimneys and cookstoves hung in a thick layer above the houses. So Adam had written an inspirational novel. The world was rife with surprises.

"Do you know about Daybreak?" she asked. "Has Adam told you anything about this place?"

"No, ma'am. We've only met through correspondence."

"I see." Charlotte mused for a minute. "My late husband and I founded this community in the years before the war. I presume you know which war I mean."

Kellogg nodded.

"We were a pair of young idealists who thought we had found the answer to the world's problems. Or at least James did. He traveled the country giving lectures on the evils of greed and the benefits of common ownership. By the time we acquired the land in this valley, he had a couple hundred followers. We lived as a common-ownership community for a number of years."

"A utopian community, then."

"We didn't care for that phrase. But as you wish. Adam was born here early in the war, and we had our struggles, let me tell you."

"And now? How do you live now?"

"We're just a regular town. Timber company came in and broke us up some years ago. Threw a lot of money around. Before we knew it, the commune was dissolved and people were selling off tracts of land. Some of us stayed, some of us left. And of course, once the timber was gone, the company disappeared too."

"That's quite a story."

"Not exactly one with a strong moral element or an inspirational conclusion."

"No. I doubt it would sell as well as Heaven Holler." He leaned over the railing and glanced down the side of the ferry. "She's an energetic young thing."

"Hm? Yes, that's true." Charlotte, distracted, followed Kellogg's nod to Petey's furious cranking. The girl needed to let the current do the work. Once she had set the ferry to the proper angle, the water flowing over the oarboard would push it across. But Petey had never been one to adapt herself to the pace of nature.

She'd always been this way, a demon for work, and Charlotte supposed she'd had a lot to do with that. A trait that skipped a generation, or came down through the mother's line, perhaps.

"You don't talk much, do you, ma'am?" Kellogg said.

"Mr. Kellogg, I'm seventy years old. I live alone. I have lost the habit of making small talk."

And now she felt abashed by her poor manners. She leaned over the rail, matching Kellogg's posture, and studied the quiet water below. The St. Francis had never run entirely clear, but she thought it had gotten muddier through the years as dirt from the hill slopes washed down, loosened when the first wave of logging cleared out the oversheltering pines. And now the tie hackers were taking the oaks. Not that she blamed them. Twenty cents a tie was poor money, but better than none. But the pines were gone, the big oaks were going, and every rain washed more dirt and cherty gravel into the streambeds.

"I was short with you, Mr. Kellogg," she said. "I apologize for that. Have you ever been to our part of the country before?"

"No, ma'am," he said. "Never been south of the Meramec River."

"Then I imagine our roads did come as a shock."

"Yes, ma'am, worse with every mile. Though I can't say that the streets of St. Louis are any more pleasurable."

"Is that so?"

Kellogg's face puckered. "Not the sort of thing one speaks of to a lady." To Charlotte's amused smile, he added, "Horse waste."

"I believe we have some experience with that down here."

"Not on our scale! Half a million people—more than that, even—packed into a few square miles, and all the riding horses, draw horses, omnibuses, wagons, streetcars, and whatnot to go along with that. The city fathers try to stay ahead of it, but who could hope to? And the smell in the summer is something I'd just as soon not talk about." He patted the steering tiller of his automobile. "If these things catch on, it'll be the salvation of the city."

Charlotte let her mind roam while he talked. Another young man with grand notions. No harm to that, although she'd seen enough grand notions sputter.

A moment later, the underside of the ferry grated against the gravel of the western bank, and Petey sprang to lower the ramp. "I'll run and find Papa," she said.

Kellogg smiled. "Actually, I thought you might enjoy riding into town on this thing, if your grandmother approves."

The man deserved credit for charm. Petey's excited face overbore whatever resistance Charlotte might have wanted to express. She scrambled onto the upholstered leather seat while Kellogg unfastened the crank from its holder and inserted it into a hole in the side of the vehicle. After a few labored yanks, he brought the engine racketing into life, and the two of them clattered up the road toward Daybreak, leaving Charlotte to wave at their departing forms and consider the rest of her morning. The automobile would draw everyone in the village, and she supposed she should be with them. But she didn't feel like it.

She had seen innovation upon innovation through the years, each one the salvation of humanity—telegraph, gaslight, telephone, electrification, and now this thing. She didn't like to think of herself as old and cynical, but she hadn't counted any decline in human misery with their advent. Perhaps city dwellers like Mr. Kellogg were happier. Or perhaps they merely reached their fates more quickly, and with better lighting.

At the fork where the road turned off to Daybreak, Charlotte stayed on the main road, following the river as it flowed south. She would join the festivities in her own time. For now, the bright morning promised greens to gather and sunshine to enjoy, so she strolled on.

Curly dock, prairie dock, dandelion. No lamb's quarter yet, or perhaps she was looking in the wrong places. Another week, maybe two, and mushrooms would appear.

In the early days, they all dined together in the Temple of Community up the hill, befitting their principles, and a dozen of them would have been out gathering greens for the common pot. But after the commune broke up everyone started eating in their own homes every evening, lunch time too, the communal instinct fading with every act of individualism. She missed the spirit of those times, the sense of shared purpose, a shared fate.

Thoughts of her past made her wistful, so she avoided them most of the time. The commune gone, two husbands buried, the war and its privation—enough loss for a lifetime, though balanced by the daily joys and sweetness of her life, to be sure. To keep her face turned forward felt more sensible, safer. The past was dead. Why rush to join it?

But seeing Petey leap into that motorcar brightened her spirits, made her feel less like a creature of the past, a relic from whom the future slipped away with scarcely a backward glance, and more like her old self, a person unafraid of new things. Petey was part of that future, dashing ahead, and if she wanted to be useful to her granddaughter she had better leap into the unknown as well. So she would indulge herself in memory this morning, if only for a few minutes.

She passed the fields, newly sown, and reached her house at the south end of the village. Her half-filled basket vexed her, and she considered following the river farther, past Charley Pettibone's place, to find enough at least to fill her skillet. But as she paused she saw a form emerge from Daybreak, walking her direction at a quickstep, so she waited. It was Newton, and seeing him bustle toward her from this distance, pausing every hundred yards to catch his breath, made her realize that he had, in middle age, grown fleshy and soft. Too much time behind the counter at his store, not enough time out in the fields as in the old days.

Newton reached her at the yard gate, huffing. "That man and his machine," he finally managed. "You saw it?"

"Oh, yes. Petey was on it like a duck on a June bug."

Newton nodded. "Still is. Anyway, he's going to stay the night at my hotel, then I'll haul it by wagon to Lucinda in the morning to catch a railcar."

"Tires gone bad?"

"No." Newton smiled. "Didn't pack enough fuel for the journey. Said his maps led him astray."

Charlotte had to smile to herself, inwardly, at Newton's "hotel." Two empty rooms he had added above his general store when he won the post office contract. But she couldn't fault the man for keeping an eye to the main chance, unlike so many of the ambitionless souls around the village. "He's not the first ill-prepared traveler we've seen."

"Here's the thing." Newton lowered his voice though there was no one to overhear within a quarter mile. "This book Adam wrote. Have you read it?"

She shook her head. "Only from Adam's brave talk about it."

"Same here. But this man Kellogg, he brought Adam a check for a thousand dollars, and that's just for the first three months. Says they can't keep them on the shelves."

There was a sitting bench just inside her yard fence, under the big maple, and Charlotte was glad of it, for she needed to sit.

"I've gone entire years and not made that amount," Newton said.

She could tell from the pained look on Newton's face how much it irked him. "What's it about?"

Newton lifted his chin and raised the pitch of his voice to match Kellogg's languorous drawl. "'A moral tale peopled by humble hill folk, much like yourself,'" he mimicked. "And he is having a big confab at Adam's tonight. Says he has a business proposition that will benefit us all."

"Us humble hill folk."

"That's the size of it."

Charlotte let her gaze wander across the river to the patch of flat ground beyond, an irritation to her for decades, good ground for pasture or planting had she ever had the capability, but to her chagrin perpetually overgrown with greenbrier and sprouting cedars. Chaos and disorder staring back at her every morning, right out her front window. An undone thing that always felt like an affront.

So, Adam had made himself rich through unexpected means. Well, good for him. Say what one might about Adam's absent-mindedness and ineptitude in practical matters, at least he stuck to his last where this task was concerned. Adam and his notebook were the joke of the town. Adam Turner, scribbling at the plow. Scribbling while hacking ties. Scribbling at the dinner table. How she could have produced two such different sons remained a mystery to her. The industrious Newton, all push and striving, and Adam the fool, Adam the dreamer, who had made himself a laughingstock during the silver craze by roaming the hills with a swindler's contraption, hoping to find the vein, while Newton ignored the furor and acquired land, planted orchards, bred cattle and sons. And yet they were hers, and she supposed they revealed something of her own contradictions.

"Very well," Charlotte said. "I suppose we had better turn up to see what glorious future Mr. Watson Kellogg has in mind."

Chapter 2

Mr. Kellogg had come prepared. Seated at the head of Adam and Penelope's kitchen table with a stack of Adam's books beside him, he wore the satisfied expression of a schoolmaster about to embark on a familiar lesson. Petey sat down the table from her parents, and Newton and Sarah fidgeted on the opposite side. Their boys were nowhere to be seen. John Wesley, the oldest, had stayed behind to tend the store in case of late-arriving customers, and Teddy and Junior were deemed too rowdy to manage during an adult conversation. They played outside in the dwindling light. Charlotte, sitting at the lower end of the table, could hear their shouts as they chucked corncobs at each other.

"They'd better not break a window," Adam muttered. He had brought out his best suit for the occasion, perhaps his only suit, for Charlotte could not remember another. It was black with a fine white stripe in it, and with his loosely knotted scarf around his neck, his carefully unkept mop of dark hair, and his painstakingly trimmed mustache, he looked like the photograph of Edgar Allan Poe they had all seen in the encyclopedia.

"They won't," said Newton.

Kellogg cleared his throat. "If I may." He waited a beat. "First let me say what a thrill and honor it is to be here among you fine people. Mr. Turner, your book has arrived at a most propitious time."

Again the throat-clearing. "Mr. Kellogg, may I bring you some water?" Penelope asked, and Charlotte detected something mildly sardonic in her tone.

"No, no. Nervous habit. To continue. Propitious moment. We live in a sordid age, a greedy age, one in which almost anything seems within our grasp materially but our spiritual bank account, so to speak, is badly overdrawn. Your book has spoken to that longing in a way that, quite honestly, none of us envisioned. When we brought out this book, we thought of it as charming, uncomplicated, a good add-on to our usual fare. Something we could throw in as a bonus on large orders. But here we are, six months out, and the demand grows greater every week. You have tapped a deep vein, sir."

He paused again and drew a breath. "We are a religious publishing house, but we are also a profit-seeking enterprise, and for that no apologies. Your book has already made us more money than we ever imagined. But this is no time to let up, the crest is still ahead of us, and I have a plan to take us, together, even farther down the road to riches."

He had been keeping a map case on the floor beside him, and now he brought it out, a long leather cylinder with a snap top. He opened the case, shook out the map, and rolled it out on the table, holding down the corners with copies of Adam's book. It was a city map of St. Louis.

"The greatest exposition the world has ever seen, or at least better than Chicago's," he said, tracing with his finger a broad rectangle of land at the city's western edge. "The nations of the earth gathered in one place. That's the plan. You should see it now. Clearing the woods and excavating the ground, putting in streets and bridges. Shoot, they're building lakes and rivers, miles of 'em."

They gazed at the map in silence for a moment as Kellogg let their imaginations fill in the blankness. Of course they'd heard about the great fair's planning, the wrangles in Congress, the blue-ribbon committees. Who hadn't?

"All the land within the fairgrounds is spoken for, of course," Kellogg continued. "Official exhibits and the like. But here—" His finger drifted north of the street that marked the boundary of the fairgrounds. "Here will be the unofficial exhibits, attractions, amusements. And my father and I have managed to acquire a half-acre property right on the street."

He drew a breath. "Mr. Turner, your work has aroused a great deal of curiosity, not just about the setting, but about you personally. I would not be surprised if your quiet valley is visited by the occasional curiosity-seeker wishing to learn if your actual habitation is like the Heaven Holler of the book, peopled by godly rural folk who live by their word and the sweat of their brow. But I have in mind a more direct way for your readers to make your acquaintance."

Kellogg shook the map case, and out fell a smaller rolled-up sheet, a pencil sketch of some buildings on a city lot. He spread it before them.

"Heaven Holler, reconstructed. The old family cabin in this corner, the Healing Spring in the other, and a great mountain between, with the Lost Silver Mine beneath it. We'll sculpt the mountain in cement over a wooden frame, and use the interior for storage. The whole lot will be tightly fenced, with comfortable apartments on the second story of the entrance building, above the admission gate. Twice a day, *tableaux vivants* will be performed, acting out favorite scenes from the book. The sensation will be grand!"

Adam, at forty-one still oddly boyish in his demeanor, tried to hide his excitement behind a look of concentrated interest. "Very good, very good," he said. "A fine design for your exhibition."

"But here's the thing," Kellogg said. "To truly draw the crowds, we will need more than a make-believe Heaven Holler. We will need a real one."

To their uncomprehending looks, he pointed to the floor plan of the entry building. "In the foyer, a small museum. Artifacts mounted on the walls and in display cases. 'Heritage of the Hills,' I'm calling it. And behind it all, quiet and away from the hustle and noise, a sitting room with a sofa and desk where you can greet your adherents, pose for photographs, and sign copies of our special Louisiana Purchase Exposition edition, handsomely illustrated, available only within the exhibit." His broad gesture took in them all. "And on the grounds, authentic hillfolk. Demonstrating the old ways, making soap, spinning yarn."

"Mr. Kellogg, no one around here has spun yarn for fifty years," Charlotte murmured.

"Something else, then," he said, flushed with enthusiasm. "The point is, people are hungry for these things. The world is changing too fast. I've thought long and hard about the appeal of your book, Mr. Turner, and that's the conclusion I've reached. Your book offers a glimpse into a simpler time, when men lived by their word and sensed the greater power that guided their lives. We need that glimpse to remind us of our better selves."

A grin crossed his face. "And if that reminder is housed in a roaring adventure story that makes us all as rich as Midas, then so much the better."

Charlotte didn't answer. Wasn't that what she wanted, what they all wanted, when they came out here nearly fifty years ago? The simple life, the benevolent power of nature.

Newton stood up. "Do I understand that you want to set up a make-believe country town with people play-acting like bumpkins so that Adam can sell his books? Is that what I'm hearing?"

"It's a grand opportunity," Kellogg stammered. "We would charge a reasonable fee for photographs, sell handmade wares, perhaps a souvenir book—"

Newton cut him off. "This is none of my concern. I have a store to keep and a farm to run. I can't be chasing up to the city to pose for pictures."

"Think of the educational aspect. The greatest agricultural and mechanical display the world has ever seen."

Newton gave no answer but simply nodded to Adam and Penelope, then strode to the door, with Sarah close behind. The silence of their departure was finally broken by Kellogg's soft cough.

"I still hold with the educational value of this venture," he said with a glance out of the corner of his eye.

"You don't have to sell me on your plan, sir," Adam said. "I'm all in. All the nations and races of the world brought together, and us just across the way. Petey will get the education of a lifetime just being there."

Across the table from Charlotte, Petey looked as though she was about to levitate from her chair with suppressed excitement. And why shouldn't she, this knowledge-mad child? Her cousins treated her as a figure of fun, spending half the day with her nose in a borrowed book and the other half pestering the tradesmen who passed through Daybreak for the secrets of how their gadgets worked, the clock repairmen and the farm implement salesmen and the sellers of home-improvement devices. But Charlotte and Penelope protected her from their jibes and let her curiosity roam, although there were times when more conventional help around the house would have been welcome.

Kellogg continued. "I have to tell you before we go too far that this is a project we cannot finance on our own. We would ask you to come in with us as a partner, to share in the risks as well as the rewards. This is not a casual undertaking."

A more reasonable man would have inquired about the specifics of the commitment, the provisions for sharing expenses and profits, who would perform the calculations and on what basis. But Adam was not that man. Indeed he seemed to pride himself on his disregard for conventional approaches, and this moment was his chance to shine. He took Kellogg's check, and with a flourish he signed its back and handed it to him. "This is not a casual undertaking, and I am not a casual man. But when I hear a good idea I recognize it, and I will not hesitate to act. There's my down payment on the exhibition."

"Mr. Turner, are you sure?" Kellogg said. "Those are your entire earnings up to now. Hymnbooks and Bibles sell steadily, year in and year out, but novels come and go. You may never see a check that size again." He sneaked a glance across the table at Penelope, whose expression was unreadable.

Adam laughed. "Don't those Bibles you sell say something about the mustard seed of faith? This is a sign of my faith in you, sir, and my faith in this book and the ones to come. I see this as an investment not to be missed."

Penelope had said nothing during the whole exchange, but now she leaned forward and gazed intently into Kellogg's face. "Mr. Kellogg, I have a home to keep. But I will not object to Adam's going."

Reasonable enough. For although she concealed it well, Penelope had been troubled since birth, with hips that never quite joined right, and she usually stayed close to home. Traveling bothered her above all else.

That left Petey, whose face had flushed to the point that her skin was very nearly the same color as her freckles. She stood up abruptly then sat down again. "Sorry," she said. "I just had a thought that was trying to get out." Her eyes flicked between her father and mother.

"So let it out, dear," Penelope said. "I think I know what it is."

Petey was cautious. "Mr. Kellogg mentions the educational value. I think he may have a point."

Of course he did, for they had all been reading the news accounts of the great fair to come, the convocation of scientists, the assembling of artwork, the scouring of the earth for anything new or exciting. And now her father was going but her mother was not. Naturally she was wary.

"Certainly!" Adam said. "Petey, it looks like it'll just be you and me, in one of the great cities of the world. We'll have a cracking time!"

Charlotte saw the imploring look that Penelope sent her and returned the briefest of nods. Their eyes connected momentarily, and Charlotte knew that she would be back to talk another day.

For they both understood that amiable, inattentive Adam could never be trusted with the care of a young girl in the city, especially not someone as innocent and inquisitive as Petey. Not that there was any malice in the man, but simply that some people paid attention to things around them and some did not, and Adam was among the second group.

As she walked home in the dimming light, with the gravel crunching under her feet and her knees aching from the day's exertions, Charlotte thought of her granddaughter's quick mind and infinite potential. She could not deny that the experience of the fair would enlarge Petey's perspective beyond anything possible in their beautiful but remote Ozark valley.

And she knew that she would be the one who went to St. Louis to take up residence in the apartments above the exhibition to look after Petey and Adam—although she was uncertain as to who would need the most looking after. And she would be the one who would somehow manage to become, whatever it meant, a hillbilly of Heaven Holler.

Chapter 3

The next day, Watson Kellogg loaded his motorcar onto Newton's dray wagon for the trip to the railroad stop at Lucinda, once a busy sawmill town but now down to a cluster of huts and a post office that doubled as a depot. Charlotte considered riding along for the novelty and conversation, but decided against it. If Kellogg's plan came to pass, they'd have more time for conversation than they'd know how to use.

Instead, she settled down with a copy of Adam's book, left by Kellogg as a parting gift. She opened to the engraving on the frontispiece: A two-room log cabin with a shake roof and a rickety porch, an old bearded man standing on that porch, pointing a Kentucky long rifle at a cloaked horseman whose face was hidden in a flour-sack hood.

"There they are," she murmured. "The famous hillbillies." She turned to the opening page.

Jeremiah Clem paused for breath a moment, then continued his ascent up the mist-clouded eminence known to local folk as The Old Man's Mountain. The healing powers of the Old Man of the Mountains were the subject of much discussion around the firesides and spinning wheels of this remote section of the Ozarks, but no-one could tell him exactly where the Old Man lived.

"Jest hie thee up that trail yander," said an old uncle he met on the path, pausing to spit a great stream of tobacco juice before continuing. "If thy intentions are pure, he'll come find ye. The Old Man can sense these things."

"Oh, my," Charlotte said.

She flipped ahead a few pages.

Little did our mountain maiden know that looming behind her, hidden in the shadows of the mighty pines, was the man known to hillfolk as The Dark Rider, a cloaked, enigmatic figure occasionally seen in late-night glimpses, and whose intentions remained as mysterious as his origin.

"Oh, my," she said again. She put the book down.

Over the next few days, she picked up the book, read a passage, and set it down again, torn between curiosity and dismay, alarmed by the casual way Adam presented her home and neighbors—*his* home and neighbors—as some kind of cutout figures, barely recognizable, full of mythical lore and superstition, buried treasure and incomprehensible accents. But she also was compelled by the story, which drew her despite herself: pure love, utter villainy, revenge, sacrifice. Blunt, brute emotions.

Josephine Bridges, who operated the mill at Lucinda with her husband, showed up at Charlotte's house after breakfast one May morning, a copy of the book in her hand.

"Have you read this?" she demanded, thrusting the book in front of herself like it was an infant needing its nose wiped.

"I blush to say I have," Charlotte said.

Pages fluttered under Josephine's thumb. "Mountain maidens, mysterious riders, messages from beyond the grave. I've never read such malarkey." Josephine, never one to mince words, looked ready to chew glass. "He makes us look like fools, is what he does. Superstitious bumpkins who call up spirits and live on squirrels."

"Well, it's just a story." Charlotte let the silence grow between them while trying to decide what to say and how far to let the conversation go. She saw in the younger woman's face that she was doing the same. Forty-some years of living in close proximity had given them a deep well of aggravations and pleasures they could draw on if they chose. But with a mutual shrug and sigh, they let the past lie.

"I hear the thing is practically coining money," Josephine said. "Is that true?"

Charlotte turned the book over in her hands. "I guess so. We haven't talked about that." She stepped back and opened the door wider. "Come in and sit. I have a kettle on the stove, and we'll have tea."

Josephine shook her head, but flashed a smile that reminded Charlotte of the great reputation for beauty she had possessed in her earlier years. Josephine had carried her good looks into middle life, aged and broadened to be sure, but still striking, nonetheless. A fountain of gray now emblazoned her long, lustrous black hair, giving her a slightly maddened look. But Charlotte knew her to be anything but mad. In fact, her perceptions were so precise and unvarnished that she made people around her nervous. Especially men.

"Just for a minute," Josephine said. "J.M. needs me at the mill."

Josephine had a swift way of moving that made her seem to be barging into places wherever she went. But Charlotte, having observed her since she was a baby, knew that Josephine just moved faster than the rest of the world, and in so doing had made a habit of shouldering past those who failed to anticipate her direction. So she stepped back and let Josephine through, let her bang open the door on the cookstove and toss in a couple of sticks, let her rummage through the shelves to find her favorite jar of tea. By the time the tea was made and sweetened, Charlotte had settled into her chair.

"Anyway," Josephine said, handing her a cup. "We have more to discuss than your son's unexpected fame. How are you doing through all this? That man who came through last month with his automobile—"

"Watson Kellogg."

"That's the one. He seemed quite pleased with the whole endeavor. Said you could expect to see hordes of tourists in your doorway."

"Nothing of that so far, but he and Adam have struck a deal to build an exhibit at the World's Fair."

"So I heard. I think J.M. and I will try to come up and see that thing. Sounds quite grand."

Charlotte cradled her cup and contemplated Josephine. She felt a little envy for her, so abrupt and businesslike, so wrapped up in the running of the mill. She was a woman of authority for sure, a modern woman, the epitome of all the things Charlotte had aspired to in her own life but which had not been available to her a generation earlier.

"And how's the business?" Charlotte said.

Josephine puffed out her cheeks. "Between scrounging for decent timber, which is getting harder and harder, and finding decent help, which is harder to locate than timber, I wonder sometimes why we bother. But we make do, day to day."

"Sounds rough."

"No rougher than times we've had before. You know how that goes."

Charlotte nodded, and they didn't need to say anything further. Josephine's upbringing had been as hard as they come, an illegitimate child whose mother ended up marrying a brute, a man who ultimately left her permanently harmed. Josephine had never talked about whether Michael Flynn's monstrous behavior had extended to herself, but Charlotte guessed the worst. Perhaps that childhood accounted for some of Josephine's hard edges and fanatical devotion to work.

As if Charlotte's thoughts were a silent cue, Josephine jumped to her feet, her tea half-drunk. "Enough flapping my lips. If I want to be sure of daylight all the way back to Lucinda, I need to get to Newton's and load up my supplies. Time waits for no man, as they say." And with that she was out the door in a blazing bustle.

Charlotte liked work, too, and considered what she would do with the rest of her day. She'd turned over the running of her farmland to Newton and his boys, so no obligation called her anywhere; but idleness repelled her. Years ago, she'd seen a handwritten prayer that Frances Wickman, the mother of Sarah and Penelope, had scribbled on a slip of paper and tucked into her kitchen window. "Lord, let me not live to be useless," it said. She had gone home and written herself the same prayer, and she had tucked it into her small-clothes drawer, where it would only be seen by herself.

Newton and the boys would be tending the crops and minding the orchard, Sarah would be holding down the store. Petey would be helping her mother while Adam did whatever it was that Adam did. There were no sick to look in on, at least not that she had heard, and no babies needing brought into the world. So she would visit the cemetery to tidy the graves and bear flowers to the unremembered.

But first she would stop at Charley Pettibone's down the road, the last of her generation still in Daybreak, and a good man to talk to in any circumstance. She had helped Charley and Jenny with all their birthings, though in truth Jenny hardly needed help after the first, and as their children grew she had watched in amusement from her back porch as the Pettibones' house backed its way up the hillside, room added to room, the children marrying and starting their own families, but too straitened to launch their own homestead. By the time the oldest had saved enough to put down a deposit on a piece of ground, a younger one would find a mate, marry, and take over the elder's quarters, and up the hill another room would rise, until the whole array looked like a vole's tunnel reaching into the pasture. Now, as the last of the children departed, people in Daybreak wondered if Charley would demolish the additions as they had been built, room by room by room, or leave them to be occupied someday by the next generation of offspring.

Charlotte was surprised to find him up the hill behind the house with a mule-drawn dirt slip, digging out the sulfur spring that seeped into the fields.

"My heavens, look at you," she said. "The picture of industriousness."

Charley loosed the reins on his mule and let it graze while he pulled a bandana from the pocket of his dungarees to wipe his face. "Oh, I'm full of surprises, Mrs. Turner. You know that."

"What's this all for?" The hole he had dug out was deep and steep, not the ideal shape for a pond even if livestock were drawn to the muddy, rotten-egg water of the spring. Charley rubbed his face; Charlotte noticed that he hadn't shaved in a good many days.

"Ain't you read your boy's book?"

"Yes, but I don't remember anything about a giant mudhole! Maybe I missed a passage. I occasionally spend my time working, you know. I don't just sit by the fire and read."

Charley held up his hand. "I know. Thing is, in that book there's an Old Man of the Mountains who tends a healing spring. Since this fellow Kellogg says we should expect a parade of curiosity-seekers coming our way, I figured they'd need a real Old Man of the Mountains." He gestured toward the hole. "And here's the healing spring. I'm going to line it with rocks and put a roof over it, benches all around. And if they need a place to stay, well, I've got rooms to rent."

"Old Man of the Mountains, eh? Thus the beard, I suppose."

"Yes, ma'am," he said. "Gotta look the part."

"I have to say, I always felt like that spring had some properties, so you may be onto something. And Lord knows you've got plenty of stories to tell a visitor."

Charley was gazing southward, his attention drawn by a one-horse wagon driving slowly in their direction. Charlotte didn't recognize its lone occupant, who sat motionless on the seat, letting the horse choose its pace. "Maybe here's your first customer," she said.

Charley squinted into the distance. "Maybe."

They walked together to the road, Charley casting a watchful eye behind himself at the mule, which grazed placidly in the new grass of the pasture. "That load of dirt should hold him, but you never know," he said.

As they stood at the Pettibones' yard fence, Jenny came out to join them, a dish towel in her hand. She nodded to Charlotte as they waited. The wagon neither sped up nor slowed down.

When the wagon got within a hundred yards, Charlotte realized that the driver, muffled in a canvas jacket and with a large felt hat pulled down over his face, was a black man. The others recognized it at the same time.

"Well, now," Charley said. "Here's a rarity."

"What do you suppose he wants?" Jenny added.

Charlotte didn't answer, studying the man as he approached. She judged him to be around thirty, and his clothes were those of a laboring man, though not a farmer. A factory worker, perhaps, or a journeyman in some sort of trade? Hard to tell. He was muscular and clean-shaven, with a round face that glistened faintly from the heat of the day.

The wagon reached them, and the man reined to a stop.

"Hello, young fellow," Charley said.

"Hello," said the man.

"Need water for your horse?"

The man looked over the reins as if the horse had only just now appeared. "I suppose I do," he said. "It's not my horse, though. I just rented him."

He climbed down from the wagon, stiff, and took the bucket from its peg on the end post of the watering trough in front of the house. He dipped out a bucketful of water and held it for the horse to drink, bracing the bucket on his thigh. "Thank you, sir."

"Don't mention it. Where you headed?"

"Can't rightly say," the man said. His accent was soft and hard to place. Southern? Not quite. "I'm not sure where I am. I rented this rig in Annapolis and they pointed me in this direction."

"I hope you'll excuse our gawking," Charlotte said. "A passing stranger is what counts as entertainment around here."

"I can stand the scrutiny, ma'am," the man said. The horse had finished drinking, and he carefully returned the bucket to its peg. "I wonder if you might be able to help me. I'm looking for a parcel of land."

Charlotte glanced at the other two, whose faces were blank. "All right," she finally said. "What do you know about this parcel?"

The man walked to the other side of the wagon and took a packet of papers out of a worn leather satchel. "This is what they sent."

Charley reached across the wagon to take the papers, but Charlotte wasn't surprised when he merely fussed through them for a moment and then thrust them at her. Charley had never been that strong a reader. "You take a look," he said. "I ain't got my glasses."

Charlotte laid the papers on the wagon bed, which, she observed, was only lightly packed. On this trip, at least, the man was not coming to settle.

"Let's see," she murmured. A deed of trust, made out to one Ulysses S. Canterbury. A legal description, incomprehensible. The northwest quarter of some section—it looked like a hundred and sixty acres somewhere in the township. And then what she was hoping for, a marked plat map. She smoothed it out and studied it, looking for landmarks.

"You're Ulysses S. Canterbury, I take it," she said.

"Yes, ma'am."

Charley snorted under his breath. Last of the Southern sympathizers.

There it was, the river, undulating north to south on the plat map with great loops that swung out around the mountains. She traced it with her finger till she found Daybreak, and her acreage.

"Here's where we are now. You came from this direction, west off the map."

"Yes, ma'am. I see that."

She straightened up. "Son of a gun, Mr. Canterbury. If that square marks your acreage, we're practically neighbors. This plot is just north of Daybreak, this side of the river. Go to the ferry crossing and head upriver. But I have to warn you . . . "

She could sense him scrutinizing her from the corner of his eye. "What?"

"That's rough ground, ridgetop mainly. I imagine you bought this from the timber company." He nodded. "Honestly, there's not even a road in there. You'll have to clear a lane."

"You bought a quarter-section of cutover land from the company?" Charley said with a little more amusement than proper. "Tree stumps and thin soil, friend. How much did you pay for it?"

Ulysses S. Canterbury knew not to say anything back, but Charlotte could see his jaw tighten. He gathered the papers and tucked them into the satchel, one by one. "Well, I've been saving my pennies and nickels for as long as I can remember to buy up a piece of ground," he said. "I'm close enough now, might as well go see. A dollar seventy-five an acre seemed like a fair price."

Charley sniffed. "You'll have Dathan across the river from you. You can paddle across and visit him now and again."

"Who's Dathan?"

"Colored fellow, been here since before the war. Up in years now, obviously."

"What's his last name?"

"Don't think he has one," Charley said with a shrug. "Renounced his old name after the war, and I think he just goes by 'Dathan' nowadays."

Canterbury's curiosity seemed piqued by this tidbit. "I may just pay him a call." He climbed onto the wagon seat and took the reins.

Charlotte spoke up. "If you need anything, just stop by," she said. "That's my house just down the way. I'm Charlotte Turner, and this is Mr. and Mrs. Pettibone."

"Thank you, ma'am," he said. He tipped his hat. "Mrs. Turner. Mr. Pettibone, Mrs. Pettibone."

"Sure, come by anytime," Charley added. "I used to be the deputy sheriff around here. Now they call me the Old Man of the Mountains." Behind him, Jenny rolled her eyes.

Canterbury muttered his thanks and chucked the reins, clattering on with his wagon. They watched him go, his back hunched, the horse reverting to its steady walk.

"Horse seemed well tended, anyway," Charley said.

"'Old Man of the Mountains,' said Jenny. Charlotte stifled a laugh.

"I'm stove up, honey," Charley said. "The farming life has beat me down. If I can make a living by play-acting instead, you better believe I'll do it."

Ulysses S. Canterbury had passed her house and nearly reached the main part of Daybreak. "You shouldn't tease that poor man about the land he bought," Charlotte said.

"City boys, coming out here to live the agricultural life," Charley puffed. "He ain't the first and he won't be the last. Damn fools, ripe for the plucking. You couldn't grow a cedar sprout on that soil." He took a last look as Canterbury disappeared around the corner of a house. "He did right to get on out of Annapolis, though. That's pretty much a sundown town over there."

Chapter 4

Nobody knew for sure when the next family moved onto the timber company's cutover land. They simply appeared at Newton's store one June morning, an old woman, her son, and three children, while Charlotte was visiting Sarah.

"We need to start a tab," the woman said. "We're homesteading up the hill from you." She was a broad woman with ash-gray hair, grown long but tied into a thick knot in back. She advanced to the counter while the children, two boys and a girl, fanned out to explore the corners of the store, and the young man leaned against the doorframe.

Sarah didn't turn to take down her account book, but faced the woman with both hands flat on the counter, her eyes darting to take in the children's movements. "Up the hill, you say?"

"That's right," the woman said. "We had thought to trade at the store in Lance, but then we heard about you all. You're closer, and we don't mind a walk through the woods."

"So you mean up to the north," Sarah said.

"Yep. We're on the old mine grounds. Not much to look at, but the building is snug. We're making a home out of it."

"I seen that," the young man said from the doorway. He didn't seem to be speaking to anyone in particular, but the younger of the boys took a tin of corned beef from under his shirt and replaced it on the shelf.

"You're living in the old mine headquarters?" Charlotte said.

"That's right," the woman said. "Good water and plenty of room. What else does a family need?" She extended her hand. "I'm Esther Renick, but everybody always calls me Grandma Renick. That's my son Bobby and his young'uns. That's Blossom, she's twelve, and Hardy is eleven and Little Bobby is ten. Their mama ain't around anymore."

Charlotte shook her hand. "Charlotte Turner," she said. She turned toward Bobby. "I'm sorry about your wife."

"Don't be," Bobby said, still propping up the doorframe. "She didn't die, just took a hike."

Sarah spoke up. "I need to tell you, we don't extend credit indefinitely. We're friendly people, but this is a paying business."

"Tell me something I don't know," Grandma Renick puffed. "I'd be offended at such talk if I wasn't a forgiving person. You just now met me, and here you are doubting my soundness."

"I look out for my own, same as you," Sarah said. "I don't apologize for being careful when somebody walks into my store and the first words out of her mouth are asking for credit. Especially when I hear they're living on some of the rockiest ground in the county. I have to ask myself, how are these people going to make even half the money they'd need to pay back the grocery bill they'd run up? It's a reasonable question."

"We didn't come hunting charity," Grandma Renick said. "There's ways to make that patch pay. Ties to hack out, stave bolts. Firewood to sell. Bobby's a fine man with an axe, and the children and I know how to turn our hands to labor."

"All right," Sarah said, still suspicious. But she drew the account book down from the back shelf and flipped to a blank page. "Have you got a list?"

"Got it all in my head," Grandma Renick said. "Fifty pounds of flour, a bucket of lard, a side of bacon and two hams, twenty pounds of beans. Sack of sugar, five pounds of coffee. Some hard candy for the children, and that should do us to start."

Sarah had been writing it all down. "We don't have those amounts in stock. My husband will pick them up for you on his next trip into town."

Grandma Renick looked slightly miffed. "And why couldn't we just go into town and pick them up ourselves?"

"You could do that," Sarah said. She closed the account book and stood with palms on the counter, calm.

"Oh, all right," Grandma Renick said. "We'll have to bring a wagon either way. Come on."

The children trooped toward the door, but Blossom paused. "Grandma, can we take the sack of candy with us?"

Grandma Renick looked, grim-faced, at the child and then at Sarah. "Put it on our tab," she finally said. Sarah nodded and wrote the purchase into the account book, then shook a generous sackful of candy from the jar and handed it to the girl.

"Thank you, Mrs.—"

"Turner."

The children dashed outside. As the adults moved to follow, Bobby Renick paused. He was a young man, thirty or so, Charlotte guessed. He was not half bad looking, but appeared to be missing some of his back teeth, which made his cheeks sink in. To cover the hollows, he had let his facial hair grow in wild, random patches, which made him look vaguely like a muskrat.

"Want to hear something crazy?" he asked with a chuckle. He didn't wait for a response. "There's a nigger living in a tent up in the woods north of you. We passed it this morning." He laughed. "Didn't say what he was doing out there. Just living in a tent, marking off acreage. Looks like he's going to try to farm."

"Takes all kinds," Sarah said, noncommittal.

Charlotte spoke up. "We hold school in the big stone building you passed on the way in. Send the children down this fall if you like."

Now it was Bobby's turn to be circumspect. "We'll see," he said with a shrug. "Lots to do between now and then."

Then they were gone, and in the long minute's silence that followed, Sarah paced the store, straightening the shelves where the children had been and, Charlotte suspected, checking for missing items.

"You just watch," Sarah said after a while. "That woman will send the children down for her groceries, maybe not the first time, but soon. Because she knows it's harder to turn away a child when the bill mounts up." She paused, and then spoke the word they both knew was in the air. "Trash."

"We've only just met them," Charlotte ventured.

"I know you love to stick up for the downtrodden, but there are practical necessities," Sarah said, her lips drawn tight as the string on a sack of onions. "The wholesalers and the men at the mill expect to be paid on time."

Charlotte didn't want to quarrel with her daughter-in-law, especially knowing that she was largely right, so she left her responses unspoken.

Fortunately, the inquisitive Petey appeared in the door, scouting the store's interior.

"I thought I saw some new people coming down the path," she said.

"You did," Charlotte said. "A family has moved in where the old silver mine used to be."

"Any kids?"

"Three little ones. None your age."

Petey's face fell, but only for a moment. Petey didn't stay down for long, and the thought occurred to Charlotte that Petey lived a lonelier life than anyone noticed, the only girl her age in the valley, and none but her rambunctious cousins for friends. But at least she had two good parents, and a home in the bottomland, and a well for her water, unlike those kids on the ridgetop, where the soil was three inches on top of bedrock if they were lucky. They'd be hauling water up from the river every day.

Which reminded her of something.

"Petey, I need to go visit Mr. Dathan across the river," she said. "How would you like to come along? I warn you, I have a motive for asking. They will likely have chores to be done that they can't manage, and neither can I. We need a lively young sprout like you."

But Petey was already out the door and heading for the ferry. Charlotte followed, but at her own pace; the hill across the river was a half mile's climb before it leveled off, and even someone with as much pepper as Petey would have to stop a few times to puff. She picked up her snake stick where she had left it, leaning against a tree, and contemplated Petey's retreating form. Had she once been a child like that, all motion and engagement? She supposed she had, but it was hard to remember.

Charlotte had a twin sister, lost in childbirth a half century ago, and sometimes in Petey's expression, or a tilt of her head, she caught a glimpse of her long-gone Caroline. Not that they were anything alike; Caroline had been a prissy sort, given to playing the coquette, which became her undoing once she married her lieutenant and followed him to the west Kansas frontier. She didn't have the strength for such a place. Whatever Petey's future might hold, it would surely not be wasted chasing after some unworthy man.

Petey cranked the ferry across, and they started up the hill. There was promise in the bright air, a sense of possibility, flowers setting fruit on the branch.

Dathan and Cedeh's house, set back a hundred feet from the road, bore the same temporary look that it had for decades, as though someone had pitched a camp, shored up their lean-to with planks, and accumulated doors and windows haphazardly through the years, never painting anything or squaring up the corners. It was more sound than it appeared, but Charlotte suspected that Dathan kept it looking ratty on purpose, to avoid attracting attention.

He was sitting on his porch in a weathered rocking chair. "Ho, Cedeh!" he cried. "Look who's come to call."

Charlotte didn't see Cedeh, but the bustle from inside made it clear she'd been seen. She stepped on the porch and shook hands with Dathan.

"Sorry for not standing," he said. "With my knees, you'd be halfway home before I ever made it up."

Dathan had always looked old to her, even when she was a young mother and he an unexpected, and disconcerting, arrival in the community, with his long silences and uncertain origin. But over the years they had grown friendly; sometimes a smile would crack his leathery face and he would allow himself some gentle teasing. She wondered how old he really was. Seventy-five? Eighty? The deep black of his skin had developed a gray cast, the color of the dolomite outcrops they walked past on the way, and the creases of his face seemed to swallow light.

"We had a notion that we might clean your cistern today," Charlotte said.

Petey's nose wrinkled, once, at the chore ahead, but only Charlotte noticed.

"Hear that, Cedeh?" Dathan called. "Get your bucket." He turned to Charlotte. "Now what made you think of that today?"

Charlotte didn't answer him at first. She walked with Petey behind the house and pushed the lid off the cistern to peek in. As she had guessed, it was getting low, a perfect time for cleaning.

"Well, here we go," she said. She and Petey drew out as much of the water as they could and poured it into their rain barrels and washtubs. With the last gallon Petey washed her feet, and then she lowered herself in. Cedeh appeared from nowhere with a wooden bucket of vinegar water and a scrub brush.

"Good girl," she said. "Not lazy like most."

Cedeh was Creek, and her facial expressions were perpetually masked; but Charlotte felt a friendliness from her anyway, despite their minimal ability to communicate. Cedeh called a few words in Creek to Dathan, who had remained out front.

"Don't miss the corners," Charlotte called down. She returned to the porch and settled down beside him. "I was wondering if that new man from across the river had come to call on you."

"That new *colored* man," Dathan said.

"That's the one. I guess he has."

"He has indeed, and we had a nice chat." He chuckled. "Ulysses S. Canterbury. I am calling him The General."

"What did you think?"

He gave her a sideways glance and rocked back in his chair. "I think the company boys back in New York or wherever think they have unloaded a quarter-section of worthless land to an ignorant city fool. And you never know, they may be right. But they may have underestimated the stubborn-headedness of the Negro working man. He will work that patch until it kills him."

"But what will he do with it? It's timbered off."

"Oh, he's planting vegetables. Summer squash, beans, melons, anything that will grow through fall. He's going to take them to town to sell, so he says. Got a whole big plan. Living in a tent but he's going to start squaring logs for a house. "

"Dathan, he's going to starve out there."

"No, he won't."

"How can you be so sure?"

Dathan stopped rocking and turned to face her. "Because we won't let him. Cedeh and me never had any children, and now here's this lonesome young colored man in the woods across the river. Climbed right up the bluff to come see us, it's a wonder he didn't get snakebit coming and going. He's our boy until he proves himself unworthy of it, and we know how to keep a poor man's farm a-going. I'll show him what I know, and if he gets tired of beans and squash, well—"

At that moment Cedeh came out with some corn cakes hot from the griddle, different from the way Charlotte made them, softer and chewier, with something mixed in. An old Indian recipe, she supposed. Charlotte took one and bowed her thanks.

"We've lived more than one winter on these hoecakes," Dathan said. "And they'll feed more than two when need be." He struggled to his feet. "So let's bring the girlie up out of the hole, and give her a share."

Chapter 5

The first visitors arrived in late July, a timid couple from Memphis who had read the book and decided to see for themselves. Adam spent an afternoon with them, flattered by the attention, then sent them to Newton's hotel for the night. "This could be the start of something," Adam said to Charlotte, stopping by her house in the evening.

"What were they like?"

He shrugged but could not hide his pleasure at the attention. "Pleasant. Uncertain. They kept looking around as though they expected bandits to ride in at any moment."

"Can you blame them? You've got bandits and night riders popping up in every chapter, kidnapping people, burning things."

"Readers like that kind of stuff," Adam said with a laugh. "It didn't help their confidence when Charley Pettibone showed up telling yarns about riding with Jesse James."

"He didn't! The shameless old so-and-so."

"He did indeed. Lucky they're leaving in the morning, or he'd be over in costume with a pistol in each hand."

It was good to laugh with Adam, who routinely seemed abstract or inattentive. But the moment passed quickly, and as he shifted from foot to foot she knew he had come to say something.

"Watson Kellogg sent a letter, wants me to visit and see the exhibit."

"You should go. You can make better plans after seeing the place."

Adam rubbed his chin. "The thing is, Petey wants to come along. I thought you might join us. She could use the company."

So this was the beginning, Charlotte thought. Her turn as chaperone, substitute mother, or whatever one called it.

Not that she minded. She and Petey had always connected well, from the early days of keeping a snack ready whenever she appeared at her back door, to teaching her how to milk the cow, and just as important how to find the cow in the evening, her favorite grazing and resting spots out in the woods. But there was a distance between being the benevolent grandmother and being the responsible party. She would have to reset her thinking for this new role.

She paused to calculate the days ahead. An early departure to town to catch the train, most of the day in transit, a day or more in the city, and then the same for the return. No point in fussing about it. She was going to do this thing, so she might as well get in the spirit of adventure. Petey had the right approach: forge ahead until forced to stop. And if Adam saw the Fair as a great stunt to sell his book, let him. He'd lived his entire life in the shadow of the competent Newton, the leader Newton, the Newton who carried on their father's legacy. Now it was time for Adam to have his moment.

"All right," she said. "When shall we leave?"

"Day after tomorrow, if that's all right."

So she found herself packing, arranging with Sarah to tend her garden in her absence, and riding the spring wagon along with Adam and an overexcited Petey to board the train.

It was the local, creeping along from stop to stop, every siding and wagon crossing peopled. Farmers with vegetables to market, stonecutters with loads of granite for the city, families out on a visit. The train barely made walking speed before it stopped at Knob Lick. When they finally reached Bismarck to catch the main line, half the morning was gone.

As they picked up speed heading for Irondale and the bridge over the Big River, she began to hum the song, unconsciously at first, then noticing herself she glanced around and realized half the car was humming it as well. Of course they were. Who could ignore the great event of last year, the Iron Mountain Baby, thrown from this very train as it crossed this very bridge, the miraculous discovery like something out of mythology, the elderly couple who rescued the child and were now raising him as their own. The timbers of the trestle rattled beneath them. Charlotte leaned toward Petey.

"This is the bridge."

"I know!" Petey whispered back. "Do you think—" She craned to see out the window. "Do you think that's their place?"

Charlotte glimpsed a little nothing of a house, its clapboards whitewashed. "I don't know. Maybe." An odd miracle, one that was a hair's width from a murder. Had the old man found the suitcase a day later, the ballad would have been entirely different.

A mother unkind, a father untrue –

So it always was, she thought, miracles and tragedies divided only by brute chance or as some would have it, the hand of God.

"I hear people are always knocking on their door," Petey added. "Curiosity-seekers, women claiming to be the mother."

"Oh, do you now?" Charlotte gave her a teasing smile. "And what great newspaper delivered this information to you?"

Petey blushed. "Oh, you know. People talk."

"They do indeed." Charlotte tried to find a comfortable position on the slatted bench. Foolish, she knew, to try to protect her from the hard things of life, illegitimacy and abandonment. Petey was no babe, not far from womanhood, and surely she had delved into the irregularities of humankind.

Still, the impulse to shield her from all unpleasantness—from knowledge, from people, from the slaps and bruises of life—was irresistible. Charlotte glanced at Adam, seated across from them on a facing bench, to see if he was following their conversation. But he was gazing out the window at the small farms and brushy fields they passed, lost to them.

Adam had always resembled his father more than Newton had, and as the years passed that resemblance grew ever stronger, until at some point they reached a crossing place, when Adam had passed the age at which James died and there was no longer any image for him to reproduce. So now the only picture of James she could conjure was a dim overlay, someone sort of like Adam, but taller, more outgoing, and more connected to the world around him.

She mused. Perhaps she should tell Petey about James and his failings someday. He had wounded her grievously in her younger years, wounds that still pained on odd days, the way people said a war veteran's scar ached when the weather was about to change. And then he had gone off to a war, a real war, and come back incapable of wounding anyone, haunted and distractable, his fine mind a tangle of troubles. Perhaps her own story could armor Petey, at least a little, from the wounds to come.

Adam became aware of her eyes on him. "What?"

"Nothing. Idle ruminations."

He gave the briefest of nods, then returned to contemplation of the passing scenery. What was it Mr. Tolstoy said? Happy families, unhappy ones. She supposed they were among the boring happy ones. Petey was happy, no doubt. From all appearances Newton and Adam appeared happy in their own ways. As for herself? She wasn't unhappy. Perhaps she had reached the point at which happy and unhappy were no longer the proper terms.

They could smell the city before they realized they were properly in it. Enough years had passed since Charlotte's last visit that she had forgotten the odor: the factories, the stables, the array of cattle and dairy farms that lined the roads and railways leading into the city, a few big operations but mostly a patchwork of sheds and small barns, each with a couple of penned cattle fed on brewery swill, breeding, calving, and dying in the perpetual dim. She leaned toward Petey.

"I forgot to mention," Charlotte said. "Don't drink milk up here. The water's cleaner. They pipe it in from the river and clean it somehow, but milk is another matter." As if to reinforce her warning, the train slowed as they approached downtown, and out the window Charlotte saw an enormous cesspool beside the tracks, the swallower of decades of garbage and carcasses, with a ring of shacks around it.

Watson Kellogg, immaculate in the dust with a brushed bowler and a paper flower in his lapel, met them at the station and led them to a waiting three-row surrey, shiny black with red leather seats. He helped Charlotte and Petey into the last row and then climbed into the second row along with Adam, nodding to the driver.

Petey ran her hand over the bright upholstery, but her voice was disappointed. "I thought you might—"

"Broke down," Kellogg said with a sniff. "I'm starting to regret buying that thing."

"I bet I could fix it," Petey said.

"I've no doubt you could. I may have to introduce you to my machinery shop man."

The driver set off down Market Street at a trot. "I thought I'd show you the work before dropping you at your hotel," Kellogg said over his shoulder. Charlotte, weary from the trip, wished he had asked whether they wanted to see the work before resting, but the surrey was well in motion by now. So she chose to appreciate the fine padded leather of the upholstered bench and rest as best she could.

It wasn't long before the crowded street opened out into a patchwork of small plots, clusters of houses, pastureland, and isolated factories. "You just watch," Kellogg said in a pleased tone. "Next year at this time, all this will be roaring with activity. This fair's going to turn a lot of people's fortunes."

No doubt true, Charlotte mused, as their carriage passed a steady stream of men walking toward the fairgrounds. Men looking for work, any sort of work, the endless hunger of men to feed their families in a world of scarcity. A few tipped their caps as they passed, but most simply trudged on. These would not be the ones whose fortunes turned at the coming of the great fair; these men would do as they always had done, labor until there was no labor, accept their pittance, and move on.

The carriage slowed to a walk as they reached a rise in the landscape, and then as they topped it Charlotte could see the fairgrounds before them, stretching out for miles, and she had to catch her breath.

She had never seen anything like it. No, she took that back. She had seen something like it once, back in the War, when Price's army brushed by Daybreak on its way north. She had been right glad it was only a brush, because the full weight of that army was too much for any village to bear. And in the fair's building she saw that same weight, thousands and thousands of men, the equipage they required, and the mules and horses, the wagons and drays, the foodstuffs and iron and all the other things needed to make progress, like a moving city in constant need of resupply.

But here the swarm was not in search of an enemy to battle. Here the battle was with the earth itself, men in long lines with shovels and scrapers creating streams and lakes where none should logically exist, and along the banks of those streams-in-the-making hundreds of other men building—what? They looked like buildings from a dream, the skeletons of giant domes and cupolas rising above immense open spaces, a hodgepodge of cathedrals and palaces made of light lumber and wire. Some appeared to be finished but for a coat of paint; others still showed their framing as plasterers flung trowel-loads against the lath; a few so ephemeral that they would have been more at home on the architect's sketch pad than on the dusty landscape before them.

"Ain't it grand?" Kellogg cried. "By springtime this will all be finished. People won't be able to recognize it. All that waste ground turned into a paradise."

Petey could barely keep herself in the surrey, so enthralled was she with the bustle and noise. "What's that?" she said, pointing to a wooden tower in the distance.

"Pleasure grounds, other side of the fairground," Kellogg said. "That's the observation tower. 'Captive Airships,' they call it. You can ride up and see for miles."

"Oh, Grandma!" she cried. But she stopped herself out of politeness.

"Yes," Charlotte said. "We'll come out to see the pleasure grounds tomorrow, while your father and Mr. Kellogg are at their business."

Charlotte leaned back into the shade of the surrey cover. Something about the air in the city. She knew it was no hotter than back home, but it had a closeness, an acrid tinge, even out here in the open ground.

"Splendid," said Kellogg. "A streetcar runs right past your hotel. You can come straight out. But let's see how Hillbilly Holler is looking."

The driver chucked the reins, jolting them all backward as they continued down the wide boulevard, the fairgrounds to their left and a long row of new buildings going up on the right, no less fanciful than the fair buildings, but smaller and closer together. Two stories, three stories, with scalloped silhouettes and ornamental facades, vying for the attention of the casual passerby. A few of them already had signs up: Jim Key the Wonder Horse, the Temple of Mirth.

"Stop here," Kellogg told the driver. "I don't want to get too close. They'll stop working and come over to talk."

The driver pulled the surrey to the side of the street, and from where they sat Charlotte could see the construction crew, thirty men or more, swarming over the site where Adam's attraction rose. It was a tall building with a flat blank front facing the street and only one entrance, a broad double door. Charlotte understood: no one could come inside, or even get a peek, without passing the ticket-taker. The framing for a high fence surrounded the entire property, and at the far back corner an artificial mountain was taking form, heavy timbers supporting an irregular shape of crossmembers and uprights. Charlotte could imagine its silhouette rising behind the main building, a citified echo of their village and the Daybreak Ridge behind it.

"You know the best part?" Kellogg said, noticing her gaze. "We're going to have a waterfall running down it, all the way from the top."

"Oh, fine," Adam said. "Fine indeed."

"Running water through the whole place. Don't have that back home, eh?"

"Not unless you count the river," Charlotte said, peeved by the man's superior attitude, although the idea of simply turning a handle to bring a flow of water for washing or cooking into the house sounded like some kind of fairy-tale conjuring. Years ago, Josephine had agitated for them to harness the river and springs of Daybreak, to build a tank high on the hillside and run pipes down to the houses, but had been laughed out of town meetings as something close to a lunatic. She'd be pleased to hear of this.

A thought struck her. "I want a garden," she said.

"What?" Kellogg said. "We have markets all over town."

"I know that. But if I'm going to come up here next spring to show how the hill folks live, I'll want a garden."

"They'll trample it. They'll steal your vegetables."

"Not if I fence and tend it. And I'll have all the water I want right to hand." Charlotte couldn't help but smile at the notion of dipping her bucket into Watson Kellogg's grand waterfall.

"All right," he said with a sigh. "How much space do you need?"

"As much as you can spare."

Ahead of them, directly across from the building site, a single-seat gig had been parked since before they had arrived, and at first Charlotte had assumed it to be empty. But then the horse stirred, and she realized that behind the curtained sides of the gig a man had been sitting, motionless in the afternoon heat. She couldn't entirely see him, but his gaze appeared to rest on the work crew, then glance away, as if he were watching but not watching. "Who's that?" she said to Kellogg, nodding toward the gig.

"Supervisor. Name's Langland."

"Should we introduce ourselves?"

His voice was curt. "No. He's not our sort. I'm told he's a bit of a rough. When I need something, I go through his employer."

Then the gig stirred again and the horse started toward them, a fine big bay of easily fourteen hands, well-muscled and shiny. As it passed, the driver leaned out to tip his hat. They looked each other full in the face.

He was a large man, filling the seat of the gig, and judging by the way he had folded himself into the seat was well over six feet tall. His face, broad and florid, bore the traces of a smile in the center of his lips, but the corners of his mouth remained downturned so that the smile seemed to combine with a look of distaste. He had an unexpected elegance in his dress for a construction supervisor, a wide silken tie and a gold pin across his collar. And the tip of his hat revealed a rich wave of well-oiled black hair.

"I've seen my share of roughs. This one looks pretty dandified to me."

"I'm just telling you what I was told," said Kellogg. "I hear he's not one to mess with."

He was the sort of man one might well have called handsome, and indeed Petey giggled a little at his accentuated politeness. But his look was emotionless and appraising, the look of a cattle buyer viewing a potential purchase.

She had seen men like him before in her life, men who looked at other human beings with that same dead gaze, and she knew why the builders had been scurrying in such great haste. With such a man for an overseer, fear was a constant co-worker. And she knew that in his idle gaze and polite greeting, they had all been seen, measured, and recorded.

Chapter 6

Charlotte kept her promise the next day, riding the streetcar with Petey to the Highlands, where they ascended the Captive Airships, not airships at all but observation cars hoisted on pulleys to the top of the tower, and indeed they could see for miles across the countryside and into the city, and more important into the fairgrounds across the street, giving them a sense of scope. And the scope was hard to grasp. Buildings as large as a good-sized pasture, monumental statues gleaming white in the sun, and to their left a broad, rolling acreage, set to become the Philippine exhibit, or so said a woman beside them in the car. The woman shuddered a little as she spoke of it, lowering her voice to speak of the primitive tribesmen who would be imported to people the various villages and glancing nervously at Petey as she whispered the story she'd heard, that some of these people spent their entire lives in a state of total nakedness, cavorting about the forest in the costume God gave them. "Don't know how they'll keep order," the woman murmured.

At dinner that evening, Petey could not stop talking about what they had seen. A boy on the street had been handing out placards, and she read it aloud twice. "I bet Uncle Newton will want to see the Palace of Agriculture," she declared.

"I expect he will," Adam said, unperturbed.

Charlotte held her tongue. She couldn't deny the excitement of the thing, the grand scale of it all, but something disturbed her about it as well—the gangs of men building enormous structures out of steel and plaster, the conquered people paraded as if in a Roman triumph. It was all too imperial, too uncomfortably large. Perhaps farm life had accustomed her to a smaller scale of existence.

On the return train, Adam, who had been out late with Watson Kellogg the night before and smelled heavily of cigars, fell asleep as soon as they cleared the station, despite the to-and-fro yanking of the cars on the unevenly bedded rails. Petey sat pensive, gazing out the window in unaccustomed silence. Charlotte let her muse. As they waited on a siding for a freight to pass through, Petey finally spoke.

"With all these books Papa is selling, I reckon we're going to be rich, or something like it," she said.

"Something like it."

Petey considered. "Then I shall have to think of a worthy use for this money in case it ever comes my way."

Charlotte suppressed a smile at the girl's simple benevolence, but her words also brought a shiver. She sounded just like her late grandfather, idealistic and earnest. How long ago had it been now? Fifty years, just about. They had come out to the valley with a group of followers, some rudimentary ideas for social improvement, and the enthusiasm of the uninformed, ready to change the world by force of example. The village of Daybreak, no longer a grand experiment in radical equality, still bore the marks of its origin. Come to think of it, she had noticed Petey leafing through James' tract *Travels to Daybreak* a few weeks ago, taking care not to bend the brittle pages.

"I'm sure a use will suggest itself."

This answer seemed to satisfy her, and she returned to scenery-gazing. Charlotte herself had been an inward child at times, given to flights of mad fancy and moods of gloomy introspection in quick succession, though with a frivolous sister to tend, she usually kept her moods concealed. So Charlotte didn't mind giving space for her granddaughter's musing.

From the depot in Fredericktown they hitched up the mare and headed for home, and with every mile Charlotte felt increasingly strange, as if she were traveling backward in time. Lanterns powered by electricity, water flowing into the kitchen basin at the touch of a finger—these were not the someday miracles to be celebrated at the fair, but everyday conveniences in the lives of ordinary people. Would they ever experience such things in their lonesome valley? She couldn't imagine it. And when she thought of the marvels being projected for next year's fair, telegraphs without wires, human voices stored up and placed on a shelf like books, she felt even further behind. She watched Petey study her placard for the hundredth time, and the thought rang in her ears: *We are going to lose this girl to the city.* And then a smaller, echoing voice that she tried not to hear: *Perhaps that is for the best.*

Back in Daybreak, Adam drove the wagon to Charlotte's house to let her off, while Petey hopped out to show her cousins the souvenirs and treasures she had brought home. Charlotte fussed a little at the special trip to her door but was inwardly grateful. She was ready to wash her face and go to bed.

In the morning Charley Pettibone stopped his horse outside her fence, his beard grown out to the point where it was clearly something intentional and not merely oversight or inattentiveness. "Had two more people looking for Heavenly Holler while you were gone," he called. She sipped her coffee on the porch, an indulgence on what was shaping up to be a hot late-summer day, but one she was not about to surrender.

"That's Heaven Holler," she called back. "If you're going to cash in on this thing, you should at least get the name right."

"Yes, ma'am," Charley said with a light shrug. "I can always count on you to keep me on the straight and narrow. Which reminds me, can you come help me paint my sign later on? I have a mind to put up a sign."

"What do you need me for? Your boys can read and write."

"Oh, I can read fine. It's the spelling that throws me. Throws the boys and Jenny, too. Ain't none of us right spellers." Charley was dressed for travel, in canvas pants and heeled boots, with some empty sacks thrown over his saddle bow.

"All right, I'll come by. You're at it early. The businessman's life must suit you." She felt a little guilty at teasing him, but not enough to stop.

He gave her a sheepish look. "My lodgers need some provisions. The kind your boy don't carry."

So that was it. Off to town to fetch whiskey, which Sarah adamantly insisted she wouldn't stock in the store. Charlotte took another sip of coffee. "You'd better get a move on, then."

His face took on the look of sly delight it always wore when he had news to share. "Oh, I don't know. Grandma Renick and her boy have set up a little operation. First couple of batches were halfway rough, but they seem to have gotten their recipe figured out. Good price and half a day's ride closer."

"Grandma Renick? Up at the old mine?"

"The very one." He grinned into her pause. "Come now, you don't have to frown so hard."

Charlotte tried to lighten her mood. She was no abstainer, but had seen enough harm caused by drunkards to last her a lifetime, especially the kind of man who would ride out into the countryside in search of a jug. "Sorry."

"I know, wine is a mocker, strong drink is raging."

"Charley Pettibone! Two Bible verses in a single conversation. I need to go lie down."

"Two Bible verses and a whiskey run, comes out about even, I'd say."

Charlotte laughed. "Say, what's this I hear about you telling people you rode with Jesse James during the War?"

Charley scratched his beard thoughtfully. "I can't say I didn't. I rode with some hard customers in the War, and we didn't always exchange calling cards. So I'd say it's pretty likely I did, at one time or another."

This recollection made them silent, for Charlotte knew that Charley had indeed ridden with hard men, and been one himself, in ways that neither of them wanted to revisit. But Charley brightened in an instant. "But enough of old times. Tell me about the great city, and the coming fair!"

Charlotte had reached her dregs, and she tossed them off the porch. "For that, you'll have to get off your horse. This subject requires a true conversation."

"Very well," Charley said. "Tell me about it when you help me paint my sign. By then I'll be able to offer you a nip."

"No thanks to that. I've never had a taste for corn liquor and don't care to try to develop it now. But a good talk is never unwelcome."

"All right, then." And with that he was off, relaxed in his seat as always, though she knew that his comfortable slouch concealed a life's worth of aches and pains. Never one to show unease, that was Charley.

And what would she tell him about the fair? What would she tell any of them? She hadn't settled her own thoughts yet, much less gotten them ready to share.

Meanwhile, there were weeds to pull, beans to harvest. High in the trees, a cicada began its late-summer grind. Charlotte felt a kinship to that cicada, up there grinding out its brains to some uncertain purpose and making a sound that was perhaps its great song of songs, but which to other ears was merely a racket. Not everyone could create the song of the lark. But the cicada sang all the same.

Chapter 7

Summer slid inconspicuously into fall, the beans came to an end, and apples ripened in Newton's prize orchard. Sarah's joke that Newton cared more about his apple trees than about his family met with a stammered deflection from him and a wry wink from everyone else; of course he cared more for his family in the abstract and ultimate sense, but in any particular moment he would no doubt have chosen to spend his time plucking beetles off the leaves or pruning stray branches.

Charlotte liked to flatter herself that Newton inherited his attitude toward work from her. For although James had been a man of great energy, he loved more than anything the launch of a new project. Once the tasks became predictable or repetitive, he was off to the next new thing, leaving others to pick up the details of the last one or let it languish. Newton's steadiness—his conventionality—would have been antithetical to James, the sort of slavery to routine he had rebelled against all his life. But Charlotte liked the rhythmic progression of everyday tasks, weekly and seasonal. They were comforting. Laundry on Mondays, persimmon-gathering after the first frost, hog-butchering on the first clear, cold day after Christmas.

And up the road one morning in her wagon came Josephine Bridges, who persisted in shopping at the Daybreak store even though their mill at the Lucinda whistle stop was closer to Annapolis. Charlotte suspected she came to Daybreak for sentimental reasons, to return to the scenes of her childhood and visit the people she grew up with, although Josephine's reputation for gruff unsentimentality prevented her from saying so and Charlotte from suggesting it. But Josephine always came inside and took off her hat.

As usual, she got right to the point. "This man Canterbury."

"What about him?""He's come looking for a job. Says you know him."

Charlotte, pouring tea, paused. "Well, not in the same way I know you, of course. But yes, I know him. He's been around all year."

"And?"

"Determined. Hard-working. And—"

"Not inclined to take any man's guff, white or black."

"Yes."

They left the implication unspoken. It was obvious enough: taking a hard-nosed black man into a mill crew would be courting trouble. Josephine cleared her throat.

"But a hard worker, you say."

"I doubt you would find anyone to match his pace. You should go up on the ridgetop and see what he's done with that patch of scrub."

Josephine wrinkled her nose. "I don't want to encourage him into thinking a decision has been made. J. M. wants to hire him, naturally. Just like him, to believe that an earnest attitude can solve all difficulties." But Charlotte heard the note of pride in her voice. "It might work out. This is a new venture he's planning." She lowered her voice, a little too dramatic for Charlotte's taste. "Matches."

"Matches! But isn't that dangerous?" They'd all read the news accounts, the factory fires, the workers disfigured by phossy jaw.

"There's a new process, safer. Keep this to yourself for a while. There's considerable outlay involved if we decide to go ahead."

"But matches, of all the things to manufacture. I don't follow."

Josephine barked a short laugh. "Two things in endless supply around here—scrappy pines and men in need of work. Put 'em together and you've got yourself a matchstick factory."

"That sounds a little cynical."

She nodded with a barely perceptible shrug. "It happens when you have a payroll to meet."

So it did, Charlotte thought, the pressure of the necessary, inevitable and unrelenting. Meet the payroll, feed the young'uns, tend the home. What was it someone had said to her once? *Eat. Struggle. Mate. Die. Put off dying for as long as you can. Take pleasure where you can, for pleasures are always cut short. Defend your ground.* The burdens of existence hardened them all.

"Well, don't blow yourselves up," Charlotte said.

Josephine dismissed the thought with a wave. "If we do, I guess you'll hear it. Well, can't stay to jabber." And flourishing her purchase list she turned, abrupt as ever, and walked out toward her wagon to head on to Newton's store.

Charlotte watched her down the path, her hair pulled back into its long braid, her arms swinging, the march of someone ready for all eventualities. Defiance of convention, that was Josephine from the start. A troublesome child, a sharp-tongued youth, then as a young woman someone whose impossible beauty should have drawn everyone to her, but who instead carried with her an aura of disruption, an air so intense it was almost audible, a crackling hum like the sound of a swarm of hornets flying through the woods in search of a place to nest. Part of that aura came from the obsidian edge of her observations, always truthful but never blunted by kindness. And part came from the singular tale of her origin, known to all at some deep level but never discussed, not even in whispers. Illegitimacy. She bore the mark like a badge, daring anyone to speak of it, and no one ever did. Josephine's birth had nearly broken the colony in those early days. Josephine, the unsanctioned child of pretty young Marie Mercadier and Charlotte's own husband, James.

Forty-odd years, and she still could not think of that time without pain. Even the freethinkers of the community had been strained to the breaking point by the revelation. Charlotte knew that many people expected her to feel shame over the incident, but she never did. Had she driven James from her, had she ever spurned him when he reached for her? She had not. Her other burdens left no room for the weakness and fault of her husband. Long ago, she had made her peace with Josephine—it was not the child's choice to be born the way she had been born—but the sight of her still felt like a needle in the palm. Never had she been more relieved to see someone leave Daybreak than when amiable J.M. Bridges from faraway Delaware had arrived in the valley, somehow managed to pierce Josephine's armor, and persuaded her to marry him. The little mill town of Lucinda, west over the hills, was not far away, but it was far enough to provide Charlotte with respite from the awkwardness of daily encounters.

But enough of that. It was a fine fall day, with work to be done. What further need was there to brighten one's perspective? All she lacked was a direction in which to point herself.

Standing in the doorway, watching Josephine's wagon rumble north toward the main part of Daybreak, Charlotte remembered an old joke from the early days. A band of pioneers passes through town, and as they stop at the general store they brag to the proprietor. "Our group is perfectly organized," they say: "This man will start a blacksmith's shop, this man a tannery. This man will operate a grist mill, and his wife a bakery. Every member of the party has a place."

"I don't know," says the storekeeper, pointing to a decrepit old man in the back of a wagon. "What's his job?"

"Oh, him?" cries the leader. "He's going to start the cemetery!"

Before we inhabit the graveyards, Charlotte thought, we must tend them. She went to the shed and gathered her tools—a rake, a pruning hook, a bucket and brush. And before leaving home, in a half-formed notion she added a jar of blackberry jam from a batch she had cooked up the month before and a loaf of bread.

The cemetery was on the north end of Daybreak, past the big stone Daybreak School, which Charlotte always remembered as the Temple of Community from the early days. Vestiges and remnants were everywhere. The building as it is, the building as it was, the space that existed before there was a building.

All her life she had insisted on looking forward, not behind; dwelling in the past was a sure path to despair, for its glories were gone while its regrets remained. Yet in the late months she found herself thinking backward more often, to the losses and sorrows of her life, betrayal and death, partings and war. Why had she fallen into such a state? And now to court these feelings by choosing to spend half a day in the cemetery. No wonder her sons shook their heads and sighed in her direction from time to time. She was three kinds of stubborn, just like they said.

But she had made up her mind, and as she walked through the village, she made a point of greeting everyone she met with a cheerful word and a wide smile, as if to remind herself that even the most ill of feelings could be willed away with enough effort. She had to stop once as she climbed the slope behind the schoolhouse, a concession to age she resented a little.

In the graveyard she started with the pruning hook, clearing out the clumps of overgrown grass around the tombstones. Newton had been up here with the sickle mower in the summer, and the long swaths of cut grass lay wet and brown in helter-skelter piles. Too bad he hadn't returned and raked it for hay.

The bittersweet she had planted so many years ago had twined up into the trees, died out, regrown from its roots, spread into the woods at the edge of the graveyard, and migrated into other places, till she could no longer say if it was her bittersweet or not. That was all right. The price of planting something that would outlive you was that it would take its own shape and become unrecognizable, even to yourself.

She dipped her brush into the bucket and scrubbed the lichen off James' tombstone. Tenacious stuff, this, tempting to moralize upon. Lessons from nature. Small and low-growing, persistent, untiring. Just the sort of metaphor James would have enjoyed spinning in one of his lectures, or an article for the *Daybreak Eagle*. The triumph of the commonplace. James was always one to seize on correspondences.

A dozen yards down the hill, the grave of her second husband, Ambrose Gardner, married twenty-plus years after James' death and widowed ten years later. Ten good years Ambrose gave her, and she gave him in return. Which was better, the flush of youthful love or the sweetness of love found in later years? Hard to say. Loss intertwined itself into love like bittersweet into the hackberries that supported it, until at some point they seemed like one tree with two sets of roots, impossible to separate without destroying it all. No moss on Ambrose's stone yet, just a little discoloration from the leaching of minerals out of the limestone.

And who would tend his grave when she was gone? He had no one but her. And who would tend hers? Not that it mattered. But she remembered her younger years, when her sister had died, and how the thought of her uncared-for grave out West had sent her mother into something like madness. There was something to it, the knowledge that one's bones would rest in a civilized place, where people made the effort to brush off the moss and plant peonies.

Up the hill came the answer to her question, her daughter-in-law Sarah, who resembled her in few other ways but who at least felt the same profound pull, the tie that binds. She was carrying a basket that no doubt contained some of Newton's prize apples and God knew what all else. Sarah did not stint.

"Saw you up here," Sarah said as she drew near, puffing from the climb. "You are some kind of mind-reader. I've had this job in my head I don't know how long, but never got to it."

"I'd guess you've got plenty to think about."

"True enough, but no excuse." She set down her basket and took out a pair of grass shears. "Looks like you've done these. I'll start with Mama and Papa's."

Back up the hill, close to James. Old John Wesley Wickman and his wife had been original settlers, with Frances a great friend of Charlotte's through all their troubles, and Charlotte vividly remembered John Wesley placing a split-log bench up here after Frances died. In the evenings he would sit on the polished cedar bench and muse. He could be heard talking to her all the way down the valley, sometimes, his presence a fixture until the day came when old age took his mind from him and he could no longer be trusted to come up here on his own. Since that time the bench had deteriorated, and now it was a pitted crumble, indistinguishable from the ordinary branches that fell from the trees and rotted in the ordinary way. Charlotte picked up a chunk and tossed it into the nearby undergrowth.

Next to Frances and John Wesley were two small humps with wooden crosses driven into the ground at one end. Charlotte and Sarah knew, because of course they would, that these marked Mary and Lucy, Sarah's older sisters, swept away along with so many others in the cholera that ravaged Daybreak in its first year, before Sarah and Penelope were even born. Sarah gave one of the crosses a gentle tug with two fingers.

"I need to get to the blacksmith and have some permanent ones made," she said. "After we're gone, no one will know they're here."

Charlotte nodded. "Mary and Lucy were quite a pair. Lively girls, full of fun, maybe even a little too full of fun now and then."

Sarah went to her basket, and to Charlotte's surprise, removed a large bouquet of cut wildflowers, tied together with ribbon. Charlotte recognized them: tall bellflowers and blue lobelia from the bottomlands, asters from the rocky slopes, and a few sprays of goldenrod from the roadside, a bouquet gathered by someone who knew where the best wildflowers grew and who was willing to make the effort to get them. Sarah laid them between her parents' graves and brushed away a tear. "I'm a sentimental fool sometimes," she said with an embarrassed laugh.

"Not in the least. It's the task of the living to remember the dead, and to do so with love when we are able." Then Charlotte smiled at herself. "I'm full of high sentiment myself today."

Her comment lightened the mood, and the two of them stood back to inspect their work. "Not bad," Sarah said at last. "It'll keep things clean till Decoration Day, when we'll have more help. Shall we walk down together?"

"You go on. I want to stay a little longer."

Sarah nodded and gathered her things. With a final pat on her father's tombstone, she set off down the slope. "And leaves the world to darkness and to me," Charlotte murmured into the quiet.

One more grave to dress, where the bittersweet vine originally rooted. Now who was the sentimental fool? Adam Cabot, her long-ago sweetheart, with whom she had exchanged no more than a half-dozen mad kisses. But each one remained chiseled into her memory far deeper than letters on stone. She scrubbed off the moss and trimmed the weeds.

Would she be happier now if the clock of her life had jumped a notch, way back when, and she had met and married Adam before she had ever fallen under the great and loving sway of her James? Who could know? And of course there was Adam's irresistible attraction to duty, which led him to throw away his life in the great war before it had properly begun. No altered future there. Adam was a man born to die young in a large cause, and he was lucky to have a tombstone for someone to scrub. Better this than some muddy trampling like the ones she'd read of, with hundreds of men thrown into a trench or sinkhole, with no place for loved ones to visit and remember.

She shook off the chill and headed uphill into the woods, for the task she had been intending all along.

The climb was hard. But it had always been hard. As a young woman she had prided herself on making it in one unbroken climb, but those days were past, and there was no shame in stopping for breath. So she took her time, pausing every fifty feet, until she reached the level ridgetop and could follow the old footpath that had been better worn in the old days, when the mine was in operation.

How far was it along here to Canterbury's patch? A half mile? She missed some of the old landmarks but had no fear that she could find the place. All she had to do was bear north and stay on the ridge.

Sure enough, after a few hundred yards she caught the sound of an axe. She followed it until she reached a clearing, high ground that sloped abruptly to the river at the far end, with a small cabin—barely more than a hut—halfway to the edge and the makings of a fence around the clearing's perimeter. Ulysses S. Canterbury was chopping a pile of wood as if he had a grudge against every stick, some headed for firewood and some the length of fence rails.

"Hello!" she called.

Canterbury, startled, whirled and grabbed his coat from a nearby post. Whatever else one might think of him, it was nice to see a man who observed the proprieties.

"Ma'am," he said, uncertain.

Charlotte put on her broadest smile to alleviate his uncertainty. "I've not been much of a neighbor. Thought I'd come by and say hello."

"Well. Not much here to see yet." His wave encompassed the whole of his property, the river valley, the world in general.

"It takes time to build a place for yourself. Especially on your own."

He nodded briskly. "I'm not sending for the missus until I have a place fit to bring her to."

"Oh! There's a Mrs. Canterbury."

"Yes, and a Canterbury Junior, too. I'll show a picture sometime."

"Somehow I'd pictured you as a single man, though I don't know why."

Canterbury shrugged. "Half of what we know is a guess, and the other half wishful thinking. Not you, personally. Just making a general observation. No offense intended."

"None taken. And not only did I not take you for a married man, I wouldn't have guessed you to be a hard-nosed philosopher." She took the bread and jam from her basket. "But to the purpose of my call. This jar has been sitting in my cupboard long enough. I thought you might like something different for your breakfast."

He took the jam from her, holding it as if it were something from across the ocean, rare and precious.

"Ma'am, my breakfast has been sparse to nonexistent these days. I am more grateful than I can say."

The hardened expression had dropped from his face and, for a moment, he seemed near tears. Charlotte, awkward, would have liked to turn and leave, but that would have felt abrupt, even rude, just to hand off the jar and depart. So she waited, feigning an interest in the horizon while she watched him out of the corner of her eye. And as she gazed around herself, naturally, she saw more to be interested in without pretending. Wasn't that always the case? The more you looked, the more you saw.

The land Mr. Canterbury had bought was rough ground indeed, six inches of clay soil atop the granite, and no amount of tending and cultivation would ever change that simple state of affairs. He wouldn't be the first homesteader to work himself to death on an unforgiving patch of earth, though having company was surely no comfort in such a condition. Past his cabin, the slope dropped sharply toward the river in a tumble of cedars.

"You must get some fine sunrises up here," she said.

Her words brought him back from whatever distance he had retreated to. "Please," he said. "Come and sit. My mother would smack my bottom to see me letting a lady stand in my yard."

He dashed into his windowless cabin and brought out a chair. He placed it on a level spot and ran inside again, emerging the second time with a dipper of water. Charlotte sat in the chair and drank, thankful. She hadn't realized how thirsty the climb had made her.

"How long have you been married, Mr. Canterbury?"

"Three years. Got married as soon as I left the Army."

"Oh! So you were a soldier?"

"Yes, ma'am. I signed up when all the excitement started with Spain." A cloud fleeted across his face.

"Young men and excitement," she said.

He nodded. "I figured it was the best chance for a man of my complexion to see the world."

"And did you?"

Canterbury, meditative, took the empty dipper from her hands and rested it upside down on a piece of cordwood. "I saw all I care to. They sent me to the Philippines. And if you don't mind, that's all I'd like to say on that subject."

Charlotte felt a sympathetic ache. Another generation of young men dashing off to find adventure and returning with a wound they could hardly even describe, much less heal. As if a wound could be healed by covering it over.

She wanted to tell him that she, too, had been through war and knew its costs, that her husband had come home damaged and mute, pursued by troubles he could never bring himself to speak of, and that after his early death she had found her second husband doing what Canterbury himself was attempting, a retreat to a rocky hilltop in an attempt to quiet his mind. She reached out to pat his hand. He flinched but did not pull away.

They sat for a moment, then Charlotte remembered her conversation with Josephine Bridges earlier in the day. She tried to think of a tactful way to broach the subject.

"I expect you've figured out by now that farming is hard way to earn a living," she ventured.

Canterbury's laugh was rueful to the verge of bitterness. "You could say that," he said. "You could probably even say that the land agent saw an ignorant and foolish man coming from about a mile away and sold him a patch of ground that a goat couldn't live on. But that is no matter. My name is on the title, and I will make do as I can."

"From the desperate city you go into the desperate country and have to console yourself with the bravery of minks and muskrats."

He looked at her quizzically. "What's that?"

"Oh, just something I read in a book once. Don't know what made me think of it. But I know what you mean about making do. Ownership is no trifle. I've had to fight to keep my land more than once, and would do so again. We'll do about anything to keep what is ours." Charlotte stood up. She didn't want to descend the ridge in twilight, and the visit had gone on long enough. "But if you find yourself in need of outside work to keep your books balanced, I may have a suggestion or two for you. The mill at Lucinda may be hiring soon. It's run by good people."

"Well, thanks," Canterbury said. "And thank you again for the jam and bread. I'll put it to good use."

"I'm sure you will." They shook hands, and for another moment Charlotte lingered before turning. "You've met Mr. Dathan across the river, I understand."

"Yes, ma'am. I've already learned a great deal from him and his missus."

They looked northward, up the river valley, as the slanting afternoon light cast a firelight glow over their features, faces uniformly pointed toward the distance, like the statue of Lewis and Clark she had seen in a magazine not long ago. In such a light, she thought, even their commonplace faces could look heroic. And across the valley, on the next ridgetop north, she could see the tiny figures of Esther Renick and her family, stirring about in their hilltop clustering, most of them up top bringing in firewood but one down at the water's edge, where the old mine entrance still gaped. A bigger figure, probably the son, moving purposefully in and out of the shadows at whatever task preoccupied him.

Canterbury pointed west toward a grove of pine trees that rose out of the surrounding scrub oaks like a floating island of green. "You ever notice that batch of trees?"

"Not really," Charlotte said. "But now that you point it out, it's quite something, isn't it?"

He nodded. "That's Dathan and Cedeh's allotment. He told me about the breakup of your old community, how everyone got some forestland and some farmland. That's his grove."

"I see. He never logged it off, then."

"No, ma'am. He walked me out there the other day. Showed me a big flat rock that he has fixed up with a backrest and cushion. Said he used to come over and sit there for half a day when he was younger, just to listen to the wind in the pines and contemplate. He calls it his lookout."

"Contemplate? Dathan has never struck me as the contemplative type."

At this Canterbury's expression grew veiled. "Well, ma'am, I get the impression that Dathan is a man who guards his private thoughts."

Canterbury's words were careful, but Charlotte recognized the truth in them. Dathan had always been a man of legendary silence. When he first appeared in Daybreak, in the chaotic years after the war, he had simply showed up and began to work, speaking to no one, demonstrating his value to the community through fierce, relentless labor, unsettling in his wordless intensity. "I wonder what he contemplated," she mused.

"Man's inhumanity to man, is what he told me."

A fit subject for a former slave. "God knows there's plenty of that to meditate upon."

Canterbury turned away from her unexpectedly and covered his face. When he turned toward her again, his expression was composed but his voice was husky.

"Out there in the Philippines, ma'am, we killed whole villages," Canterbury murmured. "Every man, woman, and child. I'll never forget that."

And before she had time to respond, he turned his back and disappeared toward his cabin at a near-run, shoulders slumped, the low light fracturing in the tight curls of his black hair.

Chapter 8

Winter approached and then arrived, blowing in all of a sudden like a freight train shielded by hills, with nothing to warn of its approach but a distant and uncertain rumble until it appears with a great clash and clatter, altering everything. Petey's reading, ever voracious, increased to the point that people began to avoid her when she came around the corner with another clipping in her hand, always about the great fair. "Look here. They're going to have singing gondoliers, brought over all the way from Venice. You climb in the little boat and they paddle you around, all the time singing."

Charley Pettibone completed his excavation and lined it with native stone, creating a circular pool where bathers could submerge themselves in the muddy, odorous water, and then built a bathhouse around it with lumber taken from unused outbuildings. Over its barn-red painted exterior, he hung another sign: Healing Spring. Some in Daybreak teased him, but Charlotte held her tongue. And true to his prediction, people came, to soak in the smelly water and to seek out the famous author. The bolder ones went up to Adam's door and knocked, but most merely walked up and down in the street for a while, hoping for a glimpse, with occasional success.

Charlotte was dismayed over the ease with which Adam slipped into his new fame, receiving the adulation of his admirers with smug grace and dispensing bits of folk wisdom like a mountaintop oracle. At first, Newton resented Adam's sudden rise to prominence, but the increased trade at his hotel and store alleviated his ire, or so it seemed to Charlotte. She resolved to follow his example and accept the altered circumstance as another lark of the jokester gods, plucking Adam from obscurity into unexpected and possibly undeserved attention.

J. M. and Josephine commenced operations of their match factory, in a separate building a hundred yards from the main mill to confine the damage should things go wrong. Perhaps the new process was safer; but the place still reeked of sulfur and ammonia and other odors that couldn't be identified. J. M. announced to all comers that because of the factory's difficult working conditions employment would be open to anyone willing to bend to the task, regardless of race; so the match mill became by default a colored man's workplace. In a few months the workers had built themselves a small barracks to save themselves the hours of walking or riding to the mill, and by New Year's Ulysses S. Canterbury had joined them, throwing in the towel on his infertile acreage. Charlotte saw his figure trudge by in the Monday morning darkness and wondered how he managed to wake himself up in time to make the trip, for it was several hours' walk with no clock and little light to guide a man. The force of need, she supposed.

The Renicks' whiskey business prospered as word got around, and Charlotte realized that it had not been the fine water or the inspiriting vistas that had led them there, but the relative isolation, far enough from any main road to escape casual notice but close enough to town for easy access, and the existence of the old mine itself, a deep network of tunnels and shafts capable of holding—and concealing—any amount of apparatus and barrels the Renicks should choose to place there. Charlotte had never heard of a tax man visiting the area, and given the number of distilleries in easier locations she imagined such a man would have a lifetime's work arresting scofflaws within forty miles of the nation's capital. Still the myth persisted of revenue agents roaming the countryside, chasing down the locals for their dollar a gallon. So concealment was the standard practice, and as long as rowdies didn't gather, no one in the neighborhood thought of complaining. Charley pronounced their product to be rough but improving.

And then it was spring, and time to gather their belongings for their stay at the Fair. Petey's enthusiasm had infected them all, even Charlotte. Who could not feel anticipation? The size and scope of the thing, the celebrated visitors. Perhaps the President himself would pay a call. Watson Kellogg insisted that they should wear rustic garb and demonstrate native artisanries, another of his two-dollar phrases, whenever they were in residence at the exhibit. The first of his requests was easy. If her simple shift and apron, and the gardening bonnet she habitually wore during warm weather, weren't rustic enough for Mr. Kellogg, then he would just have to go fish. The artisanries proved more troublesome, but Charlotte and Petey decided after consideration that corn shuck dolls might have appeal. It seemed strange to pack up a crate of corn husks to take to the city, but such were the ways of the world these days. Their task was to serve as props to Adam's tableau, so they might as well jump into it.

But first she wanted to make another trip up the ridge. She didn't need to talk to the industrious Mr. Canterbury; she just enjoyed him, liked his grit. Of course too much grit could get a man into trouble, but surely he had mastered that balancing act by now.

So on a Sunday afternoon with the air still sharp but carrying the scent of spring behind its initial bite, Charlotte ascended the hill and followed the old path, newly re-worn from Canterbury's traversing. Canterbury was outside, as she had guessed, but he was neither plowing nor clearing. Instead, he had dug out a plot on the site of what had been his vegetable garden, fifty feet square, the clay-thick soil heaped at the lower end, exposing the red granite beneath. He had a hammer and a rock drill and was working his way along a string that he had stretched taut across the bared surface, pounding out holes along the line. He stood and groaned as Charlotte came near, stretching out his back.

"This is a new twist," she said. The holes Canterbury drilled were starting to form a grid, but if he planned to cover the rock face with this pattern, he had a couple hundred more to do.

"Won't grow crops, so it might as well grow paving stones," Canterbury said. "Good market for these up in the city, is what I'm told. Eight cents apiece."

"How do you plan to get them out?"

"Been filling the holes with water. We get a couple more hard freezes, might start to see some cracking." Canterbury looked over his handiwork with a satisfied expression. "Otherwise, I'll get a little powder and pop 'em out."

"Ever worked with blasting powder before?" Charlotte hated to ask, but it seemed like an obvious question.

"You worried about me, ma'am?" She sensed a note of sarcasm. "I'm honored."

"I'll admit, I'd rather not see you brought down the hill with a hand missing. That seems reasonable, don't you think?"

Canterbury snorted. "I've worked with black powder and brown, smokeless too. Still have all my fingers and toes."

He seemed unaccountably peevish. For a moment she thought she had misread his tone, but a second glance dispelled that thought. She knew a scowl when she saw one.

"I'm sorry. I didn't mean to interrupt your work."

Canterbury waved his hand. "It's nothing. I need to stop more often. You get in a rhythm with that hammer and forget to rest."

"Then I serve a purpose of some sort." Canterbury didn't answer, but turned away, hefting his hammer. "There's something I wanted to mention to you."

He looked back at her. "All right."

"I'm going up to St. Louis in a few days with Adam and Petey, and I thought that if you wanted to send a message to your family, I'd be happy to take it up to them."

"Post Office works for colored people same as white."

"I know that. I just thought—"

"Thought you'd get into my business a little more, see what I say to my family. Am I right?"

"Certainly not!"

His face tightened. "You just figured she can't read, didn't you?"

This thought stopped her. "I didn't think that. But perhaps it entered my mind without my actually thinking of it, and for that I am sorry."

The suspicion and defiance left his face, leaving only the look of complete exhaustion they had been masking. "I'm sorry, ma'am. I ain't myself. All this work—" His gesture took in the land, the valley, the entire world. "She wants me to come home."

Charlotte was unsure how to proceed. "I'm sure she misses you," she ventured.

"I'm sure she does, and our savings too. I used them up buying this piece, and now the taxes are due." He shrugged. "I just wanted something to leave behind for our son. Something besides a hole in the ground."

"You're a young man! Don't sing 'O Misery' just yet. Most of the county has to patch together a way to make a living, just like you."

Canterbury snorted. "Dipping matches and breaking rocks. I got a cousin in prison don't work this hard."

Though his words were rough, his voice was not, and Charlotte had to smile. "You're grousing like a native already."

"Oh, I'll never be a native." His expression grew somber. "You know why Susie really wants me back? Because she thinks it's not safe for me down here."

"Not safe? That's absurd." There were rattlesnakes down the bluff, no doubt, and of course the match factory could catch fire any instant. Then she stopped, and recognized his tone, and regretted what she had said.

Canterbury waited for her thoughts to finish working. "Yeah," he said at last. "I don't see this place the same way you do. That fellow over in Joplin last year? Hung in front of hundreds of people, and only two go on trial. And both of them let off."

"There are good people here." It was weak but the best she could do.

"Good people everywhere, and sometimes they kill a man. But I can't dwell on that. I've got work to do. Paving the streets of St. Louis with this rock, or so my buyer tells me."

He returned to his hammering, leaving Charlotte to walk back to Daybreak, meditative and uneasy at the thought that this countryside, so familiar and easy to her nowadays after long years of acclimation, was to this man a frightening and hostile place, and rightly so. Of course she had heard of the Joplin lynching, and the one in Pierce City before that, but those were rough towns, railroad towns, with rough people. That was a rationalization, of course, and she knew it. She'd seen it herself—the excited madness of a mob, the sheltering anonymity of darkness, the next-day regret and refusal to meet anyone's eye. Anyone was capable of anything.

At the property line she paused, reluctant to leave the conversation as it had ended, burdened with ill omen. But what could she say to change it? Better to wait for another day and start fresh.

But sleep did not come easily, and when she awoke the next morning the sun was well above the horizon. Ulysses S. Canterbury had already passed by on his way to the match mill. And under her door were two neatly folded sheets of paper, sealed with a thumbprinted blob of beeswax, with an address in neatly penciled lettering on the blank side, and above the address the inscription: "To Mrs. U. S. Canterbury. Thank you."

Chapter 9

At last the day came to make the journey, and it seemed as though everyone in Daybreak turned out to help them load the wagon for their trip to the railroad siding and to press Adam for the chance to spend some time as part of the Heaven Holler exhibit, a way to see the fair from the inside and save fifty cents. True to his nature, Adam told each one that he thought highly of them and would try to fit them in.

And no doubt he would. One thing about Adam, he was the sort of man whose good intentions could not be doubted, though his good sense might. After they boarded the train, Petey was pensive, even melancholy, resting her head on Charlotte's shoulder as the miles clicked away.

Halfway through Washington County, after Adam strolled to the back to stand on the observation platform, it came out. "I don't want to play-act like I'm one of the people in Papa's book." Petey's voice was soft.

"I can understand that. I don't care much for the idea myself. But if it helps your father…"

Petey twirled a strand of hair around her finger, an absentminded gesture that Charlotte knew signaled worry. "They're going to make fun of us. Barefoot hicks."

Charlotte put an arm around her while trying to think of something to say that was comforting yet honest. Of course mockers and scoffers, foolish city folk, would stroll by to laugh, as if their own parents or grandparents hadn't tilled the soil, as if it was grander to wear a top hat and ride a streetcar to work than it was to plow a furrow or hew a tie. Most people's talk about the nobility of labor ran no deeper than their desire for clean hands and a comfortable chair.

"Sometimes people laugh at what they don't understand," she said. "We don't have to respond in kind. People will come because they love your papa's book and want to meet him. We're just part of the scenery."

Petey sighed as though the unfairness of the universe had come to rest on her slender shoulders alone, but Charlotte could tell that her words had achieved their desired reassurance. She reminded herself that despite her brave face and eager attitude, Petey was at heart a sensitive child, unformed in many ways. And yes, she would be wounded by the remarks of smug passers-by, and Charlotte would need to mind her closely until she acquired the city kids' tough shrug. In certain slants of light they were all barefoot hicks, but that was all right. Smile, and pose for the Kodak, and take their nickel. It was a simple enough recipe.

Petey's worry had spread to her, and she looked out the window of the train at the blur of sprouts and greenery they passed. "I'm going to miss my sarvis this year," she murmured.

"What?"

"This is the week I go out into the woods and mark the sarvis trees, so I can find them later in the summer, when the berries are on."

"Oh!" Petey pondered a moment. "Those little strips of ribbon?"

Charlotte nodded. The berries were the devil to spot in midsummertime, so she always bought a couple of yards of bright ribbon in the spring and tied strands to a prominent branch on each tree. Not that it helped her outrace the birds, but perhaps it evened the contest.

Petey laughed and then covered her mouth. "I always thought those were decorations! That you had gone out and ribboned the trees to celebrate spring. It seemed so gay and romantic."

"What's gay and romantic can also be useful," Charlotte said, ruffling Petey's hair. In truth, there was something special about the sarvis blossoms, splashes of white in the forest's winter gray, earlier than any other tree and so quick to disappear. They spoke of hope that winter's end was not far away, though chill and snow yet threatened. James often angled to walk with her into the woods on her ribboning trips, for spring made the sap within him rise as well, and indeed at times they had found a mossy bank and taken their ease, returning to Daybreak with a shared secret and twigs on the back of their clothing. But that was not a story to be shared.

"I'll write your Aunt Sarah after we get settled in," she said. "She might have time to mark the trees for us. And then, who knows? We might find ourselves out in the woods at berry-picking time."

Charlotte knew that Petey's worry over being made fun of had not gone away, despite her words, and she searched for something else to tell her to ease the sting. But her mind was empty. Of course they would be figures of fun. Experience had taught her that the world was full of fools, and Petey was just beginning to learn to manage them.

But by the time they had passed through the growing clusters of houses that had grown up between the Barracks and the city, and slowed for the sharp turn around Mr. Shaw's garden, her mood had lifted, and a sudden rush of passengers to the left side of the train brought Petey out of herself as well. Someone claimed to have seen the great Ferris wheel, still under construction, off in the distance. But the sighting must have been a mirage or a trick of imagination, for no matter how the people craned their necks and speculated, no sign of the wheel could be detected. "You damn fools, it's ten miles to the fairgrounds from here if it's an inch," a man snorted. "You'd need eyes like telescopes that could see through buildings."

"I saw it, I tell you," another man said. "Gleaming in the sun, it was."

Petey nudged her. "Will you ride it with me, Grandma?"

"Of course."

"Not afraid of the height?"

"Not enough to stop me."

And with that they were off the train, and onto the grand new electric streetcar line that ran to the fairgrounds, crowded with people already though the fair's opening was still weeks away. Watson Kellogg awaited them at the Heaven Hollow attraction, his Derby hat firmly in place as always and a look of mild displeasure on his face.

"We agreed on five, Mr. Turner," he said. "The attraction needs five people to run properly." He tipped his hat to her, almost an afterthought. "Though I'm always pleased to see you, Mrs. Turner, and you too, Petey."

Adam waved away his question. "No worries, Kellogg. We'll have a full complement by opening time."

Kellogg remained peevish. "One to work the door, one for general cleanup, two to walk the house and grounds greeting visitors, and then yourself." Then he checked himself and sweetened his tone. "I'm sure you will do as you say. Let's get you settled in."

He led the way through the building's oversized double doors and around an L-shaped counter into the large open area of the main floor, where workmen labored over paint and plaster. "Once these fellows finish and we get the floors cleaned up, we'll bring in chairs and decorations," he said. "We'll dramatize scenes from the story during the day and hold musical performances at night."

Off to the left of the high-ceilinged open area, a doorway led to a smaller room, already furnished with stuffed chairs, a writing desk, and a sofa in the corner. "This will be your receiving room," Kellogg said to Adam. "The idea is, they come in through this door, meet you, receive a signed photograph, and then leave through that door." He gestured to a door that led out back toward a small building. "More mementoes of their visit. Tobacco pouches, coin purses, dolls for the children, that sort of thing. And then behind you—" he turned the knob of an unobtrusive door, paneled to match the wall, at the room's corner "—is the staircase to your quarters."

Kellogg led their way up the long staircase, which, as nearly as Charlotte could figure, ascended across the front side of the building to a landing at the opposite corner from where they started. Only the light from a window at the top landing showed their way.

"Here we are," Kellogg said, opening the door.

They entered a long hallway, again with a blank wall on the front side and doors opening to the right along its length. "Unusual layout, I know. I'm sorry for the lack of light, but we're expecting a lot of noise," Kellogg said. "Thought you might be better off with a solid wall and then a hallway between you and the Pike."

Charlotte nodded. "That makes sense."

"But to compensate, we added this." He stepped to the wall and turned a wooden knob mounted near the door frame. In an instant, three electric lamps along the wall snapped into brightness, casting a yellow glow down the length of the hall. Petey clapped her hands with glee.

"Thought you'd like that," Kellogg said, pleased with himself. He pushed open the first door to reveal a large kitchen with a table and chairs in one corner. "All the rooms have electric light. But here's the best thing."

Kellogg walked to the counter, where an iron pipe emerged from the wall over a washpan. He turned the valve on the pipe, releasing a stream of water that, Charlotte thought, at least didn't smell or look too cloudy. "Indoor plumbing," Kellogg said triumphantly. "Here and—um—over there." He waved in the direction of a closed door in the outside corner of the room.

"Mr. Kellogg, we know what indoor plumbing is," Charlotte said. "You don't have to flourish like a magician."

"Sorry, ma'am, I just get carried away. We just want you to be comfortable."

She supposed it was that "barefoot hicks" idea still preying on her mind, however much she might try to reassure Petey and steel her for the remarks that would inevitably come. Of course they were hicks, gawking and goggle-eyed at the wonders of the city, so they might as well own up to it.

She laid her hand on Kellogg's arm as they re-entered the hallway. "I know you do," she said. "You've done a great deal, and I appreciate it."

Four bedrooms opened off the hall, one for each of them and one for the additional pair of authentic hillfolk, who Adam had not given a moment's thought to, as far as Charlotte could tell. "I've set up the end one for Mr. Turner, with a writing desk by the window," Kellogg said. "The others are all pretty much the same."

Charlotte took the bedroom nearest the kitchen, and Petey the one next to her. For a few minutes they separated to inspect. Charlotte took stock: a bed, a dresser, a bedside table, a standing closet, and a comfortable-enough-looking chair beside the window. She tested the chair and sank into it gratefully. Out the window she could see the broad back yard, with a high wooden fence around it to keep out the cheapskates, and with a miniature fake Ozarks filling it—fake mountain, fake waterfall, fake cave behind the waterfall, and pathways running throughout so that paying customers could experience the spectacle from all angles.

Then a small thing caught her eye and made her smile. At the base of the mountain, a small plot, with a fence and a gate, and inside, a mound of topsoil, raked and leveled. Mr. Kellogg had remembered his promise to build her a garden after all.

On Sunday, Charlotte tucked Ulysses S. Canterbury's letter into an inside pocket of her coat and walked to the streetcar stop on DeGiverville Avenue. She showed the address to the conductor, who frowned. "That's not a part of town you should be visiting unaccompanied, ma'am."

"I see." Charlotte paid the fare and sat behind him. "But as it is Sunday, and the middle of the day, I believe I'll risk it. Let me know where to change cars."

The conductor, a thick-bodied, German-looking man with a face as pale and lumpy as a turnip, looked up and down the street as if hoping for a supervisor to appear and tell him what to do. "It's a rough neighborhood up there, I tell you. Can't your husband escort you?"

"Sir, I am a widow."

The streetcar zigged and zagged through the streets north of the park until it reached a broad crossing avenue, newly bricked. “This is Taylor,” the conductor said abruptly. “St. Ferdinand is a few blocks up that way, maybe ten or twelve. I don’t know. Please, if you don’t like the look of the place when you get there, just stay on the car and ride it back down here.”

“Very well,” she said. “I promise.”

The day felt abnormally damp and cold, with spits of moisture stinging her face, so she was glad to see the connecting streetcar arrive. The driver took her transfer wordlessly and let her off at the stop, and as she expected the rough neighborhood didn’t look any rougher than a dozen places she knew, just poor. Poor, and from the smell of it, not a part of town that had completely gone over to indoor plumbing yet. And the real cause of the conductor’s consternation: It was a neighborhood that had black people in it, just walking around like everyone else, as if that were enough to endanger an old lady. Perhaps the old ladies of his experience were cut from softer cloth.

A pair of teenage girls darted past her, their dark hair tied up in scarves, chattering in a language she did not recognize. Charlotte supposed she should be afraid to be in this strange place, surrounded by strange people and strange words, but instead it was thrilling, like being in a foreign country yet only a few hours by train from her home. Perhaps she needed to get out of Daybreak more often to experience this new America.

She walked along the avenue past the rows of closely-set, flat-roofed, square brick houses, uncertain of the one she was looking for. An old woman was beating a rug in front of one; she stopped and showed her the address.

The woman pointed with the handle of the rug beater. “I know the gal. The big house at the corner, upstairs on the left.”

Charlotte followed her directions and found herself at the door of the upstairs apartment of a four-family house that filled a corner lot. A woman answered her knock, wiping her hands on a towel; she was younger than Charlotte expected, maybe twenty, and darker, with deeply colored skin that almost looked purple in the dim light of the interior hallway. “Yes, ma’am?” she said, with a dubious look.

“My name is Charlotte Turner. I’m a neighbor to your husband, down in Madison County, if you’re Susie Canterbury.”

Susie’s look turned to alarm. “Is he all right?”

Charlotte smiled. “Oh yes. I’m sorry to give the wrong impression. He’s fine. I’ve come to the city to spend some time at the Fair, and he sent along a letter for me to give you." She took the letter from her pocket and handed it over.

"Please, come in," Susie said, opening the door wider. "Have a cup of tea." Susie tucked the letter into her apron. "I'll read this later."

The tiny apartment had a pair of chairs in the front room with a table between them, and a picture of a bouquet of roses on the wall. Susie disappeared into the kitchen, and Charlotte heard her throw some coal into the cookstove. Charlotte didn't particularly crave tea at the moment, but couldn't think of any way to decline without seeming unmannerly. In a few minutes Susie returned with two mismatched cups, brimming with warm, sweet, weak tea.

"So you're neighbors?" Susie said.

"Yes. We're down in the valley south of him, and he's up on the ridge. He comes through a couple of times a week on his way to the factory."

Susie wrinkled her nose. "I don't like the sound of that factory. And now he's blasting rocks, as if working in a match factory wasn't dangerous enough. Can't he make a living by farming?"

What to say? A simple "no," while truthful, seemed less than kind. "It's tough ground and thin soil up there on the ridge," she said. "It's been timbered off, so no money will be made from that for several years."

"What about fruit trees? The land agent said it was good ground for planting fruit."

Charlotte hesitated. "My son has an apple orchard. But again, that's down in the valley, and it's not his only occupation. He also runs a store and post office."

"And the house? Is he living decently? Eating properly?"

"I'd have to say the house is still a work in progress. As for what and how he eats, I can't judge."

Over her teacup, she studied Susie Canterbury. She was slender but round-cheeked, with eyes that never stopped moving and an expression that some would call pert. Not that it mattered; she had been called pert herself at that age. And Susie was smart enough to know that she was being studied, and wise enough to allow it.

"I'm sorry to badger you," Susie said. "He's spoken of you in his letters. He says you're the one with the most sense. So I can't pass up the chance to find out the real story, as much as I can." She stood up and went to the window. "Excuse me, I have to check on the boy."

Susie opened the window and leaned out, letting in a swift waft of cold air. "Ulysses!" she called. "Stay where I can see you!" A faint voice answered.

She shut the window and turned back inside, letting out a long sigh. "Ever since I've known him, he has talked about owning land. 'No one is a full man without owning property.' And I'm not one to deny a man his dreams. But I have to wonder if we are walking down a path to disaster."

Another person who thinks I'm wise, Charlotte thought. But she didn't feel wise. In fact, she wondered why she had stepped into the dealings between the Canterburys. It felt meddlesome. As the man had said, there was the Postal Office to carry their messages. Maybe she should examine her own self the next time she thought about launching into the lives of others.

But that was for another day, and right now Susie Canterbury sat in front of her with an expectant look. "I was just a little older than you when I came out to Daybreak," she said. "I was with my husband, not alone like Ulysses. But in the same way, I was in unfamiliar territory and had no idea of the future. My point is, we never know where our decisions are going to take us." She took a sip of tea. "We make our decisions one at a time, based on hope and instinct, and it's only looking back when we see that we have made a path."

"I appreciate your philosophy, Mrs. Turner. But my question is simple. Is he in danger down there?"

She was right, of course, and Charlotte regretted overcomplicating the matter. She took a breath.

"Yes, I suppose he is, and in ways I can't grasp. But more danger there than here? Of that I'm not certain." She placed her teacup on the table and stood. "I imagine this is your only day off, and I'm taking it up with my unannounced visit." Charlotte wanted their conversation to end well, so she put on her brightest smile as she wrapped her coat around herself. "One thing's for sure. I've never seen a man work harder than your husband, and few as hard. Perseverance and hard work will carry a man a long way."

"You sound just like him. Sure you haven't caught whatever disease he's got?"

"If what he has is catching, I know a few people I'd like to infect."

Their shared laugh set the tone Charlotte had hoped for as she moved toward the door.

"And you're here for the fair?" Susie said. "It ain't even open yet."

"We're not spectators, we're on exhibit. Hill-billies of Heaven Holler, live and on display." She did a mock pirouette. "That'll cost you a quarter once we're open for business."

"Ulysses Junior has been begging about the fair already. Don't even know what the word means, just hears it from the bigger boys."

"Well, bring him down. We're on the Pike, and we have rooms on the second floor. Since I took advantage of your kindness to drop in unannounced, I'd be glad to have the chance to even the scales."

"We'll see," Susie said, and her gaze wandered to the window. "They say that colored people will be welcome anytime, but I'll believe that when I see it."

And there it was again, the great gulf between them, the reason why she could simply step onto a streetcar and go anywhere she wanted and Susie Canterbury had to calculate carefully whether it was safe to take her child to the fair. She took both of Susie's hands in hers. "I know the people who operate the match factory, and they are good people. They will not let their workers come to harm or take shortcuts on their safety. As for the rest of the fabric of life down there, it is no worse than you might imagine, and unfortunately, probably no better. But I promise you that I will look out for his interests to the limits of my power."

In the chilly drizzle waiting for the streetcar, Charlotte thought of Ulysses S. Canterbury on his barren plot north of Daybreak, in his burrow composing another letter to his wife and child, or perhaps out chiseling in his bed of rock to make the very stones on which the streetcar ran. Ulysses. To strive, to seek, to find, and not to yield, or so the poem went; and who was she to say the poem was wrong? But behind all this relentless, endless striving, as heroic as it might be, she saw other figures, less heroic yet present on the scene: a lonely, frightened wife, and a son left alone to find his way as best he could.

Chapter 10

Finally it arrived, the great day of opening, although painters and plasterers still swarmed many of the buildings and the Ferris wheel stood unfinished, surrounded by scaffolding. Adam, who couldn't bear to miss a ceremony, attended the festivities and took Petey along. Charlotte was glad to stay behind and mind their own exhibition; she didn't feel the need to witness the ceremonial pressing of the key to release the waters of the Cascades, or the speeches that would come before or after it. Adam had indeed failed to bring another pair of authentic Ozarkers to their exhibit, so he had gone to a vaudeville hall and hired a young married couple to play the parts. Charlotte heard them out back, rehearsing their dialect and practicing jokes.

She did crave to hear Mr. Sousa's band perform, though, so when the strains of distant music could be heard, she locked the entrance door and stepped out into the street to listen.

How crisp and bright the band sounded, even from a few blocks away! She couldn't quite catch the melody, but she could hear the higher instruments—a cornet, a piccolo, and something else she couldn't quite place—above the general sound. Even with crowds thronging the ceremony, the Pike had strollers on the broad avenue, eyeing the facades of the amusements: the Streets of Seville, the moving picture show, the Infant Incubators, the Hereafter.

It took a few minutes for her to realize that among the strollers on the Pike was a young woman who had passed before her three times, up and back and up again, with no apparent destination. She wore a red and white striped dress, fashionably cut, and her cheeks were rouged brightly, though a little awkwardly. She walked in a slow, odd gait, stepping her toe out and then skipping to it like a child, and as she walked she sang: *She's only a bird in a gilded cage, a beautiful sight to see,* and then trailed off as though she had forgotten the rest of the chorus.

Charlotte watched her, curious, as she skip-walked to the end of the avenue, then turned and began her return. The girl appeared to pay no attention to passers-by, twirling a strand of her blonde hair in her finger, singing more or less to herself in a thin but pretty voice. As she came closer, Charlotte drew back into the exhibition's entrance alcove so as not to seem to stare.

A policeman ambling by was less polite, fixing the girl with a glare and stepping into her path. "Are you lost, Missy?"

She never stopped twirling her hair. "No, sir," she said. "Not a bit."

"What's your name?"

"Rose."

"Rose what?"

"Oh, just Rose."

The policeman moved his bulk a little closer to her. "All right, just-Rose, suppose you tell me what you're doing."

"Waiting on a friend."

"Indeed, now. And who's this friend?"

For the first time, she looked up and directly into the policeman's eyes. "Big Bill Langland."

The policeman stepped back, startled. The two of them regarded each other for a long moment. "Well, if I see him, I'll tell him you're looking for him."

"Oh, I'm not looking for him. I'm just waiting on him."

The policeman seemed perplexed by this distinction but said nothing more. He stepped aside and walked on, looking over his shoulder a couple of times.

Rose, if indeed that was her name, continued her aimless meander down the thoroughfare and renewed her song at a new line, newly repeated: *Her beauty was sold for an old man's gold, she's a bird in a gilded cage.* Her obliviousness continued as well, until a young dandy in a shiny brown suit tipped his hat to her, and she stopped abruptly.

"Do you like my singing?" she said.

"I do indeed, miss."

"And do you like to dance? Here for the fair, I gather."

The young man's tone grew more guarded at her familiar attitude. "Yes, I like to dance. I cut a fair step, I'd say."

"Well, if you like to dance and hear pretty girls sing, I know just the place for you."

"Do you now?"

She pointed toward the main entrance of the fair. "Go out the gate and straight across the train tracks. North a block and it's on your right. Tell the man at the door that Rose sent you."

"Rose, eh? And will you be there later tonight?"

"I will. And I'll sing for you."

"And will I get robbed, or rolled?"

"No, sir. It's not that kind of place."

"And—" He leaned in as if to whisper something, at the same time with his hand sneaking out to pinch her bottom. But Rose spun expertly and skipped away with a teasing laugh, leaving him six feet away in awkward mid-grope while she continued down the street. She turned and wiggled her fingers at him, then pointed to the main gate and northward. Another moment, and she was lost in the throng, leaving the young man to adjust his hat and look around to see if anyone had noticed. Charlotte couldn't help but admire the slickness of the move and the easy way she avoided the man's fumbled effort, and she recognized it as a maneuver that only came from practice. So this was her world for a while, where ladies of the evening walked about unimpeded.

Then a man on a camel came by, advertising the Cairo exhibition, and Charlotte's thoughts moved on.

Over the next few weeks they settled into a routine. Charlotte and Petey took turns at the entrance while the other walked the compound, greeting visitors and selling trinkets. Adam stayed in the "study," ostensibly writing a sequel to the Heaven Holler book but actually spending the day posing for photographs and signing copies of the World's Fair edition. He invariably grew bored with this about halfway through the day and strolled out to see the fair, sometimes returning an hour or two later with an anecdote of an encounter or attraction, and sometimes simply resuming his place at his desk. Petey likewise burned to explore the fairgrounds. But her excursion reports were far longer and more enthusiastic, as she carried on about the latest wonderment she had come across: the enormous locomotive, the elephant made out of almonds, the replica coal mine.

Charlotte ventured into the fair less often. Its immensity intimidated her. Of course the buildings and statues were intimidating, or at least impressive, which was just intimidation with a smile on its face. Forty-foot statues, hundred-foot ceilings. And the crowds made her nervous with their racket and boister.

In the evenings, they retired upstairs while the vaudeville players performed their Zeke-and-Martha comic bits and acted out scenes from the book. Watson Kellogg had booked a band to play old-timey music some evenings, and they could hear it through the floor. Sometimes Adam wandered down to mingle, but Charlotte preferred sleep to entertainment, not that sleep was likely in such a situation. A jug band beneath them, the distant rattle of gunfire from the South African war re-enactment down the block, and the nightly firing of cannon provided the main themes of her night, while the ebb and flow of brass bands as they marched up the street and the barkers with their megaphones played the descant.

On an evening with no band downstairs and a smallish crowd milling outside, Petey returned from one of her expeditions with some company. "I've made a new friend," she announced as she reached the top of the stairs. "I hope it's all right that I brought him here without asking beforehand."

"Of course," Charlotte said, but she swallowed her words when the visitor reached the landing.

"This is Nimuel Baccay," she said. "He is part of the Philippine exhibit."

Nimuel was a small, trim young man who looked to be about seventeen, finely featured, no taller than Petey herself, with lustrous black hair oiled and combed to perfection. He wore a cream-colored suit, and his skin was the color of polished walnut. He stepped forward and bowed. "Madam."

But Nimuel, despite his dapper appearance and exotic good looks, bore a guarded look, a look of cautious melancholy, that contrasted with Petey's delight at having found someone new to bring home.

"Nimuel plays an important part in the exhibit," Petey said. "He is their guardian and interpreter, and mediates for them with—with—"

"Professor Pinckney," Nimuel said.

"He speaks to all the tribal elders. Nimuel says they are very wise."

"I'm pleased to meet you, Nimuel," Charlotte said. "You're very welcome here."

"Nimuel speaks more languages than you can count," Petey piped up. "English, Spanish, and—what are the others?"

Nimuel shrugged. "Tagalog, mainly, and a little of the tribal languages. It's not so special. Everybody speaks Spanish and Tagalog, and even in the city people keep some of their ancestors' language. English was the hard one for my learning."

"I can only imagine," Charlotte said. "It's hard enough for a native speaker."

"Where's Papa?" said Petey.

"Back in his room, reading."

Petey steered her new friend toward the study in the back of the building. Charlotte watched them with a mixture of concern and nostalgia. Petey was not old enough to be getting interested in boys! But of course she was. When she was Petey's age, her interest in boys had been intense but hypothetical, like an astronomer peering at Mars and discerning canals and roadways. She imagined Petey's experience to be about the same.

A few minutes later, the two of them emerged, Petey still flushed and triumphant, Nimuel still guarded and expressionless. Charlotte reflected how disorienting it must be for even the most adventurous young men to be displaced across the globe like this, no matter how spirited. "May I offer you something to eat?" she said to him. "Come sit with us a while. Petey, run upstairs and fix a plate." She gestured to the long table at the front of the exhibit, where they were planning to greet visitors.

Nimuel sat down but waved a hand at Petey. "No food, thank you. They already make us eat too much, and everyone is sluggish and miserable. They have complained, but so far no success."

"I don't understand," said Charlotte. "How can people be made to eat too much?"

Nimuel shrugged. "Professor Pinckney says it is for the exhibition. The Igorot must make the show every day."

Charlotte looked from Nimuel to Petey and back again. "Perhaps I'm just dense."

"Let's talk about this later," Petey said, a little nervous, but Nimuel waved his hand.

"It's not pleasant, ma'am," he said. "When the Igorot want to celebrate, say a wedding or a victory, they hold a feast. They kill a dog and make a great pot of stew." Seeing Charlotte's nose wrinkle, he added, "I told you it was not pleasant. But for them it is a great occasion. Over here, the dog feast is every night for the show, and the Igorot grow sick and listless. They are used to rice and vegetables, and maybe when they find them, some—" He groped the air as if to pluck a word. "*Setas.* Mushrooms."

"I see. And how did you come to be in this show, or whatever it is? Are you an Igorot?"

"No, ma'am. They are mountain people. I am from Manila. But when they perform the feast, I am there to translate, and I feel necessary to eat with them, out of respect. Their elder is a very wise man and I would not want to offend him."

"I see," Charlotte said, although she only saw dimly. But she understood the need to respect the customs of one's company. "So there are big differences between people from Manila and from the mountains?"

For the first time, Nimuel smiled, a broad and delighted smile that flashed across his face like a glint of sunlight through a cloud. "When I was young, I thought the mountain people were not even human. Something close to human, maybe, but not like us. But then I learned that my mother and father both came from mountain people, and even spoke their language sometimes. We spoke Tagalog at home, but I learned Spanish when I was small, like most children in my country. And when the Americans came, I learned English. I was hired as Professor Pinckney's servant when he came to the mountain provinces. And there I met some of the mountain people and learned their languages."

"You have quite a talent," Charlotte said.

Nimuel shrugged again. "Conquered people must learn the language of their conquerors. And now here I am, making money to send home and eating dog with Sky-Face every night."

"Sky-Face?"

"The elder of the Igorot. His name is Chaia-ngasup, which signifies a man who turns his face to the sky. When he was born, he gazed into the sky and would not look away. So his mother gave him this name. In their people, a man turns his face to the sky so he can speak to Lumawig, who is the son of the great god and who came to earth to marry one of the Igorot. So he was marked from birth as an *insupok*, someone who speaks with the gods and spirits." Nimuel paused and thought. "That's all I could understand of the story he told me, but I think there was more."

They sat at the table in silence.

"Yes," Charlotte murmured. She looked up at the ceiling of the exhibition and thought of the nights when she too had turned her face upward to drink in the light from ten thousand stars above the Daybreak valley. Here they would be lucky to see the moon through the smoky haze. "Sky-face."

Chapter 11

Charley Pettibone showed up at the end of May with the declared intention of adding some color to their exhibit, although Charlotte suspected he was more interested in boosting business for his lodge. He had let his beard grow to a startling length. It reached the top of his trousers, a dirty gray with a dark streak down the middle. "You're looking Biblical these days," Charlotte teased.

"Jenny don't like it," Charley said, stroking its length. "Says I look like I'm holding a possum to my breast everywhere I go. But I keep it clean. I tell her a man's got to look the part, but so far she ain't convinced."

"I'm on her side." They were settling him into the empty room next to Adam's. "Long beards are out of fashion these days."

"Be that as it may. I don't blow with them winds."

"No one will ever accuse you of being a slave to fashion, Charley. Do your customers like the look?"

"Oh my, yes! They think they're lodging with Daniel Boone himself. And the healing springs are starting to draw folk—locals and out-of-towners both." Adam emerged from his room in a new white linen suit. "Hey there, Big City. You're looking nifty."

"Trying to look professional," Adam replied, a little grumpy. "Just because I write about country folks doesn't mean I have to look like one."

"Certainly not," Charley said. "I'll do enough of that for both of us."

In his suit Adam looked as though he were trying out for a part in a stage play about a young Mark Twain, but Charlotte knew he was sensitive to comparisons and kept her counsel. If Charley Pettibone could dress for a role, why couldn't he? It was all bluster and show anyway.

"What news from home?" she said. "Tell us everything."

"Well, you ain't exactly been gone a lifetime. Not much to tell. Sarah cut off Grandma Renick's credit at the store, and she pitched a royal fit. But I expect you saw that coming."

"Just a little," she said with a smile.

"And your friend from up the hilltop passed through as usual, so I guess the match factory's still a going concern."

"Did he say anything to you?"

"Him? Nah. That boy don't favor conversation a great deal." Charley rubbed his hands together. "Where's that child of yours? Now there's a girl who likes to talk. I'll wager she's had some fine adventures already, and I want to hear about them all."

Adam glanced about absentmindedly. "Oh, she's around somewhere. She'll turn up." He headed downstairs with a sheaf of papers in his hand, ready to take his spot in the receiving room.

Charley stroked his beard. "Maybe they send letters back and forth."

"Who?"

He nodded toward the staircase. "Him and his missus. They must write each other a lot. Otherwise I'd think it strange that he never asked me a word about her."

Charlotte wagged a finger under his nose. "Charley Pettibone, you old gossip. Almost as old as me, and you still haven't learned that there are two kinds of business in the world, yours and everybody else's. And the path to happiness goes through tending to one kind only."

"Dang, Mrs. Turner, I have missed your pearls of wisdom back home," Charley said with a sly smile. "I believe I have backslid considerably without you around to see to my improvement."

She ignored his sally and took his elbow as they stepped into the kitchen. "Backsliding or none, Petey will be glad to see you. The observation wheel is finally running, and she's been itching to ride it. Your arrival is the perfect excuse."

Charley looked skeptical. "I hear it's fifty cents a ride. Pretty rich for us regular folks."

"Charley, you've been crying poverty ever since I've known you. You have to turn loose of a few coins every now and then."

She suspected that Charley's real motivation might be uncertainty about the immense apparatus of the wheel. Charley liked grand talk, but at heart he was still a country kid, an orphan who had appeared in Daybreak one day, penniless, with his goods in a gunnysack, and through all his life's adventures still carried that mark. She herself felt a little uncertain about the great wheel, especially after a couple of workmen had fallen to their deaths while assembling it, but it had been revolving in stately safety for a couple of weeks now. Couples clamored to have their marriage ceremony performed at the top of the ride, and a daredevil had recently made the circuit on the roof of the car, performing handstands and somersaults along the way.

So in the late afternoon they made their way south and west from the Pike, into the heart of the fair itself, past some of the immense palaces, the beds of flowers, and the peace monument, to the high ground where the observation wheel overtopped them all. The line was not long. "Told you it was too rich for the common folk," Charley muttered.

Their car was only about half full, and Petey beelined for the swivel seats in the upper rows, where they could get the best view. For a moment the car sat solid and motionless on the platform, and the passengers laughed and talked in their groups, some waving to friends in the broad outdoor beer garden nearby; then the gears engaged, there was a lurch like that of a train leaving a station, and they rose into the air, slowly, gracefully, gripping the arms of their seats in response to the strange sensation.

Was this how the soul felt, ascending to Heaven? This unworldly, effortless rise, no wind in their faces, all frivolous talk gone silent for the time being as people took in their new perspective? Then another lurch brought them all back to reality as the wheel stopped to take on the next load, one car down. They hung, swaying a little, as the passengers boarded.

Then they ascended again, and again, and again, and again, until they were three-quarters of the way to the top. Petey and the other young people in the car chattered like a nest full of baby blackbirds at the sights they could see, the Cascades in the near distance, the electric railway a little farther on as it cut through the greenery of the park, and beyond that the houses and buildings of the city, red brick and slate roofs obscured by smoke.

"What can you see, Grandma?" Petey said. "Can you see the river, or the famous bridge?"

"No. Maybe when we're at the very top."

As they dangled, waiting for the next movement, Charlotte became aware of the depth of the silence around them. She could see a brass band, marching down the Pike to promote who knows what, but the strains of its music were fragmentary tinkles, a note here and there and the rattling of the drums more a suggestion than an actuality.

Charley was gripping the arm of his seat with a madman's ferocity. "You all right, old soldier?" she murmured to him.

"Fine," Charley answered in a low voice, keeping his eyes fixed on the horizon.

A memory came to her, uninvited but not unwelcome. Her second husband, Ambrose Gardner, had come her way a couple of decades after James's death. Everyone considered Ambrose eccentric and professed not to understand what drew Charlotte to him. But Charlotte saw the tenderness and principle that lay beneath his surface oddities, and she grieved just as hard for him when illness took him as she had when James had been killed, what seemed like a lifetime earlier. Ambrose had a great fondness for heights; nothing pleased him as much as finding an aerie from which to overlook a broad scene and gain the wider perspective. His original homestead was built on a bluff above the Black River, valueless land to all except turkey vultures seeking a morning air current—and Ambrose Gardner. But that vantage was not enough. Ambrose had contrived an oversized sling in the tops of the pine trees that crested the bluff, a secure perch from which he watched the world turn beneath him, and in which he sometimes spent the night. And one night in particular he had taken Charlotte up into his nest among the pines, and they had made a fine, sweet thing between themselves in that tight-knotted web.

Something about the altitude and the gentle rocking of the car brought that memory back to her, so vivid that she flushed and looked over to see if Petey had noticed. But Petey was too entranced by the vistas around her. As the car moved up again—one level from the top now—she leaned out in one direction, then another, straining to see everything.

Petey on her left, casting her intense, blue-eyed gaze into the far distance, and Charley on her right, gazing into the same prospect but with fear-frozen eyes. And herself in the middle, reminiscing, an indulgence she rarely allowed herself. Perhaps there was more value in the exercise of memory than she had recognized. Besides, the memories weren't what she avoided, but the sloppy, sentimental longing for days gone by. Lord knows she was no uncritical adherent of modern life with all its haste and hustle, but people who made out as if the days of their childhood were somehow purer or even simpler were spouting nonsense, and Charlotte had no use for it. The human heart had never been pure or simple.

And then one final upward swing, and they were at the top. The car grew quiet as everyone took in the view.

What they could see differed little from what they had seen at previous stops along the circle, but something about the perspective—the lack of apparatus to block their view, the knowledge that no more heights remained—gave them an air of mountaintop solemnity, like stout Cortez in the poem. From here, even the enormous exhibition palaces seemed proportionate to the landscape. Her vision ranged out to the horizon's blurry edge, and the fairgoers below lost all distinction—no young or old, no black or white, just human beings gliding like ghosts along the silent pathways.

As much as anything, she missed the silence in Daybreak. Not that Daybreak was a silent place, but its sounds were distinct and separable: the bawl of a calf, the click of a gate, the creak of a branch, the hum of a cicada sitting on that branch. Here in the city all sound merged into a low roar from which only the loudest sounds stood out, a roar that went unnoticed until the moment came, like this one, when it ebbed and one was left alone, startled, briefly disoriented by its absence.

Petey slipped her arm into the crook of Charlotte's elbow and laid her head on her shoulder. "I miss Mama," she murmured.

"Of course you do, honey. Tell you what, let's go home for a while. Charley can keep your dad company."

"You don't think he'll mind?"

"Certainly not. He'll understand. I expect he'd like to take a break and go home himself, if it weren't for the fact that he's the main attraction here." Petey gave her a dubious look, and Charlotte reminded herself that she was no longer someone who could be spoken to like a child. "Honestly. I miss home too. Charley and your papa can batch it for a few days while we go check on my garden."

Petey leaned across her to speak to Charley. "Is that all right with you, Mr. Pettibone? Maybe you and Papa can try out some of these exotic restaurants up and down the Pike."

"Maybe," Charley said. "Though I have to say, in a place where you pay fifty cents just to ride up one side and down the other, I might end up begging for scraps."

They laughed together. Then there was another lurch, and the wheel groaned forward another partial turn, and Charlotte's stomach lurched along with it as the downward motion took her by surprise. The movement set everyone in the car talking again, as bright and lively as they had been before, and as the car slowly descended, stop by stop by stop, the chatter grew as everyone rehearsed what they intended to tell their friends below. By the time they reached the bottom, the anxious ascent, the breathtaking pause, and the sudden-seeming return had all been swept into one fine story, and groups of fairgoers charged off, arm in arm, in search of the next excitement to write home about.

Their walk back to Heaven Holler was slower and more thoughtful.

"Before I come up here," Charley said, "I found a blacksnake in the corn, back toward the hill, three-footer or more. Now Jenny is death on all snakes so I knew what she would want, but these boys eat a lot of mice and rats and what have you. So I just turned over my hoe and got the crook of it underneath him and lifted him up. And you know what? Once you get a snake off the ground he just freezes, don't fight or nothing. A snake is a ground creature, he feels the ground all along his body and it tells him everything, and if he loses contact with the ground he don't know what to do." He looked back at the Ferris wheel. "And I just learned that I am a creature of the ground too. I ain't going to get my feet off the earth anymore."

"A wise man knows his limitations," Charlotte said.

It was still too early for crowds on the Pike; only after the main fair closed at six did people start to swarm the broad brick streets to the north. Some strolling families, people hurrying to the train stop, waiters and entertainers arriving for their evening shift. Charlotte thought ahead to the trip to Daybreak. The whole idea of coming here was to advance Petey's education, to give her a glimpse into the world's complicated wonder. But Charlotte already felt a little tired of the world's wonders, and suspected that Petey felt the same, at least sometimes. A few days in familiar terrain would do them both good, rest them from the daily chase after a new sensation. Time spent in the predictable rhythms of farm life might sharpen their appetite for further adventure.

But adventure, or something like it, was closer at hand than she imagined. They turned the corner into the entrance to Heaven Holler and stumbled over the unconscious body of a young woman leaning against the inside wall.

Petey gasped in shock.

"What on earth?" Charley said, bending over her.

"I saw this girl out front," said Charlotte. "Her name's Rose."

Chapter 12

The three of them carried Rose inside, startling Adam and a pair of visitors in the parlor. "Let's take her up to my room," Charlotte said. Adam stood irresolute for a moment, then leaped to help. The men took her shoulders, and Charlotte and Petey took her feet.

"She don't weigh as much as a sack of grain," Charley said, but by the time they reached the top of the stairs he was puffing. After a moment's pause, they carried her the rest of the way to Charlotte's bed.

"Avert your eyes, gentlemen. I'm going to loosen this young lady's clothes," Charlotte said. "Petey, stay close in case I need you." Charley let out a muffled snort and gave her a look, for her clothes were bright and saucy in a way that suggested, to those who wished to see such a thing, that they were easily loosened and had often been so. But now was not the time for such observations, and under Charlotte's hard glare Charley had the good sense to keep his mouth shut. The men stepped away and gazed at the floor.

Charlotte leaned close. Rose's pupils were constricted into pinheads, and her breath was slow and shallow. From her mouth came a strange, sickly-sweet odor.

"Fetch me the dishpan from the kitchen," Charlotte said.

Petey dashed away and returned just as fast. "What's the dishpan for?" she said.

"I just have a feeling." Sure enough, no sooner had she spoken than the girl lurched upright, then rolled onto her side and heaved into the dishpan.

Charlotte held her hair back as she vomited. "That's good, honey. Get it out." Rose said nothing, just fell back into the bed and lapsed into her stupor.

"Is she drunk?" Petey whispered.

"Perhaps. We'll see." She handed the basin to Petey and pushed Rose onto her side at the edge of the bed. "Better rinse this out and bring it back, just in case."

Rose groaned and tried to roll onto her back, but Charlotte shoved her onto her side again and propped her with a knee. "Oh, no you don't, honey," she said. The girl couldn't have weighed more than a hundred pounds.

Adam shifted from foot to foot in the doorway. "I'd better go tend to my visitors." And with that he was gone, squeamish as always.

"What are we going to do?" Petey whispered. "Should we send for a doctor?"

Charlotte shook her head. "Not yet. We'll wait and watch." Half of the job of doctoring was to sit and watch anyway, so she felt little urgency to pay a stranger for what she could do herself. She tucked a strand of hair back from Rose's forehead and studied her face.

The girl was pretty enough, she supposed. Pretty enough for her line of work, anyway: her nose and cheeks round and smooth, her bosom full, her waist narrow but not cinched tight in the modern style. She didn't have the thin features of a Gibson girl, but who did? "Fetch me a cloth and a little water," she told Petey.

As the girl trotted off, Charley touched Charlotte's shoulder. "What do you think?"

Charlotte shrugged. "Opium, maybe. I've never seen it but it's as good a guess as any."

They watched her in silence for a moment until Petey returned with the water and cloth. Charlotte wrung it out, folded it, and wiped Rose's forehead and cheeks, not sure whether she was trying to cool her brow or wipe off the excess face powder. Whatever the reason, the touch of the wet cloth roused Rose. She flailed weakly with one arm, her eyelids fluttering, then lay still again.

"Well, she's alive," Charley said. "We know that much."

Half an hour later, Rose roused some more. Charlotte and Petey helped her sit on the edge of the bed and sip some water. "Where am I?" she said.

"You passed out in our doorway, so we brought you upstairs," Charlotte said. "You're on the Pike."

Rose tried to stand up but only got halfway before plopping back. "Has anyone come looking for me?"

"You've only been here a little while, honey." Charlotte took the water glass from her and set it on the bedside table. "Hardly enough time to be missed."

"I've got to get—" Rose's voice had a worried edge. "I've got places I need to be."

"Of course. Let's just get your feet under you."

Rose looked suspicious for a moment, but the sight of the three of them—the old man, the old woman, and the girl—must have been harmless enough to ease her mind. She lay back into the pillows. "Who are you people, anyway?"

"We're the Heaven Holler exhibit," Charlotte said.

"The hillbillies! One of my friends has that book. I haven't read it myself yet, but maybe I can get her to share." She paused. "Are you really hillbillies?"

Charley laughed. "You can pull my beard. It's genuine."

"You don't look like hillbillies. They're supposed to be dirty and ignorant."

There was an awkward pause. Sensing her overstep, Rose backtracked a little. "Well, thank you so much for helping me. I must not have eaten properly, or perhaps it was the warm day that made me faint."

"Oh no, miss!" Petey burst out. "You were right sick. I was afraid you were going to die, but Grandma got me to calm down."

It was time to break into the conversation before Petey strayed into problematic territory. Charlotte stood up and brushed down her apron. "We'll leave you alone for a while to get your head clear. Don't try to get up too soon." She waved Petey and Charley from the room. "A girl needs a few minutes to herself."

She stopped in the doorway. "We're right next door, in the kitchen. Call out when you feel ready to stand up."

Rose caught her eye. "I wonder—"

"Of course. You two go along, and I'll be right behind you." She shooed them out and closed the door.

"A friend of mine will be worried and looking for me," Rose began. "Maybe you could send word to him that I'm all right."

Charlotte hesitated. She had little doubt about what kind of friend Rose wanted to contact and even less doubt about her lack of desire to serve as a go-between for Rose and her pimp. But if passing along a message could keep the girl from a beating—

"How would I find your friend?"

"Oh, you wouldn't have to find him. Just find a policeman and tell him that you need to get a message to Big Bill. He'll know who you're talking about."

"Really."

"Oh yes! He's a very important man. Just tell him to tell Big Bill that Rose had a fainting spell, but is safe and well and will be back soon." She smiled, a little shy. "That's my name, Rose. He'll know who you're talking about."

"Rose, it's good to meet you. I'm Charlotte Turner, and the people you met earlier were my granddaughter Petey and our friend Charley Pettibone. And I'll carry your message on one condition." Rose's eyes narrowed in suspicion. "You have to finish that glass of water and stay in bed another twenty minutes. Whatever it was that made you pass out—" she let the pause hang for a moment—"has also dried you out. You need water, and plenty of it." Charlotte turned to the door. "And if you feel sickness coming on again, use the basin." And with that she was out the door, with Rose's words of thanks behind her, and the unspoken relief in her voice that Charlotte hadn't lectured her on morality or made some impossible demand about reforming her life.

She poked her head into the kitchen, where Petey and Charley sat at the table. "I need to run an errand for this girl. I'll be right back, but she should be okay."

Out in the Pike, she looked up and down the street. Nothing but strolling fairgoers, naturally, just at the moment that she was seeking a policeman. She worked her way toward the train station, where pickpockets and bunco men usually guaranteed the presence of a policeman or two. Sure enough, as she neared the station she saw a tall, thin officer leaning against the wall of the Tyrolean Alps, idly scanning the passers-by. She walked up to him.

"I need your assistance."

He gazed down at her with mild interest. "All right."

"I've been asked to convey a message to someone named Big Bill, and was told that a policeman could do that for me."

The officer snapped into attentiveness and studied her closely. "Is this some kind of joke?"

"I assure you, it is not."

He looked around in the crowd as if suspicious that someone was watching. "You hardly look the type to have dealings with Big Bill."

"I don't. I've just been asked to get a message to him."

"Do you know him?"

"I do not."

The policeman laughed. "I guess you don't! There he sits." He gestured toward a table in the open-air section of the Tyrolean Alps beer garden, where a large man sat alone, a newspaper and a glass of beer in front of him, though neither appeared to be of much interest; his eyes constantly moved, scrutinizing the crowd, and before too long they settled on her. Then they moved on.

"I'd better walk you over," the policeman said. "Big Bill don't like to be approached uninvited."

They walked over to the table; as they approached, Big Bill stood up and tipped his hat. He looked over at the policeman, silent.

"This lady says she has a message for you."

Big Bill nodded curtly and pulled out a chair. "Please, ma'am." He glanced at the cop, who swiftly disappeared.

Only when she sat down did Charlotte realize with a start that she had seen this man before. He was the man in the carriage, supervising the construction crew, who had unnerved her in the early spring. Well, that wasn't going to happen again. She drew a breath and let it out slowly to settle herself.

Big Bill was a large man indeed, perhaps six-four, barrel-chested, dressed in a cream-colored summer suit and a flat-top straw hat. "So," he said.

"I'm from the Heaven Holler exhibit down the way. A young woman passed out in our doorway a short while ago, and we took her upstairs to recover. She's doing fine, but she wanted to send word about her whereabouts." Charlotte considered how to phrase the next part. "She says her name is Rose. Says you're a friend of hers."

A waiter had appeared at her elbow, but she waved him away. "Thank you, I won't be staying."

"Are you sure, ma'am?" Big Bill said. "The food and drink here are quite fine, and I run a tab."

"I'm sure. I need to get back."

"And you say she passed out?"

"Yes. She was unconscious for about twenty minutes, I'd say."

His face closed up as if pulled by a drawstring. "Do you have any notion as to what might have caused this?"

"I'll not venture a guess," Charlotte said, not wishing to be drawn into whatever lay between the two of them.

"You're no gabster. I like that." Big Bill stood up and adjusted his hat; despite his size, he was nimble and quick. "I'd like to see her."

Charlotte hesitated. The man exuded an unsavory air but had given her no cause for refusal. "I suppose so. Please understand, she may not be capable of much conversation."

"Certainly." He extended the crook of his elbow and she took it, unwilling to be rude even to someone of troubling reputation. As they walked back down the Pike toward their building, people stepped aside and tipped their hats.

"You seem to be well known here," she said.

"I've lived my whole life in this town. Grew up in the Kerry Patch and belong to one of the Democratic clubs. So yes, people know me."

"I believe I've seen you before. We came up to see the exhibit in the spring and I believe you were overseeing its construction."

Big Bill's glance was appraising and impressed. "You have an excellent memory, ma'am. You'd be surprised how many people I meet who forget the simplest things." He chuckled to himself. "Especially when they owe me money."

Charlotte laughed. "True the world round. I haven't been complimented on my memory in a long time, so I hope you will forgive me for taking it as flattery."

"I never flatter, ma'am. 'He does me double wrong that wounds me with the flatteries of his tongue.'"

"Shakespeare! I wouldn't have taken you for a literary man."

"Nor I you. I was under the impression that you were simple country people."

"Oh, we are. But we can still read. I still have my father's copy of *The Complete Works.*"

They had reached the entrance to Heaven Holler, where the male half of the vaudeville couple had shown up to take tickets. "Hello, Jack," Big Bill said. "Still playing the Century?"

Jack the ticket-taker looked as if he had just stepped in front of an oncoming train. "As often as I can, Bill," he muttered. "Thanks for asking."

"And playing here too?"

"Rustic bits, some songs and patter. Lizzie's doing it with me." His eyes darted from one to the other. "You two know each other?"

"We just made acquaintance." Big Bill leaned forward. "And I understand my friend Rose is here, and not feeling well."

The darting eyes grew wild. "She is? Bill, I had no idea. If I'd known, I would have sent word right away—"

But no further words were needed, as Rose stumbled out from the main hall and burrowed into Bill's embrace, her eyes still glassy but her smile broad. "I knew you'd come looking for me!" she cried. "I'm sorry if I made you worry. I just got a little—a little—faint or something. And these people have been so sweet."

If Big Bill was skeptical of her explanation, it didn't show in his face. He disentangled himself from her a little and patted her hair. "It's all right, kid. We'll stop by the doc's to make sure you're okay."

Petey and Charley appeared, trailing behind, and from the looks on their faces Charlotte could tell that Rose's departure from the upstairs bedroom had been sudden and unexpected.

"Are you sure you're well enough to walk?" Charlotte asked.

"Oh, yes, ma'am," Rose said. "I'm practically skipping."

She wasn't skipping, or anywhere near it, but her obvious desire to appear light and vivacious was so palpable that Charlotte would have felt cruel to contradict it.

"All right, then," Big Bill said. "Let's go. Mrs. Turner, and friends, thank you so much for taking care of our little dear." He held out his hand as if to shake hers, but Charlotte could tell he had a silver dollar concealed in it. Perhaps this man was indeed the great crime figure everyone treated him as; but the day had not yet come when she would take a dollar for doing her Christian duty by some poor girl who collapsed on her doorstep. She grasped his hand with her left, over the top, so that the coin could not be passed.

"I'm glad to have met her, sir, and to have made your acquaintance as well," she said, meeting his look with a firm, knowing gaze of her own. He nodded, smiled, and returned his hand to his pocket.

"Here we go, chicken," Big Bill said, and with a sudden sweep he lifted Rose off her feet with as little effort as Charlotte would have used to pick up an actual chicken from the floor of the henhouse. "I think Mrs. Turner is right to question your strength, so I'll pack you to my carriage." Rose squealed in pleased surprise and laced her fingers around his neck. In a moment they were gone, disappearing down the Pike in the direction Charlotte and he had just come.

Everyone stood in silence for a minute. Charlotte turned to Jack, the vaudeville player. "Tell me, what's the 'Kerry Patch'"?

Jack recovered from his shock. "It's an old neighborhood down by the river. Not a place I'd go without an invitation. Why?"

"I heard it mentioned earlier today. Just curious." Charlotte had some thoughts to work through, but none she wished to share.

"That was some excitement," Charley said. "Are all your days this exciting?"

"No. And I've had all the excitement I care to for the day. Petey, make sure you're ready to catch the morning train back home."

Chapter 13

On the train the next morning, Charlotte studied the timetable and repented the abruptness of their departure as she considered that writing ahead would have meant that Newton or one of the boys could have been waiting for them at the Ironton depot, but now they would have to hire a horse and cart for the trip. Given the time and trouble involved with that task, they'd likely end up spending the night—not that they couldn't afford the hotel, but Charlotte had no fondness for avoidable expenses.

But to her surprise, there was Newton with a team of horses, and not just the old farm wagon but the nice carriage, the one he kept under canvas out in the barn. Thoughts of his psychic abilities disappeared, though, when he hurried to the front car to greet a well-dressed couple who stepped off, unaware of Charlotte and Petey two cars back, until Petey called out.

Newton waved to them, then bustled the couple into his carriage before dashing to greet them. "Look at you!" he cried. "Making a surprise inspection, eh? Never fear, we've been looking after your house, and your garden, too. Can't say it's as clean as you keep it, but we do our best."

"No surprise inspection," Charlotte said. "We just got a little homesick, I guess. But it's a happy surprise to find you here. Do you have room?"

"Sure. These folks didn't bring much luggage."

And so they all bundled into the carriage, Newton driving from the rooftop seat and Petey, Charlotte, and as they soon discovered a Mr. and Mrs. Blackwell, newlyweds from Louisville and devoted purchasers of the Kellogg Publishing Company's output, who were simultaneously thrilled to be riding with the mother and daughter of their favorite author, apprehensive about being driven into the spectacularly savage countryside they had been reading about, and relieved to see that it was far less savage than they had imagined.

"So who's the real-life inspiration for the Old Man of the Mountains?" Mr. Blackwell asked.

"I can't say there really was one," said Charlotte.

"Oh, but there has to be! He's so *true*." Blackwell gazed out the coach window with consuming curiosity. "I feel like I'd know him a half mile away, I have such a picture in my mind. Or I'd know him just by shaking his hand."

Charlotte decided to leave that opinion where it lay. "Come all this way from Louisville, I hope you're planning to go up to the Fair."

"My, yes!" Mrs. Blackwell burst in. "It's the final stop on our tour." She glanced at her husband for approval. "We started out at the Mammoth Cave, and then we went to Memphis."

"Stayed at the Peabody Hotel," Mr. Blackwell added with satisfaction. "Mammoth Cave was grand, once you got through the scoundrels at the train station who tried to tell you it was closed."

"What would they do that for?" Petey said.

"Take you to their own cave. That countryside is rotten with caves." He considered. "There's a cave in Heaven Holler, too, isn't there?"

"Yes, sir," said Petey. "It's not mammoth, but I can show it to you. It's more mud than anything."

"Well, that would be just fine, young miss." The inside of the carriage was hot and getting hotter. He tugged at his collar and fanned himself with his hat. "Jefferson Davis stayed in the Peabody Hotel, you know. After they let him out of prison. The bellman took us to see his rooms." He leaned forward and whispered, conspiratorial. "They don't say much about it to the public. I reckon it's a touchy subject even now."

"It's a touchy subject here too, for those of us old enough to remember it," Charlotte said. She didn't want to sound pinch-faced, but memories of the war still pained her, even now, and the notion of people making a shrine and tourist attraction out of the habitations of that blackguard Jefferson Davis filled her with disgust. But the past was past, and she tried to soften her voice into friendly neutrality. "You are too young to remember this, but that war broke families apart, put neighbors on opposite side." She considered the wisdom of speaking further; what difference would it make? But something about the man's lazy pretense to knowledge provoked her. "I myself shot a man down in the door of the schoolhouse of Daybreak, my closest neighbor and the son of a dear friend."

In the shocked silence of the carriage Charlotte gazed out at the familiar landscape. Now why on earth had she gone and said that? It sounded like the idle boasting of the GAR boys on the benches in front of the courthouse, the whittle-and-spit crowd whose exploits grew more heroic each year. As if shooting somebody was an act to be proud of.

Worst of all, she caught a glimpse of Petey out of the corner of her eye, and the child looked proud. Some words would need to be had later on.

But the comment had achieved its effect of quieting Mr. Blackwell, so they rode in silence for a while. When Charlotte changed the subject to the fine prospect of Black Mountain in front of them, they rushed to embrace the new topic with grateful haste.

And before they knew it they were rolling into Daybreak from the south, a sight that brought a lift regardless of how long she had been away: the narrow passage between the bluffs and the river, the slow opening up of the valley as they approached, then the Pettibones' cluster of buildings; Newton said as they passed, with careful neutrality, "Fella here's built a bathhouse out from his mineral spring. I can't claim it's a healing spring, like the one in the book, but what do I know? You might want to give it a try." Leave it to Newton to be scrupulous even with his competitors.

Then the fork in the road where the Daybreak road branched off, with the main road to town following the river; and just off the fork, her house, with its big maple shade tree out front, the deep ridges of its bark running in rough furrows down the trunk. Newton helped her down from the carriage. "Come for dinner tonight?" he said.

"All right." She felt more like running over to hug her dear old shade tree, then stepping inside to lie on her bed and imbibe the silence. But people would want stories, news, accounts of all the celebrated and strange. She had plenty of the latter, much of which she would keep to herself, and blessed little of the former. Petey would bring her mother up to date; so that left her Newton, Sarah, and the boys. And presumably the irritating Mr. Blackwell and his simpering wife. Charlotte let herself into her house, dropped her valise to the floor, walked into the bedroom, slapped the dusty bedcover a couple of times, lay down fully dressed, closed her eyes, and let her head sink into the pillow.

When she awoke, twilight had nearly arrived. She felt groggy and out of sorts, unaccustomed to the notion of sleep during daylight. She sat on the edge of the bed, settled her feet beneath herself, and then walked into the kitchen.

A few years ago, Charlotte had had the boys install a small hand pump at the end of the kitchen counter, connected by a pipe to the big pump outside. What a modern miracle it had seemed, saving her the many trips outside, in fair days or miserable, to pump water and carry it in. She had found a wide porcelain bowl to place underneath it for everyday use, and kept a galvanized bucket nearby for bigger jobs. Now, she pumped the little handle over and over again, for her weeks of absence had allowed the water to siphon back into the well. Eventually a trickle began to flow, and then a full stream. Charlotte washed her face and arms, then stepped to the back door to fling the soapy water into the yard.

Where was their pride in modern convenience now? This little hand pump seemed so paltry. She had seen the fountains and cascades, flowing endlessly from the faraway Mississippi, the kinetoscope, the incomprehensible phenomena of voices traveling on beams of light and even through the empty air itself. As if she wasn't feeling anachronistic enough in ordinary life, as the people she met seemed ever younger. The city had endless wonders, and she had an indoor pump.

But no one had ever made anything better by complaining, so she returned the bowl to its place beneath the spout and headed up the road to Newton's house.

Chapter 14

Charlotte awoke the next morning refreshed, grateful for the familiar lumps and contours of her own bed. She didn't sleep much anymore, even in the quiet of her own house, so it came as no surprise to her when her eyelids popped open in the dimness of near-morning, one rackety wren outside the window singing his fool head off, and a list of tasks for the day already forming in her mind. Sweep the house. Check in with Jenny to let her know that Charley was doing all right. Look in on Penelope and Petey, take the temperature of the situation there: the absent-minded Adam had in all likelihood not stayed in touch, so she might need to sit down and talk a while. Then down the lane to the store; Sarah would have news and mail, if there was any. Then home, rest, tidy, see what the remainder of the day would bring.

Her mind felt jangled after all the events of the past few weeks. Attentive Filipinos, unconscious prostitutes, large and vaguely scary criminals: it was all a bit much. Whatever one might say about their remote valley, Heaven Holler or not, at least its perils were familiar. She lay in bed a while longer and listened to the wren. What did he have to be so excited about? Marauding hawks and snakes, noisy wrens, boys with slingshots. All right, chirp all you want.

But she couldn't rest for long, and soon she was at Penelope's table, coffee in hand, while Penelope served crumb cake. "Where's Petey?" she asked.

Penelope shrugged. "Who knows? Off right after breakfast. Turning over rocks, probably, just to see what's underneath." She smiled, faintly. "I credit a good bit of that to you."

"Credit or blame?" They laughed.

"Enough of both, given the occasion," Penelope said. "But tell me about the Fair, your lodgings, St. Louis! I want to hear all."

So Charlotte set in on the experience, the immensity of everything, Nimuel and Sky-Face, the rushing throngs and the constant noise. When she reached the part about Rose, she paused for a moment, for such things were unseemly to talk about. But she pressed on, for this was Penelope, and of the two sisters Sarah might be the steady one, reliable and solid as a well-set cornerpost, but Penelope was the sharp one who concealed her wit and wanted to know everything. Sarah would frown and wave her hand in front of her face as if to dispel the odor of immorality; Penelope would lean in and ask for details.

"So has this girl returned to your exhibit?" Penelope asked. "One might think she'd come back to say thanks."

"No. I think she recognizes the difficulty. As long as she's outside and keeps moving, no one bothers her, but coming inside is a step too far."

Penelope leaned back and smiled. "Finally, I get to hear what's going on up there! Petey has to be coaxed for every tidbit, and Adam's letters are like the market report in the paper: wheat up a penny, hogs down a penny. 'An interesting gentleman from Pennsylvania stopped by yesterday, I signed fifty books and a dozen photographs.'"

It was good to talk with Penelope, someone who thought the way she did, more or less, or at least used the same vocabulary. Charley's wife Jenny was simple but good-hearted, too busy keeping track of kids and grandkids to think, and Sarah tended to think in straight lines—long ones, but straight, nonetheless. Charlotte enjoyed the meander and dip of Penelope's mind.

But it was time to move along if she hoped to accomplish all that she had set her mind to, so she said her good-byes and walked to the store. She sensed something was wrong as soon as she walked in.

She could see Newton in the back room, sitting at a late breakfast with the newlywed Blackwells, while Sarah stood at the front counter with a tense expression. Sarah put her finger to her lips as Charlotte walked in, and Charlotte followed her glance to the corner of the store, where Ulysses S. Canterbury stood examining a row of shovels and pickaxes with a look of fixed determination on his face. Charlotte walked closer to Sarah, who leaned over the counter to whisper.

"He won't leave," she hissed. "Says he's just browsing. Our paying guests have objected to his presence, and Newton's trying to keep them calm."

Charlotte nodded. She eased over to him the way one would approach an injured dog, carefully and slow.

"Well, good morning," she said. Canterbury glanced at her in surprise.

"I thought you were up in the city."

"We were. But Petey and I both got to feeling a little homesick, so we decided to make a quick trip back to Daybreak." She edged closer and spoke so as not to be overheard. "I was able to pay a call on your lovely wife while I was up there. She wanted to know if you were eating properly."

He chuckled. "That's her, all right. And the boy?"

"He was outside playing, so I didn't exactly get introduced. But I saw him from a distance. He looks like a fine, healthy lad."

The news from home, sparse as it was, had its effect, and Canterbury's tense face relaxed. Time to speak. "Sarah says you might be looking for something?"

Canterbury glanced over his shoulder to the counter, where Sarah stood with lips pursed. "Actually, I was hoping to get a word in with Mr. Newton back there, but he doesn't seem to want to come out. But maybe you can help me."

"Let's walk outside where we can talk freely."

They stepped into the street. Charlotte marveled to herself how such a simple thing—a man standing in a store—could become so fraught because of faulty perceptions, and she reminded herself to bear that thought in mind.

Canterbury cleared his throat. "I am looking for a lawyer. Thought you might recommend one."

"A lawyer! Are you in trouble?"

He snorted. "Far from it. Just the opposite. It's those Renicks that are going to be in trouble. They're encroaching on my land, claim it's theirs. Cut down six of my trees the other day. But I have a deed! Goddamn it, I have a deed in black and white." He stopped himself. "Please excuse the outburst, ma'am. My feelings are strong here."

Charlotte waved his apology away, thinking. Surely Ulysses Canterbury, young as he was, was not so naïve as to believe he could start a legal action down here, even if he could find an attorney, which she doubted, and prevail, a single black man against three generations of a white family. Things had improved since the war, but not that much, and not around here.

"Lawyers cost money," she ventured. "And the outcome is never certain. Perhaps we can find a way to resolve the problem informally. When I first came to this valley, we had disputes over our land title, too. The titles on some of this land go a long way back." She looked away to avoid his suspicious gaze.

"You are right about the money," Canterbury finally said, grudgingly. "I'd have to take out a mortgage to pay the lawyer, and then where would I be, even if I won? Over my head in debt, just with a new boss to answer to. No good to come from that."

They walked down the gravel street toward the ferry crossing, Canterbury's anger slowly subsiding. "Are you sure it was Renick who cut down your trees? Did you see him? Did he say anything?"

"Waited till I was gone to work. Got home after dark, didn't notice they were gone till morning. Young hickories, not hardly even big enough to cut an axe handle from. Haven't spoken to them about it, but there's a fine new stack of hickory wood out in plain sight up against their shed, cut to bolt length."

Charlotte felt disheartened but not surprised. From what she had seen, Grandma Renick was not one for subtlety. "All right," she said. "Let me gather some people. People who might have some sway. We'll pay a call on you, and on them, and try to get this straightened out. Nobody wants trouble in the valley."

Unless it suits their purposes, she thought grimly.

They'd had their own disputes, back in the early days. It had not been their best moment, she and James, wrangling over deeds with their neighbor, the previous inhabitant of Pettibone's place. To be sure, he had been a bad man, but that didn't mean he deserved to be treated badly, and to this day she felt a pang of shame about how she had acquiesced in James' tactics at fighting off that lawsuit. Everyone had bent the rules during the war, or tossed them aside entirely, but her regret was curiously persistent, even all these years later. Strange how she eventually forgot about the wrongs received, or at least the pain of them grew dull. But the wrongs she had inflicted burned like a poker.

By this time they had reached the edge of the village, and she stopped. Charlotte's mind raced with the trouble ahead. Say she gathered some local lights and took them to the scene, and say they found it all just as Canterbury said. What then? It was hard to picture Grandma Renick offering sweet apologies and compensation for the lost trees.

"I suppose you know," she said, "This could all come to nothing."

"I know that," he said with a tight nod. "I've had to swallow my pride before. Doesn't make it any easier."

They turned back toward Daybreak, where Newton was pulling out with his carriage, the Blackwells sitting grandly behind him, the missus in a wide-brimmed hat and morning outfit as if she was on her way out shopping.

"So what shall I tell her?" Charlotte said, changing the subject to something more pleasant. "Your wife, I mean. Are you eating properly? She'll ask me, the next time I see her."

"No doubt she will. Well, she'll be happy to know that your friends the Bridges pay a decent wage at the match factory, and Mrs. Turner charges fair prices at the store." He snapped his fingers. "Mercy sakes! I was so upset over my trees that all I could think about was finding a lawyer. I'll lose half a day's pay at the factory." Canterbury trotted down the road, calling over his shoulder. "I'll stop and talk more on my way back, if it's not too late and I see a lamp lit."

Charlotte stood in the roadway and waved at his receding form to show that she had heard. She hadn't intended to come home only to embroil herself in other people's property disputes, and yet here she was, neck-deep on her first morning, and for what? For her abstract ideal of justice for the black man, so that man could hold just dominion over his hickory trees. She felt like kicking herself. Of course she believed in equal treatment for all, but did it have to devolve into an argument over a boundary line? It felt like a great expenditure of effort over a trivial matter. Easy for her to say. They weren't her trees.

But it was a fair, bright morning, and she refused to let a squabble over a property line rob her of her pleasure in it, no matter how justified Canterbury's outrage might be.

She had a notion about where she might find Petey. In her younger days, Charlotte had made herself a little refuge, a sitting spot, on a great sloping ledge of rock that slanted into the river, across from her house. Shielded from view by bushes and tall grass, the slab of limestone proved an ideal spot to sit and reflect, to be alone with her thoughts and answerable only to herself, even if for a few minutes. Over the years, she had visited the place less and less. But recently she had introduced it to Petey, who had adopted it as her own, and the two of them had spent many afternoons there, trailing their hands in the water and hatching schemes.

Charlotte supposed she would stop by there and check on the girl. But since the appeal of the place was its seclusion, its freedom from intrusion, she felt no rush. Let the girl have her quiet.

Daybreak Ridge shimmered in the distance behind the village, the warm breeze ruffling the leaves on the trees like an indulgent father tousling his son's hair. Down the road she watched Canterbury disappear on his way to Lucinda, passing the Pettibone boys half-heartedly hoeing corn in their fields. They stopped to gawk, as they did with every available distraction. Canterbury paid them no mind, jogging with his head down until he disappeared from view.

The hunger for property, the power of land. Those boys would likely never experience anything close to what it was like to be someone like Ulysses S. Canterbury, a man born without house or holding, someone who had to scratch for everything he owned, just as their father had. They would coast along on their daddy's enterprise, and when he passed away they would divide it up and keep or sell as they pleased. Once upon a time, the inequity of this had troubled her—the labor of some, the feast of others—but nowadays she had begun to think it was a reflection of man's fallen state, the human race struggling but unable to rise from the mire of greed and selfishness where it had always existed. Or, she thought to herself, perhaps she was merely indulging in the self-justifying rationalization that came to those who were already established in the world.

She continued south, the river behind its screen of bushes on her left hand and the fields of Daybreak on her right. This time of year, it was wise to keep an eye on the road ahead, as snakes crossed out of the undergrowth in search of mice and voles, and returned to rest and digest in the protective shade. The cornfields, wheatfields, and pastures they labored so carefully to preserve were nothing more than a new kind of hunting ground to these creatures, and now that she thought about it, Charlotte could imagine the snakes probably welcomed their efforts as a way of creating ever-larger populations of mice and moles for them to eat. A foolish conceit, to be sure, the notion that brute animals thought about humans one way or another except at a moment of threat or disturbance. The human habit, to always place themselves in the center of the picture.

By now she had reached her house, where the little road from Daybreak rejoined the main road, and stopped for a drink of water and a rest on her porch. Another couple hundred yards down the road, she could see Newton's carriage stopped at Charley Pettibone's establishment. The newlyweds had stopped to enjoy Charley's healing spring, she supposed. Even when that spring was in its original state, an intermittent muddy flow that emerged halfway up the hill from a cave entrance behind Charley's barn, Charlotte had sensed something beneficial in its water, and she'd often used it for plasters and poultices. Who knows, maybe Adam's imagination had landed on something real, and Charley's embellished version was its inadvertent confirmation. Stranger things had happened in Mother Nature's domain.

By now she felt rested enough to continue with her day, and she supposed that now was a good time to pay her call on Jenny Pettibone, as the distraction of paying customers would suffice to keep her from embarking on her tedious recitation of the doings of each child and grandchild, in order, which usually took an hour. Not that Charlotte didn't want to hear all about the Pettibones, but Jenny's dosage was often too large to easily swallow.

Newton's grateful expression at her arrival confirmed her guess that Charley's absence had wound Jenny's watchspring a little too tight. "Good morning, Mama," he said, clamping his hat onto his head. "Excuse me, I need to step out to check on the horse. Be right back."

Charlotte took his arm. "Don't run off. I need to talk to you about something."

"I can't run off. I've got customers here."

"They're in Charley's mineral baths?"

"Yes, and they asked not to be disturbed."

"You don't suppose—" Charlotte stopped what she was about to say and gave him an amused glance, while Jenny covered her mouth in horror.

He shrugged. "They just said not to disturb them, didn't say why. Maybe one of them has a condition that needs healing."

"It's not even ten o'clock in the morning!" Jenny cried. "What kind of establishment do they think we're running?"

"Calm down," Newton said gruffly. "We don't know what they're up to, and besides, they're legally married. We were young ourselves once." And with that, he tipped his hat and left the house.

"Easy for him to say," Jenny huffed. "Men always go on about how reputation is no great matter, until it suits them otherwise."

"I can't disagree with you there," Charlotte said. "But I came to bring word of your husband. This will probably come as no surprise, but he's having a grand time up there, playing the bumpkin and drumming up business. You'll have a parade of visitors before long, I expect."

This news seemed to please her. "That sounds like Charley, all right. He's got a gift for talking to strangers like I never had. Nor most others, neither."

"We've only had a couple of mishaps. One was when we all took a ride on the big Ferris wheel, and I doubt if it will come as a surprise to you that Charley didn't like that one bit."

"Oh, he's deathly afraid of heights."

"Then we had a girl pass out in front of our exhibition. You might hear about this from him. We took her in to revive her, but Charley has some doubts about her character."

This brought a sour look. "Oh, does he now? I'll hear about it, all right, but he'll slip it in sneaky-like, as if it just occurred to him to remember. I don't put up with any foolishness, and he knows it. One thing I'll say, though. He's never given me any worry on that account."

Jenny's self-satisfied tone was irksome enough that for a moment, Charlotte wondered if her distaste for her attitude might show on her face. She'd spent enough of her life around village biddies and had no wish to become one herself. She turned away. "Anyway, I thought I'd let you know that he's doing well, but he misses you."

"Me, or my cooking?" But her smile showed that she was joking. "Well, when you go back, tell him I miss him too. And his dog misses him. Won't come out from under the porch."

"I'll tell him. Why don't you come up sometime? The fair is something to behold, even if you only stroll the avenues."

Jenny shuddered. "All those people! I don't see how you can stand it."

Charlotte remembered when Jenny had first come to Daybreak, as a young lady's maid to a wealthy traveler shortly after the war, and had stayed behind when the old lady returned to Philadelphia. Charlotte always figured that it had been Charley, not social reform, that had attracted her to Daybreak, for the two of them married quickly and settled into their life of placid procreation. Charley's job as a deputy sheriff had brought its anxious moments, but in their simple, straightforward way they had gradually become pillars of the community. Not bad for an orphan boy and a serving girl.

"That's the truth," Charlotte said. "People throng the streets day and night. Sometimes I can't get to sleep till midnight or past. But if you'll excuse me, I need to have a word with Newton."

She stepped outside, where Newton stood brushing down his horse. "I need your help."

Newton didn't stop his labor. "All right."

"There's trouble on the ridge that I hope to head off. The Renicks and Ulysses Canterbury are disputing their property line, and Canterbury says they've cut down a bunch of his trees."

"And how is this my problem?" Newton said, straightening up.

"It's not, directly. But you know how these disputes can fester. I'd like to settle it before it spreads."

"Settle it how?"

"I thought to take a deputation up there, respected people in the community, to look things over and decide on the boundary. Save everyone the expense of going to court and hope to tamp down hard feelings."

"Uh-huh. And you want me to be one of these Silas Do-Goods."

"Yes, and I thought I'd ask J. M. Bridges, and anyone else you might think suitable."

Newton sighed. "All right. Not that I think it's a good idea to involve myself in other people's disputes. But the Renicks are a trashy bunch that take and take and take, and they need to be put in their place. Sarah's been moaning about them since they first set foot." He walked back to the carriage, took a rag out of his pocket, and dusted off the seats. "But I need something from you in return, and it involves your pet project, Mr. Canterbury."

Charlotte followed him, curious and a little apprehensive.

"Not everyone is as broad-minded as you." Newton avoided her gaze, and gestured toward Pettibone's mineral spring. "I spent twenty minutes calming those people down this morning after Canterbury came a-waltzing through the front door of the store. Had to convince them I run a respectable establishment."

"Are you going to let a couple of kids from Kentucky boss you around?"

He grimaced. "Mother, I have liberal views, but I also have a store to run. I don't want to lose anybody's business, but if I have to lose someone's, I know which one I'd choose. So I'll serve on your deputation if you'll talk to Canterbury. Tell him to bring a list of what he needs to the back door and we'll fill it. But no hanging around inside the store."

"The man's your neighbor. You want to humiliate him like that?"

"Neighbor or not, I have customers from all parts of the country to serve, and some of them have very fixed ideas." He sighed. "Okay, he'll only have to come to the back if I have guests who might object. But you need to let him know, so he'll understand what's going on if Sarah waves him off."

Charlotte gritted her teeth. "All right." She turned to leave.

"Where are you going?"

"Off to enlist Bridges for my deputation." Charlotte pointed down the road.

"That's a long walk on a warm day. Why don't you wait till tomorrow morning? I need to take these lovebirds to the siding at Lucinda to catch the northbound train. They're in a great rush to get to the Fair."

"You should come up too, sometime. Free lodging, and Petey will give you the tour."

The look of distaste that passed over Newton's face was shocking in its intensity. "Come up and bask in secondhand glory, eh? I think not." He turned away and walked into Pettibone's house.

Of course Newton resented Adam's sudden wealth and fame. The two of them had always been opposites, one of the great oddities of family life, children a couple of years apart whose temperaments resembled each other's no more than a pair of random strangers. She had known that all along.

And the practical Newton was right about one thing. There had been a time when she could have walked to Lucinda, transacted her business, and walked home again, even if the last couple of hours would be after dark. But she was past those days now. Compromises and accommodations. The longer one lived, the more one became accustomed to them.

So she would wait till morning and ride in the carriage, and she would do her best not to antagonize the Blackwells, for Newton's sake. But it would be a long ride indeed if anybody referred to Ulysses S. Canterbury as her pet project.

Chapter 15

Word had gotten around about the trip to Lucinda, for in the morning Petey was sitting beside Newton on the driver's bench, half-turned around in her seat, peppering the Blackwells with questions about Kentucky and Louisville, which Mr. Blackwell informed her was the most promising city in the middle states, soon to surpass Cincinnati by virtue of its superior climate and industrious people, and a city that had no Negro problem whatsoever. Charlotte suspected last comment had been tossed in to bait her into a debate, but ignored it, and was grateful for Petey's peppy energy as she continued the conversation without a pause. When Petey learned that the Blackwells were headed to the Fair, they exchanged delighted confidences for the rest of the journey.

Charlotte liked the road to Lucinda, though it was not a road to like if you were in a hurry. The narrow path south between the mountain and the river, then the abrupt turn westward through French Mills and up Marble Creek, the road getting rockier and more difficult with every mile; then the flatwoods trail around Black Mountain followed by a sudden rise up over a ridge, steep and harrowing in its test of horses and wagon wheels, and the descent into the Big Creek valley where Lucinda snoozed on the creekbank, its more robust days behind it but still with the commercial advantage of a whistlestop on the main line from St. Louis to Little Rock.

They reached the siding in plenty of time, so they all climbed down from the carriage, feeling leisurely, and stretched in the light breeze. Bridges' mill was running full tilt, its circular saws keening at a high musical whine, and a stream of sawdust blasting from the blow chute. Charlotte strolled down the rail line to inspect the neat stacks of crossties and barrel staves awaiting shipment. A pretty harvest, resilient lumber for the railbeds and whiskey casks of the nation. Farther down the platform stood a stack of crates emblazoned with skulls and crossbones and warnings to keep away from heat: the famous matches, no doubt.

She walked to the main office, which stood along what passed for Lucinda's front street, a track of packed earth that ran alongside the railroad tracks. The mill office, the post office, a little store, a blacksmith's shop, a stable, all lined up in a ramshackle row like the town militia. She stepped inside the mill office, where Josephine Bridges sat bent over an account book.

"Well, look at this!" Josephine exclaimed. "I heard a wagon pull up, but figured it was just another load of logs." She leaned to look out the window. "Turns out it's a whole delegation." She stood to shake Charlotte's hand.

"Newton had a couple of guests who needed to catch the train, and Petey and I came along for the ride. But I do have a bit of business to talk over with your husband, if he's around."

Josephine gave her a quizzical look. "Sure. He's at the match factory. Let's walk back."

They came out the front door and waved to the rest of the group, clustered around the pile of the Blackwells' trunks. "Ten more minutes!" Josephine shouted. "They're pretty reliable." Newton waved in return. "If I know anything, he'll want to leave the minute those people are on board," she said under her voice to Charlotte. "We'd better pull foot."

The match factory was up the hollow from the rest of the town, and they walked briskly up the street to reach it. When they arrived at the door, Josephine took hold of the cord of a small iron bell mounted beside the door and rang it sharply three times.

"No one's allowed inside unannounced," she said. "Not safe."

In a moment J.M. Bridges appeared at the door, a canvas mask over his face. He stepped outside, shutting the door behind him, and wiped his sweaty face with a bandanna.

"Good morning, Mrs. Turner," he said, panting a little. "This is a pleasant surprise. I'd invite you in to tour the works, but we just uncapped a new batch of chemicals and the fumes are strong today."

"That's all right," Charlotte said. "I'll visit again. Today I just came by to ask a favor."

"Name it," he said. "You've done plenty for me over the years."

"Never say 'yes' to a favor until you know what it is," she said with a smile. "But I'll take the sentiment. Your employee, Mr. Canterbury, is embroiled in a dispute with his neighbors over their land boundary, and I need some distinguished members of the community to go up there and settle it."

"Why not ask Charley Pettibone? He's the justice of the peace."

"He's in St. Louis, and I'd like to get this taken care of soon."

Bridges nodded. "All right. Canterbury's a good worker. I want to see him done right by."

"I've enlisted Newton in the cause as well. Can you come over tomorrow?"

"I'll ride over early. Perhaps we can have this matter settled by midday." He turned to go inside, and as he did Charlotte caught a glimpse of the interior of the factory: lines of men, stripped to the waist, bending over machines and tables, glistening with sweat. The air that emerged from the building reeked of sulfur and pitch.

As they walked back to the main part of the village, Josephine murmured under her breath: "Distinguished members of the community. Aren't you distinguished enough?"

Charlotte caught Josephine's eye. "For this job, I need distinguished members who also wear pants." They walked on.

Charlotte knew that Josephine didn't need reminding about the handicaps their sex labored under. She was smarter, more capable, more ambitious, and more energetic than her amiable husband. That was as plain as a fly in milk. But of course J. M. had his name on the letterhead, the company papers, the correspondence, while Josephine labored in the front office, sought out new customers, and scanned the industry circulars for opportunity. Not that Bridges wasn't a fine man, gentle and bright, deserving of the respect he enjoyed. But without Josephine, Bridges Enterprises would have been a mere note in the county history by now, if it had existed at all. They both knew it, and so did J. M., and so did all who cared to look. The world demonstrated its unfairness daily.

It was a treat to ride home in the fancy carriage and with his duty done, Newton let the horses set their own pace, urging them on only when they started to loaf as they climbed the hill out of Lucinda. From there it was all flat or downhill, more or less, following the fall of the streams. Petey sang most of the way.

"What news from your mother, Petey?" Charlotte asked her at a pause in her performance. "Is she doing all right without you?"

"Oh, sure. She said she misses me, and Papa too, but I think she's fine. She's never had the house as tidy."

"Do you want to stay here or return to St. Louis?"

"Well . . . " Then her face brightened. "Who's to say I can't do both? Papa said not to worry about the price of the train ticket."

Charlotte saw Newton's back stiffen at the mention of Adam's lack of concern for expense. Adam had never been one to notice costs. "We'll see," she said, trying to sound neutral. Petey appeared to take the hint. "Then I shall speak to Mama. If she wants me to stay, I'll stay. But if she's all right with my leaving, I'll return with you for a while longer. I've just begun to explore the Palace of Fine Arts, and there are several other buildings I've not even set foot in."

Charlotte smiled to herself. Now where had she gotten that decidedly firm tone? From her grandma, most likely.

When they reached her home in the Daybreak valley, Newton helped her down from the carriage. "Bridges agreed to come help settle this business," she told him quietly. "He'll be by in the morning." She hadn't spoken of it on the trip. Not that she expected any great trouble, but there was no reason to alarm Petey.

Newton nodded. "I'll be waiting."

~

In the morning she woke early, her usual practice, and was clean and dressed by the time she heard the sound of a man on horseback, coming up from the south. She stepped into the dawn to meet him.

J. M. Bridges was riding at a slow walk, with a second horse trailing on a lead rope. He waved from the front gate.

"I had a notion that your son would have a horse saddled for you, but wanted to bring an extra just to be sure," he said.

"Good man," she replied. "Prepared for all eventualities."

He helped her into the saddle. "This is Josephine's little riding pony," he said. "Not a mean bone in her body, and she rides well, too."

"What's her name?"

Bridges chuckled. "Venus. Nothing to do with love nor beauty, obviously. Venus was bright in the sky the morning she was born, so that's how Josephine picked it."

"I'm sure Venus and I will get along just fine."

Newton was standing in the doorway of his store, and just as predicted he had a second horse saddled. "I knew there was something I liked about the way you thought," he joked to Bridges. "Yours looks like a better choice. Mine's a little too tall. Give me a minute while I turn this one out." He took off its saddle, bridle, and blanket, and turned it out into the barnyard with a slap to the rump. "He's a grateful animal. Doesn't much care for hill climbing."

He opened the top of his saddlebag to reveal his oversized copy of the Hixson county plat book. "Thought this might come in handy," he said.

From Newton's, it was an easy climb to the schoolhouse and the cemetery behind it, then a steeper rise into the woods, where the path narrowed. They dropped into single file and picked their way. "Keep a watch," Charlotte called. "This is a snaky patch."

"I'm not worried," Newton said from the head of the line. "One thing I like about this horse, he's not afraid of snakes. Twice I've sat on this horse while he stomped a snake to death."

But no snakes showed up to illustrate Newton's claim, and before long they emerged onto Canterbury's breezy hilltop. His rock quarry had doubled in size since Charlotte had last visited. They picked their way around its edges on their way to his cabin.

"A man could break a leg going through here in the dark," Newton said.

"Snakes and broken legs. You're a regular Jeremiah," said Charlotte.

Canterbury was waiting for them outside his door. He tipped his hat as they approached.

"Got your deed?" Bridges called to him.

"Yes, sir."

"All right, let's go have a look."

They tied their horses to some saplings and walked north. After a couple of minutes they reached the spot where six hickory stumps stood, the foliage of their tops withering on the slope below.

"You see there?" Canterbury said, pointing into the distance. They could make out the Renicks' cluster of sheds and outbuildings on the next ridge over. "Up against that low-roofed one." Charlotte could make out what appeared to be a stack of cut logs.

"First things first," Bridges said. He spread out the deed on the stump and gestured for Newton to lay the plat book beside it. They bent to examine both documents.

"Okay, Section Thirteen," Newton said. He pointed to the book. "Southeast quarter of the northeast quarter. Here." His finger stabbed a spot on the plat book.

"So where are we?" Bridges asked. He pulled a compass from his pocket and let it settle. "This way's north. So that puts us right about here," he said. His finger landed near Newton's."

"Agreed," he said. They straightened up and looked around. "Deed says the corner is marked with a stake in a rockpile."

Canterbury cleared his throat. "I know right where that is. I marked off my corners the first day I got here."

"Well, that makes sense," Newton said. "Let's see."

Canterbury led them about fifty feet down the slope toward the river. Just as the ground started to drop off sharply, a mound of rocks was stacked around a slender cedar post.

"That's a survey marker, all right," Newton said. "Which way's west from here?" he asked Bridges, who consulted his compass. Bridges pointed toward the shoulder of a distant hill.

"Those stumps are yours, then," Newton continued. "Now to check that cut wood."

Bridges interrupted. "Ulysses, I'm going to make a suggestion. Now that Mr. Turner and I have confirmed the property line, perhaps you should go on to work. You can still get in half a day. I'll catch up with you on the road and let you know how the conversation went."

He didn't state the obvious, which was that if Canterbury accompanied them the conversation would turn ugly in a heartbeat, but that if he was absent a slight chance existed that such a turn could be avoided.

Canterbury hesitated. Charlotte could sense him weighing the choice, for surely it would be a pleasure to confront Bobby Renick face to face, but just as surely he knew that such a confrontation would be too risky to undertake. "Yes, sir," he finally said.

"Good man," Bridges said, a little apologetically. "We'll stick up for your interests."

Canterbury didn't answer. He started down the path to Daybreak and the mill beyond it.

None of them spoke further as they re-mounted their horses for the ride across the ridge. Charlotte thought of Canterbury and his pride of property, the thing for which he labored so mightily. A bitter pill, having to rely on near-strangers for the protection of something you valued. She hoped they were up to the task.

As they rode close, Bobby Renick came out of the house and stood watching them draw near, his gaze flat. Grandma Renick was close behind, followed by the children.

"Good morning!" Bridges called in his most cheerful voice. "Looks like a fine day ahead."

"Maybe so," said Bobby. "I ain't exactly the Weather Bureau. I see you all messing around over there."

"Is that so?" Newton said. "What do you suppose we were doing?"

"Getting ready to stir up trouble, is my guess. Grand delegations always mean trouble, is my experience."

"I wouldn't know about grand," Newton said, "but we are here on business. Don't know what your policy is on discussing business in front of the children."

Renick appeared to notice their presence for the first time. "They ain't that delicate."

"All right. We want to take a look at those stave bolts you've got stacked up there." They climbed down from their horses.

"Stave bolts, you say?" Grandma Renick said. "I had thought to use those for firewood." She contemplated the stack. "I guess some of those might make a decent barrel stave. You in the market for some?"

Newton didn't answer. He walked to the stack of wood and examined the butt ends of the logs, then looked to Bridges and Charlotte for confirmation. They both nodded.

"The problem is, you cut this wood off somebody else's land," he said. "We were just up there checking the deed."

"Who said anything about me cutting the wood?" said Bobby. "Besides, what business is it of yours? And that deed's probably fake."

"We're concerned citizens," Newton said. "His deed has the recorder's seal on it. We want to maintain harmony in the neighborhood and keep any disputes from getting out of hand without the sheriff getting involved."

The mention of the word "sheriff" thickened the atmosphere. "Perhaps there's been a mistake," Charlotte said. "Perhaps your deed just isn't clear."

Bobby eyed her suspiciously. She could tell he was trying to figure out if she was offering him a face-saving way out of an accusation of theft, or attempting to trap him into a damaging admission. In all likelihood, their deed was perfectly clear—or else they didn't have one to begin with and were simply squatting.

"Who the hell keeps their deed around the house?" Bobby said. "We sure don't. It's in town, where it's safe."

"So back to the beginning, and leaving aside who cut what," said Newton. "That there's a stack of wood that doesn't belong to you, and this needs to be made right. Beyond that, we need to agree on the boundary and how to respect it."

Renick waved his hand as if shooing a fly. "All right, tell your little friend I'll sell the wood and bring him the proceeds. I should charge him for the labor, though."

"That's a new one on me, charging somebody for cutting their trees uninvited. I wouldn't try that on your other neighbors if I was you. I think we'll be better off if you just take him back the wood."

"I ain't hauling that wood up across that slope!" Renick said with a spit. "I got better things to do. If he's so troubled about his wood, he can come get it himself."

"It's not fair, you people coming up her to blackguard my boy!" Grandma chimed in. "You can go talk to the sheriff, as far as I care."

"It's all right, mama," Bobby said. He turned back to the group. "I've said what I've said. He can have the wood, but he'll have to come fetch it."

Newton gazed at the stack for a moment, contemplating. "All right. I count twenty-seven pieces here, and that's what I expect to be here when we return." He walked to his horse and mounted. Charlotte and Bridges followed suit.

"I want my credit back at the store!" Grandma burst out. "That ain't fair, you treating us like dirt."

Newton sighed. Every deal needed a little something to close it out. "Thirty days, and then we'll see how we stand. We can't carry you indefinitely."

He reined his horse abruptly, as if to end the negotiations before any further demands were made. They fell into line behind him. "I'm bringing the boys up here with the wagon tomorrow," he muttered as he passed Charlotte. "If Canterbury comes over by himself, there'll be trouble I can't predict."

Still, the redress had been achieved, and Charlotte felt a measure of satisfaction at how Newton had handled the matter. She hadn't asked him to take the lead, but he had, and she had to admit that he had effectively trod the line between tact and confrontation. Sarah would not be happy to hear that the Renicks had credit for another month, but the concession seemed modest.

And as they passed the waist-high stump that served as the Renicks' gatepost and horse-hitch, Bobby spoke out in a voice that was not a shout but meant to reach their ears, clear and distinct: "Nigger-lovers."

A younger Charlotte Turner would have reined her horse around and challenged him, would have called him to account for his nasty remarks, especially in front of his own children, and at least tried to shame the man even if shame was not within his capacities. But the older Charlotte just sighed and let the words pass. They'd gotten what they wanted, with less fight than expected, really. So perhaps the best idea was to shrug their shoulders and let Bobby have his moment of ugly triumph.

Chapter 16

Charlotte awoke the next day feeling refreshed, despite the stress and travel of the previous days, and resolved to spend the day putting her house and grounds in order. Petey showed up after breakfast, though it was unclear whether she came on her own or was sent by her mother. Either way, Charlotte was glad to see her. They beat the rugs and swept the floors, pumped buckets of water to wash down the windows, and then walked to the springhouse for a dipper of water.

"I think I'm ready to go back to St. Louis whenever you are," Petey told her. "Mama says she'll be fine."

"Very good, dear. Tomorrow is your uncle's weekly trip to town. Pack tonight and we'll catch a ride with him in the morning."

Charlotte would have enjoyed a few more days of rest, but she couldn't fault the enthusiasm of the young. And of course catching the train from Fredericktown meant relying on the Belmont line, less than ideal, but surely the branch would be running on time. If the train didn't show up, or if it showed up too late to make the transfer at Bismarck—well, they'd just have to spend the night somewhere.

She found Newton in the barn that night, brushing down the horses, and told him of her plans. He shrugged. "Sure, come along," he said. "I was planning to go to the station anyway. There's a man coming down from St. Louis I'm supposed to pick up."

"Another literary devotee?"

He cleared his throat, a little nervous. "No. This fellow is looking to do business with me."

"Oh, really! I'm intrigued."

Newton glanced at her. "You won't like it."

"How do you know?"

"I know you. You know that piece of flat ground across the river? The old Flynn place?"

"Of course." That acreage had been a challenge and an affront to her ever since they came to this valley, flood-prone and sandy-soiled, and no one had ever been able to turn it to productive use. Not its original owner; not Flynn, who had bought it after the war; not Newton, who had bought it after Flynn's death.

"Well, this man is interested in buying it."

Charlotte didn't answer. Newton was right. She didn't like it much. Sure, the land resisted improvement, but it was theirs. She understood his desire to profit from the property but hated thinking about someone else—a stranger—taking it over. "Another would-be farmer?"

"No. This man says he represents a group from St. Louis that's looking to build a hunting and fishing club."

"Think that's true?"

Newton shrugged again. "Hunting club, farmer, makes no difference. I'll see if he's real and what price he'll pay, and decide whether to sell then. Either way, he's taken a room in our hotel, so we won't lose."

Charlotte walked home in the warm evening darkness, reflecting. She'd come a long way since her younger years. Once a radical enthusiast of the communal life, now as property-minded as a banker. Oh well, the parcel wasn't hers to dispose of anyway. Newton could do as he wanted.

The prospective buyer wasn't mentioned when they rode into town the next morning. Charlotte guessed that Newton was putting on his deal-making poker face and didn't want his thoughts to break through. So she kept her thoughts to herself as well. If Newton wanted them, he'd ask.

At the train station she leaned into the booth. "Is the northbound on time?"

The clerk tipped his cap. "Was when it left Marble Hill. Should be on the siding now, waiting for the southbound to pass." He checked the clock on the wall. "Southbound'll be here any minute."

"Good enough." She bought their tickets and sat down on a bench.

The southbound train rolled in on time, stopping just long enough for alert passengers to jump off. Newton's pickup was easy to spot, an older gentleman with gray mutton-chops who was dressed far better than anyone else who stepped onto the platform. Newton walked over to shake his hand.

"Hope it wasn't too much trouble to come fetch me," the man said. "I'm Bob Callender."

"No problem at all, Mr. Callender," Newton said. "As it turned out, I needed to bring my mother and niece up to catch the northbound." He gestured to Charlotte, who stood up and extended her hand.

"Ma'am," Callender said, raising his hat. "It's a fine day for travel."

"Indeed it is," Charlotte said. "I understand you're from St. Louis."

"Yes, ma'am." He held out a card: Robert M. Callender, President, Callender Corrugated Box and Fiberboard Company.

"You are a maker of boxes."

"Correct. The paper box is a significant advance over wooden boxes in many instances, much lighter weight and surprisingly strong."

Charlotte smiled. "I can see that your success comes from a true belief in your product. I won't detain you. Our train is on time, or so they say, and you'll want plenty of time to look over the acreage in daylight."

"True and it's a bit of a ride," Newton said. "Enjoy the Fair, Mother."

"Ah, headed to the Fair!" Callender said. "Now there's a grand thing."

"So they say." Charlotte didn't elaborate, since the reason for their visit to the Fair was a sore point with Newton, and waved them on their way.

A half hour later, the northbound train arrived as promised. "Seems longer than usual," Charlotte said to the conductor, who nodded.

"Two extra cars," he said. "Seems like we've brought half of Arkansas up here in the last month. Special charters, whole towns full."

"All good for business, I suppose."

"Good for the owners, anyway. Me, I just have to hoof it from one end of the train to the other like I'm running a foot race."

In moments they were off and settled into their seats, whisking past the stop at Mine la Motte, pausing at Knob Lick to snatch up a passenger, angling north and west through the flat country. Petey's curiosity got the best of her, and she wandered toward the back cars to find out about the special charters. She returned a few minutes later as they pulled out from Delassus.

"They're from Charleston, Missouri," she said as she plopped into the seat. "They grow cotton." She sniffed. "They seem a little backward, if you ask me."

Charlotte eyed her with amusement. "Is that so?"

Petey blushed. "I sound like a right fool, don't I? Sitting in judgment on people I've just met."

"The seat of judgment is usually a precarious spot." Point made, she said no more, and gazed out at the passing landscape of scrub oaks and scratched-out farm holdings, a diminished territory pockmarked by abandoned tiff diggings.

It seemed as though everything around her these days was diminished territory: lumber mills turning out matchsticks, mines used for whiskey storage, farms that made more money by selling the rock beneath than the production from the surface. As if the whole area was hollowing itself out and was reduced to consuming the remaining scraps to keep itself alive. And now this man and his hunting and fishing club. The trees, the rocks, the very creatures of the earth itself, all to be harvested and hauled away.

By the time they reached Union Station, there was little time to admire its immense gold-leaf-and-limestone grandeur before hustling to find the right streetcar. It was past suppertime when they arrived at the Heaven Holler exhibit, and the Pike was in full swing, with bands and barkers intermingled with the swirling crowd. And there on the corner a dozen yards from the entrance, singing "Sweet Genevieve" in her bright, thin voice, stood Rose, in a pink-and-white striped frock and matching hat, as unconcerned about the jostling throng as if she were standing on the bank of a mill stream.

Charlotte glanced at Petey, who in her youthful self-absorption hadn't spotted Rose. "You go on in," Charlotte said. "I'll be in directly. I want to watch the crowd a little while." Petey obeyed without a second glance.

Charlotte leaned against a lamppost and considered. Surely she needed to say something to this girl, who had obviously taken up her old line of work with little pause. But what to say that she hadn't already heard? The risks, the people she dealt with, all were plain. And no doubt she'd already heard and dismissed the moral argument.

While Charlotte pondered, a man stopped in front of Rose. "I like your hat," he said.

"Do you?" Rose took it off and studied it, revealing a loose knot of blonde hair tinged with red. A practiced gesture. "I was thinking about selling this hat today."

There was a pause.

"I might buy that hat," the man said. "I like the looks of it."

She looked directly in his eyes. "I don't know," Rose said. "I would only sell it to someone who would take proper care of it."

"Oh, that I'd do."

"What would you want this hat for anyway?"

The man leaned close and whispered.

Rose lowered her eyes, smiling, and turned the hat around and around in her hands. Then she looked up and surveyed the crowd quickly. She spotted Charlotte.

"Just a minute, I need to talk to this lady," she said. "Wait right here."

She walked to Charlotte, and they regarded each other for a moment. "Keeping an eye on me?"

"No." She gestured toward the suitcase at her feet. "Just got back from a quick trip home. Do you need someone to keep an eye on you?"

Rose snorted. "You sound like Big Bill. He treats me like a child."

A number of retorts occurred to Charlotte, but she decided not to follow the path of retorts. "You are well again then? I'm glad to see it."

"Fit and fine. Never better."

"That's good." A passer-by jostled her elbow. "Any time you want to sit for a cup of tea and a chat, stop and say hello. I'm always in need of good conversation."

"And what makes you think I'm any good for conversation?"

"I don't know. Maybe you're not. But I suspect you are."

Rose looked around, feigning diffidence. "I suppose I'd better get back to work. This fellow has an unusual taste in hats. I'll have to charge him extra." Her sly smile was an implied challenge.

"You cannot shock me, miss. I have seen too much of the ways of the world by now."

"I bet I could."

"Let's just remain in our separate certainties, then." Charlotte turned to go inside.

Rose pointed to the Heaven Holler sign on their building. "I've started the book. It's pretty good."

"Thank you. I'll be sure to tell my son."

"Your son wrote that book?"

"He did indeed. That's why we're all up here, to assist him."

At that moment, Adam emerged from inside. "There you are, Mother. Petey said you were still out here, and I thought you might—" He caught sight of Rose; recognized her; and tipped his hat awkwardly while reaching for Charlotte's valise. "Oh. Hello, miss."

"Rose and I were just discussing your book. She's an admirer."

"I've only read the first fifty pages, but they're quite—" She searched for the word. "Thrilling."

"Well, thank you."

Adam picked up the valise and headed inside. Charlotte followed, giving a quick wave to Rose, who had already returned to her customer. Rose waved back with a wiggle of her fingers.

"You're certainly the collector of unusual specimens," Adam said as they climbed the stairs to their quarters. "Your Filipino friend was by yesterday. He was disappointed not to find you in residence."

Charlotte thought of Nimuel and his compatriots, so far from home and family, stranded and hopelessly out of place while she sped with such ease from home to fair and back again.

"He's mainly Petey's friend, but I'm sorry to disappoint him," she said. "We'll pay a call on him tomorrow."

Chapter 17

The day came late for Charlotte, for she had not fallen asleep easily, not with the noise from the Pike filtering up and with her own head full of thoughts. So when she finally dozed off, she fell into a deep sleep that lasted far later into the morning than usual. She awoke to the sounds of deliverymen and their wagons, the customary racket of the city that she had forgotten about so quickly on her return home.

Her garden plot in back still lived, though it needed watering, and the ground around it had been packed so hard by the constant tramping of feet that she could hardly imagine it becoming productive earth again. It was like the ground in the wheel tracks of a road, concrete-hard and seemingly impervious—until a rainstorm turned it into clinging muck.

Charley Pettibone, in full country getup, was setting up a display of carvings in the front room, willow whistles and tiny figurines. "You've been busy," Charlotte told him.

"It's my natural state, to sit around and whittle," he said.

"Far be it from me to contradict a man in his own opinions," Charlotte teased. "I expect you know yourself best."

"Nickel for the whistles, dime for the miniatures. Figured I'd put a little jingle in my pockets as long as I'm hanging around."

"Speaking of which, you had some paying customers at your medicinal spring." Charlotte told him about the visitors from Louisville.

"Bless their hearts, is all I can say," said Charley. "I'm not claiming the spring has some kind of power of stimulation, mind you. But you can't deny there's a potency in it."

"You don't need to preach to me, Charley. I've used those waters for plasters and poultices all my life."

Charlotte found Petey in her bedroom, reading. "I thought I might walk over to the Philippine exhibit," she began, and Petey was up and putting on her shoes before she finished the sentence. They walked out together into a day that was breezy and dry, a light taste of summer before the real summer arrived.

As they drew closer to the exhibit on the far west side of the fairgrounds, the crowds became thicker and thicker, until they could hardly pass on the fair's broad sidewalks. "What's going on?" she asked a vendor of badges and ribbons. "I know it's a popular spot, but this—" The vendor shrugged. "Anthropology week is what they tell me. Whatever that is."

"I remember this from the pamphlet, Grandma!" Petey said. "Famous scientists from the government and universities are all coming to visit the fair and see the tribesmen. It's supposed to be quite an event."

"I see." They continued toward the exhibit, although Charlotte felt a growing sense of unease, both from the throng of people and from the sense that their visit was occurring at an inauspicious time. Who would want to receive visitors while being examined by a bunch of scientists? But here they were, so they might as well carry on.

The exhibit was immense, and once they passed through the gates the crowd dispersed in all directions. The Igorot village, though, was jammed. A long strand of twine, stretched between hastily-driven stakes, separated the crowd from the scientists on the other side, who were walking among the huts and talking with the villagers.

"This is annoying," Charlotte said, more to herself than to Petey. "We won't be able to talk to Nimuel."

"You remembered his name!" Petey exclaimed. "I thought perhaps you wouldn't like him."

"Why wouldn't I like him? He seemed like a perfect gentleman."

"Just—" She paused, embarrassed. "He's different. And they say some of the tribesmen walk around with no clothes on."

Charlotte laughed. "Everyone seems to think I'm easily shocked." She pointed to a hut where seven men squatted in a circle around a chair where an elderly man sat, dressed in a linen suit and wearing rimless glasses. "Besides, it looks as though the guardians of morality have already arrived." The tribesmen had all been outfitted with shorts.

But Petey had spotted something else: Nimuel, standing discreetly to one side, translating. "There he is!" she cried, waving.

Nimuel seemed too far away to see them among the crowd. "Let's walk on," Charlotte said. "We can come back."

They followed the makeshift fence around the perimeter of the village, where on an ordinary day fairgoers would have been able to mingle with the villagers as much as they desired. Charlotte was struck by the sight, once again, of bare, packed earth, worn slick by thousands of feet into hardpan the color of terra-cotta. The earth itself could not withstand the unending pressure of humanity, footfall after footfall slowly wiping away all signs of nature. She remembered something that old George Webb, the original settler of the valley, had told her once, when the brakes on someone's wagon had failed coming down the hill into Daybreak and dumped a load of manure into the river: "A river cleans itself in a hundred yards." A comforting thought, though she doubted its accuracy. But could the earth clean itself after such a trampling? A year, a dozen years, a hundred years? What would this park look like after the fair had gone? She couldn't imagine.

They found their way to the far side of the exhibit, where a high wall separated the buildings from the empty ground on the other side, the trainyards and the garbage incinerator. To their surprise, there stood an older tribesman in his traditional loincloth instead of the odd-looking shorts, smoking something that looked like a Mayapple root and gazing at the wall with a moody expression. He started at their arrival, and for a moment they gazed at each other suspiciously.

"I'm sorry to disturb you," Charlotte said. "Please excuse us." She bowed slightly, then took Petey's hand to walk away.

Evidently, the tribesman recognized them as no threat. He smiled broadly and waved his arms in the air. "Welcome!" he cried. "Miss and miss! Welcome!" He followed with a stream of language, none of it comprehensible to her.

It appeared that "welcome" and "miss" constituted about two-thirds of the man's English vocabulary, for the rest of his monologue was in that same unrecognizable language. But his friendly manner and gap-toothed grin allayed Charlotte's concerns. He took Charlotte by the hand and led her around the corner of the building, little more than a dirt-floored shed, with Petey following. They bent though a low doorway to the inside. The interior was dim, but Charlotte could make out a circle of benches along the walls and a firepit in the middle. The building was as redolent as a smokehouse.

"*Itokchok,*" he said, gesturing to a bench. They sat down, their eyes adjusting to the windowless room. The man held out his hands to them palms outward. "*Aunika.*" Then he said it again, this time as a question. "*Aunika?*"

"What's that mean?" Petey whispered.

"I don't know," Charlotte said. But it seemed clear the man's intentions were good, so she smiled and nodded. He dashed out of the building, surprisingly agile for someone who seemed so old.

"Lordy, I hope he doesn't bring us a dog," Petey said.

Charlotte squeezed her hand. "I don't think you have anything to worry about."

And so it was, for a few minutes later he returned with a dipper of water and a shallow wooden bowl containing some bananas and another kind of fruit she didn't recognize. After another moment an elderly woman entered the room, wearing a one-piece, brightly printed dress that fitted snugly around her torso. She greeted them with a bow. "Eat," the woman said.

Charlotte had tasted bananas a few times before, as a novelty food on special occasions, but she wasn't sure about Petey. So she peeled the banana and took a bite, trying to show her how to eat the fruit without being overly ostentatious about it. It was chewy and sweet, vaguely exotic, something like a pawpaw but without the big seeds. The other fruit had a soft skin, and Charlotte wasn't whether to eat it like an apple or try to peel it. Sensing her confusion, the woman took a large knife from her sash, stepped forward, and split it in two, then sliced off several chunks of the fruit from a large central pit.

The bright orange fruit was sweet, excessively so to her taste, but Charlotte smiled brightly at the woman to show her appreciation. They traded smiles and nods for a few moments. "Are you two man and wife?" Petey asked. The two stared at her in incomprehension. "Man and wife?" she repeated, then clasped her hands together and mimed a look of loving bliss. Understanding her question, the man rattled a burst of words to his companion; they howled with laughter.

"I'm not sure they understood you," Charlotte said. "But if they did, I'm pretty sure they're not married."

The couple exchanged a few more words, and the woman excused herself. They sat in silence in the shed, which felt awkward to Charlotte although the man sat on his bench with a look of composed relaxation. The silence deepened, mellowed, grew comfortable.

Charlotte cleared her throat. "Thank you for your welcome, and for the delicious food," she said. She knew he wouldn't understand her words, but hoped that the tone of her voice would convey her meaning. "Petey and I have been eager to visit you in your temporary home and to meet your countrymen." She sounded formal, even ceremonial. But that was all right.

She took a surreptitious closer look at him. How old a man was he, anyway? His wrinkled face and gappy smile could be deceiving.

The man replied in equally calm and measured tones.

"I think he's happy to see us," Petey said.

"Of course he is."

In the dim hut she contemplated Petey. Such a bright and fearless girl, curious about all things, someone she could imagine becoming a scientist or business leader like the ones they saw every day here, walking around with an air of command over other people, the knowledge of how things are done, over the bright earth itself. But of course she was a girl, and such a destiny was hard to imagine for her. What was a bright and fearless girl to do? She could follow the path of Josephine Bridges and find an understanding, compliant man to marry, a man who would help smooth the roadblocks that would lie in the path of her desires. But such a stratagem seemed a defeat of its own.

Perhaps the world would change by the time she reached adulthood, and Petey would become whatever she wished to become. Hadn't they been reading of the exploits of Madame Curie?

She sighed. Perhaps the world would change, and perhaps a band of angels would swoop down and carry them all to paradise. Either seemed about as likely.

There was a stirring at the door, and the woman came back in, accompanied by Nimuel. He bowed to them, but Charlotte noticed the appraising sidewise glance he gave the man.

"Ladies, I am overjoyed at your visit," he said. "Regrettably, my presence is required elsewhere in the reservation. There is a delegation of eminent men touring today, with a plan to include us in the Congress of Arts and Sciences this fall. I am needed to translate." He gestured to the others. "I see you have met Mr. Chaia-ngasup."

"Chaia-ngasup?" Charlotte tried to duplicate the pronunciation, and the old man bobbed his head in response to the sound of his name.

"The gentleman I told you about earlier. Sky-Face. The elder of the Igorot delegation. But I really must go."

Nimuel wore the same suit Charlotte had seen him in before, though it seemed more worn and wrinkled than she remembered. But his smooth, cheerful face was as bright as ever.

"May we accompany you?" Charlotte said.

Nimuel rubbed his face. "I don't see why not."

"I hope we didn't offend your friends," Petey said. "When they brought us food, I thought maybe she was his wife, but they made it pretty clear that wasn't the case."

He chuckled. "I wouldn't call them my friends, but we are fellow countrymen, anyway. No, she is from a different part of the island. In fact, her people and his people were long time at war with each other, until they finally came together. There was much head hunting in those days."

"What brought them together?" said Charlotte.

His look was carefully neutral. "Fighting the Spaniards. And then the Americans."

"Oh! They were our enemies?"

"Not for long. They soon saw the, what do you say, the handwriting on the walls. Americans, Spaniards, *insurrectoes*, all the same. They come and they conquer, they take things." At the sound of the word *insurrectoes* Charlotte noticed Chaia-ngasup stiffen and look from face to face, trying to follow their conversation. She smiled to try to reassure him, and Nimuel uttered a rattle of phrases in Igorot. "He suffered much from the *insurrectoes,*" he said to Charlotte and Petey. "They enlisted the Igorot in the fight against the Spanish, and then against the Americans. But when they made peace with the Americans, the *insurrectoes* turned against them and proved to be harsher enemies than the others combined. Chaia-ngasup lost three sons."

Of course he had. It was always the ordinary who suffered the most. Charlotte thought of her own experience of war, so many years ago. Its barbarism, its cruelty, the way it erased even the simplest acts of neighborliness and courtesy. No wonder his face was lined and weary.

"But now we must depart," said Nimuel. "People are waiting."

They left the shed and walked toward the center of the compound, where a ring of villagers stood around a tall, athletic American in canvas pants and a white shirt with rolled-up sleeves, the very picture of authority. He was giving instructions to an Igorot man standing in front of him, while at the same time addressing a group of older white men in jackets and ties who were grouped at the side of the circle. Charlotte and Petey stopped in the doorway of one of the houses.

"That is Professor Pinckney," Nimuel said. "He is the man who brought us here."

"Is he speaking their language?" Charlotte whispered to Nimuel.

"He is trying his best." Nimuel stepped out into the group and began to speak.

"Ah. There you are," Pinckney said. "Tell Balagie here that I need to take some measurements." He reached into a satchel at his feet and pulled out a large set of calipers. "Don't want to frighten him."

Nimuel spoke to the man in a few short phrases which were answered with several other phrases and gestures. After a little back-and-forth, he turned to Pinckney. "He is all right, but does not want the examination to hurt."

"Oh, it won't hurt a bit." Pinckney took the calipers and demonstrated on his own bicep. "See? Just measuring." The man looked uneasy but submitted to the measurement.

"Notice the ratio of the bridge of the nose to the widest point of the lower nose," Pinckney told the group. "In the Negroid race this ratio is considerably higher than in the Asiatic racial groups. Thus we can determine that the Igorot should be classified as Negroid, not Asiatic."

"But the skin tone?" someone said. "Surely you would agree that this is not your classic Negroid skin color."

"Mere skin color varies widely among all races of men," Pinckney replied confidently. "Judging race is never as simple as looking at skin color. It's a complex calculation." Looking back toward the village, he spotted Charlotte and Petey. "Who are those people?" he asked Nimuel.

"They are friends to me, currently residing at the Heaven Holler exhibition on the Pike," Nimuel said. "Allow me to introduce you."

"Heaven Holler, eh?" Pinckney walked over. "That's a show I haven't visited yet. But I've heard about it."

"I'm Charlotte Turner. And this is my granddaughter, Priscilla." She extended her hand, and Pinckney shook it, studying her face.

"Mountain people. Classic Scots-Irish features, I'd say." Charlotte didn't reply. "Over there visiting with the headman, I see. I should have known the old scoundrel would get out and about."

"We've just met. I'd have to say I find him more agreeable than many of the civilized people I've met in my life."

"You'd be surprised. Old Skyface has claimed more heads than he can remember." He leaned closer. "Listen. Don't try to civilize this man, or soften him. Someday he'll return to his village, and he won't need to be civilized. He'll need to be ruthless and hard if he wants to stay headman. And if he doesn't stay headman, then—" Pinckney cleared his throat. "I don't want to get into what happens to a man when he falls from power in a primitive society."

"You needn't worry." Once again, Charlotte thought about saying more but decided not to. There was so much more to say, about the primitive and the civilized, and about the soft and the ruthless, but she didn't want to step into that wallow. Perhaps it was just too fatiguing to imagine arguing with Professor Pinckney, or perhaps she wanted to follow the old wisdom that silence conferred dignity. Either way, the professor would think he had silenced her. And maybe he had.

She turned away. All said and done, what business did she have here anyway, milling around behind the scenes while a bunch of white-mustached men made these tribespeople perform calisthenics. Nimuel followed. "I'll walk you back," he said.

"That's all right. I'm sure you have a great deal more to do."

"It can wait." He spoke a few words to the villagers, who nodded and murmured.

"Nimuel!" the professor called. "Just a moment." He hurried over to them. "Mrs. Turner, I'd like to visit your exhibition one day soon, if I may." He handed her a card.

"Certainly," Charlotte said. "Our admission charge is quite modest."

If he understood the slight, he didn't show it. "I failed to make the connection. You must be kin to the novel-writing Turner of the Heaven Holler books."

"Yes, he is my son, and Petey here is his daughter."

"I see. Tell me, are there more of your kind at your exhibition?"

"That depends on what you mean by my 'kind.'"

"Authentic hill people. Ozarkian hill folk."

Charlotte laughed as she thought about the performance Charley Pettibone would put on for a visiting anthropologist. "Yes, we have a few."

"Excellent. I'd like to talk to some."

"Very well, but I'll warn you not to take everything you hear at face value."

Pinckney smiled, a little indulgently it seemed to her. "Oh, no concern about that. I've always been a most scrupulous researcher. I understand they still speak Shakespeare's English back in some of those deep valleys."

"If you say so."

Pinckney returned to his demonstration, leaving Charlotte and Petey to walk back through the interior of the settlement, reflecting. "Is this what their village looks like back home?" she asked Nimuel.

He considered. "Not really. The Igorot prefer taller roofs, with steeper sides. But most important, it needs a big tree in the center, to give shade over the *chapay.* The *chapay* is the open space where everyone gathers to decide things."

"And is Chaia-ngasup the headman?"

Nimuel clapped his hands in approval. "Your pronunciation is very good! No, they have no headman. Everyone talks things over until they come to agreement. Chaia-ngasup is the elder, so when they need to speak to outsiders, he does the talking."

"And if they don't all come to agreement?"

"Then they do nothing."

"That sounds familiar."

By then they had reached the small building in the back. "I am sorry to have to leave you, but Mr. Pinckney needs my assistance," Nimuel said. "Please come again, when we will have more time to talk together."

"Gladly," Charlotte said. "And please, return to see us at our exhibition."

"That may be difficult," Nimuel said. "The professor is watching us carefully nowadays. There is unrest, and he fears some may try to leave."

"Unrest? Why?"

Nimuel shrugged, uncomfortable. "Everyone was promised five hundred dollars to take home if they stayed until the end of the fair. Such an amount of money would make them the wealthiest people in their village, far and away. Now some are beginning to doubt his promise. They are homesick and want to leave."

"Why doesn't he just send them home, then?"

He arched an eyebrow. "Did you not see the press of people? They are the main attraction. They cannot go home. The visitors rush past the weavers and the craftsmen to see the naked Igorot."

"And you? Are you homesick?"

Nimuel's face grew serious. "No, ma'am. I never want to leave America. When the fair is over, I will stay. Even if I have to hide, I will stay. I cannot go back."

Chapter 18

Charlotte's encounter at the Philippine exhibit weighed on her mind as the days passed. She worked distractedly, mechanically, thinking of the homesick Igorots, not exactly prisoners but definitely not free, performing dog feasts and mock battles for the edification of strolling visitors and relying on the ultimate benevolence of Professor Pinckney. No wonder they were restless.

In the mornings, she stayed upstairs with Petey, replenishing their supply of cornhusk dolls for the sale table. The cool mornings of early June were giving way to humid overnights that left Charlotte ill-rested and damp. Petey too seemed distracted. She folded the larger husks to form a head and braided side husks to create arms, humming under her breath, but appeared to take little interest in whether the dolls were uniform or whether their corn-shuck skirts were properly fluffed out. They worked together in silence, side by side.

One morning Petey spoke up. "Do you think Nimuel is handsome?"

So that was it. Charlotte thought for a moment. "Yes, I suppose so."

"I do too! He has such deep dark eyes."

Charlotte recalled herself at that age. Where had she been living then? New York, she supposed, her father teaching at West Point and she and Caroline roaming the grounds. Caroline had been the one fixed on boys, with her pretty face and the dance steps she practiced endlessly, but Charlotte had cherished her own dreams of romance. She had mooned over a cadet from Virginia, his name lost to her now, some Old Testament name like Jeremiah or Jereboam.

All she could remember of him was his syrupy accent and the vague image of a clump of curly hair. They had never spoken. She had admired him from afar and written his name over and over in her lesson book—Jeremiah, that was it.

She traced the name on the table. What had ever become of him? Given that he was from Virginia, it wasn't hard to guess. Rebellion, departure, defeat. Probably dead by now, if not from the war then from the shocks the flesh is heir to.

Charlotte became aware of Petey watching her reverie. She returned to her cornhusk work, a little embarrassed.

"You disapprove," Petey said.

"No. I was just reminded of myself at your age. There's nothing wrong with having feelings." Then a thought occurred to her. "Has he said something?"

"No, but I think he looks at me . . . you know. Admiringly."

Charlotte held her face steady but felt inward relief. She had no idea how old Nimuel was, but some years older than Petey would be her guess, too old to be making overtures to a young girl. Perhaps they married younger in the Philippines, but this wasn't the Philippines. Not to mention the impropriety. So she was happy to learn that the whole thing could well be taking place only in Petey's mind, a name scribbled in a lesson book and nothing more.

"All right," she said. "But if you get anything other than admiring looks, I want you to come to me for advice."

"Yes, ma'am."

Charlotte thought about speaking further, but decided to leave things there for now. No reason to cast doubt on Nimuel's character with only admiring glances to go on, but it was a situation to be watched, quietly. Such things were not unknown even here.

Besides, she had other things to consider. Adam's room had been quiet this morning, well past breakfast, and when she had softly knocked to rouse him, there had been no answer. She cracked the door just far enough to see his neatly made bed, his unlit lamp.

So Adam had not been home last night, and she suspected it was not the first time. Charlotte held this knowledge close while she tried to decide what to do with it, if anything. Adam was a grown man, of course, and needed no mother clucking over his behavior. But there was Petey to think about, humming and oblivious, but not for long.

They worked on in silence until they heard Charley Pettibone's heavy boots clumping up the stairs. He poked his head through the kitchen doorway.

"There's a man downstairs, says he knows you," he said. Charley walked to the table and handed Charlotte a calling card.

"It's Professor Pinckney," Charlotte said. She stood up and brushed the corn-husk fragments from her apron. "Let's go greet him."

Professor Pinckney stood in the entry foyer, idly brushing his hat, accompanied by Nimuel and a young assistant. The professor looked tired and harried, but Nimuel wore his customary expression, comfortable but watchful.

"This lad was determined to come along," Pinckney said, waving vaguely in Nimuel's direction. "Hope it's all right."

"Of course," Charlotte said. "He is always welcome."

At that moment Charley Pettibone came downstairs, whistling, with a fresh set of wood blocks in his arms. His curiosity about the professor was evident as he sat at his sale table, pulled a Barlow knife from his pocket, and ostentatiously began to carve. Pinckney studied him across the room. Charlotte followed his gaze: the long gray beard, the weathered overalls, the pile of shavings.

"I say," Pinckney said. "Where did you find that one?"

"Mr. Pettibone is my neighbor," Charlotte said. "I can introduce you if you like."

"Certainly! No disrespect to you and your daughter, but this Pettibone chap looks much more like the authentic Ozarks type, at least as I understand it."

"No disrespect taken, sir."

"Where are you from, Mrs. Turner? Your people, I mean."

"My mother and father were both born in Ohio, as I remember, and I was born in the state of New York."

"No, I mean ancestrally! We all have accidents of birth, but our true roots go back much farther. I am of Anglo-Saxon stock myself. I believe I mentioned when we last spoke that many of you people come from the Scots-Irish branch of that tree."

"I'm afraid that's a subject I've never bothered to inquire about."

He puckered his lips. "One's heritage is often a source of great insight. Our racial ancestry dictates much of who we are."

Charlotte didn't feel much like debating with this confident young man, so she walked him over to Charley's table. "Charley, this is Mr. Pinckney. He's quite eager to meet you."

"Sit yourself down, Pinckney. Always happy to make a new friend."

Charlotte left them and returned to Nimuel. "Let's walk out back. I want to show you my garden."

The spring had been cold and rainy, so the garden wasn't much to look at.

Some spindly tomato shoots and a row of beans, waiting for warmer days to rouse them. A row of spinach and a row of carrots, not enough to feed a family for any length of time but sufficient to raise her spirits in the tending.

"So you are an agriculturalist," Nimuel said. "Are these the plants you raise at home?"

"Yes, but more, much more. My garden at home is as big as this whole lot." She gestured to take in the back area, surrounded by its high fence.

Nimuel pointed to the artificial mountain at the back of the plot. "And are you from the mountains?"

"Yes. Not as dramatic as that one, but steep, very steep, and covered with forests. We farm in the bottomland, and the men hunt in the forests and cut the trees for lumber. You're familiar with this word, 'bottomland'"?

"Yes." Nimuel stood, reflecting. "You would probably have much to talk about with Mr. Chaia-ngasup. He too is a farmer, a man of the hills. He too misses the mountains of home. He told me yesterday that he seeks a spirit here to carry him on its back out of kindness until he has returned to live where the spirits of his ancestors and of the rivers and familiar places can speak to him again."

Incomprehensible phrases. "What does that mean?"

Nimuel shrugged. "He said the spirits here are unfamiliar to him, and they speak in strange ways. He said unfamiliar spirits are not always trustworthy."

She nodded despite the strangeness of the ideas. "I don't mean to pry, but are these your beliefs as well?"

"No, ma'am. I am a good Catholic and worship the one true God."

Charlotte didn't answer. Instead, she knelt in her garden and placed her palms on the ground. Was it a mere flight of fancy to imagine spirits of the earth and trees? Or blasphemous? She could imagine herself praying to such things. The earth was warm and gritty beneath her palms.

Yes, she missed her hills, her pocked and beaten hills, with their thin pelt of trees to cover the bruises. She missed her neighbors, even the brutish and crooked ones, but the simple and straightforward ones most of all, the people about whom it was enough to say "They're good people," and everyone would know exactly what you meant. She missed the moods of the river, the way it smelled in the morning of things both pleasant and unpleasant, of mist and rot and distant flowers. And the whippoorwills, always so distant and sad, and the annoying cicadas, too close, and the infinite shades of green that surrounded her in every direction she looked except straight up. She didn't object to the idea that these things all had spirits of their own, the trees and streams and rocks, although whether they could be spoken to directly was not for her to declare.

She looked up at Nimuel. "Does he have one great god also?"

"He does, ma'am, but that god is too busy moving the heavens and clouds for us to trouble him with our little concerns."

Hard to argue with that. She stood up, brushed off her hands, and smiled at him, feeling a little unsteady.

"He says things are out of order," Nimuel said. "But order can be restored, though it will take great effort."

To Charlotte, his words sounded like the fortuneteller at the county fair. But who was she to cast doubt on the beliefs of another? She hardly knew the state of her own beliefs these days. As for disorder, well, she had plenty of that these days. "Let's go inside," she said. "I don't want to leave Charley alone with your employer too long. One of them may succeed in bamboozling the other, and I'm not sure which."

They strolled inside, where Charley and the professor were still engaged in intense conversation, with the assistant taking notes. "Indeed," Pinckney was saying in response to something Charley was telling him. "Is that so? Indeed."

Charley shot her a sly glance as she approached. "We're discussing the various wildlife of the Ozarks."

Nimuel did not appear to want to linger near Professor Pinckney. He edged toward the door and then out, noiselessly, taking advantage of Pinckney's distraction to step a couple of feet into the pedestrian throng of the Pike, where he stood and watched the flow of people. Petey followed, standing a few feet away, ready to converse if he spoke in her direction, but for the moment they stood in silence.

Charlotte saw an opportunity to question Charley discreetly. "Did you see Adam go out this morning?" she murmured.

Charley's brow furrowed, though Charlotte couldn't tell whether his expression of deep thought was real or feigned. "No," he said after a while. "Of course, I did sleep in a little, and I wasn't exactly looking for him either."

"Did you see him go out last night?"

He squinted up at her. "Is something going on?"

"No, I don't think so. I just can't find him."

"Well, he's a grown man. He doesn't have to report in."

Charlotte left him there and walked toward the entrance, feeling evaded. If Charley knew something about Adam's whereabouts he certainly wasn't telling.

So what if Adam had gone out for a night on the town? As Charley said, he was a grown man. What would it have hurt him to say, "I'm going out tonight. Don't wait up"? Some notion of respectability or concealment, she supposed. The conspiracy of men to evade being held accountable for themselves.

And here he came in the door, whistling a tune, a newspaper tucked under his arm. "You look like the cat that just found the cream," she said.

"Why shouldn't I? It's a beautiful morning, Mr. Kellogg says the books are selling like peanuts at a ball game, and I am given the chance to meet my readers. Life is good. Who's the lad out front that Petey is casting doe eyes at?"

Charlotte suppressed her urge to inquire. All in due time. "He's the assistant and translator for the gentleman over there." She tilted her head toward the table at the other side of the foyer, where Pinckney and Charley were still deep in conversation. "That's Professor Pinckney. Something of the ringmaster of the Philippine exhibit, I'm led to believe."

"I've heard of him. Very celebrated."

Adam smelled of *Eau de Cologne.* Charlotte could see him trying to decide whether to join Charley's conversation or leave it alone. Finally he elected to sit in the corner chair. He fluffed his newspaper with one eye on the pair, ready to stroll over and be introduced if invited. He spent a minute scanning the pages before glancing up at Charlotte. "I have a bit of news myself."

"Do you now."

"You remember that lady of the evening who fainted outside a while back? The one we brought in?"

"Of course."

"I bumped into her last night out on the Pike. Turns out she's a country girl, just like us. From a good family. Surprisingly well-read."

"Including your book, I suppose."

A faint blush came into his cheeks. "She says she's started it. Anyway, she wants to read some of my poems. I don't mean to sound naïve about this, but I think this girl might be capable of redemption."

"And how do you propose to achieve this?"

Adam cleared his throat. "Conversation, the building of trust. A gradual unfolding of the knowledge that no one's life is permanently ruined. There's always a way to turn oneself around, to become a new person."

Charlotte turned away, unexpectedly emotional. She thought of herself as a young woman, how she too had believed in the infinite capacity of human regeneration, that with the right people, the right circumstances, the proper knowledge, and a touch of luck, a person could become something new. One could become someone freer, more moral, even more spiritual than the ordinary man burdened by the dead hand of society and the tyranny of wealth. Had she given up those beliefs or merely allowed them to wither? People said they grew wise with age. But perhaps they only grew tired and jaded, unwilling to make the effort to advance their ideals.

She would not become one of those complacent old people who believed in fate or the fixity of human conditions. She turned back to Adam.

"All right," she said. "How do you plan to accomplish this?"

"The way anything of value is accomplished, through patience and reason."

Charlotte could find no words to answer this directly. So she focused on practical things.

"Before you go too far with this, I'd ask you to consider a couple of things. The first is how this venture might affect your reputation and your book sales if it got into the newspapers. Not to mention how it might affect your family life."

Adam hunched his shoulders. "I am wanting to do the moral thing here. Publicans and sinners, you know. I know cynics might see it otherwise, but good things are often misunderstood. So I will just have to accept that, although I hope my activities won't reach the papers. And I will inform Penelope at the right time."

"My second point." Charlotte glanced out the front door. "Even if nothing ever reaches the public, you need to consider how to tell Petey about what you are doing. She is a bright girl and ahead of her years, but she is still innocent in many ways, and you will need to explain to her how this young lady makes her living."

"Actually," he said with a grimace, "I was hoping I might enlist you to perform that task."

Chapter 19

Charlotte sat alone on the southbound train, her hands idle for once, for she had forgotten to bring anything to work on, not even a sock to darn. For she had left abruptly, pushed into movement not by Adam's notion of rescuing that girl, but by the arrival of a messenger boy from the Western Union office, a skinny kid in a white shirt and tie, and a floppy cap two sizes too big. Both Adam and the professor had stood up expectantly, at opposite corners of the room, but the kid called out "Charlotte Turner!" and handed her the telegram.

Her heart sank when she heard her name, for no good news ever came by telegram, at least not for people of her station in life, anyway. A parade of catastrophes raced through her mind as she fumbled with the flimsy slip of paper and noticed that it had been sent by Newton. But it was no extraordinary catastrophe, just an ordinary one, an old friend dying at a ripe old age, but even so the news struck her hard. For it was Dathan, very nearly the oldest of friends. Newton's message was characteristically obtuse: OLD DATHAN DIED LAST NIGHT. NOT SURE HOW. As if she needed a reminder that Dathan was old, or the cryptic information that Newton wasn't sure how he died. What was that supposed to mean?

Of course Charlotte would have been forgiven for not attending Dathan's funeral. She wasn't sure there would even be a funeral, given Dathan's secretive nature and his lack of churchgoing. Who would hold it, and who would attend?

Still, she felt compelled to travel home, alone this time, to perform the duty of the old: to send off another member of their fraternity with the respect they deserved.

The repeated train trips fatigued her, and she thought about staying home longer this time to rest and regain strength, to hoe her beans and listen to the cicadas in the evening. But she did not relish leaving Petey for long. Too many unsettled things. So the beans would likely have to wait.

A nearer concern, how to get from the Fredericktown train station to Daybreak. She would have to hire a rig, she supposed, a nuisance and an expense. She hadn't bothered to wire back to Newton, just packed a case and left, since a telegram would likely have taken a day to deliver anyway. But lo, when she embarked from the train and set off for the livery stable, there sat Grandma Renick on her box wagon, her back straight, looking out over the travelers like a general surveying troops. Their last encounter had not been pleasant, but Charlotte hoped that the code of neighborliness might outweigh that tension. She walked over to her.

"Good afternoon, Mrs. Renick," she said.

Grandma gaped at her for a moment. Then she snapped her lips shut and mustered the closest approximation of a smile Charlotte had ever seen on her face, which usually had all the friendliness of a cornered possum. "Sorry," she said. "I'm not used to hearing 'Mrs. Renick.' Everybody calls me 'Grandma' these days."

"I know what you mean. Whenever I hear 'Grandma,' I always look up, even when it's a voice I don't recognize. Are you here to pick someone up?"

Grandma's eyes darted to the back of the wagon, which was covered with canvas. "No. I come up here some days when nothing's going on at home. Many's the traveler has our product on his mind the minute he steps off the train."

Proving her point, a man walked up to the wagon and tipped his hat. "Are you the person I'm looking for?" he said.

"Depends," Grandma said. The man glanced at Charlotte. "She's all right. Back to your question."

"I've been told there's a woman at the Fredericktown station who can help a man out with his thirst."

"That's a reasonable thought. May I ask you to open your coat?"

The man unbuttoned his coat and displayed the inner lining. "I'm not a robber, if that's what you're worried about."

Grandma snorted. "Never crossed my mind. It's the tax boys I think about. They generally wear their badge on the inside of their coats."

"I'm no tax man. How much?"

"Fifty cents a gallon, twenty-five cents a quart."

"Is it aged?"

Grandma snorted again. "You want aged, there's a tavern at the end of this block that'll fix you right up, for three times the price or more. I hear it ain't bad, either."

"No, what you got suits me fine," the man said. "I'll take a quart." He produced a quarter, which Grandma tucked into her dress pocket.

"How about handing me your satchel," she said.

The man lifted his valise into the wagon. Grandma Renick took it, slid it under the canvas, and unsnapped the catches. Charlotte could hear the sound of liquid sloshing.

"There you go," she said, snapping the case shut again and handing it to the man. "How long you here for?"

"Week or two. Got some buying and selling to do."

"Should have got yourself a gallon."

"If I like the quart, I'll be back for the gallon. Can I find you here?"

"Depends," Grandma repeated. "But for now, I better get a move on. That tavernkeeper don't like seeing me around here. Says I hurt his business, which I do." She picked up her reins, and the man tipped his hat again and walked away. "Nice talking to you, ma'am, but I need to head on home."

"Wait, Grandma," Charlotte said. "Can I catch a ride with you? I came back in a hurry, and no one's expecting me."

"Of course! Climb on up. If I'd a known you needed a ride, I wouldn't have kept you standing there like a serving girl. I do apologize."

Charlotte climbed into the seat beside Grandma Renick, and they headed south through town toward Daybreak.

What the Renicks did for a living was technically illegal. She knew that, depriving the government of revenue or whatever the actual crime was. She also knew that this illegality didn't matter much to most of the people in the county, the tavernkeepers excepted, with the prevailing belief being that if somebody wanted to risk their health buying Renick's rotgut to save a few pennies, that was their business. But it was a topic that mainly did not come up.

So as they sat together on the spring seat of the wagon, Charlotte tried to ignore the constant clinking of jugs and bottles from the bed and talk about safer topics, although such topics felt increasingly difficult to find as the miles dragged on.

"Your people came from Bollinger County, do I remember that right?" she ventured.

"That's right. Old settlers, as they say. But my daddy fell on hard times and we had to move west. Lived in Yount for a while, then I married Mr. Renick and moved out toward Cornwall with him." She looked over at Charlotte. "Hard years, those."

"I'm sorry to hear that. This was after the war?"

Grandma Renick nodded. "It wasn't three years before Mr. Renick took sick and died. Not that he was much account anyway. But he left me to raise the boy alone. We lived in some shacks that make this old mining camp we're living in look like the Temple of Solomon." She gazed straight ahead, her lips tight. "Most landlords are sons of bitches. You learn that in a hurry. Or maybe I should just say most people in general." With that she leaned over to Charlotte. "But I don't need to be carrying on to you about my woes. I'll venture that you've had troubles enough to last you."

Charlotte didn't reply. It went without saying that everyone at a certain age had experienced woes and losses, enough to last as Grandma said, so it hardly seemed necessary to recount her own. Everyone bore wounds.

When they reached the fork where the road to Silvermines branched off, Charlotte climbed down. "Thanks so much," she said. "You've saved my legs a lot of work. Another hour and I'll be home."

"Ride on with me," said Grandma. "From our place you can take the footpath. You won't have to ford the river."

"That's all right. I want to stop at Dathan and Cedeh's along the way and pay my respects. I guess you heard that Dathan died."

Grandma Renick showed no expression. "That's what happens to old people." But after Charlotte had taken her case from the wagon, she spoke again. "I have something on my mind."

They regarded each other across the distance. Charlotte waited.

"My Bobby was in the wrong about that stave wood, so I didn't say anything then," Grandma said. "I had to take his side because he's family, but that was all."

"I know," said Charlotte.

"But it don't sit right with me to have you and your fancy people all riding in, taking sides, acting all high and mighty. I know you're an old settler and all, and you think you're pretty fine." She bobbed her head for emphasis. "But you're not so fine that you can just break the laws of nature. This is a white people's world, and don't you forget it."

Charlotte glared at her. But this was no time to start an argument, not with miles yet to travel and the day growing long. "We're going to have to disagree on that," she said. She turned on her heel and headed south, the road following the ridgetops until it began its descent into the river valley. Her case banged against the outside of her knee with every step, making her grateful for light packing.

And there at the top of the ridge, just before the road dropped steeply down, stood Dathan and Cedeh's house, which always appeared at best half-inhabited but now bore a look of utter emptiness. Charlotte walked to the front door and knocked. She knocked again.

The door opened to her push. Inside, the air smelled stale and dense, like the interior of a root cellar, and there was no answer when she called Cedeh's name. But she called it again a couple of times as she walked through the house, just to relieve the oppressive silence.

The bedroom was about as she had expected, small and dim, with one sash window to bring in light. The bedcovers were thrown back as if someone had just leaped out to start their day. A large dry stain darkened the center of the bed, blood or who knows what. She folded the covers over the stain and walked outside.

She felt spooked at being alone in the house, so silent and empty. Perhaps that would be her house someday, neighbors walking through it in her mortal absence, going through her things. She needed to think about what she wanted people to find, and not to find.

As Charlotte stood by the roadside, catching her breath, she had the sudden sensation that she was not alone. "Cedeh?" she called, one more time, turning in a quick circle to listen for an answer. But instead of Cedeh, the person that stepped from the bushes by the road was Ulysses S. Canterbury.

"Oh," Charlotte said. "I had imagined that you would be at work today."

"And I thought you were up in St. Louis."

"Well." She gestured toward the cabin. "I got the news yesterday, just the minimum. What can you tell me?"

Canterbury glanced away. "I can't add much, but what I can tell you is strange. I won't blame you if you disbelieve me."

Charlotte waited for him to find his voice.

"Night before last, I was about to bed down after dinner when I heard a knock at my door. It was Cedeh, and don't ask me how she made it across the river because I surely don't know. I asked her in to eat a bite but she said no, she was on a journey and had miles to travel before she stopped." He paused to survey her reaction. "Now, summer evenings are long, and the moon is bright, but who starts a journey at that time of night? Something was wrong, so I asked her what."

He cleared his throat again. "That's when she told me that Dathan had died, and she asked me to come over in the morning and take care of things. And off into the night she went. So in the morning I fetched Mr. Turner and sure enough, here he was."

Charlotte pondered. It was a crazy story, but plausible enough. Much to decipher.

"This is the part no one's going to believe," Canterbury said. "Before she left, Cedeh told me that she and Dathan had talked it over, and they agreed that they wanted me to inherit their property when they passed away. That's all she said, and then she was gone."

His expression was almost a glare, his jaw set, as if daring her to dispute him. Charlotte met his look calmly. She had no such intention, but he was right about one thing: Nobody else would believe him.

Dathan and Cedeh's land. A hundred acres on the ridgetop, nothing special, and forty acres of choice bottomland near the ferry landing. Nobody would care much about the forest land, but the bottomland acreage was something to fight over.

"So she just said that to you?" Charlotte asked. "No papers, no deed?"

"It didn't seem like the time to ask for paperwork."

Charlotte took a breath. "True. But that time will come soon enough. There won't be any trouble if you want to move into this old house. It's bigger than yours, and it has a solid cistern. No more trips to the river for your drinking and cooking water. But without a proper deed transfer, that cropland will go to probate. If Cedeh doesn't have the papers, the public administrator will take over. I expect the land will go to auction eventually."

Canterbury looked dissatisfied, but nodded. "I figured something like that. Just thought I'd tell you."

"I know," Charlotte said. "I understand." And she did understand, that for a young man like Canterbury, who struggled every day simply to maintain his existence on the Earth, a forty-acre plot that simply dropped into his possession in the middle of the night must have felt like God's own grace.

But she couldn't talk any more about deeds and cisterns, not with an old friend newly dead and his wife out on some kind of travel. She turned away. "Could you tell what killed him?" she asked.

"No, ma'am. I'm not so good at medical things. He looked peaceful, though."

"That's good to know." Her voice suddenly felt constricted and thick, and she paused a moment to swallow. "Well, I guess we'd best be going."

Canterbury cleared his throat. "You go on ahead. I need to go back over to my place and take care of some things."

Charlotte couldn't imagine what tasks were so pressing that they couldn't be put off, but decided not to push matters. She glanced at him out of the corner of her eye. "Will you be down later?"

"Oh, yes." And with that he was off into the woods, down a path she could scarcely discern, worn by traffic between the two homes, she supposed. For what else lay in that direction? A steep drop, the river, a steep climb up the other side. And Cedeh had made that journey evening before last. The world was a strange place indeed.

Chapter 20

The descent into the river valley was easy, and in a bit of good fortune the ferry was tied up on her bank. So she didn't have to ring the bell and wait for someone to appear. She untied the ferry, pushed off from the bank, and let the current do most of the work while she cranked the windlass. A few minutes later she walked into Newton's store.

Sarah ran out from her usual spot behind the counter to hug her. "Why didn't you send word?" she asked. "We would have met you at the depot."

"That's all right. I wanted to get down here as soon as I could. What have you learned about Dathan? And where's Cedeh?"

Sarah glanced toward the back of the store with an uncomfortable expression. "Newton's out back. I'll go get him."

"Don't bother." Charlotte walked through the store and the living quarters, stepping out the back door into the yard, where Newton usually had a project or two going. She could see Newton in a distant shed, laboring over something at a workbench. He straightened at her call and ran to meet her.

"I had an idea you would show up," he said. "Thought you'd want to be in on the decision."

"What decision?"

He led her to the shed, where a wagon stood in the breezeway, covered with heavy canvas. "What to do with him." He pointed to the wagon.

"Dathan's in there?"

Newton nodded.

The presence of the body, so unexpectedly close at hand, cast a pall. Lord knows she had been around plenty of dead bodies in her life, but somehow each one was sobering. This one in particular. "I ran into Mr. Canterbury up the road. He told me the strange story about Cedeh."

Newton shrugged. "I've got nothing new to add. Nobody's seen her since then."

"I don't understand."

"I can't say that I do either. After Canterbury turned up here yesterday morning, I went with him to check, and sure enough, Dathan was dead in bed, peaceful as you please, arms crossed, kind of a happy look on his face. But no Cedeh. I went on to town, sent you the message, then came back and loaded him up. So here he lies."

"What do you think is going on?"

"I don't want to speak ill of those who are not here to speak on their own behalf. But if you ask me, I think she's gone off to find her people, maybe out west in the Nations. You've seen their shack. What does she have to stick around for?"

It felt unseemly, the idea of going off and leaving a body behind. Especially the body of one's lifetime love. But what did she know? Dathan and Cedeh might have had some kind of prior understanding. Besides, if you truly believed that the spirit had flown, what was there to stay behind and tend?

"All right," she said. "What's your plan?"

Newton walked to the wagon. "Thought I'd wait till evening, just in case I'm wrong. If the missus shows up, then we'll listen to what she has to say about a funeral or whatever. If not, then I'll take him back up to their place, bury him out back of the house."

"What, out in the woods? Like the family pet?"

"You have a better idea?"

"I certainly do. Dathan lived here before we did, Newton. It's only right for him to have a place in the Daybreak cemetery."

Newton started to speak, then stopped himself and walked away.

She knew the objection. She was no foolish soul who thought a person could remake the rules of society without consequence. And burying a black man in a cemetery that up to now had held nothing but white people? Well, that was remaking the rules in a big way. But the alternative was unthinkable. An unmarked grave on the rocky ridgetop? Not if she had anything to say about it. There was an old slave cemetery down by the river, which Dathan himself had maintained until the years got the best of him, but since then the forest had reclaimed it, sprouts that turned into saplings and then into something close to harvestable timber, with buckbrush and grapevines to clutter one's passage. Only Dathan knew who was buried where, and now that knowledge was lost forever. So that graveyard was little better than the deep woods, with only a few slab stones and rounded cairns to mark a burial site. Not the honorable resting place he deserved.

Charlotte walked to the wagon and lifted the canvas. Dathan did indeed have a peaceful expression on his face, as far as she could tell, though his skin had turned gray and rigid. Newton had placed pennies on his eyes to keep the lids closed. Charlotte studied the Indian head on them: with her flowing locks and thin, fluted nose, the ostensible Indian maiden on the coin looked no more native than she did. With her feathered headdress and decorative necklace, she certainly looked nothing like Cedeh, who usually kept her hair in a scarf, and had never worn any kind of adornment that Charlotte could recall.

Down deep, she knew that Newton was right. Cedeh had fled, who knows where. And though her motives couldn't be known, Charlotte could guess them. An old woman, alone, no family near, and subject to the dangers of being the wrong color in the wrong place. She might have flown to the Indian Nations herself in such a situation. They could wait till morning, but ultimately they would be the ones to decide what to do with the body.

Newton came up behind her. "He was a tough old bird," he said.

"That he was. We should send word to Josephine. They had some kind of a special bond that I never quite understood."

"Of course." She nodded. Back when Daybreak was still a commune, and not just a little town like any other, Josephine and Dathan had lived in adjacent houses. The bond between them was a mystery. An alliance of outcast spirits, perhaps.

Charlotte thought about telling Newton of Canterbury's other statement, his land claim, but decided to keep it to herself. She didn't doubt his honesty, but the timing felt inopportune.

And there came the man himself, rounding the corner of the house. Canterbury stood beside them at the wagon.

"Damn, son, you're quiet!" Newton said. "Did Cedeh teach you some of her Indian tricks?"

The working of Canterbury's jaw told Charlotte that he was considering his response. Finally he said, "No. Me and my brother used to play Deadwood

Dick around the neighborhood all the time. I suppose that's where I picked it up."

"I'm glad you're here," Charlotte said. "We're discussing what to do for Dathan's funeral. If Cedeh doesn't appear soon to make her wishes known, we'll have to decide ourselves."

"Tell you what," Newton said slowly. She could tell by the way he drawled his words that he was thinking as he spoke. "I know the old fellow that preaches at the A.M.E. church in town. He barbers during the week. I doubt if Dathan ever attended, but I imagine he'll come out to perform the service just to be proper. I'll go to town and tell him, and start the boys digging a grave." He looked up the valley to the cemetery in the distance. "Everybody needs a place to lie down, when the time comes."

"All right," Charlotte murmured. She didn't think it wise to ask what had prompted his change of mind. Some things were better off simply accepted.

"You want to put him up there?" Canterbury said.

"Sure," Newton said. "Why not? He'd be the first colored person ever buried in that cemetery. Sign of respect."

Canterbury walked to the end of the wagon and squatted down, his hands on the tailgate. He stayed there a long minute before straightening up and returning to them.

"I mean you no disrespect," he said. "But have either of you ever been up to Dathan's forest property?"

Charlotte and Newton looked at each other. "I'm sure I haven't," Charlotte said. Newton just shrugged.

"If you like, I can take you up there," Canterbury continued. He pointed to the great hill behind them to the west. "It straddles the ridgetop, comes down the slope a little. Those tall pines you can see are part of it."

"All right," Charlotte said, uncertain of where the conversation was heading.

"It's about like my land. All rock, not much soil. It'll grow trees, though." He paused to take a breath. "Dathan took me up to see it when he first came to visit me."

From here the words tumbled out. "He told me it was the most beautiful piece of land on Earth, because it was his, and that I should think the same about my plot. That whatever labor I put into it was worth it. Because it was something that would last beyond me, into the next generations. He had a favorite spot up there, a big rock outcrop where he liked to sit and look out over the valley, your valley right here. I've mentioned it to you before, ma'am. And

I'll tell you one thing. He'd ten times rather be buried at the base of Dathan's Lookout than in your white people's cemetery."

He took a step back. "All right, I've had my say. I've got no more right to decide where to bury him than anybody else, but I felt the need to speak my piece."

Charlotte didn't know what to say. A dozen objections popped into her mind, but Canterbury's passion stopped her from voicing them. But Newton wasn't deterred.

"And how do you propose to get a dead body up to that spot? And would you have us hold the funeral up there too, out in the woods? I never heard anything like this."

"No, hold your funeral down here. But when you think about a final resting place, don't imagine that you'd do him any honor by putting him in the far corner of your graveyard, out where it's obvious he's a second-class citizen. It might make you feel good, but that's all."

He started to walk away, but Charlotte called out to him. "Wait a minute. That first question. How would you transport Dathan up the mountain?"

Canterbury glanced at the half-finished project on Newton's workbench. "That's a coffin, I take it." To Newton's nod, he said, "A coffin is a narrow thing. With the right mule and a handcart, I could take it straight up the footpath to my place, and then follow the ridgetop over to Dathan's property. Or we could take the long way around and come in past Renick's."

"And what would be the right kind of mule?" Newton asked. "You seem pretty sure of yourself."

"Sure-footed and not prone to spook. I'm not a teamster by trade, but I can handle horses and mules."

"All right, here's what we'll do," Newton said, eager to reclaim the initiative. "I have just such an animal. We'll wait and see if Cedeh makes an appearance, and if she doesn't, we'll hold the funeral in the schoolhouse." He drew a breath and pointed a finger at Canterbury. "And then you and I will take Dathan up the mountain together, because I don't trust other people with my mule. And besides, I'd like to see this burial site myself. You talk like it's the land of glory, but I want to make up my own mind."

"Fair enough," Canterbury said. "I hope you'll excuse me now. I have an idea that digging that grave will be no simple task." And with that he turned and was gone, as briskly and unceremoniously as he had arrived.

"He's got that right," Newton muttered. "Chiseling out a grave in solid rock."

And occasionally that afternoon they heard small explosions coming from the mountain, Canterbury blasting out troublesome chunks.

In the morning the preacher arrived first, a lean old man on a mule, who went straight to the schoolhouse without stopping anywhere in the village. Charlotte walked up the hill to meet him.

He removed his hat as she approached and took on a somber expression, which was accentuated by his worn black suit. "Morning, ma'am. I'm Clarence Abernathy. Hope you don't mind my coming up to think and pray a little before the services."

"Of course not. I'm Charlotte Turner. Dathan was my neighbor for many years."

"Yes, ma'am, I spoke to your son, I believe. Can you tell me a little about the deceased for my remarks? I didn't know him from church."

She looked out across the village. "Well, from what I know, Dathan grew up down at the south end of the valley, on what we call the old George Webb place. That was before the war." Abernathy nodded his head, catching her drift. "At some point he went to Louisville, but after the war he came back here. Lived in Daybreak for a while. Then after the community broke up, he took a parcel up on the ridge and one down here by the ferry. Lived up there and farmed down here until he got too old, then Newton started farming it for him and taking him the proceeds." She paused. That forty acres of bottomland, Dathan's legacy.

"Yes, ma'am," Abernathy said, breaking her reverie. "Lived up there, farmed down here."

"Yes. And of course he was married to Cedeh for, what, forty years or so."

"Will she be arriving soon?" Abernathy's face took on an even more lugubrious look.

"No, sir. Nobody is able to find her. She is Creek, and there is some thought that she might have left for Oklahoma."

"You don't suspect—"

"Oh no, nothing of the sort. No foul play of any kind."

"You're sure, ma'am? As much as I wish to honor my duty to the bereaved, I cannot involve myself in anything that…well, you know. Anything that suggests irregularity."

"Certainly, Mr. Abernathy. And I can assure you, everyone here wants the same as you. To lay to rest a good man and neighbor who deserves no less."

"Thank you, ma'am. And 'Clarence' is enough for me, or 'Reverend Clarence' if you prefer."

Up the road from the distance came Josephine Bridges on her wagon, her shoulders hunched, looking for all the world like a vulture on a tree limb. She had to have left early to make it here by morning, but Charlotte was happy to see her. At least this ceremony would be a little less lonesome.

Josephine climbed down with a groan. "Who has coffee?" she said. "I'm in no mood to ask twice."

"Sarah keeps a pot on the stove. She'll take care of you." Josephine walked to the store.

And from down the hill came Canterbury. his usual inscrutable self.

"Everything all right?" Charlotte said. Canterbury nodded, and she led him up to the schoolhouse, where the preacher stood at the door, his hands clasped behind his back. "I'm not sure you've met. This is the Reverend Clarence Abernathy, and this is Ulysses S. Canterbury, our neighbor."

The two men shook hands. "I've heard your name," Abernathy said. "You should stop by for Sunday services sometime."

"I may just do that," Canterbury said in a tone that indicated the time would be in a distant future.

"You kin to the departed?"

"No. But he and his wife made friends with me."

"I understand she is not to be found."

Canterbury's glance darted between them. "I guess so. She came by on the night he died, said Mr. Dathan had passed away, and told me to come down here to take care of things. Didn't hardly give me time to express my condolences."

"She just left?" Abernathy said. "Was she on foot?"

Canterbury scratched his head. "I suppose she was. I didn't hear anything outside that made me think she had a horse or mule. Mind you, I wasn't expecting her when she came knocking. So I didn't exactly mind the details."

Abernathy sniffed the air. "Perhaps she will find her way here, then. But who knows when? I have tasks to attend to in town. I mean no disrespect, but…"

"Of course. I think everyone is here who intends to be here." Charlotte saw Josephine climbing the hill, and behind her came Newton, Sarah, and the boys, all in a line like ducks, with Newton leading the horse and wagon up the path. She felt grateful that they had brought the boys, if for no other reason than to fill out the attendance a bit. Even the least of humankind deserved a few people at their departing. She wondered about Penelope, whom she had failed to visit yesterday. But Penelope's limp made it hard for her to climb the slope, so her absence was understandable. Charlotte resolved to call on her later in the day.

Her mind wandered as the preacher launched into his sermon. She'd heard it all before, the comforts of memory, the promise of future bliss. The better place, free of suffering and trials. Who was he talking to? Himself, the tiny congregation, the universe? The one bereaved soul who needed comforting was not here.

Or so she thought until she glanced over at Josephine, who sat apart from everyone, still as stone, but with tears streaming down her cheeks and dripping off her chin. Occasionally she wiped them with the back of her hand. Mostly, though, she simply let them soak the bosom of her dress. No sobbing, no sound, just silent tears that would not stop.

Clarence Abernathy finally reached his conclusion. They all murmured the Lord's Prayer together, and then Abernathy peeked up from his bowed head when Newton audibly shuffled his feet. "All right," he said. "The Lord bless you and keep you. Time for these men to get to their work." With his Bible in his hand, he led them down the path toward the village. Newton and Canterbury waited until they were out of earshot before disappearing behind the schoolhouse, where a mule had been tied up, a jerry-rigged handcart bound to its harness with leather straps.

She caught up with Josephine and linked elbows with her as they walked in silence until they reached the rail where Josephine's horse was tied. "Stay for lunch," Charlotte said. "I'll fix us up a little something."

"Already missed half a day of work, and he's missed two," Josephine said, nodding in the direction of Canterbury. "I doubt if either of us can afford to miss much more." She cleared her throat. "Up there at the funeral—"

"It's all right."

"No, I want to tell you. There have been a lot of years in my life when very few people treated me with kindness. Often because I treated them unkindly myself." Charlotte squirmed a little, inwardly, knowing that she herself had often been harsh toward her, though in fairness she had to say that Josephine's memory was correct. She had been an unpleasant child, smart-mouthed and prickly, and though her hard shell undoubtedly stemmed from her illegitimate origins, she had never endeared herself in the community. "But this man Dathan never dealt with me on any terms other than kindness and understanding. Never in my worst moments."

"He always scared me a little," Charlotte confessed. "There was that glare he could turn on a person, and when he did, you knew you had been glared at."

Josephine managed a chuckle. "Amen to that. But there was a soft center to that hard shell. Like an old turtle sitting on a log."

Charlotte nodded. "Sounds about right. Close up tight and back into the mud when danger threatens."

Newton's oldest boy, John Wesley, walked over to them, a thoughtful expression on his face. "Preacher wants to know if you want him to talk to the monument man in town, maybe set up a marker. Says it's five dollars."

"Of course," Charlotte said. She had forgotten about the preacher. Of course he would want to talk. She strolled to the hitching rail in front of Newton's store, where the reverend stood expectantly. "Thank you for thinking about the grave marker," she said. "Does he need paid in advance?"

"Oh, no, ma'am. I'm sure with a lifelong citizen such as you, he'll be happy to be paid when he comes to set the stone. What kind of stone do you want, and what should he put on it?"

"Just a simple marker. I don't know the date of Dathan's birth. So perhaps just 'Dathan' and the date of his passing."

"No scripture? Or a few words of comfort?"

She shook her head. "I wouldn't know what to choose. Better to stay silent in such a case."

"Very well." Abernathy led his mule toward the road leading to the ferry, but his steps seemed peculiarly slow. Then it dawned on Charlotte.

"Reverend?" she called out. "Don't leave just yet. I'd like to offer you something for your time and trouble."

"Oh, ma'am, you don't have to do that," he said.

"I insist. Surely you deserve some compensation for the effort."

He gazed at the sky. "People do make a free will offering sometimes. But strictly of their own free will. A man of God shouldn't demand payment for being a man of God."

"One moment," Charlotte said. She stepped into the store, and as her eyes adjusted to the interior dimness she walked to the register and took out five dollars. "I'll pay you back," she called to Sarah, who gazed at her questioningly. She folded the bill into a tight packet and walked outside again.

"Again, my thanks to you on behalf of everyone in Daybreak." She pressed the bill into his hand, and he slipped it into his pocket without looking.

"God bless you, ma'am." He mounted his mule and kicked it into a trot toward the crossing.

Charlotte watched him depart, a dusty black suit on a dusty brown mule, shrinking with the distance until they became a swaying brown dot with a smaller black dot atop it. Sarah arrived beside her.

"I took five dollars out of your till to pay the man," she said. "I've got some cash at home to pay you back."

"Five dollars!" Sarah said. "That's a week's work for a man like him. He was probably hoping for a dollar and expecting fifty cents."

"Somebody got some good out of this day, then."

Sarah groaned. "There is an order in the way of doing things, and when someone disrupts that order, they create all kinds of disturbances they likely didn't intend or envision. That preacher goes home, tells everybody about the amazing generosity of a kindly woman out in Daybreak, and in three weeks we have beggars show up. Or maybe somebody comes down in the night to rob your house."

"Sarah, you have a remarkable ability to find the gloomiest corner of every room."

She grinned, but the grin faded instantly. "We all have our special talents. But I'm serious. You overpay the preacher, you hold a funeral for a colored man in a building that's only held white people up to now, people do notice. And when they notice, I hear about it."

"Is that so?"

"You know it is. And you don't feel the effects because of the respect accorded to you. But what I hear is from the yahoos who ride through here looking for something to complain about or someone to blame for their miserable lives. What I hear is 'Daybreak's a bunch of radicals, Daybreak's a home to race mixing, Daybreak's a place where the rules get broken.'"

Her words stung though she recognized their accuracy. "There was a time when people in Daybreak would be proud to hear those complaints."

"I know. But that time is not now. Daybreak's not a grand idea any more. It's just another name on the map. I don't mean to be harsh, but reputation matters in business. Newton is about to close his deal with the Hunting and Fishing Club, but they'd jump like a spooked rabbit if they thought they were buying into a radical hotbed. We have to be practical."

"I understand that," Charlotte said. "Doesn't mean I agree or think you're right, but I do understand."

Chapter 21

And now it was Josephine's turn to depart. They embraced in silent comfort. Neither of them spoke for a while. A blue jay squawked nearby.

Finally Josephine spoke. "If you see my employee, let him know that he's expected back to work tomorrow. We're all grieving, but we have orders to fill."

Charlotte smiled. "You know Canterbury. He'll probably want to work double shifts to make up the lost time. Anyway, I doubt if he'll come back down the mountain today. He had the firm idea that Dathan should be buried up there, and was quite persuasive on the subject. I'm not entirely sure that Dathan would have wanted that lonesome hilltop. He always struck me as the bottomland farmer type. Canterbury only knew Dathan for a few months."

"No," said Josephine. "But maybe he knew him differently, in ways we never could."

Charlotte considered this for a moment and knew it to be true. She and Josephine had known Dathan for more years than she cared to count, but always as a curious, alien entity, a former slave who had returned after the war to the place of his bondage to carve out some kind of life in the only home he knew. What did they have in common with that experience? Barely anything. Oh, they chafed at the restraints and prejudices they encountered for being women, the assumptions, the mockery, the legal restrictions. But they had never been someone else's actual property to be bought and sold, never been judged by strangers simply by the shade of their skin, never had to measure their actions based on the knowledge that a wrong word could lead to their death at the hands of a vengeful mob or a drunken rowdy. Ulysses S. Canterbury shared all that with Dathan except the actual condition of slavery, and surely his life was far closer to Dathan's than theirs could ever be.

She took Josephine's arm. "Let me pack you a box. I have some good ham."

Josephine chuckled. "You and I have grown too much alike these days. I have a box tucked under the wagon seat."

Of course she would have. Josephine climbed into her wagon and rode off without a look back. One moment of sentiment was all she allowed herself in a day, apparently. "Stop at the springhouse for fresh water, anyway," she called. Josephine waved without turning around.

One last visit before she returned. What to say to Penelope? Charlotte didn't really want to leave so soon, for there was much to do around the house. Mice had encroached inside; she had seen the telltale signs in the pantry. She needed to stay and clean, to sweep and purge, until whatever had drawn the mice was gone. But when she thought of Petey on her own in St. Louis, the call to return felt overwhelming.

At home, she scrubbed and dusted, her thoughts on Petey. The girl grandchild. A grandmother's privilege, to single out a grandchild for special attention in a way that parents were not supposed to do. Newton's boys would be fine. They had the weight of family and property, the entitlement of their sex and color. They would go on to whatever fate their brains and willpower could support. But Petey had no advantages. If greatness lay in her future—and greatness certainly spoke in many of her habits of mind—it would have to be coaxed out from within the web of hindrances the world had placed around her.

She stood at the kitchen counter, rag in hand, and considered for a moment. Then she dried her hands and tugged at the little board that she had left unfastened on the inside of the window jamb, just at the bottom where the window met the sill. She recalled the day they had installed this window, back in the old times before the war. At the beginning they had been too poor for glass windows and had hung oilcloth over the openings, and the arrival of windows had seemed like a great achievement. The frame, nailed into the roughly cut opening of the log cabin, fit only approximately, and Charlotte had discovered one day that the board on one side of the jamb could be pulled loose to reveal a sizable gap between the window and the logs, a gap that she had used ever since as a hiding place for valuables and secret things. She reached into the alcove, half-expecting to find nothing but chewed papers and a mouse nest.

But it was all intact, a packet of letters and papers tied up with a ribbon. She untied the bow and spread them on the counter.

Letters from James, back when they were courting, filled with passion and high ideals, almost embarrassing now in their earnestness. James' letters from the war, and her father's letters, still too painful to read for all they revealed about the grinding-down of their dreams and James' descent into gloom. The letter from her father's commanding general. And then from years later, the letters she had been sent by Ambrose Gardner, her unexpected second suitor, also passionate in their own bookish, eccentric way, descriptions of birds and flowers so rich in detail they became erotic. A sprig of bittersweet, the berries long disintegrated and gone, a memento of a long-lost love. A deed to some tract of land she had forgotten about.

Perhaps she should take these things to St. Louis with her this time, lay them out for Petey and go through them, a lesson in the twists and turns of life, how certainties vanish and unexpected joys appear. Petey knew her only as a grandmother, an old lady with settled patterns, reassuringly stable, the sensible one in every conversation. Perhaps she could show her that even her grandma is a human being.

She fingered the letters and contemplated opening one to read. Instead, she tied the ribbon and returned the packet to its hiding place inside the wall, bumping the board into place with the heel of her hand. Was it that Petey wasn't ready to see these letters, or that she wasn't ready to reveal them? Something of both, she supposed. She prided herself of being the kind of person who didn't dwell in the past, and poring over old letters felt all too close to that impulse regardless of whatever motive she conjured up. But perhaps she needed to stop thinking of the past as an enemy. Not a friend, to be sure; but something else. A new thing altogether. A place one visited occasionally, perhaps. A well to drink from.

Penelope didn't answer Charlotte's knock at first, and when she did her limp seemed more pronounced. "I thought you might come by," she said, smoothing down her housedress. "Sorry, I should have tidied up. The house is a mess."

It was indeed, as Charlotte took in with a glance, although she tried not to let her expression reveal it. Penelope was a mess as well, her hair uncombed and her housedress stained. Granted, Charlotte had a few of those dresses herself for everyday use, but there was an unruliness about Penelope's appearance, something beyond the everyday mess, that bothered her. She sat on the edge of her chair as Penelope disappeared into the kitchen.

Penelope was gone a long time, and when she returned didn't look any better. She sat in the chair across from Charlotte but didn't speak for a moment. Then she said, "It's good to see you."

"It's good to see you too. Petey and Adam send their love."

"Do they?" Penelope seemed distracted. "That's good."

She didn't ask further about them, but Charlotte forged ahead. "Petey is exploring the fair almost every day. I think it may turn out to be educational after all. She made a friend from the Philippine exhibit, and I believe she's a little sweet on him as well."

Penelope looked at her blankly. "Mm. I guess that happens to everyone eventually." She stood up and walked to the window. "I'm sorry I missed the funeral yesterday. I didn't mean to miss it."

Charlotte recalled Penelope as a child, funny and observant, with a wit that was always insightful but never mean. She was Charlotte's favorite of the two daughters-in-law, a good counterbalance to Charlotte's tendency toward somber self-reflection. But that Penelope had disappeared.

Penelope turned away from the window. "I just couldn't get a grip on things, I suppose."

"My dear girl!" Charlotte said. "What's troubling you?"

"Nothing, really. Don't worry about me. I'm fine."

Charlotte wasn't sure of that, but it didn't seem the right time to pry, not two minutes after she'd walked through the door. "I always try to stay busy to keep my mind off my troubles," she ventured. But the words sounded superficial and hollow, even as she spoke them.

"I miss Petey," Penelope said.

"Of course you do."

"When she was home to visit, I felt normal again, or close to it, anyway. But here by myself—" She broke off and turned to the window again, gazing out as if a miracle were about to appear, one that must not be missed. "I think perhaps I'll get a cat to keep me company."

Charlotte felt the need to tread carefully. "Well, Newton's barn is always full of cats, so I'm sure he could pick you out a kitten to raise. But Petey will be home again soon."

"Oh, I wouldn't want an old barn cat in my house! I meant one of those lazy, fluffy ones you see in pictures. It was just an idle thought."

Charlotte reached out to pat her hand, for the moment demanded something other than words. Or at least words that she was incapable of summoning.

Penelope did not draw her hand away, but neither did she return Charlotte's squeeze. But Charlotte held it anyway, a warm soft limp mound of bones and flesh, and gave it an extra squeeze before she released it, as if one last bit of effort could impart life and energy into its recipient. She leaned in close.

"I leave tomorrow for St. Louis," she whispered. "Is there any message I can take to Adam and Petey for you?"

Penelope's face moved from blank to frown to blank again. "Tell her I'm fine."

Chapter 22

Charley greeted her at the door of the exhibit with a look of relief. "Your professor friend has been by again," he said. "He wants to hear all about our folkways."

"Our folkways?"

"Superstitions and such. I told him about planting potatoes in the dark of the moon, but he'd already heard that one. He wants new ones. I think he's getting bored with his aboriginals."

"What did you tell him?"

"I told him it was bad luck if you see a skunk cross your path."

"Is it?"

His sly smile appeared. "It is in the sense that you're about to get sprayed. Anyway, he seemed to like it. Wrote it down in his notebook." Then his expression grew more serious. "Your son's been pacing around all day like a dog with worms. I don't know what's on his mind, but something sure is."

Charlotte sighed. Family drama at both ends of the rail line. She brushed through the reception room, where Adam was busy regaling a group of admirers with tales of Heaven Holler, and took her valise upstairs to unpack. Petey was nowhere to be seen. She lay on the bed and closed her eyes. Now that full summer was upon them, the upstairs of the building seemed to accumulate heat, no matter how many windows were open. The only solution was to lie still and wait for nightfall.

Fifteen minutes later, she heard his footsteps on the stairs. She took her chair by the window and waited for his knock. He came in a few steps and cleared his throat.

"Everything all right at home?" he said.

Charlotte took a breath. "I have to tell you, your wife is not well. She is sad and lonely. She is not taking care of herself. I am concerned about her situation."

Adam fluttered his hand between them as if waving away an odor. "She's fine. Her letters are full of spirit. Lots of observations about life in Daybreak, the people, the weather. She just gets a case of the blue devils sometimes."

"You may read the letters, but I saw the writer. I'm telling you, she's not well."

He turned away. "All right, I get it. I'll write Sarah and ask her to stop in more often."

"She doesn't need Sarah. She needs Petey and you."

"I understand! All right? I'll talk to Petey."

Charlotte wanted to emphasize her point one more time, but she had learned that badgering only brought more resistance. Time to change the subject.

"Dathan's funeral went as well as one could hope. For some reason Cedeh was nowhere to be found."

"Nowhere to be found? They don't suspect foul play, do they?"

"No. The best guess is that she sized up the danger of her position and took off for Oklahoma."

"Hard to imagine any danger. She's been there all her life."

Charlotte tried to keep any exasperation out of her voice. "Adam, she's an Indian, who was married to a black man, and who is now a widow with no family. Surely you see the precariousness of her life."

"Well. Now that you put it that way. That's about the beatinest thing I ever heard."

He pursed his lips and cleared his throat. "I have a bit of news myself, as it happens. You are aware of my efforts on behalf of Miss LaBelle, of course," he ventured.

Charlotte felt a spreading chill in the pit of her stomach. What now?

"While you were away, I had a long conversation with her about her life and how to improve it. She is a bright young woman, and I believe she is in earnest."

"Oh, Adam, you're not involved with her somehow!"

"Mother! How could you think such a thing!" But the haste with which he assured her only made her doubt him all the more. "My relations with Miss

LaBelle are governed by a true concern for her well-being, not by—by whatever you want to call it."

What she wanted to call it. A couple of words came to mind but she let them pass.

"The source of her problem is her reliance on codeine," he continued. "She drinks codeine to numb herself to the things she must do in her occupation, and has become so reliant on it that she must perform the work in order to buy it. I've told her it is an unending circle with disastrous effect."

The cold sensation in her stomach only deepened. "You've had quite a conversation."

"A series of conversations over the past several days. But the upshot is, she has agreed to remedy this situation, and I have agreed to help her. I have formed a plan, but I need your help."

"I see."

"Here's my idea. We will house Miss LaBelle here for four or five nights, long enough to get the poison out of her system. I'll tend to her, but I would need your help with meals and, ah, personal care."

"So you think you will cure her of her codeine addiction in four or five days."

"I'm not that naïve. But we can get her through the worst. After that, we'll see. I can make up her lost income for a time."

"And where will she be housed?"

He shifted from foot to foot. "That's where I need your help. My thought is to move her into Petey's room, and ask Petey to move her bed into your room for the time being. With your permission, of course."

Charlotte stood up and walked to the window, her face burning. People were milling around in the back yard as usual, climbing the pretend mountain, dawdling all too close to her garden. She fought the urge to run downstairs and out, to protect her threatened tomato plants.

"You say you're not naïve, but indeed you are," she said. "You think you are this young woman's savior, that because you've attained success with the Heaven Holler book you are now some kind of moral guardian to the world, and you can just talk your way into any goal you set for yourself. Well, you can't. Have you even talked to Petey about this business?"

His silence told her that he hadn't.

"Perhaps you should think about that. 'There's a little whore around here that I've gotten fond of, and I'd like you to move in with your grandma while I see if I can help her kick the dope.' I'm sure she'll understand."

Adam swallowed. “You don’t need to speak in such cruel terms, Mother.”

“Apparently I do.” She labored to bring her temper under control and gestured to the building and grounds. “This is your great venture, and you are entitled to run it as you see fit. You may house whomever you want and behave in whatever ways you think best. Just don’t ask me to smile on it and tell you it’s fine.”

Charlotte walked out of the room and into the kitchen. She could leave, or threaten to leave. But common sense told her never to threaten anything she wasn’t ready to do, and the idea of leaving Petey in an increasingly troubling situation was inconceivable. She could demand to take Petey home with her. But what if he refused? It was a welter of undesirable choices.

She heard Adam’s footsteps come down the hall and pause at the door, but didn’t turn around to look. “Whatever you decide to do, don’t cloak it in the language of morality,” she said. “You have a personal interest in this. Describe it how you will, but don’t act like it’s not there.”

The footsteps moved on.

Charlotte spent an hour upstairs, tidying and scrubbing to keep her mind occupied, before descending to the main floor to greet visitors. She passed Adam in his alcove, engaged with admirers as usual, without a glance in his direction. There would be time to return to their conversation later, or at least so she hoped. Charley sat at his table across the way. He tried to catch Charlotte’s eye, but she merely waved and walked on.

And where was Petey? Something didn’t feel right.

Outside on the Pike, the throngs of people hurried up and down, bumping into each other, each intent on some goal. It reminded her of the beetles she would see along her path back home, laboring endlessly at some obscure task. The tourists clutched their guidebooks in their hands, and their expressions were strained and intent as the barkers called out to them, each caller crying out that this pleasure, not those others, was the sublime attraction of the street, the one not to be missed in the precious time that remained to them.

She walked on. The moving picture display house, the Hagenbeck animal show, the Irish village. No Petey.

Charlotte supposed she could have taken advantage of her absence to sneak off to visit Nimuel. Adam wouldn’t notice, and Charley wouldn’t tattle. But Petey had never been one to sneak. Her fault, if it was a fault, lay in being too open and straightforward about her feelings, not in concealing them.

“Best mind your path,” a close voice said. “Pickpockets are about tonight.”

She looked up, startled. It was Big Bill Langland, decked out as always, his boots shined to a high polish and a maple walking stick in his hand. And by his side stood Petey, with an intense look of discomfort on her face.

"Mr. Langland," she said, recovering herself.

He tipped his hat. "I found this girl wandering around in my neighborhood. And I assure you, my neighborhood is no place to wander around unaccompanied."

"You just found her? You have a way with coincidences."

Langland shrugged. "We are at the crossroads of the world, Mrs. Turner. Walk the Pike long enough and you shall see everyone you desire. And I will admit, I have eyes and ears all over the city."

They had reached the Tyrolean Alps, near the entrance to the Pike, and a waiter rushed over to show Langland to a table.

"Will you sit with me a minute?" he said. "I'd like to talk a bit."

"We have talked here before, you may recall. And I don't remember it being particularly pleasant."

"Then let's try again. I don't like to leave things on an unpleasant note with someone if I can help it. And I have a feeling we may have common interests."

Charlotte sat down, distrustful, but recognizing that Langland might have a point. At the very least, she could listen to him. "All right," she said.

"In private, if I may. I have a feeling our young friend here may need to get back to your exhibition before she is missed."

Charlotte nodded. "Petey, I'll talk to this man a little while and then join you at the sale table. I think we have enough dolls to start out." Petey's face was still clouded, but she had the manners to nod briefly and excuse herself. They watched her pick her way through the crowd toward Heaven Holler.

"Fine young lady," Langland said. "One of my boys reported that an unknown girl was wandering the neighborhood, so I had him bring her in. Of course, I recognized her immediately. She didn't tell us what she was doing there, but she seemed upset."

"You're a very courteous man for your line of work," she said.

Langland laughed. "Mrs. Turner, you're wise in the ways of the world. I expect you know the usefulness of good manners, even in an occupation that has its rough moments. Besides, I deal with respectable people every day. Courtesy matters."

"I'm abashed. And I apologize for casting you in such a light. If experience has taught me anything, it's not to prejudge."

A cup of coffee appeared at Langland's elbow. He cast a querying look in Charlotte's direction. She shook her head, and he waved off the waiter with a flick of his finger.

"What is it that you think I do?" he said.

She considered. "I wouldn't presume to speculate. But from what I have observed, it would appear that part of your occupation includes being a procurer."

He cocked an eyebrow. "All right. Cautiously spoken, but fair enough. I do manage the affairs of some young women who are under my watch. Call it what you will." He sipped his coffee. "But that only occupies a fraction of my time. I spend most of my time in politics, business matters, the regular affairs of life. I supervised the crew that built your exhibit, as you recall."

"I do."

"I have a way with people, that's my skill. I know what they need, what they want, what they are willing to do to get it." He leaned over his cup of coffee, his heavy body hunched. The coffee cup looked like a child's toy in his hands. "I supposed I learned this skill in my youth. As a child, it was important to me to sense every whim, every mood, every possible action of my father, for to mistake his mind was to invite a beating."

"You must have resented that immensely."

He scoffed. "'Resent' is a soft word," he said. "I hated the man, not just for what he did to me, but what he did to me mother. He thought he was so fine, strutting about on the stage like the poor player in Shakespeare, and never understanding that he was the idiot signifying nothing. He lost his position from the drink after a while, and then he took off for the South, where he'd heard a man could make a living treading the boards, and they didn't care as much whether he was drunk or sober. That was the last we saw of him. Somebody told me years later that he'd died, and I didn't much care. Would have liked to kill him myself, was my only regret. I hated him then, hate him now, and if we ever meet in Hell I'll hate him there, too ."

Langland stopped himself. "But I've gone distracted. My point was, from an early age I've been able to read people. Their weaknesses and their strengths. And then to play on those things to achieve my own goals, which may or may not coincide with theirs. In that respect, I am not so different from every other businessman in the city, except that my business takes me into avenues where others do not tread. I work the night shift, so to speak."

"You speak about business as if it's something close to murder."

"Who's to say it's not?" Langland said with a chuckle. "I've heard legitimate businessmen wish things upon their rivals that you don't even read in the Old Testament."

"I don't doubt that," Charlotte said. She thought back to her own brushes with the world of big business and could think of no contrary examples.

"Not to make false equivalencies," Langland said. "I'm well aware of all that separates me from the legitimate world. It's a small-time crook who pretends to be anything else." He leaned toward her, close enough that she could smell the coffee on his breath. "A man can be a criminal and yet not devoid of understanding, that's what I'm saying. And as I said, I think we have interests that coincide."

"Having interests in common doesn't mean we must act in common."

Langland's blank expression didn't change. "I don't seek to persuade, only to point out. What you do with this knowledge is your own business. Just be aware that I rarely offer opportunities to cooperate, and those opportunities, once withdrawn, are never extended again. I usually end up achieving my aims another way."

"I'm sure you do," Charlotte said. "Exactly what interests are you talking about?"

Langland turned his coffee cup around and around in his hands. "I have a number of girls who work for me," he said slowly. "Their goal—and mine—is to earn as much money as possible while making sure they stay healthy and on the good side of the law. Beyond that, how they make their money is pretty much up to them."

Charlotte noticed that as he spoke, Langland's expression never altered, but his eyes remained in constant motion. What was he watching for? Dangers, acquaintances, opportunities?

"Every so often, a gentleman will fall in love with one of the girls. I don't mind that," he said with a shrug. "It creates a steady customer, and it makes the girl feel special. As long as the income stays the same, all's to the good. But there's one thing I can't tolerate, and that's a gentleman who decides he's going to be a hero and rescue a girl from the life. A life she's chosen and at which she makes a damn sight more money than any schoolteacher or governess you'll find."

"So you're their guardian angel now."

Langland snorted. "I told you already, I'm a businessman. My job is to protect my investment. And a girl who runs away with some infatuated young man is a lost investment." He stood up and brushed himself off. "There is a personal aspect to this as well, which I won't go into. Suffice it to say that your son is at risk of making a fool of himself, or far worse, and my girl is about to run herself into a world of trouble as well. You and I can prevent any number of bad consequences."

Charlotte looked up at him but did not rise. "Mr. Langland, through all of this I've heard you speak only of protecting your investment. Not once have I heard you mention what's in the best interest of Miss LaBelle."

"She is a silly young flibbertigibbet who has no idea of her own best interests," Langland said with a dismissive wave. "That's my job." He studied Charlotte for a moment. "I hope you're not mistaking me for someone who can be dissuaded."

He leaned toward her in a sudden move that startled Charlotte, although she tried not to show her surprise. "*The girl is mine*," he hissed. "*I will not give her up*." Then he straightened and put on his hat. "May I walk you back to your residence? The crowd grows ever thicker."

"No," Charlotte said. "I might decide to order something after all. Thank you, though."

"All right," Langland said in a tone equally as flat as hers. "Good evening."

And with that he was gone into swirling mass of fairgoers, disappearing like a rock dropped into a turbulent stream. A momentary disturbance in the flow, and then nothing.

Charlotte sat at the table another minute, until she felt sure he was gone. Then she stood up. Langland had not left a tip for the waiter; she felt in her pockets and found a nickel, which she left on the table. The great and the small, what difference did it make. Cheap sons-of-bitches could be found everywhere.

She didn't want to return to the exhibition, but what other choice did she have? She had even less desire to join the aimless milling of people in the street, in search of the next bit of distraction. That left Hillbilly Holler, like it or not.

She found herself following the path of a pipe and drum band, some kind of imitation-Scottish group that blew out "Garry-Owen" again and again, while the drummers pounded out the rhythm with an enthusiasm bordering on mania. Another night on the Pike. At least they cleared the crowd as they marched so that Charlotte could follow easily. Langland was right about one thing; pickpockets could feast in these crowded passages.

And he was right about something else, Charlotte reflected as she walked. Adam was on the verge of making a right fool of himself, with actions that were likely to cost him a lot of money, his reputation, his family happiness, and perhaps even his safety.

Of course she didn't want that. So they had a convergence of interests after all. But the farther she walked, the stranger this convergence became. She doubted Adam's claims about the nobility of his motives, but at least he had noble motives to claim. Just like his father, unable to distinguish his ideals from his own desires, persuading himself that his passing wishes were universal goals.

But was it worse to be a misguided idealist or a clear-eyed, cruel realist? All Big Bill Langland wanted to do was to add to his money and increase his power. If Rose LaBelle died from her codeine addiction, he would pause and sniff sadly, then head to the train station to recruit a new, lost girl. Hardly a man to ally oneself with.

Yet here they were, on their own in a city that wasn't their home, not the kind of place where it was wise to make a powerful enemy. There was Petey to think about, as well as herself and Adam.

She passed through the entrance turnstile and stood in the foyer for a moment. Charley and Petey at their tables, selling their mementoes. The musicians tuning up in the big open area in back. Visitors examining the displays on the wall and lining up for their turn with Adam. Was she the only one who noticed how flimsy the building's construction was, built to last for one season and no more? The corn shuck dolls and miniature carvings, destined to be thrown in a closet or toybox to gather dust upon their return to Asheville or Schenectady or wherever. It all seemed so temporary and inconsequential. The high claims of the World's Fair to foster harmony and global understanding seemed to have resolved themselves into trinkets and show.

Charlotte settled into the chair beside Petey, who still looked miserable. "So what were you doing off in the rough districts?"

Petey didn't meet her eyes. "Something's going on with Papa and that woman, isn't there? He carries on about the hard life she leads and how she needs to be saved from it."

Charlotte didn't know what to say. A customer came and went.

"So I decided to go see this hard life she lives," Petey continued. "Doesn't look that hard to me. Silk dresses and piano music."

Charlotte drew a deep breath and let it out slowly. "There are different kinds of difficulty in this world. Sometimes a hard life doesn't look that way on the outside."

"I suppose so," said Petey, but she didn't sound convinced. Charlotte thought about her conversation with Big Bill. She had no doubt that he could make a person's life as miserable as he wanted. Rose LaBelle was a slight girl, who despite her spirit appeared to have little judgment about her own best interests. What was it her father used to say? *Man is a wolf to man.* And Rose LaBelle, in such a world, was a sheep.

"Perhaps something is going on with your papa and this Rose," she said. "But I asked him about it, and he insists there is not. So I suppose I'll have to take him at his word."

She understood Adam's yearning to bring good into the world, to rescue the sheep. She even understood how that yearning could blind him to the darker yearnings that she could see. But what to do with a sheep who wouldn't be rescued? *The girl is mine. I will not give her up.*

Charlotte stood up from the table. "I think your father means well. Please be patient with him." She eased past the line of Heaven Holler enthusiasts waiting to speak to Adam, their souvenir editions clutched in their hands. But she paused and leaned in before climbing the stairs to their quarters.

"All right," she said to him softly. "Let's see if we can get this girl out from under her cravings, or at least lift them a little. I'll move Petey's things into my room." She straightened up. "I hope you know what you're doing."

Chapter 23

Rose LaBelle showed up a day later, a small valise in her hand, moving uncertainly through the exhibition like the rest of the tourists. Adam leaped from his chair to show her upstairs, while Petey gaped and Charley Pettibone cast dark looks. "I take it you were aware of this idea," Charlotte said to Charley when they were out of earshot.

"Aware but unconvinced that he would follow through," Charley said. "I advised against it. I dealt with dope fiends many times during my years as deputy sheriff. They will lie to your face and steal without remorse." He began locking his bedroom door and carrying his cash box around with him wherever he went.

It was clear to Charlotte that Adam had given Petey only the vaguest of descriptions of their new housemate's occupation. "Papa says she's a troubled soul, and we must be kind to her," she said as they washed dishes after breakfast the next morning.

"That she is, and indeed we must be kind to her as we are to all who come our way," Charlotte answered.

"He says she's had to sell her body to make ends meet."

"That's true," Charlotte said. But from her quizzical look, she could tell that Petey had only a bare idea of what that phrase meant, so for the next half hour they stood in the back yard while Charlotte explained the economics, mechanics, and logistics of Rose's existence.

"Would you excuse me?" Petey said after she finished. She wobbled inside, and Charlotte guessed she needed time alone. She had not held back on her explanations of the desires of men and the rigors of the prostitute's life. The romances that girls carried around these days were full of talk about courtesans, but entirely vague on what it meant to be one. If Adam was going to enlist them in his efforts to redeem Rose LaBelle, they all might as well know what she was being redeemed from.

After a while she walked inside, but found that Petey, instead of brooding in her bedroom or hiding in the bath, had gone to Rose's room, where the two of them sat together on the bed in what appeared to be complete harmony. "I'm telling Rose about Daybreak and the farm," she said. "She grew up on a farm too."

"Is that right?" Charlotte said.

"Yes, ma'am," said Rose. "Ohio."

"Your folks still there?"

"As far as I know." Her expression was as blank as a statue.

Charlotte wasn't sure how far she could take her inquisitiveness, so she refrained from asking further about the Ohio home. Rose did not seem particularly troubled or ill, but Charlotte guessed that the cravings for her drug would only increase as time passed. For now, though, she sat with Petey looking for all the world like the big sister Petey never had. Charlotte excused herself and walked downstairs, where Charley was setting up his display for the morning.

"This situation ain't good," Charley muttered. "I don't know what you were doing, letting him move that girl in."

She unpacked the dolls from their box beneath her table and laid out the supplies for making new ones. "I can't say myself," she said. "Maybe I don't know what I'm doing. All I know is that he's a full-grown man, so it's not a question of my allowing or not allowing. My choice is whether to stay or leave, and for now I think I'll do more good here than down in Daybreak."

Charley grumbled but didn't answer. "Ain't good," he finally muttered.

Charlotte couldn't disagree. But at this point in her life she knew that making choices wasn't between good and bad, but between difficult and less difficult, or between not-great and entirely terrible. Adam might think he could work miracles, but she focused on holding back the tide of disasters that lurked behind every sunrise.

Petey came downstairs a half hour later and sat beside her, fussing with the display. "You didn't react to my little talk about the facts of life the way I expected," Charlotte said to her.

When Petey looked over at her, Charlotte could see that her eyes were full of tears. "Oh, Grandma," she said. "She's had such a hard life, and so young too! I hope you don't mind, but I think Miss LaBelle needs a friend more than anything. I've resolved to be her friend."

Petey's innocence and optimism touched Charlotte's heart, and she reached over to give her granddaughter a hug. She held back on her misgivings. It seemed inevitable to her that Rose LaBelle would prove to be far less of a friend to Petey, but such things were only learned through experience, and the bearer of such a gloomy prophecy would only be remembered as the messenger of prospective disappointment.

Rose showed up on the main floor a while later, in a striped blue-and-yellow pinafore tied with a broad yellow sash. It looked vaguely like a mock school uniform from an Offenbach operetta. Charlotte was relieved to see that she hadn't painted her face.

"Well, don't you look spritely," she said.

"See, I can be respectable when I need to," she said in a playful tone.

By now, the gates to the Pike had opened, and the first wave of visitors was streaming down the street. They could hear the growing murmur of voices outside. "Is there anything I can do to help?" Rose said.

Charlotte thought for a moment. "Just walk around, chat with people. Make them feel welcome." She didn't want to appear to endorse Rose's presence in their exhibit, but on the other hand, here she was. She might as well be put to use. Out of the corner of her eye, she could see Charley following her movements with a disapproving look on his face, but with his gaze fixed on the gentle sway of her hips.

And so it went with the general flow of visitors. Rose greeted them amiably, walked them around the exhibit, and spoke of the stories of Heaven Holler as if she were a native, when Charlotte wasn't even sure if she had gotten past the first few chapters. Men laughed at her jokes and submitted to gentle teasing, while women looked on uncomfortably, sensing something amiss although it would have been impossible to say what. The easy familiarity with which she bantered, the confidence and lack of deference in her conversation, made them nervous.

In the early afternoon a man paid his way into the exhibit and stood in front of Charlotte's table. He took off his cap, revealing a tangled hummock of red hair. His stocky build and dusty clothes marked him as a working man, and he held a parcel under his arm. "You'd be Mrs. Turner, I take it?" he said.

"I'd be," she said.

He tapped the parcel. "Big Bill sent me. Said as long as Rose is going to be staying over here, she'd need a change of clothes or two."

"All right," Charlotte said. She reached for the parcel, but the man held tight.

"He said I'm supposed to deliver them personally."

Charlotte turned in her chair to look, but Rose was nowhere to be seen. "Well, you've paid your admission. Walk around and see if you can find her. She's greeting guests."

The man wandered into the exhibit hall, leaving Charlotte and Petey to exchange glances. "One of the roughs," Charlotte said.

"You can say that again," said Charley in a low voice from the other table.

After a while the man reappeared. "Can't find her. Are you sure she's here? Big Bill said there are some rooms upstairs. Maybe I should go look there."

"Oh, no," Charlotte said. "Those are our private quarters. But I can send my granddaughter up to see if she's there. Who shall she say is calling? Mister—"

"She would know me as 'Two-Eyes.' It's a nickname."

"I guessed as much."

"It comes from a humorous remark I made once, which does not bear repeating."

"I see." Charlotte didn't take her eyes off the man. "Petey, could you run upstairs and see if Miss LaBelle is there? If so, tell her that Mr. Two-Eyes is here to pay a call." Petey scampered off, and the man walked to the front entrance to stand, looking out.

"How long you been in the crime business?" Charley called to him.

"I'm sure I don't know what you mean," said Two-Eyes. "I work in politics."

"Well, then, I stand corrected," Charley said with exaggerated politeness.

The man said nothing but gave Charley a glare that would cut metal.

"Spare me your dirty looks," Charley said. "I rode with Jesse James back during the war. I've seen worse than anybody's dirty looks."

"Jesse James is twenty years dead." The man resumed looking out the door.

After what seemed like an excessively long time, Petey returned downstairs. "I'm sorry, sir," she said. "Rose is in bed with a bad headache and says she can't see you. She told me to thank you for the clothing and to leave it with my grandma."

Two-Eyes squinted at her through watery blue eyes. "I hope she ain't fooling, miss. Bill can't stand being trifled with."

"Nothing of the sort, I assure," Petey said, with an assurance that surprised even Charlotte. "I saw her myself lying in bed with a damp towel draped over her head."

"That much I can believe," Two-Eyes said. "I've seen her the same way more than once." He laid the parcel on the table in front of Charlotte. "You'll see she gets this?"

"I'll consider it a duty."

Two-Eyes clamped his hat onto his head. "Then I'll take my leave."

"Feel free to look around some more. You can meet the author."

"Him I've heard about. No, ma'am, I can't stay. I have other things to tend to, and I don't read much anyway."

With that he was out the door, and Petey stood up again. "Rose told me to tell her when he left." She started for the back, but Charlotte touched her arm.

"I'll go. Perhaps I can help with that headache."

"It's not really that bad," Petey said with a blush. "I think it was more of an excuse, but I didn't want to press her."

Charlotte nodded. "No matter. Hold the fort here. Sell some dolls."

She took the parcel under her arm and went upstairs, her footsteps quiet. Before she walked to Rose's room, the next-to-last room at the end of the hall, she stopped in the kitchen and closed the door behind her.

Charlotte untied the string and opened the package gently. A couple of dresses were neatly folded on the top. Beneath them, stockings and undergarments, laundered and folded as well, and a stack of embroidered hankies. Two corsets, tightly rolled.

She unrolled the corsets and found what she had been looking for. At the center of each roll, with the corset stays wrapped around it to conceal its shape, was a pint bottle of North Star Lung and Throat Balsam, its contents glowing murky yellow in the afternoon light.

Charlotte meditated for a moment, then set the bottles in the back of the pantry, re-rolled the corsets, and assembled the packet to its original form, tying the string into a tight knot. Then she strolled down the hallway to Petey's old room, where Rose lay on the bed with a folded damp towel over her eyes. She peeked out from under the towel as Charlotte entered.

"Is he gone?" Rose said.

"Yes. You know him?"

Rose nodded. "One of Bill's men. Anytime you need a ballot box stuffed or a shopkeeper roughed up, Two-Eyes is your man."

"He brought you some changes of clothes." Charlotte laid the parcel on the bed.

"I bet he did," said Rose. "Probably a dead rat in there." Rose tugged at the knot for a moment before digging into her bedside drawer for a small clasp knife to cut the string. "Or a live one. Let's have a look."

But when she opened the package, revealing the dresses and underthings, Rose's suspicious expression melted into near-tears. "My favorite dresses!" She held one to her face. "And freshly washed, too. He knew these were my favorites."

She laid out the items on her bedspread, her headache suddenly gone, and drew in a breath. "I know you think Bill's an awful man, and I do myself, sometimes. But there's a sweet side to him, if you know where to look."

Charlotte sat on the bed. She couldn't explain why, but she felt oddly protective of this woman, little more than a girl, now that she had thrown in with the idea of helping her end her habit, as fruitless and destructive as she knew this idea to be. "I know you believe that," she said. "But I have to ask myself, what would be his motives for sending you these clothes, if not to soften your resolve and get you to come back to work?"

She shrugged. "I know. He says I'm his biggest earner. But he can still have feelings, too. He likes for me to look nice. He knows it makes me happy."

"And does he like for you to be addicted to codeine?"

"Of course not! That just shows how little you understand." Rose sat up, draped the towel over her headboard, and pulled her knees close under her chin. "Bill has told me many times to get off the stuff, but I just can't seem to manage it. It's my own doing, plain and simple."

Charlotte walked to the window and looked down at the milling visitors. She needed to get back downstairs. It was shaping up to be a busy day, and Petey could not handle it alone, especially not with Charley in a pout. And she had found out what she had come to find out—that Rose LaBelle had not sought out the bottles in her packet and was unaware they had been sent. Or at least she had found that out as far as anyone could penetrate.

"Well, come down whenever you're ready," she said. "So far, you don't seem to be showing any ill effects."

"No. Those usually show up on the second or third day."

"So you've tried before?"

"Oh, yes."

"Alone? Or with help?"

Rose's expression was once again veiled and indecipherable. "People have tried to help before. More than once."

"Other admirers, I suppose."

Her expression hardened into something almost a glare. "That's one word. Pick whichever one suits you."

Charlotte left the room before an argument could begin. Of course there had been other admirers, men who had decided they would be the one to rescue this fallen angel with the pretty voice and open legs. Men, their weaknesses, their arrogance. Hadn't Bill Langland told her as much already? And this girl was no fool.

The rest of the day passed as the others had, a blur of hurried conversations with a passing flow of visitors, each of whom had something they were determined to say. Charlotte could only greet them, listen to their thought, and move them along, but that modicum of attention was sufficient for them.

Throughout the day she felt anxious and watchful, for the situation around her seemed unsettled in every direction. Rose LaBelle showed up after a while and circulated around the exhibit, but she avoided the front room and displayed less interest in talking with visitors, strolling distractedly among the groups as if she were a fairgoer herself. In the afternoon, sitting beside her at their sales table, she overheard Petey humming "I'm Just a Bird in a Gilded Cage," low and melodious. Rose's influence was everywhere, it appeared.

That night, she awoke with these unsettlements circling her mind, which brought her out of bed and into the kitchen. She left the lights off, for electricity still made her nervous despite everyone's easy acceptance, and the idea of summoning it to course along behind her walls would only add to her sense of discomfort. She sat at the kitchen table with a cup of water and gazed out the window at the distant lights of the city.

From the room next door, Charley Pettibone's gentle snoring vibrated like the bass string in some dull tune. The sound didn't bother her, though. Her husbands had both snored, James only rarely, the gasping rattle of a young man who suffered from occasional catarrh and who was too full of ideas to sleep anyway, and Ambrose regularly, the deep snore of a man who took to sleep with the gusto other men took to fishing. It was the sound of a human being at rest, and who could complain about that?

The rest of the building was quiet, and Charlotte took comfort in that. The everlasting noise and tumult of the day wore on her. She knew that she should return to bed. Tomorrow was likely to be difficult, and she was not the kind of person who could sweep through the challenges of a day without a good night's sleep. Still, she let the peacefulness of the moment wash over her for a minute, like the breeze through the window, calming and restful no matter how temporary.

Down the hallway she heard someone's bedroom door open, and someone else's bedroom door close. And from this she knew that the thing she anticipated, and dreaded, and already knew in her heart of hearts, was true, and that tomorrow was going to be even harder than she had imagined.

Chapter 24

Rose began to show signs of distress the next morning, although at first they didn't look like distress. She acted snappish and ill-humored, announcing that she was coming down with a cold and was going to stay in bed. "Do you think I should stay with her?" Adam murmured to Charlotte in the hallway.

"No, you have work to do. I'll check in on her from time to time." Charlotte wished now that she had poured out the bottles instead of putting them in the pantry. Lord knows what that girl might do once she got desperate.

At ten in the morning she climbed the stairs to the kitchen and made a pot of tea. Tea had always soothed her, so perhaps it would do the same for Rose LaBelle. She knocked on her bedroom door, paused, and then stepped in with the tray.

Rose stood by the window, gazing down into the back enclosure where visitors would soon be wandering. "This place is boring," she said. "Is this all you ever do? Chit-chat, chit-chat, sell your little dolls?"

"Pretty much," Charlotte said. "I try to find interest in the people I meet. You know what they say, everyone has a story."

"And it's usually boring. Tedious people with tedious thoughts."

Charlotte wasn't in the mood to take her bait. She set the tea tray on the dressing table without responding, stirred some sugar into her cup, and took a sip. "Milk or sugar?" she asked Rose.

"I don't drink tea much." But Rose edged over to the table and sniffed the brew. "Maybe some sugar."

Charlotte stirred up a cup and handed it to her.

"It smells funny," Rose said.

Charlotte shrugged. "Likely so. I can't remember where I bought this batch, it's been so long." But neither of them put their cups down. It tasted fine to Charlotte.

Rose couldn't stay still. She walked from the window to her bed, sat on the bed, then immediately rose again to adjust her curtains. She seemed to be sweating, although Charlotte couldn't tell whether that was from the warmth of the day or from the ill effects of her codeine withdrawal.

"I know you don't want me here," Rose said. "I understand that."

"It's not that I don't want you," Charlotte answered, choosing her words. "It's that I don't quite understand what you're doing here."

"Ask your son. I wonder myself. Don't get me wrong, he's a good man, with good intentions, but it's pretty obvious I don't fit in here."

If you're expecting me to try to talk you out of that idea, Charlotte thought, *you're in for a long wait.* She said nothing for a moment. "Have you come to any conclusions on that question?" she finally said.

Rose looked diffident. "He thinks I need saving."

"What do you think? Do you need saving?"

"Sure. Don't we all? I don't mean 'knight-in-armor' type saving, but saving from ourselves, from our worst impulses and instincts. I bet you need that kind of saving too, don't you, Mrs. Turner?"

She had a knack for putting her finger directly on the sore spot. "I do indeed."

"So you see. If someone comes along determined to assist in your salvation, of course you'd take advantage of that offer, no matter how nonsensical it seems."

And especially take advantage of the man making the offer.

Once again Rose seemed to read her mind. "And since it gives Adam such satisfaction and sense of purpose to believe he is saving me, it would be downright mean of me to deny him that pleasure."

"So you're doing him a favor."

"You could say that."

Rose set her teacup down on the tray with a whack. "I can't drink this anymore. Something about it doesn't taste right to me." She retrieved her copy of

Hill-Billies and climbed back into bed. "He's always wanting to talk to me about the characters in this book, so I'd better finish it."

Charlotte left, miffed at the abrupt dismissal but determined not to let it become a confrontation. She needed to keep in mind that she was on Adam's side, and that creating a situation where he had to choose between her and Rose would help no one. She hoped to let him pass through this infatuation by himself, if possible, and let Rose move of her own accord to whatever ultimate destination awaited her, probably back to her addled state and degraded life.

In the kitchen, she rinsed the cups and pot and turned them upside down to dry, then quietly opened the pantry door and took out the bottles of medicine. She poured them down the sink. It had a nasty odor, a smell like grease or kerosene, and she wondered if the pungent aroma would reach Rose and intensify her cravings. Too late to worry about that now.

Adam eyed her as she passed his alcove, and she gave him a nod and a smile. How much did he think she knew? Not much, she guessed. Men always believed their obviousness to be invisible.

At lunchtime she sent over to the French Village for a container of soup and took it upstairs. She found Adam tending to her in her bedroom, grossly improper at ordinary times but marginally excusable at this moment of illness. She gave them both a long look and set the soup onto the dressing table. "See that she eats some," she said, returning downstairs with a feeling of deep dread. There was something about the solicitous way he leaned in to that girl. What if she had underestimated the degree of infatuation? What if, instead of a passing cloud, this turned out to be a lasting storm? What kind of damage would it do—to him, to Petey, to the absent Penelope? The prospect of sitting by and allowing this to happen felt ever more untenable.

Back at the doll table, she leaned over to Petey. "You understand what's going on with Rose LaBelle?"

"Papa says she's going to be fighting through her cravings for a while."

"That's the sum point of it, but I don't think he knows how this will all unfold. I don't know it myself. So we must all be watchful, and not build up our hopes too much." Her words felt uncomfortably like a stratagem to her, but she wasn't sure yet how much she could count on Petey, or take her into her confidence. The child should be protected as much as possible from unpleasant knowledge, although her umbrella could extend only so far.

She spoke again. "I took her some soup, but I have my doubts if she'll want to eat it. In twenty or thirty minutes, I'd like you to go up and see. If the soup's still there, fire up the stove and reheat it. She's not helping herself if she doesn't eat." Surely Petey's coming and going would squelch anything untoward.

But thoughts about Rose LaBelle has to be set aside, for here came Watson Kellogg through the door, wearing a morning coat with a striped silk cravat as if he were about to pose for a photographer, and with the same expression of benign satisfaction that he applied to every situation. "Mr. Kellogg! What a pleasant surprise!" she said.

Kellogg tipped his hat. "Good afternoon, Mrs. Turner. I thought I'd drop by and say hello. I have to admit, I've been avoiding the fairgrounds since the opening ceremonies. I'm not strong on crowds." He tipped his hat to Petey, sitting beside her. "In case you're wondering, miss, I didn't bring my auto down. I took the streetcar like regular folks. But I signed up for the autoists' rally in August, so you won't want to miss that. They're coming from all over the country."

He cast his glance around the room, taking in the crowd, and nodded to Charley.

"You're dressed pretty fine for a Bible salesman," Charley said.

"Publisher," Kellogg said. "Businessman. One must look the part."

"I reckon so," said Charley. He took out his pocketknife and started to whittle a new figurine. "Don't worry, I sweep up the shavings."

"I'm sure you do," Kellogg said with a sniff.

"How's business?" said Charlotte. He looked at her in surprise, as if having a woman inquire about business matters was like hearing a cow speak.

"Thanks for asking," he finally managed. "*Heaven Holler* continues to sell well, although I have to say that our return on this exhibition hasn't been what I hoped. People don't seem as interested in the literary arts as I imagined."

Charley cleared his throat. "Maybe we should bring in some of them pygmy dancers," he said to his knife.

Kellogg gave him a look but said nothing. "*Heaven Holler* may be getting a little stale. Let's hope the second book is ready soon."

Perhaps we was expressing a general hope, or perhaps he was fishing for information. Either way, Charlotte had nothing for him. "Petey, tell your father that Mr. Kellogg is here," she said.

"That's all right," Kellogg said. "I'll just pop around the corner and say hello."

Whatever Kellogg was up to, Charlotte felt certain that finding Rose LaBelle ensconced upstairs would not be a good part of it. She considered.

"Petey, I need to ask something of you," she said. "Walk back there and ask Mr. Kellogg if he'd like some tea. Then whatever he says, go upstairs and let

Rose know we need her to stay quiet as a mouse until he's gone. This feels to me like something of a deception, and I'm sorry to ask you to do it. But I want to keep your father out of more difficulty than he's already in with this business."

"That's all right, Grandma," Petey said. "I understand." She hustled out of the foyer and disappeared.

It all felt like an increasing tangle, misdirection piled upon deception, none of them speaking the full truth to each other. The kind of situation Charlotte despised. She had never been good at diplomacy, or the keeping of secrets. Speak your mind and deal with the consequences, that was her motto, and though it had brought her pain sometimes, at least she never had to worry about keeping her story straight. She only had one story, and it was for everyone.

Charley continued to whittle, and before long he had attracted a crowd of onlookers. "What are you carving?" a man said.

He held up the stick. "I thought it was going to be a person at first, maybe a man holding a rifle. But now that I'm farther into it, I think maybe it's a weasel or an otter. What do you think?"

The man leaned closer. "You mean you don't know what you're carving when you start?"

"Oh, no. That would spoil the fun, don't you think?"

The man fish-eyed him. "That's the trouble with you people. I can't tell if you're serious or joshing."

"I am a very serious man," Charley said, fish-eyeing him right back. "I just express myself strange." He continued to carve as the man moved on. "You watch," he whispered to Charlotte after a minute. "He'll be back to buy this thing before long."

Charlotte stayed at her table, greeting visitors as they wandered through and attempting half-heartedly to correct their opinions about Heaven Holler, the Ozarks, and the book. No, she wasn't the person on whom Miss Minnie was based. Yes, she was Mr. Turner's actual mother. Yes, Mr. Turner was really here, and he would be happy to talk with you and sign a copy of your book, especially the special World's Fair edition that was available in the shop. But all the while, she watched for Kellogg, or Petey, or God forbid Rose LaBelle, to emerge from the back and give her an idea of what was going on. Twenty minutes passed before Adam and Kellogg strolled out, as cheerful as a couple of baby piglets as far as she could see, chatting amiably about the other attractions on the Pike. They shook hands at the door.

His expression dropped as soon as he turned inside. "Ugh. I guess I'll have to get to work seriously."

"What is it?"

Adam cocked his head in Kellogg's direction. "He says we're not turning over enough books to justify keeping the attraction open. If I had a second book ready, there'd be more interest."

"How close are you to having that second book ready?"

Adam shrugged. "Not close enough to have anything before the close of the fair. What can I say? I've been distracted."

"So let's go home."

He looked incredulous. "Declare defeat? Mother, you surprise me. I have commitments here."

"You have commitments back home, too." It was as close as she wanted to come to telling him directly that she knew of his nighttime shenanigans, and she hoped he had the sensitivity to hear what she was saying. He didn't answer, returning to his study with his cheeks puffed out, so it was hard to tell.

After a while Petey returned to her seat and leaned over to whisper as soon as she had a free moment. "He didn't want tea," she said. "They seemed very intent on business matters."

"And upstairs?"

"She had some soup. Said it didn't taste right, but she had some. And she says she's itching."

"All right," Charlotte said. "I'll go up and check on her in a bit."

"Have you ever dealt with people like this before? I mean, people addicted to their medicines?"

"I have. Why?"

"I just want to know what to do."

The poor girl looked so apprehensive that Charlotte reached out to stroke her cheek. "Just follow my lead, child. Here's a secret: Half the time I don't know what I'm doing either. All you can do—and I do mean all—is act on what seems right, given what you know at the time. Beyond that, none of us know what we're doing. Adults don't have any more idea than young people. They just hide it better."

To be that innocent and vulnerable again! To ponder the right and wrong of things, the way a young person could and most adults appeared to have forgotten. If grandmothers had any sort of job, surely it was to guide their grandchildren through this passage with as little harm as possible, to tell them the things their parents could not say or did not know. The dulling of the moral sense, the inevitable compromises that occurred as one moved from the robust, clear idealism of youth to the muddy, messy decisions of adulthood: such things were unbearably painful to experience. Even now from the perspective of a full life, when she could view them from a remove, having eaten her own peck of dirt, it was almost too much to think of Petey going through those troubles unaided.

She realized that she was still stroking the girl's cheek, embarrassing her. She wanted to tell Petey that she loved her so much that her heart ached with the size of it, that she would stay beside her and direct her steps until the end of her life, and even beyond it if there was any way to do so, but she had already mortified the girl enough for one day. So she dropped her hand to her lap and let the moment pass.

After a couple of hours, Charlotte's curiosity got the best of her, and she climbed the stairs to check on Rose. She found her at the kitchen sink, washing her soup bowl, her face sweaty but her lip firm.

"Here, let me do that," Charlotte said. "You need to conserve your strength." But by now the bowls and pans were washed and the counters wiped.

"Need to make myself useful around here somehow," Rose said.

She was shaky as she sat down, though, and there was something about her tentative, deliberate movements that felt familiar. Charlotte studied her for a minute, trying not to be obvious. Finally she spoke.

"Is it Adam's?"

Rose's panicked look confirmed her guess. "I can't imagine that it could be. The timing doesn't seem right. Listen, I need to get out to see a doctor. Big Bill has a doctor who takes care of these things."

"He's taken care of them for you before?" She nodded tightly. "That can't have been pleasant."

"No less unpleasant than the alternatives."

Charlotte knew the truth in what she was saying and didn't feel any desire to deny or soft-pedal it. "I suppose there's an aid society here."

Rose scoffed. "Oh, yes. That's where I first met Big Bill. He was waiting outside the door when they threw me out. Took me to the doctor that very day."

"I thought your whole idea in coming here was to free yourself from bad habits, bad influences."

"Bill's not a bad influence. He loves me." Rose's face took on its characteristic pout, and Charlotte had to turn her head for a moment to conceal her distaste. She walked to the window and spoke without looking back.

"If I were to take you to this doctor, he would send word to Bill the minute you walked in the door. And Bill would have you back on codeine that day, and whoring for him as soon as your bleeding stopped. Is that what you want?"

Her sharp response achieved its desired result. "No," Rose muttered.

"Then buckle your shoes and stop talking of love. We're considering your future here, and perhaps your very survival. You're a woman. You should know by now that love has to be set aside sometimes when larger needs arise." She turned and faced her. "Or perhaps you don't."

Rose didn't answer, but the pout had left her face.

Charlotte continued. "Your task now is to eat, gain strength, recover your balance. Don't make hasty decisions about the baby. There are orphanages. And if you don't want to take that road—" She paused. "I know ways to deal with this."

She returned to the main floor, reflecting somberly on the young women she had assisted over the years, one way or another: births, preventions, removals. Women, the bringers of life, the sustainers of life, but at some cost of their own. A fearsome price.

The rest of the day passed quietly, and then the evening, as Charlotte reflected on Adam's misadventures. Of course his pride wouldn't allow him to fold up and return home, having sold fewer books than he was needed to, at least not without a second effort to shake things up or at least a way to save face. And there was the matter of Rose LaBelle to be considered. Did he really think he could cure her of her addictions, and did he imagine some kind of future for them afterward? No fool like an old fool, as the saying went, even if the fool was only middle-aged.

Near closing time Adam emerged from his study. "I think I've got it," he said. "We need more to draw people than just books and knick-knacks. We'll double up on the music and maybe start a lecture series."

"You think that will do it?" She hated to sound negative, but she had seen the lines at the moving picture building. A lyceum hardly seemed competitive.

"It can't hurt to try. At least show Kellogg I'm making an effort. I have considerable investment in this enterprise, so I stand to lose a lot of money too."

Charlotte let it go. Adam had already made more money off his book than a person had any right to. He had made his choice and didn't need her further caviling about home and family. Not that he paid attention anyway.

As he wandered off, no doubt headed upstairs to confide the details of his new project to Rose LaBelle, the ticket-taker peeked around the corner. "There's a man outside who says he wants to talk to you," she whispered to Charlotte. "Won't come in. Just says he needs a word." She lowered her voice further. "*He's a colored man.*"

"All right," Charlotte said, amused at her disapproving tone. Hadn't she seen people of every hue and shade in the last few months? The secretive summons intrigued her, and she walked into the street.

The usual crowds and sounds assaulted her senses, the overwhelming smells of a dozen kinds of food and the racket of bands and barkers. She looked left, and then right, searching for her mystery visitor, and there he was, slouched against the wall in a gray hat and scarf, wrapped in a coat far too heavy for the warm evening. He lifted his head, and she saw that it was Nimuel.

"Mrs. Turner," he said, with urgency in his voice. "I need your help. We need your help."

Someone was squatting beside him, similarly cloaked, and from the pair of large bare feet visible beneath the figure, she guessed it to be Chaia-ngasup. He stood up as she approached. Indeed it was Chaia-ngasup, his usual picket-fence smile clouded by an expression of worry.

"What is it?"

"We need your help," Nimuel repeated. "We are running away."

Chapter 25

She led them through the building to the back yard, out of casual view, where they could talk in the shadow of the artificial mountain. "Why would you need to run away?" she said. "Can't you just leave if you are dissatisfied? You are grown men."

Nimuel shook his head. "No, Mrs. Turner. He holds us here by holding our pay. We are only to be paid at the fair's end, and so we have no money. And his men, they watch us all the time. I am a mere employee, but the Igorot are valuable parts of the exhibition. He would no sooner let them go than he would let someone carry off a carving, or a piece of fine cloth. So we cannot just leave."

Charlotte nodded. "What do you need?"

"We need a safe place to stay, one where Professor Pinckney cannot easily find us. From there we will send messages to the newspapers and to our friends. There are people in America who have seen our condition, who have called us prisoners and slaves. We will call on them for help."

"And you've tried reasoning with Pinckney?"

Chaia-ngasup had been following their words intently, and at the mention of Pinckney's name he waved his arms and launched a tirade. They waited for him to finish before Nimuel translated.

"The professor talks to us like children and thinks we are fools. He will not pay us, not even at the end, or if he does it will be a tiny fraction of what he promised. We have heard him complain again and again about how much it costs to feed us."

Charlotte considered for a moment. She glanced up at the exhibition building and saw Rose LaBelle at her window, gazing off into the distance, seemingly unaware of their presence in the darkened yard below. Waifs of all sorts. "All right," she said. "We can make you pallets on the floor for the night. After that, I don't know."

"Mrs. Turner, you are our only friends here. This is the first place he will look. We must find somewhere outside the fairgrounds."

"Does he know you're gone?"

"I don't know. I don't think so. He's giving a speech downtown tonight, so he won't return till morning. But one of his men usually checks on us sometime in the night."

She looked them over. "You're not exactly inconspicuous characters, either, if you don't mind my saying." But an idea was forming, at least the first part of an idea, something that might hold them till morning when they could think at greater length. "Wait here."

Charlotte walked inside, and the look on Petey's face told her that she was about to be peppered with more questions than she had time to answer. She raised her hand. "We'll talk as we walk. Now, run upstairs and bring down two empty valises."

Petey did as she was told, while Charlotte found a slip of paper and jotted down Susie Canterbury's address. She folded it and tucked it into her pocket, along with five one-dollar bills that she removed from her sewing kit, where she stashed money from the corn shuck doll sales before gathering it more securely. When Petey returned, Charlotte led her into the back.

"All right," Charlotte said, handing each of the men a valise. "You must pretend to be our porters until we are through the gates and have reached the streetcar stop. The lady at this address can help you find lodging for the night, and perhaps longer if it becomes necessary. Mention my name."

Nimuel translated the instructions for Chaia-ngasup, and the four of them marched through the exhibit and out the front door, each man holding one of the empty valises. Charlotte turned left, toward the entrance of the Pike, taking Petey's arm as they walked. After about fifty feet she glanced behind herself.

"You're doing fine," she murmured to Nimuel. "Just stay behind me a step."

Nimuel nodded. He could play the part of a porter with believable ease, but Chaia-ngasup, behind him, looked about as much like a porter as he did a centerfielder for the Browns. His clothes concealed his identity, more or less, but they were wrong for the season, thick and baggy, unlike anything even the poorest of men would have worn. And of course there were those enormous bare feet. Charlotte wished she could have found shoes to fit him, but reflected that even if she had, he would have probably limped in them so much that he would have called further attention to himself.

They passed the Tyrolean Alps, where she permitted herself a sideways glance for reassurance. No Bill Langland, thank goodness, although this activity was none of Langland's concern anyway. But above all else, she didn't want to have to break her stride, to stop and speak, anything that might cause notice. She was just an old woman, strolling through the Pike with her granddaughter, on their way to their hotel, like so many thousands of others. She kept her head high and did not look back.

A policeman idled at the gate, casually surveying the passers-by. Charlotte didn't worry about him; counting the hours till the end of his shift, probably. She didn't slow down.

But of all the cursed nights. "Ma'am?" he said.

She didn't look back. "Ma'am?" he said again.

It was clear he was calling to her. She stopped and turned. "Yes?"

"You're the lady from down the way, the hillbilly exhibit. Am I right?"

"Why, yes. Yes, you are."

He tipped his helmet. "Don't forget, the gates will be closing soon. You'll have the devil's own time getting back in. Have to raise the watchman, wherever he might be, and that ain't ever easy."

"Oh, of course." Charlotte tried to hide her relief. "We'll return before closing time, I hope. Thank you."

She walked on, nervously anticipating a further call from the policeman, but none came. Out of the corner of her eye, she saw him sizing up her entourage. But he said nothing, and soon they were outside the gates and headed toward the streetcar stop.

When they arrived, she wrapped the paper around the money and pressed it into Nimuel's hand. "Do you have coins for the streetcar?" she asked.

Nimuel nodded.

"Change cars at Taylor Avenue and go north. The house is left on St. Ferdinand, and this lady lives upstairs. I feel confident she'll know somewhere you can stay. If I can get away tomorrow, I'll come see you."

Nimuel took her hands. "God bless you, Mrs. Turner."

His sentiment made her uncomfortable, not to mention the fact that a colored man holding her hands would attract attention. She turned away. "Save your blessings for later. Let's get you out of here. You have a way to contact these friends in the community and the press?"

"Yes, ma'am."

"All right. I'll leave that to you."

"And these valises?"

"Take them. You may need them later, and it would arouse suspicion for us to be seen returning with them." A streetcar's bell in the distance announced its approach. "Till we meet again, then." She stepped away from the curb, steering Petey with her.

Petey dragged a bit and called "God bless!" over her shoulder. After half a block, she stopped. "What is going on, Grandma?"

Charlotte slowed to a stroll but did not stop. "The Filipinos are unhappy with their treatment by Professor Pinckney, and these two have taken on the task of flying the coop and calling attention to their plight. Or perhaps they're just doing this on their own. Either way, they have called on us for help. So here we are."

"Where did you send them?"

"To Mrs. Canterbury, the wife of our neighbor. They'll blend in with the neighborhood, and she'll likely know of a place they can stay."

They reached the gate, and Charlotte showed the gatekeeper their exhibitor's passes. The policeman was gone.

"And what shall we do?" Petey said.

"I don't know. Wait for word, read the news. I'll go visit them tomorrow if I can find a way to do it. You're welcome to come along."

"And Papa?"

They exchanged looks, and Charlotte saw recognition in her gaze. And why not? She had raised her to be observant, and the girl was not as naïve as she looked. "Your papa has sufficient troubles of his own for today. Let's not trouble him with ours unless we need to."

The two of them walked on, silent, while Charlotte considered what would come next. With patience and luck, they could outwait Adam's present infatuation and return to Daybreak, a little bruised but not permanently broken. Rose could shake her habit or not, have her child or not, as she saw fit, and could go back to Ohio or to Big Bill or wherever else she chose. And Nimuel and Chaia-ngasup could gain their pay, freedom, fame, God knows what.

What did any of these people want? What did her own son want? At least in Daybreak, one's needs were clear: bring in a good crop, tend the ground and keep it productive, be a good neighbor, mind your own business. Newton knew these rules and aspired to nothing beyond them. A good citizen, a productive farmer, an honest businessman. Nothing wrong with that. So what compelled Adam to come up here, stake a claim in the wider world, to intervene in the lives of near-strangers?

She sighed. One of the consequences of growing older, the realization that one's reach shortened with the passing years, one's force grew weaker, and that people were going to go their own way regardless of her wishes. But within that reach, one gripped with mad ferocity and held back none of that diminished force. If anything, age only increased her sense of tender determination. These children, these grandchildren, would live the best lives they were capable of, if she had any say in it. No matter how they defined that, and no matter what cost she had to pay. And even if they themselves did not recognize their best when it appeared.

She stopped in front of the exhibit. "I will speak plainly to you," she said to Petey. "You are old enough for plain speaking."

The throngs of fairgoers had dwindled to a few late strollers, and lights up and down the Pike blinked out as taverns and shows closed for the night.

"Your grandfather, my late husband, was a big thinker like your dad. He never met a grand scheme he didn't like. That's how we came to Daybreak in the first place, as pioneers of a new order. But putting firm feet under his ideas eluded him, and that led to much grief for himself and those around him." Petey rubbed a circle on the pavement with her foot. "I'm afraid your father has inherited this tendency. The success of *Heaven Holler* has given him the notion to cure all the ills of society that come within his view, and so he has taken up the cause of Miss LaBelle. And I fear that this will bring us grief as well. So it falls to us to—" She sought the right words.

"To save him from himself?"

She couldn't have said it better. Charlotte nodded, her mouth set, as she thought about the implications of their quiet understanding. They would find a way to bring Adam back. To himself, to Daybreak, to them. What it would take to accomplish this, she had no idea. Sell more books, sell no books, cure the girl, abandon the girl, succeed with the exhibition, or fail and let it fall to ruin. Wherever she saw a path to spare Petey from sorrow, that was the path she would take.

But as they turned to walk inside, the ringing of a bell sounded from far inside the fairgrounds. Then it was joined by another bell, and another. In a minute, nearer bells were ringing, urgent, the sound of alarm. Charlotte shuddered, thinking of the Filipinos' escape and of the inquisition to come. But from down the street came the cry:

"The Lumbermen's Club is on fire! The Hoo-Hoo House is burning!"

Chapter 26

In the morning, they all walked over to see the damage, all except Rose LaBelle, who murmured from her bed in tones of dejection that she didn't feel up to the trip. The walk between the enormous palaces, by the Grand Basin, and around the Cascades always made Charlotte feel insignificant, miniature, as she guessed it was supposed to. The palaces felt designed to intimidate and awe.

The ruins of the Hoo Hoo House stood in a cluster of odd buildings, haphazardly grouped: state exhibits, church exhibits, General Grant's log cabin brought up from its original site south of town. She'd never gotten around to touring the nearby state exhibits, but she liked Grant's cabin, Hardscrabble as he'd named it. It was a real building, not a fabricated replica. She'd visited it a couple of times to see the interior and drink a cup of the sponsor's coffee, and reflect that it wasn't much larger than her own house. Presidents and log cabins, the great American creation story, and even though Mr. Grant had only lived in the house a few months before moving on, it was still a more affecting place than the overloaded and ornate state exhibits nearby that sought to proclaim their importance by massed displays of products.

A crowd had formed in the walkway, watching the fire crews work as the timbers of the Hoo Hoo House smoldered. To Charlotte's surprise, she saw the man from the Hunting and Fishing Club standing among a small group at the edge of the lawn, speaking in low, earnest voices. When the group broke up, she walked over to greet him. "It's Mr. Callender, I believe, is it not?" she said, extending her hand.

It took him a moment. "Mrs. Turner!" he cried once he recognized her. "I'd forgotten that you were up here." He cocked his head toward the ruins. "There's a messy business, eh? You've got to give it to the fair planners, though. They left space between buildings so a fire in one can't spread to another."

"I hadn't figured you for a spectator," Charlotte said with a smile. "You men of business are always on the go, and don't have the time to rubberneck like us idle folks."

"Oh, this is business," Callender said. "I'm a member of this group. I contributed to its construction."

"You're a lumberman in addition to all your other pursuits? I'm surprised you find time to sleep. I'm even sorrier to see your clubhouse burn, then."

Callender shrugged. "I'm a lumberman only by investment. Wood makes paper, paper makes boxes. So I threw in my share for this building. We'll rebuild it if we can, or clear it if we must. Can't have a big hole in the ground at our World's Fair."

"What caused it?"

"Cookstove, best we can tell. Some of our members stored distilled spirits in a back room off the kitchen, and we think some spills might have found their way to the stove."

"I hope it wasn't any of the product from down our way. From what I hear, that stuff could be used as a firestarter."

Callender chuckled. "The boys up here only want bottled-in-bond. We save the wildcat stuff for our country adventures."

Charlotte had never been one of the temperance crowd, but Callender's casual attitude irritated her. A club of drunken businessmen, lolling in their swill, cutting deals while tended to by the less fortunate.

"Well, good luck on your rebuilding," Charlotte said. She rejoined her group and they began the return walk to their exhibit, dawdling in the pleasant light of the morning. Excitement or no excitement, there was an attraction to open soon, and they all needed to be on hand.

She fell into step beside Adam. She hated the sight of a building ruined by fire. She'd seen houses burn, nearly had one of her own burn, and there was nothing worse. The smell, the sense of ruin, the feeling of irretrievable loss. It reminded her that everything was temporary, no matter how solid-appearing it might seem. Even the great buildings of the Fair were secretly flimsy, built of reinforced plaster that wouldn't last the winter. All things faced destruction, all the time, and one's work in life was to hold that back, to build up walls of resistance against the creeper vines of chaos, all the while knowing that they would eventually, inevitably, be overcome. There was no time to allow bonds to weaken.

Charlotte slowed her step to let Charley and Petey get ahead. "I don't believe I've told you this often enough," she said. "I'm truly proud of what you've done here, writing this book, building it into its great success, coming up here to promote it. You've accomplished a fine thing. We differ about Miss LaBelle, but I don't want that difference to obscure my admiration."

"But? Statements like this always seem to have a 'but' attached to them."

She took his arm as they walked. "No 'but.' Only appreciation. Somebody is always ready to pull you down or second-guess, so I just wanted to let you know that I see all your work and am proud of your success. They say pride's a sin, but it's a sin I'll embrace."

The Grand Basin glittered to their left, its water so clear and bright that for a minute she could forget that it came from the Mississippi itself, piped down from the filtering plant up north, such a wild extravagance to have clean water simply flowing out from the Cascades with no dedicated use. It reminded her of the place upriver where they picnicked on occasion, above the old silver mine, where the river tumbled through boulders in a tangled skein of streamlets before it smoothed out into the rocky flats. A fine place for a picnic, though moss made the boulders ankle-turning slick, and there were always a few snakes to be found in the underbrush. Certainly preferable in her opinion to this manicured, manufactured pastoral.

And then it struck her, the longing to return to the home place. Charlotte had never thought of herself as sentimental or romantic, but the memory of that one place vibrated within her all at once, and its vibrations set off a procession of other memories that stopped her where she stood. June in Daybreak, one of the best times of the year. Early mornings in the garden before the sun rose too high. Then a walk up the road to the old springhouse, now unused by almost everyone except herself; but she still preferred the taste of its water to that of her well. The June bugs drifting aimlessly above the fields, improbable that such delicate wings could lift their fat, heavy bodies. Finding Petey and making plans for the day, fixing lunch for her family or joining in her tasks. And in the evening, the front porch, the rocking chair, waiting for a breeze, fireflies.

"I think there may have been a 'but' after all," she said. "I miss being home. I don't want to abandon your effort up here, but I think I want to go home soon."

To her surprise, Adam squeezed her shoulder softly. "I understand. I miss home too, sometimes. I've been thinking about my grand schemes lately, and I wonder if there might be better ways for me to devote my time."

By now Petey and Charley had disappeared ahead of them.

"You have?"

"Yes. Mr. Kellogg wants his second book, and a second book he shall have. But I can't produce it here, with all the noise and distraction. Perhaps it's time to retreat to our little valley for a while. I can work on the book, and the rest of you can resume your lives." He paused as if thinking of an idea for the first time. "I can rent a room in Newton's hotel, or perhaps one of Charley's cabins, for Miss LaBelle to stay in while she completes her return to health."

So that was the plan. Did Adam imagine himself to be that skilled a dissembler? Carrying on his business in the anonymity of the city was one thing, but trying to do it in Daybreak, where every eye turned toward the least anomaly, was another. It was almost insulting.

"Listen here," she said. "I don't wish to get into your business—"

"Then don't," he said, raising his hand. "I've consulted my conscience on this matter, and I can't see any way to go off to Daybreak while leaving this young lady behind. I've taken on her well-being as a personal charge. I can't just leave her to the wolves."

They had reached the corner by the firehouse, the entrance to the Pike, where the procession of massive palaces gave way to the piled-up hodgepodge of the attractions' wild architecture, each building trying to outshine the one next to it. So he had consulted his conscience, had he? It was on the tip of her tongue to say that perhaps he should try consulting his wife, when they saw Charley striding in their direction, with Petey trailing behind him, unable to keep up.

Charley's face was a thundercloud of anger. He stopped about four feet in front of them.

"The bitch is gone. And so is my money box."

Chapter 27

Adam bolted toward the exhibition at a dead run, his face contorted. He dashed past Petey, who waited for Charlotte and Charley with a look of concern. They fell into step toward Heaven Holler, Charley's lips set and his eyes fixed ahead.

"How much was in the box?" Charlotte said quietly.

"A hundred bucks, give or take," Charley growled.

Charlotte winced. Weeks of work. "Any sign whether someone came and got her, or she walked out by herself?"

Charley shook his head. "I didn't stop to look around. Didn't see anything out of the ordinary." He glared into the distance ahead. "I know he's your son and all. That's why I'm not going to say what's on my mind."

Charlotte knew enough not to answer. Charley in one of his moods was difficult enough, but Charley in a fit state, and with justification, was a different man entirely. The aw-shucks face dropped away and a look of grim, implacable ferocity took its place. As a deputy sheriff, Charley had spent many years gazing into the dark hearts of men in all kinds of settings. She would not have liked to face that gaze from the other side of a confrontation.

"What's going on, Grandma?" Petey called, trailing them. "Has Rose been kidnapped?"

"Let's not get ahead of ourselves," said Charlotte.

"Kidnapped," Charley muttered with a sniff. "Right."

When they reached the exhibition building, Adam was upstairs, rummaging through Rose's room. Charlotte took it all in: the unmade bed, the empty wardrobe, her wild-eyed son, the copy of *Hill-Billies of Heaven Holler* sitting on the bureau.

Adam raised his hand. "I know what you are going to say."

"I doubt that," Charley said.

"She didn't leave a note. She wouldn't have just run off without leaving a note. I don't believe it."

"The last time somebody stole something from you, did they leave you a note?" Charley's face had gone bright red.

"I'll find her and find out what happened. She may have just gone for a stroll."

"With my money box."

"Are you sure you remember where you left it?"

Adam's question was unwise. Charley's fists clenched as he stomped toward the door. He stopped in the doorway and turned around. "There are ladies and children present. Otherwise I'd tell you a few things about what I remember and what I think." He marched down the hallway to his room, his brogans clomping on the bare wooden floor.

They stood in the fraught silence.

"Papa—" Petey began.

"It's all right," Adam said. "He'll calm down. I expect there's a simple explanation. We'll have this cleared up by sundown."

He returned his hat to his head, adjusted it, and turned to walk downstairs. "When we open, tell our visitors that I am out for a brief time," he told Charlotte. "I should return after lunch."

And then they were alone, the two of them, grandmother and grandchild, standing across from each other in Rose's empty room. All at once it felt like an intrusion to be there, a sensation she knew to be preposterous, but felt anyway.

"What do you think, Grandma?" Petey murmured. "Is it all right?"

"I don't know. I don't think it is. Your father wears blinders sometimes when it comes to people. I'm sure that comes in handy."

"But it means his judgment can't be trusted."

Charlotte gazed at her rueful face. It was a hard day when a child came to recognize her parent's failings. She remembered her own childhood, about the same age, when the clouds of unquestioning admiration began to part, and she saw her own parents for the human beings they were and not the figures of magical perfection her childish imagination had made them.

"Yes, that's what it means," she said. "We love him as much as ever, but we have to make our own decisions about what to do next."

"I don't think I can do that."

"I understand, dear. Just follow my lead."

She would have spoken more, but a persistent rapping on the front door interrupted her thoughts. She walked into the hall; Charley's door was closed, with no sign of his emerging. So she descended the stairs herself, considering the variety of bad possibilities that could be waiting on the other side of the door. With luck, it might be an early visitor hoping for admittance. The worst—well, she didn't want to contemplate the worst.

Not the worst. Professor Pinckney, slightly disheveled, enraged, his face a color to match Charley's. Charlotte took a breath. She'd had enough of angry men to last her a while, and the morning was still young.

"Where are they?"

Charlotte saw no point in lying, and even less point in being helpful. "I can't rightly say. I saw them off last night, but I'm not sure where they ended up."

Pinckney waved his arms in the air as if calling down a curse. "What were you thinking? How could you do that?"

He was a tall man, and like so many of the big men she had known, he used his size as a weapon, leaning into her as if he could enforce his will by simple mass. She placed the palm of her hand flat on his chest and held it there. After a moment, he backed up.

"It was simple enough," she said. "When a friend asks you for assistance, you give it. They needed a place to stay, so I referred them to someone I know."

"Friend!" he spat. "These people are like children. You can't just do what they ask. If a child asked you to help him load a pistol, would you do it?"

For a moment Charlotte considered pointing out the stupidity of that rhetorical question, but that didn't feel helpful. She allowed herself a ferocious look.

"Very well. Just tell me who you sent them to, and we'll let the rest go. Is that un-hypothetical enough for you?"

"Indeed it is. But the problem is, they asked me not to tell you, and that's a promise I intend to keep."

"I should have known," Pinckney sniffed. "You seem like an intelligent enough woman, Mrs. Turner, but I've studied your kind long enough. You hill people always stick together, despite all plain logic and common sense. It's that clannishness that holds you back."

"Our kind, eh?"

"Yes." He stepped back and folded his arms. "Country people. Hill people. What earlier generations would have called the peasant class. I don't say that as an insult, but as a scientific fact. You folk are the same the world round."

"Then I suppose we have nothing further to say to each other." She turned to shut the door.

"We'll see how feisty you are when you talk to the police."

She met his gaze until he looked away. "I'll be happy to talk to them. I understand the departure of Nimuel and Chaia-ngasup has to do with a pay dispute."

"They'll get their pay," Pinckney groused. "At the end of the fair, as promised. After a full and thorough accounting, as specified in their contract, with all debts paid and expenses settled."

"So they'll receive their pay, minus expenses."

"As specified in their contract. I'm not a charity, ma'am."

"No," Charlotte said. "I can see that." She drew a breath. "Mr. Pinckney, we have troubles of our own this morning, so I can't be distracted by yours. But it's plain to me that whatever scientific knowledge you may possess, you are at heart a selfish and deceitful man, and I can't fault these folks for walking off the job. They probably should have done it earlier. Hill folk may be alike all around the world, but so are liars."

"Amuse yourself as you wish. I don't have time for your abuse." He stalked off.

Charlotte watched him leave, half-desiring that he would bring the police, for she had heard enough of Professor Pinckney to last her and would have enjoyed the opportunity to speak her mind in front of a third party. But she had a full basket of trouble already, so it was just as well that he was bluffing.

The nearer situation seemed simple by comparison. Rose LaBelle had seen her opportunity and walked off with Charley's money, and that was likely the last they would ever see of her. One problem solved, but more created. Adam could restore Charley's money without difficulty. But the hurt feelings and wounded pride would be harder to repair.

Back home, a meal would have been the starting point for the restoration of good feeling. Let everyone stew in their resentments for a few days, then kill a chicken and throw it in the pot. Fried chicken in the summer, chicken and dumplings in the winter: grievances disappeared like the steam off the frypot when people gathered around the table. But up here, that path didn't feel right.

She had a cookstove, and a good one; and markets brimmed with foodstuffs on every corner. But the indispensable element was missing: the gathering place, the common ground, the spot where they all felt equal, and free to laugh at themselves and their absurdities.

So she would have to work her way through this mess by instinct and reaction. So be it. She'd navigated messes before, though this was a big one.

First concern, Petey. Charlotte found her in their shared bedroom, her eyes a puddle of worry and mourning.

Charlotte rubbed her back. "Listen," she said. "If there's one thing I know, it's that Rose is not the sort of person to put herself into situations she can't get out of. I don't think she's been kidnapped. I think she walked out of here of her own choice, or at the very worst was enticed. Rose LaBelle is not someone we need to worry about."

Petey didn't look in her direction. "He loves her, doesn't he?"

Charlotte held her breath for a moment, then let it out slowly. She should have seen this coming.

"No. Not by any definition in my dictionary. I imagine he's flattered by the attention she gives him, and he has this notion of being her rescuer, which is something that men love to imagine about themselves. But love?" She sniffed. "No, ma'am."

"Well, he's *in* love with her, then."

"Ah—"

"I hear them at night, creeping around. It's disgusting. Does he think we're deaf?" Her voice, once trembling and uncertain, grew fierce. "I haven't told Mama yet, but I'm going to. She needs to know what kind of nonsense Papa has been up to." She glared at Charlotte as if daring her to defend him. "As for Rose LaBelle, she can go to hell."

Petey's rage came as a surprise. But then, she'd had always been more observant, and more advanced in her understanding, than anyone gave her credit for. "You are a serious young woman," Charlotte said, "and your thoughts deserve serious consideration. So I will tell you what I think. You don't have to agree with me or follow my advice. You've earned that right."

Charlotte walked to the open window. Behind the back wall of their exhibition ran the Rock Island line, and behind it the Rough Riders encampment; the mingled smells of horse stables, buffalo pens, and coal smoke, and the yells of the railwaymen and cowboys of a dozen different nationalities, gave the day a sense of chaotic energy, of infinite possibilities both grand and terrifying.

She could understand how people grew enamored of city life, with its relentless energy, its mad bustle.

That is, if you were a man. A woman who strolled the sidewalk at midday, shouting curses or snatches of song, calling to companions at the end of the block? Jail or the madhouse.

That seemed a good enough place to start. She turned back to Petey.

"We are women. We spend half our lives watching men, learning their ways and their secrets, for men control much of our lives whether we like it or not. Men fancy themselves to be creatures of logic and reason, but in truth they are not, with their mania for honor and recognition, and their endless wars. Products of irrational desire and vain imagining. But they have power, so we stand beside them and worry while they thrash about, and fight, and bully one another. And as they battle and beat their chests in pride, they harm us without even noticing. They trample us underfoot."

She paused to see if Petey was listening. Of course, she was. Whatever faults Petey might possess, inattentiveness was not among them.

"So we learn watchfulness," Charlotte continued. "We learn to anticipate which direction the battle is going, and take care not to be in its path." But enough of the exegesis. On to the application. "Your father does not know himself as we do. Me, you, your mother. We observe and anticipate. We gain knowledge and decide what to do with it. As a child, you never had to learn this skill, but soon you will need to employ it."

Charlotte sat on the bed and took Petey's hand. "Your father's passions are strong but temporary. I've seen that quality for years, and so has your mother. If you told your mother of this latest adventure, it would fit into that pattern. Get-rich schemes, grand ideas. The fact that this one involves a young woman would make it doubly painful, but the habit is nothing new."

She stood up and walked to the door. "I don't mean to be overly dramatic. But I do want you to understand. Ever since he reached adulthood, my strategy with your father has been to wait out his enthusiasms, let them burn themselves out as they always do, and then clean up whatever hurt or embarrassment is left behind. Perhaps that has not been a wise strategy. But it was done to shelter him from ridicule and disapproval, and to shelter his loved ones, too. That was probably cowardly of me. It wasn't unconsidered, though."

Petey had sat and listened to it all, her usual nervous animation stilled for once. Had she been making sense, or had she merely sounded reflexively defensive? Charlotte couldn't tell.

"I'll go downstairs and set up, and greet visitors for a while. Come join me as you see fit. Or perhaps you'll want to write your mother or make plans to travel home. If you do, I'll join you. This is not knowledge that should be delivered alone." She took a breath. "Knowledge is a bomb. A person can decide whether to throw it and when, and in what direction. But once it goes off, the harm spreads out everywhere."

Charlotte returned downstairs, thankful for the relative calm of people coming and going, the ordinary bustle of another summer day, conversations both mild and predictable. Charley glowered at his table, refusing to meet her eye, and grunted audibly when she explained to visitors that Mr. Turner had needed to step away for a while. She signed the back of their tickets for readmittance in the future.

An hour and a half later, Adam returned, his coat torn at the shoulder and dust on his face. He tried to walk past without speaking, but Charley stopped him.

"Well?"

"They wouldn't let me see her. They say she just showed up, but I don't believe them. I think they're holding her."

"And my money?"

Adam's eyes darted away. "They said they didn't know anything about that."

"Of course they did," Charley said. "You don't know how to talk to these people, is what I think."

Adam retreated into his study, and eventually Petey joined her at their table. "I'm doing what you said," she muttered. "I'm thinking about it."

"Fair enough." Charlotte had said enough already. Time to let it sink in, if it would.

People came, people passed, people spoke. Charlotte sold a few cornhusk dolls but didn't try particularly hard. She meditated on Adam, whom she loved but who was also a damned fool, and Newton, who had passed through his damn-foolishness at a younger age. As if that excused it.

Charlotte had just about had her fill of the pretensions and self-justifications of the men around her, and the sight of Charley across the room pouting as he whittled did not make her feel any more charitable. Sure, the girl had stolen his money. But Adam would make his loss good. He possessed that level of decency. And hadn't Charley bought into all the Heaven Holler hoo-raw? His lodge, his healing spring? Charley was no fragile blossom.

Maybe they should follow Petey's instinct and hash it all out in the open, confront Adam about his failings. Modern ways for modern women. But then what? What would that accomplish? Just putting Penelope in a corner, as far as she could see. She'd be forced into a decision, to break with Adam or to stay in humiliation. And how could Penelope break with him? She had nowhere to go, no family to take her in.

Charlotte made up her mind. She would take Petey back to Daybreak as soon as possible, for in Daybreak she would feel at home, if nothing else. Whatever ills befell them after that, they would be in a familiar setting to deal with them. Let Adam stay or return, let Petey speak or keep mum, they would be home.

As evening fell Charley packed up his things and disappeared upstairs. A few minutes later he returned with his hat and coat. "I'm dining out," he said.

Charlotte gave him a skeptical look. "Charley—"

"Don't try to talk sense into me. Have you ever been able to talk sense into me?"

"Once or twice."

"This is not one of those times." He tapped the top of his hat, as if for emphasis, and marched toward the door.

"Charley!" She was surprised by her own vehemence. "Listen to me! We're not at home any more. And you don't know who you're dealing with."

"I know exactly who I'm dealing with. I have dealt with men like him all my life." And with that he was out the door, his beard flying behind him.

"He's going to try and get his money back, isn't he?" Petey murmured.

"Yes, and I'm afraid he's going to come back like your father did, or worse. Charley forgets sometimes that he's an old relic, like me."

"Oh, Grandma, you're not an old relic!"

"Thank you for that, but regardless. Charley would do well to stop thinking about the days of his glory."

"He's had some good ones though, hasn't he?"

"Indeed he has. Did I ever tell you he fought for the Confederacy during the war?" Petey's sideways glance confirmed that yes, she had told her that story, probably more than once. "I never forgave him for it, either."

There was no telling when Charley would return, so they packed up their merchandise when the day was over and locked the door, trusting that he had remembered his key. Charlotte went to bed with a troubled mind, thinking of Charley out somewhere blundering, and of Nimuel and Chaia-ngasup on the run; neither of these things her doing, exactly, but both impinging on her over-developed sense of responsibility. And how the day began, the swift destruction of the Hoo-Hoo House, how quickly it went from a fine-looking structure to a smoking ruin. She lay in the dark and stared at the ceiling. If a fire broke out in their building, it would suffer the same fate, with its frame-and-lath construction and its whistling drafts through the floorboards. And with one narrow staircase from the second-story bedrooms, they'd all be roasted like Christmas geese before the fire wagons even arrived.

So she did not sleep well, and during one of her wakeful times she heard a thumping from below, not like someone knocking at the door, but a muffled thud, a heavy sound, not something she recognized. She lay still, her ears as attentive as she could manage, waiting for the sound to repeat. Perhaps she had dreamed it. She had done that before, awakened to a sound only to find that it had come from her own sleeping imagination.

But this did not feel like a dream, and although the sound never returned she climbed out of bed and crept downstairs. It would be foolish to confront a burglar, in her nightgown and unarmed, even if she had a weapon to arm herself with. But at least the noise she made might wake others, or scare the man off.

No one was downstairs. The darkened rooms were silent.

Had Charley come in yet? She'd forgotten to check. And what time was it, anyway? Fearfully late, not long till dawn.

So she went to the door, and she found it still locked. He must have come back while she slept.

But for some reason she felt compelled to open the door and look outside. And as she opened the door she felt the weight of something push it inward, as if someone had been standing on the stoop with a shoulder pressed and waiting. Of course that was impossible, and in an instant Charlotte knew the source of the thump and the cause of the push.

Charley Pettibone, his back resting against the door, fell heavily across the threshold, making no groan or huff, no sound at all beyond the thud of his arms on the floor. Charlotte had never seen him this drunk before and was about to scold him when she saw the dark splotch in his beard. She reached down. His beard was wet and gooey, and it had a rank, unpleasant smell, the smell of dirt and innards.

She opened the door wider to gain more light from the street and knelt for a closer look. She lifted the beard from Charley's chest. As she peered close, the smell was unmistakable, and in the dim glow of the streetlights she saw what she had feared.

Charley's throat had been neatly cut in one deep slash along the underside of his jaw, from earlobe to earlobe, a terrifying wound made even more terrifying, if such a thing was possible, by the evident skill and ferocity of the strike.

Chapter 28

The room where Charlotte sat smelled of cigar smoke and sweat, and its one window was so begrimed that it had nearly lost its original function, allowing only a dim filter of gray light into the confined and miserable space.

Which was only appropriate, she reflected, for this was a place of misery, where lives were ruined every day, and a ray of sunshine in the room would only serve to mock. There was a table with two chairs on one side and one chair on the other. A place where men were bullied and tormented. A place where evil deeds were confessed.

Charlotte let her gaze rest on a splotch of mold that defaced the wall across from her, the yellow paint showing through the black of the mold like a muffled cry. She didn't allow herself to think about the cause of the mold. She wasn't allowing herself to think about anything, merely to observe and take note of the physical world around her. Thinking would not be wise right now, as it would only lead her back to the events of the night before, and that would only break her heart again. Today, all she could do was sit, and watch, and breathe in and out, and answer the questions she was asked.

Across from her, the policeman labored with a stubby pencil in his ledger book. "So you didn't hear anything before the noise that woke you up?"

In another life, Charlotte would have remarked on the stupidity of the question. Of course she hadn't heard anything while she was asleep. But today she simply replied, "No."

The chair beside the policeman was empty. She supposed that when they interrogated a criminal, they used two officers, to wear down the suspect and defeat his defenses. But a mere woman reporting a crime only merited one inept and nearly illiterate policeman.

"And did you see anything?"

"No."

The policeman's lips puckered as he wrote. "But you think you know who did it."

"Oh, I'm sure of it. I know who's responsible, at least."

He frowned at her. "I can't tell you how many times somebody has come in here and made a claim that won't stand up in court. I'm not accusing you of that. I'm just saying."

Charlotte watched his knuckles clench and unclench as he wielded his pencil. Clearly not a task that came naturally to him. He finished his sentence and looked up.

"We'll go talk to this fellow Langland. We know him."

"I expect you do."

The policeman caught her implication, frowned further, but let it pass. "If we can make a case, we'll make it. Are you willing to come and testify?"

"Of course."

"Many's the time—"

"—that someone says they'll testify but then doesn't show up. I understand."

"Especially someone from out of town."

She didn't have it in her to argue. She felt nothing but fatigue, a weariness that didn't feel like it would ever lift, no matter how much or how little she slept. And she hadn't slept.

The policeman stood. "All right, ma'am. We have all we need for now." He opened the door and stepped aside, hands folded before him like a prayerful churchwarden. Charlotte walked into the anteroom where Adam waited.

"We're done here, sir," the policeman said. "You can go home now."

"All right. You have my card?"

"Yes, sir."

Adam took her elbow, the picture of solicitude. So she was a helpless old lady now, needing a boost under her elbow? Perhaps she was. She felt eight kinds of exhausted.

"I sent a wire home," he said as they walked toward the Heaven Holler building. "The undertaker says he could have him ready to take home tomorrow."

Charlotte nodded. She hated the idea of spending another night in the building, but it couldn't be helped.

When they reached the exhibition, Watson Kellogg was waiting for them at the door. He took off his hat and held it over his heart. "I am so sorry," he said. "I came over as soon as I heard." He bowed deeply to Charlotte and shook hands with Adam. "How is the young one holding up?"

"She'll be all right," Adam said. Charlotte had no idea how he divined this knowledge, for when they had left for the police station Petey was still mourning behind closed doors with audible sobs.

"I think it best if we suspend operations here for a while," Kellogg said. "You'll be inundated by the idle curious if we don't. You can stay here if you like, but we'll keep the door shut."

Adam nodded. "Of course. We'll be heading down to Daybreak for Charley's burial, probably tomorrow. I'll let you know when we want to return."

"Please do." They walked inside, where Charley's box of carved figures still sat on the table. Kellogg picked one up and examined it. "He was quite a character, wasn't he?"

Charlotte walked away. She couldn't bear to hear it. Of course Charley was a character. He had always been a character, had relished being a character. But she didn't want to see him reduced to that, a colorful figure in some people's reminiscences. She could hear it already: *Do you remember the time when Charley—*

People like Watson Kellogg, passing acquaintances who thought they knew something.

And the last words she had spoken to Charley were a scolding.

She walked out into the back yard, the trodden earth and the phony mountain, and stopped at her garden, a source of Charley's endless teasing. Half a dozen stalks of sweet corn and a row of beans. But by God, they had produced. With good luck and water, even this brick-clay earth could grow a crop.

She would harvest it before they left, even the undersized ears and the beans that had not yet plumped out, for who knew when they would return, and allowing this minor waste in the face of such a colossal waste felt like compounding the sin.

Adam cleared his throat behind her. "I need your help with something. The undertaker said he needed a good set of clothes to send Charley home in. I wonder if you could pick something out."

Charlotte nodded. Of course Adam wouldn't want that task. The handling of another man's garments, intimate things. Not his strong suit.

Upstairs, Petey remained shut behind the bedroom door. No sounds emerged. Charlotte let her be.

She had not visited Charley's room much herself. It hadn't felt proper, and her innate sense of privacy kept her from intruding when they weren't in the public areas. A person needed space. So she stood in the center of the room for a moment, feeling like a burglar, and reconnoitered for a moment before stepping to the wardrobe to look for clothing.

Charley would have wanted to be buried in his dungaree trousers, or something similar, no doubt. He was a country boy all the way. But Jenny would want him sent home in something other than his work clothes.

In the wardrobe, she found a black suit hanging, although she'd never seen him in it. Jenny had probably insisted he bring it in the unlikely event he should ever decide to go to church. In the bureau, a white shirt, boiled and starched, likewise unworn. She removed some socks and undergarments from the drawers as well.

No dress shoes. If Charley owned a pair he must have left them at home. And no necktie either. Well, she could spare him that indignity.

Searching for a bag to put the things in, she came across a worn leather hand-grip in the bottom of the wardrobe. Just about the right size, if she folded the suit carefully. But when she lifted it, the bag surprised her with its weight.

Charlotte looked inside. There was Charley's old duty revolver, the one he had carried during his deputy sheriff days.

She hefted it in her hand. "Good gracious," she said out loud. "This thing must weigh a pound and a half." She checked the cylinder. Fully loaded.

Charley had always avoided carrying the weapon on duty. His philosophy was that showing up armed only brought out other people's instincts to arm themselves as well, and that no man was such a master of arms that he could guarantee himself the victor in all situations. If the shooting had already started, that was one thing. But if no one was shooting yet, why invite it? This approach had served him well over the years. He usually brought in his man, and he rarely fired a shot.

She studied the weapon. The pistol was too big for her hand. If she let the butt rest comfortably in the palm of her hand, as one was meant to, then her fingertip could barely reach the trigger. But if she rested the fleshy middle of her finger on the trigger, the rest of her hand slid up the grip, and the gun would kick ferociously. As if a pistol that size wouldn't kick enough already.

She laid the pistol carefully in the bottom of the valise again, then layered clothing over the top, undergarments, trousers, shirts on top to minimize the wrinkles.

When she emerged from Charley's room with the satchel of clothing, Petey had opened her bedroom door and stood at the entrance, her eyes puffy and her face red. Charlotte answered the question in her eyes.

"Clothes for the burial," she said. "Your father's going to take them to the undertaker."

"When will we leave?" Petey's voice was raspy and uncertain.

"Tomorrow."

"Good." She wiped her nose. "I'd rather leave today. I don't want to spend another night in this place."

"I agree completely. But I guess we can't avoid it."

She turned to take the satchel downstairs, but Petey laid a hand on her arm. "You've been to the police."

"Yes."

"What did they say?"

The earnest, intent expression on Petey's face made Charlotte suddenly want to cry. For a moment she held it back, thinking that an outflow of tears would not improve matters, but then she dropped the satchel and reached out to take the girl in her arms. They held each other and let all their pent-up emotions flow, the sadness and the anger and regret and grief, until they finally were able to breathe again.

"Petey, my darling," she said. "We are alone in this. Those sons of bitches will be no help."

"But why not?" Petey cried, her face contorted.

Charlotte sighed. "Maybe they're afraid of the people who did the crime. Maybe they think we're just outsiders who don't deserve protection. Maybe other things. "

And why indeed? The question nagged at her. Why kill a man? Why not simply rough him up and send him home, as they did with Adam? Even for a criminal gang, such an act was extreme.

A message? If so, to whom? She tried to turn away from this question. A good man had been killed. She needed to reflect on his memory and to think about the tasks of the days ahead, not ponder this last, mad, seemingly pointless act. But like all seeming mad and pointless things, it forced its way into her mind, demanding a solution.

Perhaps there was no message at all, just the simple exercise of power for its own sake. *Look at me, I can do anything I want.* A message to the world, then. Or perhaps—and the thought gave her pause—the target was someone inside the circle. Rose LaBelle. *This is what I will do for you. I will kill for you.* Or just as likely: *This is what I will do to you if you ever try to leave me.* A thought that changed her view of things.

Petey could see her mind working. "What is it? What other things?"

"Let me think," Charlotte said. "Right now, I'm overwhelmed. When I have something coherent to say, I'll tell it to you."

She took the satchel of clothing downstairs and gave it to Adam, who glanced inside without paying much attention. "Favorite outfit?"

"Not really. But suitable to be buried in. I think Jenny will approve."

He nodded and left. Charlotte sat at Charley's table to gather his figurines, placing them carefully into the little box he kept on the floor. The melancholy job of sorting out Charley's things, choosing what to keep and what to throw away, would fall to her, of course. Women were better at the tasks of care: the handling of the body, the cleanup of the waste, the restoration and repair of the battered souls. But she would think about that later. What she needed now was some quiet time to mourn.

But that was not yet to be, as a light but insistent knock on the front door demanded her attention. Charlotte sighed and opened the door.

It was Susie Canterbury, looking worried. "Ma'am. I heard the news."

And it was that, the simple words of concern, that opened the dam and Charlotte sat down in the hard wooden chair and began to cry. Her tears came silently but hard, and they felt endless to her, as if she could sit there and cry for the rest of the day and into tomorrow. Susie sat beside her, not touching or speaking. She just sat and provided company, another person to cry to, someone who didn't need her strength or her decision-making. Just a fellow soul who knew pain.

Finally it came to an end, or at least close enough that she could draw a breath. She gulped the air and wiped her face with the hem of her dress.

"You never met Charley," Charlotte said. "He was quite a fellow."

"I expect so, ma'am."

Charlotte glanced over. "He was a hard man to get along with sometimes."

"Aren't they all?"

Charlotte nodded. "He was a man of the old ways. Fought for the wrong side during the Civil War. Never got used to me being independent and in charge of myself. I think independent women frightened him a little bit."

Susie laughed. "And yet he followed you up here. He must not have been too frightened."

"Oh, no. Charley never let anything scare him except heights." She paused before speaking further, not wanting to embark on a long train of reminiscences with someone who was, after all, a near-stranger. "Thank you for coming to see me. I'm sorry I haven't asked yet about my Filipino friends. Are they all right?"

Susie shifted uncomfortably in her chair, and from the look on her face Charlotte realized that her visit had not been made entirely for compassionate reasons. "No. They are not all right. Something must be done."

Charlotte fought to concentrate on this new challenge. She turned to face Susie. "What's going on?"

"They've been sleeping on my floor, and they're perfect gentlemen. The young one has entertained Junior with endless stories about soldiering and the jungle and great fish as large as a ship. But this morning two men came through the neighborhood. Not policemen, mind you, but Pinkertons or some such. Said they were looking for runaways, and they had pictures."

"Oh, dear."

"Mrs. Turner, are these men wanted by the law?"

"No, they've done nothing wrong. They're in a dispute with a man here at the Fair over their pay."

"Must be a powerful man, to have detectives at his bidding."

Charlotte considered. Professor Pinckney was not a powerful man, but no doubt he had powerful friends. And the prospect of an incident that would bring embarrassment to the great Fair was something they would not tolerate.

"One more thing," Susie said. "They are offering money for information. I didn't open the door to them, but there will be people who will. These men need to be out by morning."

And how was she to do that? And why should this be her problem in the first place? Charlotte didn't have to think long. She had brought Susie into this situation, so she needed to get her out of it. She had agreed to help Nimuel and Chaia-ngasup, and that meant help all the way until she could help no more. That was how things worked.

"All right," she said. "Wait here a moment."

Charlotte walked through the empty building and climbed the stairs to their rooms. In Charley's room again, she picked out some trousers, a shirt, and the oldest, most battered pair of brogans she could find. She took them downstairs and handed them to Susie.

"These are for the older gentleman," she said. "He's pretty conspicuous." She took a deep breath. "Can you have them to Union Station tomorrow morning?" she asked. "I'd like to catch the seven o'clock train, but doubt if we'll manage that. So we'll try for eight-forty-five."

Susie lifted one of the brogans with a dubious look. "Are you sure about these? That man has some feet."

"Split the sides if you need to. They won't be worn again."

A nod of comprehension passed between them. They said nothing more, but stood and went their separate directions. Tasks to perform, trials to endure.

Chapter 29

The wagoner from the undertaker's met them at the station in the morning, as promised. They had used framing nails to hold down the coffin lid, making it easier for the family to remove to get their final look. A small thing, but small things revealed much.

The wood was a good grade of yellow pine, the kind that grew around home. Fitting that Charley should be sent home in familiar wood. Charlotte laid her hand on the smooth-planed coffin.

"Did you work on this?" she asked the man.

"Yes, ma'am. I was a carpenter before I joined the firm."

"It shows, and I appreciate it."

"Thank you, ma'am. People always do what you're doing right now, lay their hands on the box, and it wouldn't be right to have them pick up splinters."

She nodded. "I guess I'd better let you get to it. You don't suppose—"

"Sit with him on the train? No, ma'am. Cargo only in that car. It ain't safe." He caught himself. "Not that this gentleman is what you should call cargo, but you know what I mean."

Charlotte had recognized Nimuel and Chaia-ngasup leaning against a far wall, with their faces turned away from the crowd. But it stood to reason that if she could spot them, so could whoever was hunting them, although for once their color served as useful camouflage, blending them in among the porters and day laborers who thronged the building. Chaia-ngasup looked no more remarkable than many of the men who roamed the streets in whatever clothing they could scavenge.

"I won't keep you further," she said to the undertaker's man. "Again, thank you for your care."

Adam appeared with their tickets. "All set. We've got half an hour before boarding. Anyone for a quick breakfast?"

Petey was still mired in gloom, and Charlotte supposed he was just trying to lighten her mood. But he didn't have to act so much like they were going on a picnic outing. Or perhaps he was trying to distract from his own part in this tragedy.

Charlotte's own gloom was so deep it felt bottomless. She still felt the weight of Charley's body, pressing against that door, and smelled the nauseating odor of his blood. The days ahead would be miserable with nothing to relieve them. Everyone would be looking to her to be strong, to set an example, to be the pillar of resilience they all counted on. But she didn't want to be a pillar of resilience today. She wanted to lie in bed and blubber like a baby.

But of course she could not. "You two go ahead," Charlotte said. "I'll be right behind." She waited until they had disappeared into the crowd, then walked to the ticket window and bought two seats for the colored section.

She found the two men and handed the tickets to Nimuel. "We can get you out of town, I think. But after that, I don't know. Do you have a plan?"

Nimuel gazed into the distance, which in Charlotte's experience meant that he did not have a plan. "I think people will rise up when they hear of our mistreatment. They will demand that Professor Pinckney give us what is due."

Nimuel's idea of what would cause ordinary people to rise up seemed doubtful to her, but this was not the time for debate. "Anyway. I won't be able to watch after you once we're down there, at least not for a while. I'll have many things to take care of. I hope you won't take it amiss if I find a place for you and then leave you alone for a few days."

"Of course," Nimuel said. "You have already been a great benefactor to us." Charlotte couldn't tell if his words were flattery or simply his habitually fulsome way of expressing himself.

"See you in Fredericktown, then." She turned and walked to the restaurant to join Petey and Adam.

Charlotte had already thought of where to put the two men. There was a woman who ran a boarding house in town for people of color. Mrs. Thorp would take them in as long as they promised to behave. She waited until the train had left the city before telling Adam and Petey about them, Yet another stratagem, but she was getting used to stratagems. Predictably, Adam reacted badly.

"To Fredericktown!" he sputtered. "And what will they do down there, pray tell?"

"Please, keep your voice down," Charlotte said. "They needed to leave town unnoticed, at least until they decide on their next step. It won't do to have someone overhear us and report them to the very man they're trying to escape."

Adam scowled but obeyed. "Seriously, what will they do in Fredericktown?" he said in a softer voice.

"They hope to negotiate with the professor for their promised payment. If he won't budge, they'll expose him in the press."

"As if anybody cares," Adam groused.

"May I go back and see them?" Petey exclaimed.

"If you wish," said Adam.

"But I'd add," Charlotte said, "that the idea is for them to be unnoticed. White people visit the colored car all the time, but it's something that gets noticed. Especially an unaccompanied girl."

Petey nodded, and the three of them settled into their seats for the grim journey home.

They spoke little for the rest of the way, and as they neared Fredericktown, Charlotte felt a growing sense of oppression settle over her like a cold fog.

Who would be waiting for them at the station? Newton, of course. He had answered their wire. But would anyone else? Jenny, or some of the children? She dreaded the thought, the demoralizing labor of the unloading, a human body in a box as if it were no more than common freight. At least if they could bring him back to Daybreak on their own, they could return him with a little ceremony, a little honor.

A silly idea, that it mattered to the dead body in the box whether it was brought to its final resting place with a spray of flowers. Charley would have been the first to tell her that, and she would have had to defend the idea against his joking insistence. Charley loved to provoke, loved to tease, loved to take an extreme position and argue it even as his debate partner grew more frustrated.

And Charley was the last person who spoke to her as a peer. Someone who knew her as a young woman, someone to be provoked and teased, not a gray-haired elder who couldn't be treated so casually. That was something she would miss terribly, that different perspective through which she was perceived, and something she wouldn't be able to explain to anyone. To everyone else, she was a mother, a grandmother, a neighbor, someone to be deferred to and treated with a respect that sometimes verged on dismissiveness. But Charley knew the old Charlotte, the woman who loved and hated, who aspired and failed. Who felt beautiful sometimes, and wronged and passionate and ashamed. No one would ever know her like that again.

Charlotte forced herself out of her reverie. Here it was, the worst day of the Pettibone family's life, and she was thinking about her own loss. Human nature, she supposed, to worry about one's own lesser difficulties before considering other people's great ones.

The train stopped with a jerk, and she looked out the window. No Pettibones, just Newton and his wagon, and she could see the slump of his shoulders even from this distance.

He scrambled over to help her with her bag. "Thanks for coming to get us," she said. "It's been a rough time."

"I expect it has," he said. "Have they caught the man who did it?"

"Not that we've heard." Adam and Petey stepped down to the landing next. They greeted Newton with subdued warmth, and the four of them stood for an awkward moment on the landing.

"Guess we might as well—" Newton began. "You know, might as well get our other passenger. I'll bring the wagon around to the baggage car."

Charlotte and Petey walked down the landing while Adam and Newton headed for the wagon. As they walked, Charlotte saw Nimuel and Chaia-ngasup step out from the last passenger car. Nimuel removed his hat as they neared, prompting Chaia-ngasup to do the same.

"So here we are," Nimuel said.

"Here you are, anyway," said Charlotte. "We still have a long ride ahead. My home is several miles out of town. But your place is just down the street." She turned to Petey, who was torn between following Nimuel's every word and gesture and pursuing Adam to the baggage landing to see the unloading of the coffin. "Honey, if you could go tell your father that I'll be along directly. I need to get these gentlemen settled." Petey dashed off, grateful for a task.

"Right this way," Charlotte said, setting off at a brisk walk. "Nimuel, I need to tell you something. We are in a tricky part of the country here, and you'll need to take care, and make sure Chaia-ngasup does as well. Life for colored people is freer in the cities, although I'm sure it may not seem that way to you. But out here our world is more confined. Be careful not to provoke an incident."

"I understand," Nimuel said.

Charlotte wondered if he did understand, being a foreigner, but remembered his stories of oppression and survival. She was not the one to question Nimuel's capabilities.

Mrs. Thorp eyed the two men suspiciously through her screen door. "How you know these men?" she asked Charlotte.

"We met at the Fair. They're part of the Philippine exhibit. They've gotten into a pay dispute with their employer and need somewhere to stay for a few days."

"Pay dispute, eh?" She sniffed. "I've had a few of those with my renters. Gets ugly." Her glance bounced from man to man. "Either of you boys speak English?"

"I do, madam," Nimuel said with his characteristic head dip, respectful without being obsequious. "My friend only knows a few words, so I generally translate for him. I am Nimuel."

"All right, Nimuel," she said, stretching it out over a long three syllables. "Come on in and we'll fix you up." She signaled her acceptance to Charlotte with a quick look and drew the men inside, but then stepped onto the porch, pulling her close. "I doubt if I'll be able to keep them long," she whispered. "There's unrest in the air."

"Unrest?"

But Mrs. Thorp would say no more, just rolled her eyes with a meaningful look as she shut the door. But Charlotte didn't have long to wonder about the source of the unrest, for as she returned to the station she saw Bobby Renick, sitting like a potentate on his whiskey wagon, in vehement argument with Adam and Newton. He jerked his head up as she approached.

"And there's the leading friend to the colored race herself, back for another funeral," Renick said. "Funerals seem to follow wherever you go these days."

"I'll not have you speak to my mother like that!" Newton shouted.

"Or what? You'll drag me off this wagon and fight me in the street? I'd like to see you try."

"What's this all about?" Charlotte said.

"Oh, never you mind," said Renick. "No need to trouble yourself by getting down into the muck with us common folk."

"Seriously, Mr. Renick. What are you talking about?" she said.

"That Canterbury boy you coddle so much. He got sassy with my little Blossom and laid his hands on her, and I'll see justice done for that."

Charlotte could hear the alarm bells ringing in her mind, insistent and loud. "Who witnessed this incident?"

Renick sniffed. "What does that matter? It happened, and that's all anybody needs to know."

Adam spoke up, trying to sound conciliatory. "Come now, Mr. Renick, surely you know how children's tales get bigger with each telling. Independent corroboration is needed in these—"

"Doesn't matter!" Renick exploded. "Doesn't matter, your independent what-you-call-it. My girl said what happened, and nothing matters after that."

"For once, I agree with Mr. Renick," Charlotte said, her voice cold. They all turned to hear her. Charlotte climbed into Newton's wagon and waited until the others had joined her.

"You are right, Mr. Renick," she said. "Funerals seem to follow me these days. I don't like it, but it's a plain fact. And I have another one to attend to, so we must be going." She glanced into the wagon bed. Newton had covered it with a blanket and had brought an extra bench for the wagon bed, to save his passengers the unpleasant choice of sitting on the unforgiving wagon floor or the coffin itself. Always a man for details, that was Newton.

She turned toward Renick again, with his own canvas-covered load. "And here's another plain fact. You're a liar, you've proven yourself to be a liar, and unless a recording angel was on your shoulder writing down everything that happened, I wouldn't believe you if you told me my dress was on fire. So it doesn't matter what you say, or what your little girl says. Blabber on as much as you like."

No one spoke a word the rest of the way out of town, and no one looked back to see whether Bobby Renick had moved on from where they left him or stayed in place. Charlotte counted her breaths to calm her racing heart, inhaling to a count of four, exhaling to a count of four.

"How's Charley's family doing?" she said to Newton after a mile of travel.

He shrugged. "Bereaved. About as you would expect."

Charlotte took a deep breath. The June air filled her lungs. Maybe it was just her imagination, but it even tasted sweet to her. She'd forgotten how pervasive the smoke from factories and cookstoves in the city became, night and day, the smoke just hanging in the air until it became the air itself.

"So what will happen with Bobby and Canterbury now?"

"Don't know, exactly," Newton said with a sigh. "You know they've had bad blood from the beginning. Can't imagine they want his land, it's such a scrappy little patch. Maybe just meanness."

"What exactly is he saying?"

"Says his little girl was playing over by their property line when Canterbury came over, yelling and screaming, and dragged her by the arm halfway back to their house. Bobby says she can't sleep nights now, she's so scared. The story gets bigger every time he tells it, too."

"I'll bet." A cold knot of dread formed in Charlotte's stomach. It was the perfect story to rile up a crowd. A black man, a white child, an altercation with no evidence to prove one thing or another. "What does Mr. Canterbury say?"

"Denies it all. And Bobby won't let the sheriff talk to the girl unless he's in the room."

"Of course not. Does Canterbury understand—" She wasn't sure how to put it. Did he understand that this kind of story got men hanged? That it wouldn't go away soon, or perhaps ever? "Does he understand the seriousness of the situation?"

"He'd better," Newton said, giving her a look. "Maybe you should talk to him."

Charlotte didn't reply. Why was it her job to talk sense into everyone? Maybe people should develop some sense on their own. They rode in silence for a few miles.

As they passed by a hayfield a mile and a half before the road began its slow descent to the river, Charlotte put her hand on Newton's arm. "Stop here for a minute," she said. "Let me borrow your pocketknife."

Along the roadside, black-eyed Susans bloomed in boisterous profusion on a sunny outcrop of soil. Charlotte cut a handful, and then she spied some firepinks farther into the brush, where there was a little more shade and moisture. She added a half dozen of them and cut some prairie grass to wrap and tie them.

"All right," she said, as she climbed into the wagon and laid the bouquet atop the coffin. "That should help a little."

And help it did, though little it was. After they reached Daybreak, they dropped Adam and Petey at their house and rode on to the Pettibones'. Although the wagon passed her own home, Charlotte felt obliged to ride the final half mile with Charley, delivering him all the way rather than letting Newton shoulder the burden alone.

Jenny fell into her embrace as they reached her house. The Pettibone boys stood by awkwardly, uncomfortable with open emotions, waiting for someone to tell them what to do. One of them made a move to unload the coffin.

"Don't do that, boys," Jenny said sharply. "Take it up to the schoolhouse. We'll have the funeral up there. I expect a lot of people will turn out to pay their respects."

The idea surprised Charlotte, who had never heard of a funeral held somewhere other than a church or home. But she saw the sense. Charley's long years as deputy and his status as a veteran would bring out a crowd.

"James, ride into town and fetch the preacher for day after tomorrow," Jenny said to the oldest. "We'll sit up with your father tonight and tomorrow, and then we'll have the service after lunch the next day."

"Yes, ma'am," the young man said, darting off toward the stable.

"Preacher?" Charlotte said. "I thought you were a Catholic."

"Not anymore," said Jenny. "I got born again."

Once again Charlotte found herself with nothing to say, so she just hugged Jenny again in hopes that her embrace would speak for her. "I'll be back later tonight to sit up for a while."

But Jenny pulled her close and whispered. "How did it happen? I need to know."

They turned away from the group, their heads close together. "Charley had the impression that a young woman at the Fair had stolen his money. He went to retrieve it, but it appears that this woman had criminal friends, and things went bad from there. I'm just speculating about that part. Nobody's talking, and the police don't seem inclined to pursue it."

Jenny's face puckered. "Charley wrote me all about this girl that your boy Adam was trying to reform, or so he claims."

"Yes. That's the one."

"Then it's your son's sin and foolishness that has cost my Charley his life."

Charlotte held her peace. She could have said that Charley showed a sufficiency of foolishness of his own, chasing after a box of money into a den of vipers, but this was not the time. Besides, she had a point.

Jenny glanced behind them and cleared her throat. "Tell your son not to come over tonight. I don't want to speak to him. He can come to the funeral, but that's all."

They turned away from each other. Charlotte felt overwhelmed by the sadness of it all, the waste of a life and now the threat of enmity between neighbors. So before they parted entirely, she reached back to squeeze Jenny's hand, and was relieved to feel her squeeze back, if only faintly.

Chapter 30

The next day passed in a leaden haze, with everyone retreating to their homes to harbor their thoughts. A stream of carriages, wagons, and men on horseback passed Charlotte's house on their way to the Pettibones'. She watched them go by, and occasionally someone would stop to visit, commiserate, or pry for details. But Charlotte's heart warmed only when she saw Josephine Bridges tie up her mule and walk to the door. She and Josephine had been through their troubles, but all that history only seemed to bind them at times like these.

They embraced in the doorway. "Well, this is a mess," Josephine said, always the one to walk straight to the edge of the cliff and look over. "Damn, I'm going to miss Charley. I know I didn't see him as much as you did, living over in Lucinda, but I'll miss him anyway. He was a bright light."

"That he was," Charlotte said. "And I hate for him to go out in such an undignified way."

Josephine shrugged. "Who knows? We all want to pass away in our beds, with our loved ones gathered round. But we don't get to choose. Besides, there's no indignity in being a murder victim. We've known some fine people who have died that way, have we not? It's the murderer who is the base one."

Charlotte couldn't disagree but hardly saw the point. Of course the murderer was the true villain. But that didn't help the family, who would have to forever live with the image of their Charley, killed in some dark place and thrown into the doorway in a distant city. But she recognized it as Josephine's brusque way of placing blame where it belonged. Perhaps someday Jenny Pettibone would recognize the truth of that statement as well.

"What's being said around Daybreak?" she asked.

"The usual stuff and nonsense," Josephine said with a sniff. "I'm told Adam has got himself mixed up in some trouble, but I didn't care to listen further."

"You'll be one of the few, then."

"I expect so." She shook her head. "Never underestimate human frailty, I guess." Sensing Charlotte's discomfort, she said no more on the subject. "I am truly sorry about Charley. He was one of the originals, wasn't he?"

"He was an original in more ways than one," Charlotte said. "I'll miss him more than I can properly express."

They sat for a moment in silence. "And you know who killed him?"

"I know who's responsible for it," Charlotte said. "Whether he actually did the deed or left that to someone else, that I don't know."

"The son of a bitch." Josephine covered her mouth and laughed to herself. "I'm sorry for my vulgar mouth," she said. "All these years at the sawmill have coarsened me."

"That's all right," Charlotte said. "'Son of a bitch' says it just right." She paused. "Son of a bitch."

They laughed together and then shouted it in unison. "Son of a bitch!" Then the somber nature of the visit came over them again. They grew quiet.

"Are you going back?" Josephine said after a while.

"No. Not unless I'm particularly needed." Charlotte gazed out of the window at another wagon on its way to Charley's house. A familiar hat: the county clerk, perhaps. "I hate to think what's happening at Adam's today," she murmured.

"Then don't think about it. Every family settles its own matters in its own way. Just be there when the rocks start to fly. Metaphorically, I mean."

Charlotte wasn't sure how metaphorical she was being. "How'd you get so wise?" she said with a smile.

"Watching you."

"My goodness! We've got a mutual admiration society going."

"I don't know about that, but I will say I've come to appreciate your way of doing things over the years."

Charlotte knew that this was as close as either of them would ever get to sentimentality. It was time to change the subject. "Tell me of your new venture. How's the match business?"

Josephine frowned. "Up and down. It took us a few months to get the process worked out. Then we had to find buyers. And now—" She stopped herself. "You don't need to hear my troubles."

"Please. Distract me from my own."

"Maybe they will, and maybe they won't. Now, we're having trouble keeping workers. Your outspoken neighbor up the valley has them all scared, and they're staying close to their homes."

"You mean Renick?"

"The very one. As long as he's out there stirring up trouble, nobody wants to venture out. We hardly have half a crew most days." Josephine cast a sideways look in her direction. "Surely you've heard about this situation."

"Some."

"Well, the men figure that Bobby will gather a mob to come looking for Canterbury one of these nights. And they figure, rightly, that if they don't find Canterbury, they'll move on to our place. One black face is as good as another once the mob gets going."

Charlotte sighed. "Have you done anything to try to head this off?"

"J. M. wants to go see Bobby, talk this out like reasonable men." Her snort made it plain what she thought of this idea. "As if Bobby Renick had any interest in being reasonable. The unreasonableness is the whole point. He just needs to get a big enough crowd to go along with him, to give him cover."

"And you?"

Josephine stood up. "As I said, I don't want to trouble you with extra burdens. You have plenty to concern you. But I will tell you this. If Bobby wants to come out and trespass on our property, he will get a warm reception. My workers will be armed and they will have my backing."

"Oh, surely this will not ease matters."

"J. M. wants to ease matters. Myself, if someone wants to be unreasonable with me, I will be just as unreasonable back. If blood is to be shed, I want to make sure that both sides shed it equally."

And with that she was out the door, as implacable as ever, trailing ripples of disruption like the wake of a steamboat. Say what you might about Josephine Bridges, when she passed by you knew she had been there.

Charlotte walked to her kitchen and absentmindedly began to make a pot of tea. She didn't really want a cup of tea, for it was too warm, but she needed something to do with her hands, and by instinct they gravitated to this familiar, comforting task.

She told herself that ultimately, Ulysses S. Canterbury's problems were none of her own. But she couldn't help feeling responsible anyway, just as she had felt responsible for Nimuel and Chaia-ngasup, and responsible for Petey, and responsible for Adam and even Newton, despite their being full-grown, middle-aged men with families of their own. Blessing or curse, it was hers, so she might as well embrace it. But whether she could do anything about Mr. Canterbury's plight was another matter.

What did she want?

She wanted everyone to be happy, and no one to come to harm.

And if she couldn't have that? Whose happiness could she wish to be blighted, whose harm would she countenance?

She didn't know. But she knew she would need to visit Mr. Canterbury and at least talk things over with him. She bore that level of responsibility. In an earlier time, she might have acted first and then sought conversation, but those days were done. At least she thought so.

From the kitchen she stepped out back into the garden, which looked surprisingly well tended. She looked closer at the rows of corn and beans, and saw recent hoe marks.

Charlotte returned inside, put on a loose shawl and sunbonnet, and walked up the road to the center of the village. Newton's store had a "CLOSED FOR DEATH" sign on the door, but she knew that Sarah would be inside, as Sarah always was, tending to unfinished tasks and cleaning things that didn't really need cleaning. Sarah could not remain idle, even in mourning.

"Thank you," she called through the screen.

Sarah came to the front and unlatched the door. "What for?"

"For tending my garden while I was away."

Sarah had a rag in one hand and a lantern globe tucked under her arm. She returned to the counter, where all the lantern globes were lined up, with half of them clean already. "You don't need to thank me. I can't bear a weed."

"I feel the same. But thanks anyway." Charlotte picked up one of the globes and looked for a lantern base to fix it to. "Do these go in any special order?"

"No." Sarah gestured to the lantern bases, lined up on the opposite counter, which Charlotte saw had already been polished to a fine shine.

"You've been busy," Charlotte said, setting the globe into one of the bases and tightening the setscrews.

"Oh, you know how it is. Idle hands and all that. I'd give this job to the boys if I didn't know they'd break half of them."

Charlotte sat in one of the bentwood chairs clustered around the now-dormant potbellied stove, content for the time being with small talk and the silences in between, though she knew serious conversation lay ahead. "Your boys are turning out all right," she said. "You have a lot to be proud of."

Sarah straightened and looked at her with an even gaze. "I do indeed," she said. "But I'm surprised you noticed."

Now it was Charlotte's turn to be surprised. "I'm not sure what you mean."

"I imagine that's so." Sarah's voice remained calm. "It's not the sort of thing you would have paid attention to. But believe me, this half of the family pays attention."

"Please. Help me understand."

Sarah laid the final lamp globe on the counter and wiped her hands. "All right. I don't wish to start a quarrel, but I believe you ask in good faith. Newton and I notice how you fuss and worry over Adam and Petey. How you indulge his every whim because, oh, I don't know, because he's the artistic one and thus deserves every indulgence. How you single her out for special treatment. Walks in the woods, alone time together. She's your favorite grandchild, I can understand that. And she's a sweet and bright girl. But there are times when it grates. Good old Sarah and Newton, noses to the grindstone, building a fine and respectable lives on our own, attracting no notice until our help is needed."

She walked to the corner and fetched a broom, then propped open the front screen door and began to sweep. As she swept, diligently, furiously, and methodically, she continued to speak.

"I don't expect you to do anything about it. Just take notice from time to time. 'Newton, come get us at the train station.' 'Newton, settle this dispute between our crazy neighbors.' 'Sarah, take care of things while we're off at the fair.' Granted, you never asked for any of these things. And we gladly do them just because it's right. But it would be welcome to be recognized now and then for our contributions to everyone's well-being, and to be acknowledged that we have important lives of our own, to us if to no one else." With a great arc of the broom, she swept a pile of gravel and dust out the front door into the street. "And now the boys are up at the graveyard digging the hole for Charley Pettibone's resting place, not because anyone asked them to but because it's their honored duty, and that white-trash bastard from up on the ridge will be down here some night looking to hang your beloved Canterbury, and once again we will be expected to do something about it."

Charlotte was stunned. She stood up and walked out the door in silence. Sarah did not follow her, and she turned toward home.

Sarah's words troubled her, but the calm, even tone with which she delivered them troubled her even more. They were not the passionate outburst of someone who had been stretched to the point of breaking. They were the thoughts of someone who had borne a grievance for a long time, who had considered her words, and who had waited for her moment to deliver them.

And worst of all, she had no reply. For Sarah's complaint had merit, and she knew it. She did favor Petey. Her counter-arguments echoed in her mind. Of course she would! What grandmother wouldn't favor the only girl in the brood? And it was understandable that she would turn her attention more to the weaker side. Adam had always been the one who cried, the one who craved notice, while Newton, stubborn and self-contained, had almost repelled her motherly fussing, even from a young age.

But all these thoughts rang hollow as she considered how such actions would appear to the less-favored ones, particularly as the years went on and instinctive responses hardened into unthinking habits. Steady, reliable Newton and his steady wife, and their ordinary children who showed none of the spark or inquisitiveness of Petey, but who possessed feelings nonetheless and could tell when they were being slighted. Remorse pierced her.

She would do better. She would show her appreciation to them more, make a point to inquire about their thoughts and plans. She would even work to gain an understanding of the boys, whose only noticeable aptitude up to this point had been devising new ways of punching each other undetected.

Charlotte reached her house and sat in the porch rocker, which she had avoided so far this morning because she didn't want to give the impression of spying on the procession of passers-by on their way to the Pettibones' house. But she no longer cared about impressions, for she had things to consider.

She felt culpable for the hurt feelings of Newton's family. But at the same time…at the same time, she wasn't about to apologize for the time she spent with Petey. Newton's sons didn't get the same time with her that Petey did, but when was the last time any of those boys had done anything around her house besides stand in the doorway and let the flies in, or hang around in hopes that she might bake cookies? It was selfish to think such thoughts, but they came unbidden.

And then there was the fact they should all acknowledge, that Petey's path forward was far more rock-strewn than any of those boys could imagine. All they had to do was obtain a little schooling, keep out of serious trouble, and pay their debts on time, and they could look forward to the future of their choosing. Stay in Daybreak and farm, move to town and take up a profession, maybe even strike out for the city. Perhaps one of them would go into politics and become state representative; she knew that Newton had secretly dreamed of such a turn in life. He treated his justice-of-the-peace duties with the solemnity of an archbishop. But what did Petey have to look forward to? A well-made marriage, a respectable home. Perhaps some acceptable outside life for a while, teaching school or charity work. But beyond that, the whole weight of the world pressed against her, no matter how many books she read about Marie Curie.

So she would favor Petey, by God, and let them complain. Who deserved the special attention, the lost sheep or the ones in their comfortable pen? Even Charlotte, no churchgoer, knew her Bible well enough to answer that question.

She sat and rocked. And what was that remark about her "beloved" Canterbury? That was beneath Sarah, who for all her frustrations know how to maintain a civil tongue. She had danced right up to that most evil of epithets, and then danced away again.

Charlotte considered, and as she considered she grew angrier yet. Sarah knew she didn't put up with race-baiting, yet that was what her comment felt like. But perhaps her thoughts were clouded. Perhaps she should let it rest, let it go by.

There was plenty to worry about besides a chance comment. Canterbury, for one, whether beloved or not. There was clear danger ahead, not just for him, but for the whole community. She had heard the stories from Pierce City and Joplin, and a basketful of other towns. A night of cathartic violence, followed by months of agonizing trials and the choosing of sides, or a generation of shamed silence. The mob broke a community one way or another.

But what was there for her to do? She saw no clear answer.

Another wagon from the north passed her gate. Another county official come down from town to pay his respects, she guessed. But the wagon didn't pass; it stopped. The driver turned in his seat and appeared to do something in the bed behind him. In another moment two men hopped out from where they had been lying in the wagon bed, out of sight, and trotted up her walk. Two men she had little space for in her thoughts at the moment: Nimuel and Chaia-ngasup, still dressed in their borrowed clothes.

"Good heavens!" she said as neared. "Why didn't you stay in town?" She led them inside.

"Mrs. Thorp sends word," Nimuel said. "There is trouble in town, and she no longer thinks it safe for men of color, especially two strangers who are not known to local folks. She says we will be safer with you."

Charlotte frowned. Mrs. Thorp was not a person to be doubted, so there had to be something to what she said. But whether the men were safer in Daybreak was an open question.

Nimuel seemed to sense her consternation. "We have written to Professor Pinckney," he said. "If he responds favorably, we will return to the city soon."

"I appreciate that," Charlotte said. "But we need to find you another place to stay."

Her mind raced. She couldn't lodge them here for a dozen different reasons, and no other house in Daybreak would have them either. They could find a bed in the workers' barracks at the match factory, a spot that would place them near the rail line; but how would a letter from the professor find them there? Canterbury's place was out of the question, the lion's den itself. But as she reflected on Canterbury, a notion came to her. She brought each man a glass of water, and carved them some bread with a thick slice of butter.

"All right," she said. "Rest here a while, and then we'll start out."

Chapter 31

As they sat in her front room, Charlotte tried to think ahead. She would need to get these men safely tucked away, then talk to Canterbury if she could, and be home in time to get some decent sleep for Charley's funeral tomorrow. Thank goodness there was plenty of daylight this time of year.

Chaia-ngasup could not sit still. He perched on the edge of the chair for a minute, then stood up and walked in tight circles around the room. He picked up objects from the tables and fireplace mantle, examined them, then carefully replaced them. He spoke a few words to Nimuel.

"Chaia-ngasup feels confined," Nimuel translated. "Things are disturbed here. People have told him of the happy valley described in your son's writings, and he would like to see this happy valley instead of the inside of houses."

"He's in luck, then," Charlotte said. "We'll be on our way."

She gathered some blankets from her bedding chest and rolled them into a large handbag. "Could you carry this for me, please?" she told Nimuel. From her pantry, she added a ham and a tin of crackers. "It will be rough sleeping tonight, I'm afraid."

"We'll manage."

They set out to the north, in the direction the men had just come from. "Here's what we'll do," Charlotte said. "I'll show you my happy valley. We'll walk along and talk. If we meet someone from Daybreak, we won't try to avoid them, but we won't seek them out either. Evasion draws attention."

"I understand." He spoke to Chaia-ngasup, who nodded and replied. "He is an old guerrilla fighter," Nimuel explained to Charlotte. "He knows how to hide out in the open."

At the junction they stayed on the main road instead of turning toward Daybreak. "My family is all up there," she said, gesturing toward the distant village. They could see the cluster of houses, the big meeting-house on the slope of the hill, the cemetery behind it. Chaia-ngasup spoke a few words.

"He smells water," Nimuel said. "When we came down in the wagon, they took us on a boat of some kind to cross a stream. We are near this stream, are we not?"

"Just ahead," Charlotte said.

They reached the ferry landing within a few minutes. Charlotte cranked them into the current while Chaia-ngasup inspected the mechanism with delight.

Nimuel interpreted his exclamations. "Very ingenious! The water itself pushes the boat across."

"Yes," Charlotte said. "It's not as fast as some, but it gets the job done."

As they neared midstream, Chaia-ngasup spoke again. "He would like to stop for a moment, if that is possible."

Charlotte stopped turning the crank. The ferry held its place in the river, the cable bending under the pressure of the current like a gently drawn bow. She didn't particularly like the sensation; solid ground underfoot was the best. But the ferry felt secure, and after a moment she grew accustomed to the soft sway of the ferryboat. Chaia-ngasup held the rail, closed his eyes, inhaled deeply, and murmured a few words.

"What is it?" Charlotte whispered to Nimuel.

He listened intently. "He says this river has a strong spirit. He greets the spirit and asks for its protection on our travels. He asks for its blessing on you and your family."

Charlotte didn't know what to say in reply. As she stood on the swaying ferry and listened to Chaia-ngasup's deep murmurs, a calm came over her. Whatever the man was praying, it seemed to work. She resolved that whatever happened in the next few days, she would simply do what she could for those who mattered to her. If ill things befell, she would try to rest in the knowledge that she had strived. What else was there to do, when it all came down?

Chaia-ngasup grew silent, and Charlotte resumed cranking the ferry across the river. In the distance ahead of them came the sound of hammers and saws.

"What's that?" Nimuel asked.

Charlotte judged the direction. "The Hunting and Fishing Club. Businessmen from St. Louis have bought all this land on the east side of the river, and they're building a lodge." She pointed downstream at the freshly driven pilings. "That's going to be their dock."

They reached the bank and stepped out, pulling the ferry a little further onto the shore. "We'll pass their lane a little farther down, but I doubt if we'll meet anyone. They're building pretty far back in the woods."

The three of them passed by the road to the Hunting and Fishing Club and began to climb the hill out of the river valley. The road was steep, and they paused several times.

When they reached the place where the road leveled out to follow the ridgeline toward town, Charlotte paused again. She remembered stopping at this rocky ledge the first time she ever came to Daybreak, back before the war, before there even was a Daybreak. Then the view from this overlook was of an empty valley, a few scratchings of a cornfield, the empty road, and at the far end the old Webb place, now Pettibone's. Now look at it: a schoolhouse, a store, a cluster of houses, tended fields and pasture all up and down. All in her lifetime.

Chaia-ngasup spoke again, his voice measured and calm, and Charlotte waited for him to finish.

"He says your village reminds him of his own," Nimuel said. "He looks upon it and thinks of home. "In the old days he would plant the crops with the other men, and then they would wait for the rains, and while waiting for the rains they would talk and tell stories. Sometimes they would decide to make war over the mountains, but usually not, for there was plenty to do." Nimuel stopped, and for a moment Charlotte thought he was finished; but when she glanced over she saw that he was waiting, for Chaia-ngasup's face was covered with streaming tears. He caught his breath and spoke again.

"He does not think the gods will allow him to return home," Nimuel said, resuming. "And if they do, the village might be gone, for the kind of war men fight today has upset everything. And the missionaries have built a church on top of the big plaza where they used to gather and talk and pray. So he will take this sight of your village with him in his dreams."

Chaia-ngasup fell silent. They turned up the road again.

"Tell him not to lose hope," Charlotte said to Nimuel. "We had war here too. Where we are walking today, a troop of soldiers came marching back then, and they had a battle down at the river."

Nimuel and Chaia-ngasup spoke back and forth for a little while.

"He thanks you, for your words are wise. The land heals itself, and people come and go. The old gods are not dead because a church has been built on their ground. They have just wrapped themselves up and gone to sleep for a while."

After a moment, Nimuel leaned close and murmured, "I remind you, Mrs. Turner, that I do not subscribe to these old beliefs. I am a good Christian."

"Don't worry about trying to ease my sensibilities," Charlotte said. "I'm hard to shock."

Soon they reached Dathan and Cedeh's old house, set back from the road about fifty feet. "An old couple lived here," Charlotte said. "Then the man died, and the widow moved away. It's been sitting empty for a little while, so keep an eye out for vermin. But you should be able to put up in it while you wait for your reply."

She started down the lane, and Nimuel followed a step behind her. "I'll send Petey to town to check for your mail," she said. "And I'll pack some food for her to bring with her as she comes. Let's hope you don't have to wait more than a couple of days."

But Chaia-ngasup stayed in the road. He tapped the side of his nose and spoke to Nimuel in a low voice.

"He says he smells a man," Nimuel said.

"Oh? He does?" Charlotte looked toward the house, which sat silent. "Hello? Hello the house?"

No answer came. She took another couple of steps forward. "Hello the house?"

They waited, uncertain. "Is he sure?" Charlotte asked.

Chaia-ngasup nodded emphatically.

Charlotte felt suddenly exposed and frightened. She fought down an impulse to run. Then a voice came from inside the house.

"Just you three?"

She relaxed. The voice was that of Ulysses S. Canterbury. "Yes. Just us."

"All right. Come ahead."

Charlotte walked the rest of the way up the lane and pushed open the door. She stepped inside the front room, which was dim with tightly drawn curtains over its small windows. It took a moment for her eyes to adjust. Nimuel and Chaia-ngasup followed her.

Ulysses Canterbury stood at the back of the room, away from the door, and in his hand he cradled a Springfield rifle. In the deep shadows his dark features, stubbled with beard, seemed even darker, a man about to disappear into the shadow. "You're sure you weren't followed?"

"I'm sure. Came up from Daybreak and didn't see a soul. I didn't expect to find you here."

He nodded. "The way I figure it, if old Renick gets up a crowd, they'll come for me in the night, cowards that they are. Better for me not to be at home."

Charlotte looked around the room. Rifle cartridges were lined up at each window. "And here?"

"Not likely that they'd find me. Everybody thinks this place is abandoned. But if they did, it's more defensible than my little dugout. From here I could take out four or five before they made it to the door, and that might be enough to give them pause. Especially if one of them was Bobby."

She shook her head. "I assure you, once shooting starts, there's no pause to be had. Not to advise a military man on tactics, but I come from a military family myself. Better to slip out the back and down into the river valley."

Charlotte noticed him peering at her companions. "Let me introduce you. Ulysses Canterbury, this is Nimuel, and this is Chaia-ngasup."

Canterbury waved a hand but did not step forward. "Filipinos?"

"You are very perceptive, Mr. Canterbury," Nimuel said.

"I recognize the coloration. And you speak English." He pointed to Chaia-ngasup. "His tribe?"

"Igorot," Nimuel said.

"I've heard of them. Never went up that way."

"So you served over there."

"Yes."

Nimuel and Canterbury studied each other politely, neither of them speaking. Chaia-ngasup kept his eyes on the rifle.

"I had intended to house these gentlemen here for a few days," Charlotte said. "Perhaps the three of you can help each other. Keep a watch, that sort of thing."

"You're on the run too, eh?"

Nimuel cleared his throat. "We are, as it were, on strike."

Canterbury laughed. "On strike! Now there's a new one."

Charlotte explained their situation as succinctly as she could. After she was done, Canterbury snorted. "You'd better hope your professor doesn't just send a Pinkerton down to drag you back. Your American upper class is not known for negotiating kindly with colored people. But at least he won't try to hang you. You're worth something to him."

Canterbury walked toward the back room of the house and gestured for Charlotte to follow. As soon as they were out of earshot, he whispered, "Are you sure you want these men here? If things go bad, they would get caught up in it. I don't want anyone else's blood on my hands."

"I don't have anywhere else to put them. Listen. I know you don't want to hear this, but perhaps you should return to St. Louis for a while. We'll watch your place. Things will calm down."

His features grew fierce. "Running away just makes them think you're guilty."

"Who, the Renicks? They don't care about guilt, you know that."

"Everyone else. The townspeople. The mob."

"You surprise me. I never took you for someone who cared about the opinions of the mob."

The torment on Canterbury's face made her regret the remark immediately. A man in imminent danger of his life didn't need a lecture from the neighbor lady. She laid her hand on his forearm. "I'm sorry," she said. "That was uncalled for. I know you're doing the best you can."

Canterbury regained his stoic expression and dug something out of his coat pocket. "Here. I want you to hold this for me." He handed her a sheaf of folded papers. "It's the deed to my property. Worst comes to worst, deliver it to my wife. If all goes well, I'll retrieve it from you."

He sneaked her a sidewise look. "I have thought about that idea, you know. Waiting things out in St. Louis. I may yet do it, if I can figure out how to keep from getting waylaid as I leave town."

"Go through the woods to Lucinda or Ironton and catch the train from there. Nobody knows you in Ironton." She tilted her head. "Or these two, either."

"I'll not take on the job of shepherd for these foreigners."

"I'm not asking you to. I'm just thinking aloud."

They returned to the front room. "I'll leave you now," Charlotte said. "Send messages by way of Petey, as she comes and goes for the mail." She nodded toward Canterbury. "I'll instruct her to make sure she's not followed, and we'll avoid any contact with the Renicks. I'm sure the three of you will find plenty to talk about."

"Lots to talk about, but maybe too painful to bring up," Canterbury said.

"Well, that's up to you. In any event, we'll be in touch."

Charlotte went to the door and peeked out before emerging. She gave Canterbury one last look. "One last thing. I am attending the funeral of Charley

Pettibone tomorrow. You remember Charley. He was a good man, but he had an irresistible urge to play the hero and defend his honor. And now I will sit with his widow and sons. I'd just as soon not repeat that ceremony with your family." She patted the deed in her dress pocket. "Which do you think your wife would want to see more, you or this packet of papers?"

And with that she was out and down the lane, and soon down the hill, her steps growing longer with the steepness of the slope, trouble before her and trouble behind her, and no sign of certainty in any direction.

Chapter 32

Charlotte had intended to return to the Pettibones' house that evening, to sit up with the family a while, but the walk up and down the mountain had fatigued her. When she looked down the road toward their house, she saw a cluster of teams and wagons tied up out front and decided that the Pettibones had plenty of company already. She lay down in the mild light of early evening, and when she awoke it was full dark.

She guessed the time to be after midnight, judging from the deep stillness and the light from the stars that illuminated her bedcovers with the barest of glows, so dim that she could hardly tell whether she was actually seeing the patterns of her quilt or just the tricks of her weary eyes. She thought about getting up and starting the cookstove for breakfast, but it was too early for that.

Charlotte lit the lamp and looked for something to read. Wouldn't you know it, *The Hill-Billies of Heaven Holler* was the only book ready to hand. Oh well, good enough.

Re-reading it now, with all that had happened, she felt an odd mix of appreciation and repugnance. Those innocent hillfolk with their instinctive moral sense. The monstrous villains with their citified ways. Did he believe these things? Surely not. Surely he had concocted the story with an eye on sales, and had exaggerated and simplified the people in it to meet his idea of what people wanted. But at the same time, there was something undeniably heartfelt in the book, and she could sense in its hero, so heroic as to be almost comical, Adam's own imagining of how a person should behave. Grand gestures of self-sacrifice, declarations of eternal loyalty and friendship, love that knew no boundaries of distance or time. Had she raised him to be such a romantic? Or had he come to that on his own? Surely the latter.

But as she read further, with the old clock ticking on the mantel in the next room, something else caught her attention. For all his overwrought prose and implausible characters, Adam had a good eye. He noticed things: the way a wren shuffled in the dry leaves of the forest floor, how a cascade of water from a wet-weather spring split and reunited as it passed over rocks on its way to the pool. Perhaps that was what drew people, his awareness of the world around him and the way he slipped that awareness into theirs. Perhaps he had been listening all along, when she had taken the children to the woods to show them the healing herbs and the edible things. It certainly hadn't seemed so at the time. The only one to show even mild interest had been Sarah, whom she had often thought of as the daughter she had never had, until lately, anyway. You never knew what the children were hearing.

She felt herself drifting.

When Charlotte awoke, it was true dawn, past her usual time of awakening, and she fussed in her kitchen, annoyed with herself at having started the day wrong. She fired up the cookstove aggressively, too hot, and sure enough burned the bottom of her biscuits. She muttered a cuss under her breath, then immediately looked to see if anyone was at the door or within earshot. Might as well face it, she wasn't cut out for cussing. Too late to start now.

Charlotte never entered the schoolhouse without thinking of its past existences. The Temple of Community they had called it at first, a grandiose name to be sure, but one that had matched the ambition of its builders. Then during the war, a makeshift fortification and storehouse, and afterwards a meeting hall, town center, schoolhouse, whatever the people needed at the time. The broad yellow pine floorboards, where she had danced in years gone by, scattering the planks with sawdust to provide a kinder footing. And now, the site for a funeral, with a stiff-looking preacher and a full row of Pettibones in the front benches.

The entire town had turned out, as was only right for such a longtime resident, and a fine showing from surrounding towns as well. Charley would have been pleased. Although he always pooh-poohed fancy people and their fancy funerals, their granite headstones, insisting that a plain pine box and a hole deep enough to keep the groundhogs out was good enough for any man, she knew that he had been proud of his achievements, and the turnout was a sign that others saw them as well. Like everyone, Charley was about two-thirds bluff in his claims that he didn't care about others' opinions.

Adam, Penelope, and Petey lined up on one bench, each looking miserable in a unique way, and collectively miserable as well. Mother and daughter bore the marks of prolonged weeping, while Adam's face was drawn and frozen. Charlotte could well imagine the conversations that had gone on at their home overnight.

At the other end of the bench sat Sarah and Newton. The boys, she assumed, were up in the cemetery awaiting their duty, probably pelting each other with clods to pass the time. Then she reminded herself that she had resolved to have softer thoughts of the boys, and silently repented. She squeezed herself into the middle of the row, between the two families. She took the hand of Penelope, to her left, and Sarah on her right. The three of them sat, holding hands, binding together the wounded families. Petey sat between her mother and father, an added buffer to ease their various bruises.

Charlotte wondered how Penelope would manage, with a husband who had embarrassed himself, embarrassed her, embarrassed the whole family. What was there to do? Nothing, really. A woman with no family elsewhere, no external source of wealth, no name or reputation to carry her into another life. Her only choice was to endure and to make the best of a bad situation, as women had learned to do since the dawn of history.

The preacher clearly had never met Charley, who often joked that he was a member of the Catfish and Smallmouth Church and faithfully attended services every Sunday morning. But he labored his way over that obstacle artfully enough, evading any speculation about Charley's eternal destination by reminding the congregation that Jesus himself had said his father's house contained many mansions. He left it up to them to imagine whether one of those mansions housed avid fishermen, and Charlotte appreciated his forbearance.

Afterward, the trip to the cemetery, usually an occasion for her to walk around and reflect. But today she had no appetite for it. Too many troubles on her mind. Meditation would just transform into worry.

Petey fell into step alongside her as they walked up the hillside. "Mama and Daddy are fighting," she whispered. "I don't know what to do."

"Let them fight," Charlotte said. "Stay out of their way. They have to fight right now. It's the only way they'll find their way to a solution, if there is one."

"I hate it! It's horrible. Yelling and then silence, and then more yelling."

"I know. Come down to my porch and sit whenever you need to." They stopped at James' grave, already a little overgrown since the last cemetery-cleaning. Charlotte thought to herself that she should come up next spring and plant some flowers, or perhaps some bulbs in the fall. No one would appreciate them but her, and that was enough. "I was also thinking you might go to town for me, to see if there's mail for Nimuel."

Petey looked nervous. "I'm not sure I should leave Mama and Daddy alone in the house. They act calmer when I'm around."

Such an overdeveloped sense of responsibility, and at such a young age. She might as well admit it: Petey reminded her of herself. Traits skip a generation, or so they said.

"That's all right," Charlotte said. "You stay home. I expect you're right. There's certainly no harm in keeping them on their good behavior."

It was true that Petey needed to be with her parents, and she didn't begrudge her that. But it also meant that Charlotte would need to check on the mail herself, for a promise was a promise. She just hoped that Nimuel and his employer would work something out soon, for she wasn't sure they understood how slippery their position was. Or perhaps they did. They had made it all the way from the Philippine forests to the hills of Daybreak, after all.

"You go on," she said, turning away from the cemetery. "I'll pay my respects later." She met Newton on the way down. "Would you mind if I borrowed Maggie for the afternoon? I've a mind to go riding."

Newton couldn't hide his surprised look, but nodded. "I'll send one of the boys to saddle her up."

Charlotte felt a passing annoyance at Newton's assumption that she needed help with the horse. She could still lift a saddle. But in the barn a few minutes later, wrestling with the gear that didn't seem so pliable to her fingers as it once had, she was grateful for Maggie's patience and John Wesley's assistance. A friskier horse would have brought her close to giving up.

The post office had nothing, curse the luck. A long ride for no benefit. But she stopped by the Madison Hotel to check the latest St. Louis newspapers, and there it was on the front page of the *Republic:* SEEK RUNAWAY SAVAGES FROM FAIR.

She bought a copy and walked around the corner to the City Restaurant, where she ordered a roll and a cup of coffee. Sitting at a window table, she read the account of how two homesick tribesmen, possibly led astray by members of the local Colored People's Association, had run off in the night. Exertions were under way to locate them, but the public should not feel alarm, for they were harmless despite their strange appearance.

Charlotte sighed. At least they had the homesick part right.

She noticed a stranger at the counter, a well-dressed man with a solemn expression, chewing his way through a slab of roast beef and potatoes with the concentration of a caterpillar on a leaf. She cocked her eyebrow at the waitress who came to refill her coffee.

"Hotel guest," the waitress whispered. "Got in last night. Didn't say what he's here for."

Charlotte studied the man's broad back. At first, she thought he might be a Pinkerton, sent to locate Nimuel and Chaia-ngasup, but something about him didn't fit that bill. Pinkertons didn't often show themselves in the broad light of day, for one thing, and when they did they usually had a carefully built cover story as traveling horse dealers or real estate scouts. This man just sat in stolid silence, grinding away at his food as if he had nowhere to go for the rest of the day.

A thought occurred to Charlotte. She paid her tab and stepped outside, then walked to the hitching rail at the corner, where she pretended to adjust Maggie's tack. In a few minutes, the man emerged, wiping his lips with his handkerchief.

She spoke to him as he passed. "I have you figured for a government man. Am I right?"

The man stopped and tipped his hat. "Ma'am. Good morning to you."

No answer was as good as an answer. "I would say you're a Treasury man. Am I right?"

His expression was blank, and he said nothing.

"I'll tell you this," Charlotte said. "If you're from the Treasury, and you're looking for operations that have avoided their lawful obligation, I could help you out."

The man blinked. "I've been down here three times, ma'am. You're the first person that has said anything the like of that to me." He looked both ways around himself, as if he suspected a trick.

"I imagine so." Charlotte knew a man from the Revenue Office would be as welcome as a wasp. So she kept a neutral tone. "But I have personal reasons for coming forward."

"Temperance lady, eh? Or maybe ratting out a rival? You don't look the type for either."

She had a moment of doubt. The man had never actually come out and said he was a revenue agent. But what else could he be? Nobody else cared about bootleg whiskey other than where to find some.

"My apologies, ma'am," the man said. "I don't mean to question your motives. Is this a big operation we're talking about?"

"It is. And I'll warn you, it's well placed. Remote location with a broad view all around. You'd find it hard to surprise him."

The man grinned. "I like a challenge. And I apologize again if I sounded too cynical. I'm usually shunned and scorned everywhere I go." He opened his coat and flashed a badge, pinned to the inside pocket. "And you are correct, I'm a government man. My name's McCorkle."

Charlotte extended her hand for him to shake. "I'm pleased to make your acquaintance, Mr. McCorkle. I'm Charlotte Turner, of Daybreak."

"And where is that?"

"Southwest of here a few miles." They had been standing there talking for long enough that Charlotte felt exposed. If she had spotted McCorkle for who he was, surely others had as well. He seemed uncomfortable, too. "Perhaps you'd like to meet me in about an hour. Take the road south to Mill Creek, and I'll wait for you on this side of the ford. It's on my way home."

"Mill Creek, eh?"

She nodded. "If you don't know the way, just ask anyone. It's a well-traveled road."

He tipped his hat, and they parted.

Waiting on the bank of Mill Creek, where she let Maggie take water and browse, Charlotte let doubt again seep into her mind. What if her idea did not disrupt Bobby's plans, but made him vengeful and rabid instead? He was not a stupid man. He could very well find out who instigated a raid. Not a pleasant outcome to contemplate. But the symmetry of it, forestalling lawlessness by resorting to a different branch of the law, appealed to her. And there came Mr. McCorkle down the hill on what had to be the oldest, most broken-down horse in the livery stable.

"You're going to have to do better than that creature if you intend to catch this man," she said.

McCorkle reached down and patted the horse's neck. "We don't work that way. Surround and surprise, that's our strategy. No need to outrun anybody." He stepped down and led the horse to a shady place near the water. "Now how about you tell me all about this local rapscallion?"

Charlotte told him the story of Bobby Renick's operation, as far as she knew it. The works up on the hilltop, the storage down in the old mine shafts. The mother, who appeared to be the intelligent one. The children, little more than unpaid laborers, as far as she could tell.

McCorkle sketched a map as she described the place. "How many gallons you think he takes out of there in a week?"

"I couldn't say. Enough to supply most of the town, anyway. A couple of wagonloads."

"And there's just the one road in and out? Where's the road go?"

"One more little homestead, and then it turns into a footpath that leads to Daybreak. They use the footpath from time to time, but it won't carry wheeled traffic."

"Does he grow his own corn?"

Charlotte chuckled. "Growing corn is hard work. He buys it or trades for it."

McCorkle took on an expression of grim satisfaction. "These people are all the same. They think their isolation protects them, when it just makes them easy to cut off." He folded his notes and tucked them into his coat pocket. "All right, I have what I need. I won't keep you any longer. I'll keep your name out of this, so don't worry about any repercussions."

"So now what?"

"I'll return to St. Louis, gather some men. Get approval from my boss and schedule a raid. In a month or so, you can express surprise along with everybody else that your friend Renick is going to jail."

"A month? I was thinking—"

"What, that you could just summon a group of Treasury men to solve whatever problem you're having with your neighbor? We don't work like that, ma'am. We have rules and procedures."

"No wonder you never catch anybody. And don't try to look so wounded. You know people aren't afraid of you out here."

McCorkle expression changed to a grimace. "A couple of big successes and they will be."

"I guess I'll go home and watch the newspapers, then. Good luck." Charlotte climbed into Maggie's saddle, not as easy a task as it once was, but one she was determined to perform unassisted. She forded the creek and swung around the shoulder of the little hill on the other side, past the scattering of houses that dotted the slope. She felt peeved at herself for imagining that some miraculous outsider would swoop in and fix her troubles. As if a lifetime's worth of experience hadn't taught her the folly of that idea. There was no easy way out of troubles. Who was she kidding? One either fought through them, succumbed to them, or learned to live with them.

She stopped at Dathan and Cedeh's old place on her return, taking care to tie Maggie to a tree back in the woods on the opposite side of the road so no tracks or droppings would show. She walked to the rear of the house and entered from that door.

The men were arrayed in chairs at the corners of the house, looking inexpressibly bored. "We were watching you," Canterbury said. "You cover your tracks like a regular old guerrilla."

"I remember a few tricks," Charlotte said. She tossed the copy of the *Republic* onto the table. "You're in the news," she said to Nimuel.

Nimuel read the article, frowning, and then translated it for Chaia-ngasup. In the meantime, Charlotte turned to Canterbury. "Everything all right here?"

Canterbury nodded with a shrug. "You don't get much more traffic on your road than I do on my little goat path. There haven't been a half dozen people go by, and none of them even looked in this direction."

"That's good." She looked around. "And inside?"

"We've been re-fighting the war. Your old friend here is more fearsome than he looks."

"I thought you didn't like to talk about the war."

Canterbury didn't meet her gaze. "You know what they say. You can't atone for your sins until you confess them first."

He followed her to the door. "Listen," he said. "You need to send these people back to St. Louis. They don't belong down here, and they'll just get mixed up in whatever trouble comes my way. Whatever happens to them up there, at least they'll be with their people."

"And what do you propose to do about yourself?"

He looked away, and then looked back. "You don't think this will blow over?"

"Not for a long time. A month or more." From the shocked look on his face, she could tell that her estimate came as a surprise. "Bobby may not be good for much, but he strikes me as the kind of man who is good at holding a grudge." She considered telling him about McCorkle and the Treasury men, who might put an end to Bobby Renick's nonsense, but that whole enterprise seemed too uncertain.

"Then I guess I'd better go with them," Canterbury said. "Get away for a while, like you said. One thing I learned in the Army: the longer you sit in one place, the more you set yourself up for an unpleasant surprise. We've only been here a day and already I'm feeling nervous."

"I'm sorry. I know it's not in your nature to back away from trouble. But for now I think it's the best course."

Canterbury rubbed his cheek but didn't disagree. "So what's your thought for our next move?"

"Like I said earlier, head west. Bobby is known in Fredericktown, and if he doesn't have many friends there, at least he has customers. So don't go that direction. Somebody will spot you sure. Tonight, come down the road to Daybreak. I'll leave the ferry on your side of the river, and you can skirt the town. Dogs won't bark at someone on the main road. You'll be too far away. Catch the train at Lucinda and you'll be home in time for supper."

"This is the same kind of shit my father used to talk about," Canterbury said in a tone of disgust. "Running around in the middle of the night, hoping the farmhouse dogs don't bark. I thought all this was supposed to be behind us."

Charlotte didn't know what to say to him. Of course they were supposed to be putting this all behind them, but it clearly wasn't working out that way, and men like Canterbury would have to find a way to survive until it did. But he knew that already, so there was no point in repeating the obvious.

"It's a mess," she finally said.

At the base of the hill, where the road sloped down to the river, the ferry rested in its worn ruts. Charlotte needed to leave it on the near bank for Canterbury and the others, so she swam Maggie across. "Sorry, old gal," she said as they clambered up the opposite side. "I'll give you a good brushing in the barn."

A wet horse and rider would have inspired questions in town, so she stayed on the main road until she reached her house, then tied Maggie out back and went inside to change her clothes. After a few minutes, Maggie was brushed and dry, looking entirely unremarkable. Charlotte led her to Newton's barn and bedded her down.

A long day, and an arduous one. Arduous almost to the point of perversity, it now seemed to her, looking back. Dashing here and there, making plans that were thwarted as soon as they were made. What did she have to show for all her effort? A wet horse and a tired body. She fell into bed as soon as she managed to put on her nightgown, hoping to sleep a few hours before the men came by, and have food and water ready to give them. But when she woke it was full morning.

Chapter 33

The sunrise brought an air of calm, like the feeling of a morning after a thunderstorm, and for a moment Charlotte wondered if it had indeed rained overnight. But a glance out her window showed that whatever cleansing rain might have occurred was only in her dreams. The path to the road was dry, the grass dewy. She wondered if the men had left some kind of sign that they had passed, a mark on the porch post or an arrangement of vegetation out front. But of course that wasn't the idea. The idea was to leave no trace of their passing, no way for anyone to follow them. She would have to wait for news from later on.

So it was an empty day, a rare commodity in her life, and she actually found herself looking forward to the simple, straightforward tasks of housekeeping. For once, tasks that always felt like drudgery now appeared as a welcome relief, a return to the ordinary rhythms of life. "Let there be laundry," she murmured to herself.

By afternoon, the sight of Petey walking down the road toward her house was a welcome excuse to step out onto the porch, pull out the rocking chairs from their place against the front wall, and plop down to await her arrival. Petey carried a basket under her arm, and as she neared Charlotte saw that it was filled with fresh ears of corn.

"I thought we might make some more dolls," Petey said. "They were such a hit at the Fair that maybe it would be nice to have some down here. To give to the people who come to see Papa, as a kind of souvenir."

"You came prepared, I see," Charlotte said with a smile. "Well, sit yourself down."

Petey set the basket between them. "These are some good old chairs."

"Did I ever tell you the story of how I came by these chairs?"

"No."

Charlotte chuckled. "My husband, Mr. Gardner—not your grandpa, but the second man I married—was mad for walking. Walked everywhere he went. Said it was the only ethical means of transportation, and had a lengthy argument about the economics, too, which he would bring out at the drop of a hat. Mr. Gardner had some odd ideas, but he was a kind and generous man, and I grew to love him a great deal."

She browsed in the basket for a workable ear.

"Anyway, Mr. Gardner walked by here regularly, and he always stopped to talk. I only had one chair to sit on, and he would perch there on the steps, like some kind of exotic bird that had just landed and was about to fly away. After a few visits, he made his intentions clear, and I had to decide whether he was welcome. So I thought about it for a while. And then I went up to see Mr. Nichols, the chairmaker, and bought the chair you are sitting in right now. And when Mr. Gardner came by the next time, he had a proper place to sit and rest his bones, instead of the hard and dirty steps of my front porch. And the rest is history, as they say."

Charlotte smiled to herself. There were other things she could say about the ingratiating ways of Mr. Gardner, but they were not for Petey's ears.

"But when he died, you changed your name back to Turner."

"Yes." Charlotte glanced over at her. "The boys are both Turners. You're a Turner. It just seemed to fit."

An idea occurred to her at that moment. She stood up and gestured for Petey to come inside. "I want to show you something. I've been meaning to do this for some time, but just never found the moment."

They walked into the kitchen, where Charlotte stood by the window and loosened the sash jamb. She pulled out the packet of letters and papers. "Back during the war, I got in the habit of hiding anything that would reveal my sympathies. With both my father and husband in the Union Army, local folks knew which side we were on. But raiders would come from all over. They were the worst. Just looking for an excuse to shoot people."

Charlotte spread the items out on the table. "Anyway, I got to thinking the other day. Just my luck, I'd pass away some day and nobody would even know these things were in the wall. I put them there for safekeeping, but it would be one of life's great ironies if they disappeared because I forgot to tell anybody about them. They're yours to look through whenever you like. Or not, as you see fit. I just don't want them to be lost through inadvertence."

"Oh, Grandma!" Petey cried. She picked up a few of the letters and studied the writing on the envelopes. "Letters from Grandpa? From the days of the war?"

"And your great-grandfather, too. He was killed, you know. They buried him on the field, and I never had the chance to visit. So these letters are the last memories I have."

Charlotte watched Petey's eyes as she examined the items, one by one, looking only at the outsides for now. But she knew the workings of Petey's mind. Petey was categorizing, classifying, making plans.

"These are a treasure, Grandma," she murmured. "Thank you."

Charlotte felt a mixture of emotions as she watched her granddaughter rummage through the papers. This moment was the reason she had saved them all these years: the chance to show someone that yes, this was her life, these were the people she knew and loved, this was her history, her struggles, her triumphs and losses. But she also realized that a bundle of papers was a paltry thing, a mere suggestion of a life. Far more would be lost than could ever be communicated, even if she sat and talked to Petey for a month. So it was, one generation cometh and another passeth away, and no matter how much she would like to protect Petey from the storms of life by telling her of all that she had endured, such a thing would never happen. For every generation had to learn through its own defeats, cherish its own loves, commit its own crimes.

"Are you sure you want other people to read these?" Petey said, a tiny frown creasing her forehead. "I expect there are some personal things in here."

"I'm sure of it. Better that you read them while I'm still around to explain what was going on, than to have you read them at some future date when all you could do is wonder."

"Don't talk like that, Grandma! I don't like to think such things."

Charlotte could have gone on further about the ravages of time and the failures of memory, but this did not seem to be the moment for those meditations. She let Petey riffle through the letters a while longer, then stood up and returned to the porch. "Now you know where I keep them," she said. "Come over anytime you want."

They continued making cornshuck dolls, and eventually Petey opened up about the state of things at her house, which were chilly but not irretrievably frozen. Her parents had begun to speak to each other again, though their exchanges were clipped and functional. "I know how that goes," Charlotte told her. "Your grandfather and I went through some troubles of our own. Just give them time. And for your own well-being, steer clear of their arguments. What they say to each other is not your concern, and it will only make you worry to hear them fight it out. But fight it out they must. Come down here when it gets too much."

The next afternoon, Petey returned with more ears of corn, and the two of them took turns making dolls and reading the letters. The next day was laundry day, leaving no time for leisure, but on the afternoon of the next day she was back.

And a couple of hours later came Newton up the road, walking for once, a rarity since he was too out of shape to travel dismounted for long. They watched him as he unlatched the gate and came up the path.

"Hello, son," Charlotte called. "Come and sit. Petey and I have just about run out of conversation topics." But Newton remained in the yard, his hand on the porch post.

"That's all right," he said. "I can't linger. Things to do, you know."

"Very well."

Newton cleared his throat but said nothing more, looking increasingly uncomfortable.

"Petey," Charlotte said, "I think your uncle Newton would like you to disappear."

"That's all right," Newton said again, but he sighed with relief when Petey stood up and announced that she would walk to the springhouse and fetch them all a drink of cold water. She took the bucket from its nail on the inside wall of the porch and strolled up the road, whistling.

"Don't know why you still insist on that spring water," Newton said. "You've got well water inside the house."

"I like the taste. What's on your mind?"

Newton cleared his throat again. "I had a couple of tourists to pick up at the train station. Heaven Holler people, you know."

"That's good."

"Suppose so. It's a craze, and like all crazes it won't last. But we'll earn some money from it in the meantime. Anyway—"

He looked down the road to see Petey's back, still headed for the springhouse, the bucket swinging in her hand.

"There was another person got off the train, a young woman, and she was asking how to find you."

A dull, icy ache filled Charlotte's stomach. "Did she say what her name was?"

"She called herself Mrs. Smith. But nobody believed her."

"What did she look like?"

"She didn't look like a 'missus,' I'll tell you that. She wanted to get a room at the hotel, but they wouldn't take her. Said they didn't permit her kind of trade."

"What do you think?"

"Oh, yeah. That kind isn't hard to spot. A little too fancy, a little too much powder. But she kept calling your name out, so I felt I had to step in." He rubbed his face. "She's sticking with the Mrs. Smith, and she insists she'll only speak to you."

"What do you mean, 'insists'? Where is she?"

"That's what I was working up to. I didn't want to leave her there on the platform, running up to strangers, asking for directions. So I brought her to the hotel. I put her upstairs and told her not to speak to anyone."

Charlotte groaned. "Is this person who I think it is?"

"Don't know who else it could be."

She stood up and brushed off her apron. "Well, let's go see."

Charlotte's mind raced as they rushed up the path toward Newton's store. What on earth could have possessed this woman to come to Daybreak, the place where she would be least welcome? And to ask for her? It was madness.

They passed the springhouse, where Petey was dipping water into the bucket. Charlotte paused. Her instinct told her to shield Petey from this troubling news, but if she was going to start treating her as an adult, she might as well start now. She leaned into the doorway. "I have to go up to Newton's," she said. "Someone has showed up at the hotel and won't give her true name. They think it might be Rose LaBelle."

"What on earth?" Petey's face worked. "What would she be doing down here?"

"I guess I'll find out." Charlotte took the dipper out of her limp hand and sipped. The world might go mad around them, but a dipper of cold fresh spring water was a blessing in any circumstance. "I think you understand that Rose's presence in Daybreak, whatever the reason, would be impossible to sustain. She will have to go. I'll not talk about this to your mother and father until I have a better idea what's going on."

"Sure," Petey said, her face continuing to oscillate between puzzlement and fear. But Charlotte didn't have time to try to comfort her. She waved and strode on.

"You didn't have to tell her," Newton muttered beside her. "I was trying to keep her from hearing this news."

"I know," Charlotte said, feeling grim. "But it's a world half insane much of the time, so she might as well start getting used to it."

She understood his desire to keep Rose's arrival secret. If word got around that a whore had chased Adam all the way from the World's Fair, there was no telling how far the ripples of scandal would travel. But why would Rose come all this way just for that? She had nothing to gain from launching a scandal. That was the mystery.

They reached the store, where Sarah stood in the doorway, her arms folded.

"Where is she?" Charlotte said.

Sarah cocked her head. "Room at the head of the stairs. I told her not to unpack."

"Good." She looked at Newton. "I gather you haven't put away the horse and carriage yet."

"No. Just water and a cool-down."

Charlotte nodded. At least they all seemed to be thinking alike. "Well, no reason to stand here dawdling." She mounted the steps and listened for a moment at the door. There was no sound from within, although down the hall she could hear the muffled, cheerful voices of the tourist couple, unpacking their things. Charlotte stepped inside.

Chapter 34

Rose LaBelle was sitting on the bed in a yellow dress, her sun hat still tied under her chin. A light cotton jacket covered her shoulders and arms and created a little flounce around her middle, but Charlotte could see past that concealment easily. So that was it.

She regarded Rose for a minute. It wasn't hard to see how the townsfolk spotted her profession. As Newton said, there was something a little too much in everything she did, a little too prettified, a little too powdered. Down here no one wore powder on an ordinary day.

Rose met Charlotte's gaze with composure. It was the look of someone who was accustomed to being viewed with scorn, a level look that went beyond and through the present moment to some distant place. But Charlotte could see the wear that had occurred in maintaining this mask. The indifferent expression of her eyes, the forced neutrality of her face; Charlotte tried to imagine the work that such a visage required. And as she looked, she gradually saw through that mask to the woman beneath. Hardly a woman, really, just a few years out of girlhood.

The longer she looked, the more she saw of the uncertain human being who was so carefully hidden. And against her better judgment, against her intentions, she felt empathy for this foolish, lost, dangerous young woman.

"He's thrown me out," Rose said. "Because I wouldn't—you know—go see the doctor."

"And so you came here. Why, in God's name, did you come here? You can't be here."

"I couldn't think of anywhere else."

"Good heavens, girl. You have parents. Soon to be grandparents."

She shook her head. "My father was very emphatic when I left. I wrote them a couple of years ago, and their reply was the same."

"Yes, but—" It felt fruitless to argue. "I can't allow you to see Adam. There's too much harm in it."

Rose sniffed. "Why would I want to see him? He'd be no help. It's you I came to see." Charlotte's confusion must have shown on her face, for she added, "I thought you might know a place where a girl could get help."

"Why would I help you? You stole from my friend. And your stealing led to his death."

Rose's voice was little more than a whisper. "I know."

"And yet here you are."

Charlotte walked to the window. The back of the hotel looked out on Newton's barn and pasture, and beyond that the slope to the cemetery and the woods line. She supposed to a city visitor it would look like a romantic, rustic vista, with the slope rising up into the forest, and the shoulder of Daybreak Ridge behind it, but to her it was home, not the setting for someone else's adventure story. And here was this girl, whose troubles had somehow become her troubles, unasked for and unwelcome. She contemplated calling out to Sarah, who she knew was listening at the bottom of the stairs, and hauling her back to the station to catch the next train north. Or south, or anywhere.

But instead she took Rose's hand and picked up her valise. "Your travels are not over for the day," she said. "I don't know if this will work out. But it's all I can think of."

Rose stood up obediently and followed her down the stairs. Newton and Sarah made way for them as they walked outside. Charlotte was grateful to see that Newton had brought the carriage around front, with Jack already in harness. She climbed into the carriage and took the reins.

"If anybody asks, tell them I had a yen to go visiting," she said to Newton. "And you know they'll ask. As you have guests to attend to, we'll take our leave. I'll see you tomorrow."

She gave the reins a flick, and Jack pulled into his harness in the direction he was pointed like the well-broke horse he was, setting a modest but steady pace toward town. Charlotte let him find his own rhythm. But when they reached the ferry landing, the steered him south down the main road, away from Daybreak and away from the direction they had come.

The sides of the roadway were overgrown with sassafras and cedar sprouts, making the wagon less and less visible from Daybreak the farther they traveled. Charlotte was grateful for the screen. They rode in silence until they reached Charlotte's house, where she hitched to the gatepost and stepped down.

"I'll just be a minute," she said.

Charlotte gathered some fresh clothes and provisions, throwing it all into a basket. Simple but filling, some bread and ham. That should do them. Then she had one more thought and pulled a black shawl and gray bonnet from her wardrobe.

She returned to the carriage and set the basket behind their bench. She pointed down the road. "That house down the way is Charley Pettibone's place. Obviously, we're not going to stop and visit. Put these on until we're out of sight."

Rose covered herself with the shawl and bonnet, and the two of them did not speak until they had passed the house and rounded the bend, where the road followed the river and became lost in trees.

"So," Charlotte said. "I want to hear what happened to Charley."

They settled into the rhythm of the ride, the easy pace of the horse that swayed them gently from side to side with each step, nothing too harsh or pronounced, just the uncomplicated rocking of ordinary travel. It felt right to Charlotte to be moving at a proper speed again. Trains and streetcars, rushing them through the world in crowded boxes, yanked people's bodies from place to place before their minds had time to adjust. In the carriage they could appreciate the landscape as they passed, the altering of the roadbed from its smooth, packed surface along the river to the rocky, lurch-filled track it became once they passed the turnoff to French Mills and climbed the creekbed west. And the almost imperceptible shift from bottomland foliage to forest's edge, and then to deep woods. Such things were better experienced at the pace of a horse and buggy.

Rose sighed. "My craving got the better of me," she said. "I'd seen your friend Mr. Pettibone carry his day's earnings upstairs, night after night, so I knew he had to have a strongbox somewhere in his room."

"Surely you knew that he would check for it every night and discover it missing."

She shrugged. "When the craving comes over you, you don't think from step to step. You only think about the one thing, and whatever happens after that is of no consequence. Maybe I thought I'd get my dose, then find a few customers, enough to pay him back. But I doubt it. My mind is cloudy on the subject, but I would guess that I didn't really care whether it would be discovered."

They grew silent as they passed a little farmstead, as if by unspoken agreement that they would not talk while they were within sight of others. Now that they had reached Black Mountain and were heading up the winding creek, no one came out to greet them and talk, for they were not neighbors. But people stopped their work to watch them pass, and to speculate on who they might be and what errand they might be pursuing. The homesteads grew farther apart.

"Anyway, I found my dose," Rose continued. "But the druggist I visited must have tipped his nose in Bill's direction. He sent men to fetch me."

Her face was blank. "Bill took the money box and told me that I had cost him more in trouble than any amount in the box. I suppose that's true."

Charlotte didn't speak. Debating with her now seemed pointless. Better to let her spill her thoughts.

"So then your son came, but Bill shooed him off right quick. That's not Adam's fault. Even the worst of the toughs knows to avoid Bill when he's on a mad."

Charlotte glanced over at her, not wanting to inquire further, but sensing that Rose had been on the receiving end of Big Bill's mads plenty of times. "I understand," she said.

Rose nodded in recognition. "So along comes your friend, later that night, and he's hopping mad. Bill had the boys throw him out once, but he stayed in the street. He yelled and hollered about how he was a man of the law, and how he was going to bring the law down on us. Everybody laughed at that, because we had two police officers upstairs at that very moment."

She paused. "I mean, anybody should have known that. Right?"

"Charley could be pretty hard-headed."

"Anyway, Bill let it go for a while, but eventually he called Two-Eyes over. He told him, 'That old man is scaring away business.' So Two-Eyes gathered up a couple of fellows and left. He came back a few minutes later." A blue jay flashed across their path with a garish squawk. "I don't know what happened out in the street, but Bill came over and told me to get my ass down to the doctor's so I could start working again. He said I was going to cost him more in payoffs than I could hope to earn in a year, so I'd better be ready to work extra and wherever he told me. I said I didn't care for the sound of that, because I was his best attraction and brought a respectable crowd in from the Fair."

Rose cleared her throat. "I knew it was a mistake to say that. But I said it anyway. Next thing I knew, I was out in the street with all my things, and instructions not to come back until I had taken care of matters at the doctor's."

She grew silent for a while, as if deciding whether to say any more. Charlotte let the silence expand around them. She had learned the hard way over the years that there were times when talking got in the way of communicating. Better to let her thoughts find their own way out.

They reached the junction where the main road continued up Marble Creek toward Ironton, and the side road, lesser-traveled, rose up the ridge to the west from which it would eventually descend toward Lucinda. She steered Jack up the side road.

"It gets rocky up ahead," she told Rose. "Make sure you've got something to grab onto when we hit a rough spot."

After a while, Rose started up again, picking up her story as if she hadn't been silent for nearly an hour. "So there I was out on the street. I didn't want to see the doctor. He's a horrible, nasty man." She made a face. "And I thought, what's so wrong with having this baby? Women do it every day. And I knew that even if I did, Bill would punish me when I got back. He doesn't like it when we get sassy."

Charlotte could feel her resolve to listen without argument or comment start to crumble. The offhand way in which she spoke of Charley's killing incensed her, and she could barely stand to listen to Rose's vapid thoughts about childbirth and her current line of work. But she had promised herself to attend quietly to the girl's thoughts until she had learned all there was to learn. So she held her peace.

Almost. "But why come here? There are charity hospitals in the city, but down here—" She waved inclusively at the deep woods surrounding them.

"Have you seen those places? No, thank you. Besides, Bill has someone on the payroll at every one of them. He'd have me clapped back in his place downtown before the end of the day, and no walking away that time. The charity hospitals are his best recruiting grounds, apart from the train station. I think he even pays off a nun or two to send him likely prospects."

"I see." Charlotte didn't know whether her claims were true, but she'd seen enough charity homes to recognize at least a nugget of truth within her thoughts.

"So here's where you come in. I got on a streetcar, didn't really think about where I was going. Before I knew it, I was way down on Chestnut Street, and you know the kind of things that go on down there." She cast a knowing look at Charlotte, who had no idea what happened on Chestnut Street, but could guess. "So I found a couple of customers, earned enough money for a train ticket, and here I am."

"What made you think I would help you?"

Rose's look to her was as blank as if she were reading a handbill. "You just have a look about you," she said. "You've always spoken the truth to me, and you seem like the kind of person who wouldn't turn away a girl in trouble."

Charlotte opened and closed her mouth a couple of times while trying to think of something to say. Was that a compliment or an insult? Hard to tell. Either way, it meant she was a soft touch for someone with a tale of woe, and she supposed that was true. Then the carriage wheel hit a rock and lurched hard to the side, and she had to mind the reins. By the time they had reached a smoother patch of road, the urge to reply had left her. They rode on in silence.

After a mile, Charlotte spoke again. "Tell me about your childhood."

"All right."

So for the rest of the way into Lucinda they took turns, Charlotte describing the years her family followed her father's military postings. She spoke of her beloved twin sister, so vivacious and full of surprises, lost so young in childbirth, and of her mother's struggles after that event. And she heard Rose tell of the small Ohio town where she grew up, her sternly religious father and her meek, obedient mother, her longing for someplace new to see, someone new to become. And the familiar story of a visiting boy, a period of intense feeling, and the predictable outcome of shame and banishment. The thought occurred to Charlotte that her own sister had missed such a fate only by luck or the forbearance of others, for certainly Caroline, for all her charms, had not possessed the fortitude to resist a young man's entreaties. Her young lieutenant had enough moral fiber, or fear of retribution, to behave himself honorably with her. Not that it had done her much good in the long run, besides affording her a proper burial spot when the childbed fever took her. And, presumably, the prospect of Heaven, if one's thoughts tended in that direction.

She glanced at Rose from time to time as they rode, and the idea came to Charlotte that perhaps she had a soft spot for this girl because of her memories of Caroline, rarely reflected upon but always present. They even resembled a bit, in the softness of their features and the vague sense of doom that lingered over them.

And with their conversation, before she knew it they had arrived at Lucinda, smelling the acrid fumes of the match factory long before they saw the first house. Charlotte stopped in front of the office and tied Jack to the hitching rail.

Josephine stepped out to greet them. "Lord, you are the travelingest woman in three counties these days. Every time I see you, you're either going somewhere or just coming back." She took in Rose LaBelle with a sweeping glance, then led them inside, where a pitcher of water rested on the front counter. A scrawny boy of ten stood in the corner, holding a broom. His pants hit him about mid-calf, and he wore a goofy grin that appeared to be his permanent expression.

"This is Roland, my Man Friday," Josephine said. "But sweeping doesn't appear to suit him. Roland, I want you to take Mrs. Turner's horse to the stable, brush him down, and give him grain and water. Half a bucket of grain, no more."

Roland scampered to the door. "Is he mean?" he asked.

"No," Charlotte said. "He's not a mean horse."

"I got bit by a horse one time. Didn't break the skin but it left a bruise I'll never forget."

"Jack won't bite you, or kick you either."

"His name's Jack, eh? I'll call him by his name. That calms them down." And with that he was out and gone.

"Where'd you pick him up?" Charlotte said.

"Just showed up one day," said Josephine. "Roland has his uses. Horses make him nervous, but he'll get over that."

They settled into their chairs and sipped their water. Charlotte decided that the best approach was to get right to it. "Josephine, let me introduce you to Rose Labelle. Rose, this is Josephine Bridges." Josephine extended her hand, and the women shook. "Rose is in a place of trouble in her life, and she came to me for help."

"I had a notion of such a thing." She turned to Rose. "But you're not from around here, I believe. Where did you two meet, pray tell?"

Charlotte started to reply, but Rose spoke up. "At the Fair, ma'am."

"I had a notion of that as well." Her bright, inquisitive eyes returned to Charlotte. "And what sort of timetable are we on here?"

"Rose will know this better than me, but I'd say six months or so. Does that sound right to you, Rose?" She nodded, eyes lowered.

Josephine took it all in and considered. "Let's talk outside," she finally said.

The two of them walked into the street. For a moment Josephine watched Roland lead the horse into the stable, until it was clear that he was managing all right. Then she turned to Charlotte. "Before we talk about this girl, I just want to tell you. Three men boarded the early train this morning. One was Ulysses S. Canterbury, and the other two I didn't know. But I am guessing you do."

Charlotte nodded. "Did they say anything?"

"No. Canterbury told me he'd be back to work when and if he could, but the other two did not seem eager to talk to anyone, including me. Then they were on the train and gone." Josephine gazed northward up the valley as if the disappearing train could still be seen. "Anyway, two trains have passed by since then without stopping, and there's been nothing on the telegraph. So I guess they made it out. Now. What's your plan with this girl here?"

Charlotte closed her eyes. Where to begin? "This girl has run away from her procurer," she said. "He is a violent and dangerous man, and she came to me for help, although I certainly don't count her as a friend. But I couldn't see a clear path to turning her away."

The obvious question remained. "She could not remain in Daybreak," Charlotte continued. "In St. Louis, Adam became enamored with her. So when she showed up, I had to get her out of there before the whole family started to break down. I'm hoping I got her out of town before anyone heard of her presence."

"Ah. I see. You have gone to great lengths for this young woman. Most people would have put her right back on the train."

"Maybe so, but as I said I couldn't find my way there. She's a small-town girl with no family who'll take her in."

"And afterward?"

"I'll write her parents. People's thoughts change when there's a grandchild."

Josephine looked skeptical but didn't express disagreement. "You seem pretty confident of my help, coming all the way here with a girl, a wagon, and a hand case." But she said it with a smile, so Charlotte knew she was coming around.

"Two more things you should know," Charlotte said. "She's a codeine drinker, and from what I saw in St. Louis, she was pretty firmly in its grip."

"I see. We don't have any here or permit it on the premises, so if she wants some she'll have to walk off to town, or sneak onto the train. And in that case she's not my problem anymore."

"True."

"And the other thing?"

Charlotte took a breath. “I told you that her procurer is a dangerous man. Here’s how much. He’s the man responsible for Charley Pettibone’s killing. He didn’t wield the knife, but he gave the order.”

“Good Lord! When you take on a challenge, you never take on the easy ones.” Josephine tapped the side of her nose. “Did she have anything to do with it?”

“Only indirectly. She stole money from Charley to buy codeine, and that’s what kicked the whole thing off.”

Josephine let out a deep sigh. “This girl spreads havoc in all directions. Well, forewarned is forearmed. Let’s go inside.” She stopped and let out a laugh. “Charlotte Turner, you have taken on a challenge to beat all. If I had heard this story about somebody else, I’d have said they’d gone soft in the head.”

Rose was perched on the settee like a pupil waiting her turn for piano lessons. Josephine pulled her chair close and sat across from her. “Can you read and write?”

“Yes, ma’am.”

“Can you cipher?”

“Yes, ma’am.”

“Can you cook?”

“A little.”

“You’ll catch on. It’s not hard. All right, here are my terms.”

Josephine took Rose’s hands in hers and held them tight. “Hm,” she said, rubbing Rose’s palms with her thumbs. “Soft hands are a casualty of life out here. Just so you know that in advance. I’ll take you in, and you will help me with the books and the housework. Do you have anything against colored people?”

Rose seemed taken aback. “No, ma’am.”

“Good, because we have a whole platoon of them working for us, and I’ll not have them disrespected in any way. You’ll help me keep the books, but you won’t handle any money, for obvious reasons. And when your time comes, we will help you through that. All right?”

“Yes.”

“Very well. Mrs. Turner has filled me in on your story. Just so we’re clear on the subject, there will be no repeat of your habits down here, nor of your former occupation. This is a mill camp, and no doubt some of the men will try their hand at drawing you into some kind of relation. But if I catch wind of any such thing, I’ll have you on the next train out, no matter where it’s headed and no matter what your condition. I have enough trouble with our neighbors as it is.”

She paused at watched Rose's face for any sign of disagreement or uncertainty. Seeing none, she continued. "As for the problem with codeine, I sympathize but can't really say I know what to do about it. We've had a few workers with one or another of such problems, drinking and the like, and I know it's hard. Not everyone succeeds at beating the urge. But it may be that hard work will distract you, and if so you're in the right place."

Josephine stood up, and the three of them walked outside. "Roland, bring Mrs. Turner's carriage up," she called. Roland, who appeared to have been lurking around the corner of the house, dashed up the street toward the stable. "That boy's like a demon imp. Just call his name and he materializes out of thin air." She pointed to her house on the hill. "We have a spare room, so that's where you'll stay. I'll introduce you to the Mister at suppertime."

Roland pulled the horse and carriage around, and Rose took her case out of the back.

Josephine spoke one more time. "I'd invite you to stay for supper, but I suspect you've provisioned yourself and would like to get back home," she said to Charlotte, who nodded. "Otherwise, you're welcome here, and we can put you up overnight." She turned to Rose. "The only reason I'm doing this is out of respect for Mrs. Turner. Don't disappoint us, and God help the person in this county who disappoints Mrs. Turner. You wouldn't find anyone to lift you out of the ditch if you did." She took a small notepad and pencil out of her apron pocket and handed it to Rose. "Mrs. Turner plans to write your folks and see if their thoughts have changed. She'll need their address."

Charlotte climbed into the carriage as Rose handed her the paper. She could see that Rose's calm demeanor had broken, and there were tears in her eyes as she mouthed a thank-you.

"Just one thing," Rose said. "My name isn't really Rose. I just picked that because I thought it sounded pretty. When you write my folks, you'd better use my real name. It's Margaret."

"Thank you," Charlotte said. "I'll remember that. Margaret is a lovely name."

Chapter 35

Josephine's question troubled her on the ride home. Would Big Bill really try to retrieve his errant possession? It wasn't impossible. A businessman would see the gains and losses, and would calculate accordingly. Why chase one runaway girl when dozens more arrived at Union Station every day? But Charlotte had a grim suspicion that Bill did not think like an ordinary businessman. Precautions would be needed.

It was full night by the time Charlotte reached home, but lanterns shone in the windows of the Pettibone house, so she stopped. One of the boys opened the door.

"Mother," he called. "Charlotte Turner is here."

Jenny came from the back, wiping her hands on a dishtowel. For a moment the two gazed at each other. Then a sense of all they had passed through over the years, and all they had gone through lately—the hard work and frustration, the struggle for every opportunity, the disappointment and grief—washed over them like a flood, and they fell quietly into a long embrace.

"I'm so sorry," Charlotte said. "For everything."

"I know," said Jenny. "I was unkind earlier. We can't have that. Not with each other."

"Yes. We don't have room for that." She took Jenny's hands. "I have learned more about how Charley came to his end. Whenever you are ready, I will tell you."

"Thank you," Jenny said. "Another day. Some quiet day when we can sit on the porch and drink coffee and talk."

"That's good." An idea came to her, as yet incompletely formed. "Charley's service revolver," she said.

"What about it?"

"Do you think I could borrow it for a few days?"

Jenny's eyebrow arched, but she didn't inquire further. She walked to the rolltop desk in the corner, unlocked it, and took out the wooden pistol box. She handed it to Charlotte. "My boys can help you out if you've got varmints. I expect you'd have better luck with a rifle."

Charlotte smiled. "You know how it is with varmints. You have to be right there at the moment, or else they get away. I'll have this back to you in a few days."

And then it was time for home, and bedding the horse, and bedding herself, and rest for whatever lay ahead.

The next morning she examined the pistol, hefting it in her hand and examining its chambers. She laid it in the bottom of her handbag, which felt as heavy as a sack of flour with it in there.

"Oh well," she said to herself. "It's a silly notion to begin with."

The sound of her own voice startled her. There were other widows around the valley she visited who talked to themselves endlessly, chattering on to their animals and garden plants as if they were sensible of their meaning, and she had always considered them foolish. Now here she was talking out loud to herself just like them.

She brushed out the horse and led him from her barn. He had worked hard yesterday, so she decided to walk him back to Newton's instead of saddling up. Everyone deserved a break now and then.

Just her luck, Adam was outside his house as she passed, trying to reset a tipped-over rain barrel at his roof corner. "Where were you yesterday?" he said. "I was looking for you."

Might as well get to it, she supposed. "I was out on an errand. I should tell you before you hear it from somebody else—it involves you to some degree."

"Does it now?" Adam straightened and put his hands on his hips.

Charlotte nodded, her lips tight. "Rose LaBelle showed up out of nowhere at the train station yesterday. She's run away from her keeper and came to me asking for help." Seeing his worried expression, she added, "Don't worry, she didn't ask for you. She appears to have put your escapade behind her."

Adam's face flicked from relieved to concerned to slightly annoyed. "Then why did she come down here?"

"Like I said, to see me. She had the idea that I would help her."

"And did you?"

"I took her to Lucinda to stay with Josephine."

Adam's cheeks puffed. "I'm surprised she didn't at least ask about me."

"Listen here," Charlotte said. "You should stop and count your blessings. This girl could have made your life difficult in a dozen different ways. Instead, she is giving herself a chance at a new start, and you as well. If you weren't so blinded by your own sense of self-importance, you'd see that. Your job now is to rebuild whatever you can with your family. Your wife and child no longer trust you, and I can't say I blame them."

She turned away from him and continued down the road, sorrowful at having scolded him in such a fierce way but relieved as well. She had finally said some things she had been holding in. She was tired of being discreet, tired of letting Adam think that his literary success had given him some sort of special dispensation. If he wouldn't buckle his suspenders and tend to his family, she had no use for him.

As soon as she got within eyesight of the store, John Wesley ran out to take the reins of her horse. "Mama says I'm to tend him from here," he said. "She says you've been working too hard to do barn chores on top of it."

"That's kind of her," Charlotte said. "Give him an apple. He's done me well the past day."

With the horse and carriage out of her hands, Charlotte felt tempted to return home and rest for the remainder of the day. But her sense of things unfinished nagged at her. She called to the boy as he walked to the barn. "If you will, I need you to saddle the mare. I have one more trip that must be made."

"Yes, ma'am," he said.

Charlotte walked on to the store, where Sarah waited at the window. "All well?" she asked.

"I wouldn't go that far. But the girl's out of the county and in good hands. What's to become of her is not something I can see clearly."

Sarah nodded but did not say anything. Just as well. Charlotte reflected that as a young man, Newton had gone through his own rough patches in life, foolish decisions and impulsive behavior. And now here they were, solid citizens, pillars of the community. Perhaps it was time for them all to suspend judgment on each other for a while.

Out in the field, Newton and the other boys were haying. The spring rains had left the hayfields lush and bent, the heavy seed tops of the grass touching the ground in some places. "That's a fine crop," Charlotte murmured.

"I suppose so," Sarah said with a sniff. "They'll have to turn it over two or three times before they put it up or else it will all go to mold."

Spoken like a true old farmer, always playing down their prospects. Charlotte could remember when working wet hay involved a whole crew of men with pitchforks. Nowadays, even Newton Junior could manage it with a team of horses and a dump rake.

John Wesley arrived with Charlotte's horse. "Not going out again, are you?" Sarah asked.

"One last thing," Charlotte said. "I need to go to town and put my mind at ease on something, and then I'll rest. Tell Newton I will be gone a while. When I come back, I might just loaf on my pillow all week."

They laughed at the absurdity of the thought, and Charlotte walked to the mounting block to climb into the saddle. She was glad for the excuse to depart, for she didn't want to reveal what was on her mind and have to argue her way through their efforts at dissuasion. Sarah followed her out.

Sarah cleared her throat. "I spoke harsh words to you the other day, and I want you to know I regret that. It wasn't the time or place."

It crossed Charlotte's mind to point out that Sarah's sort-of apology was not a retraction. But she held her peace on that subject. Sarah had enough right on her side to make a retraction false anyway. She reached down and took her hand.

"I owe you an apology, too. I resolve to do better in the future, and you are right to point out my failings. People never know their shortcomings until someone directs their attention to them, and I'm no different." And since neither of them was particularly good at apologies, she left it at that.

Charlotte rode home and packed an overnight bag, setting Charley's pistol box into the bottom. "All right, old gal," she said to the horse as she remounted and headed for town. "Double helping of oats when we reach the stable."

She crossed the river and climbed the hill, stopping briefly at Dathan's abandoned house. No signs remained of its temporary occupants, but Charlotte noticed that mice had found their way inside, and a few tentative tendrils of trumpet vine had started to climb a porch post. So it began. Mice and greenery. In a few years the roof would cave in, and within a generation the site would become a lost memory, a place where people would stop and ponder, trying to recall who had lived here once upon a time. And of course she would no longer be here to speak their names.

When she reached town, Charlotte took a room at the hotel and left Maggie for her promised tending. She walked to the café across from the train depot, where the waitress greeted her at the door.

"I have a question for you," Charlotte said as she settled into her chair. "Are you open whenever the trains arrive?"

"Yes, ma'am," the waitress said. "We probably get half our trade from those trains. Four a day, from early morning till late of an evening. We pretty much set our clocks by those trains."

"That's good to know. I'm supposed to meet someone arriving, but I don't know which train they'll be coming on. So I will take my meals here and keep a watch out."

"Wonderful! I'll save you a table by the window."

"That is most kind."

She bought a coffee out of politeness, then strolled across the street to the depot to study the timetable posted on the wall. Early morning, late morning, mid-afternoon, suppertime. Watching the trains would become an expensive proposition if she ate a meal at the café every time, but so be it. After a few days she would have to give up the idea. She walked back to her hotel room for a nap.

In the evening she returned to the café, valise in hand, and ate a heavy meal of boiled beef and vegetables while she waited for the train to arrive. A scattering of passengers emerged, none of whom she recognized. She finished the meal and left.

The same was true the next day, at breakfast, late coffee, and lunch. Passers-by and waitresses were all she saw, but she didn't mind the lack of conversation. She felt as though she had been talking too much lately as it was.

But in the evening as she sat by the window, there came Bobby Renick with his wagon, its contents discreetly covered with canvas. She watched him pass the café on his way to the tucked-away spot where he liked to park, where passengers in the know could find him.

Charlotte thought about leaving the café through the rear door, avoiding him, but changed her mind. After all, she was trying to set things right all around. Why not with him as well?

She finished her meal and walked across the street. Bobby's head jerked up in surprise as he saw her approach. But then his face took on its characteristic hard, blank expression, the face of a man determined to reveal nothing.

"Evening, Bobby," Charlotte said.

Renick nodded. "Ma'am."

"There's something I want to talk to you about."

"If it's about that man Canterbury, don't bother. I reckon he's got run off."

"It's not about him, it's about you and your business."

His face grew suspicious. "Oh yeah?"

"A few days ago, a man from the Revenue Office was here in town. He learned where your works are, and in a couple or three weeks he plans to come back and break them up. I advise you to move them to a new location, at least temporarily."

Renick's eyes grew wide. "You know all this for sure?"

"Sure as my birthday."

"How do you know all these things?"

"Because I'm the one who tattled on you. I was angry over the way you were treating Mr. Canterbury, and I wanted to get back at you."

"Hm. Repented of the deed, have you?"

"I won't say that. But country folk need to stick together, I suppose, and I don't see any point in continuing my campaign now that Mr. Canterbury's returned to St. Louis."

Renick took on an aggrieved look. "Do you know how much trouble it's going to cause me to have to move my operation?"

"I don't know but I can guess, and frankly I don't care. If you don't want trouble in your life, get into an honest line of work."

"You are a hard-headed woman, Mrs. Turner."

"Guilty as charged."

"The least you could do is apologize for putting me through all this."

"I wouldn't lie awake waiting for that, Mr. Renick. Just think, if you had found Mr. Canterbury a week ago, you'd probably have hanged him, and then I would have had to swear against you in court to try to get you hanged too. And then no matter what the outcome, our families would have been enemies for life. So from my perspective, I'm doing you a favor, and myself one as well, though I'll grant that's a little harder to see."

She was near to walking away but stopped herself. "You really would have hung him, wouldn't you?" she said over her shoulder.

Bobby shrugged. "I was on a ten-day drunk. Who knows?" The hard shell clamped back over his features, and there was nothing more to say about something that would have happened for no reason and ruined them all.

Another trainload of strangers, and Charlotte returned to the hotel. Perhaps her concerns were just idle fictions, the product of an overdramatic imagination. She would give herself another day or two before calling it quits. The St. Louis newspapers had arrived, so she bought a couple for bedtime.

And there on the front page was the headline:

SAVAGES RETURN TO FAIR VILLAGE
AFTER MYSTERY EXCURSION.

She read the news account with dismay. How a pair of villagers from the deep Philippine jungle had set out on a lark, determined to see the sights of the city. The writer hinted that the outing might have been prompted by an infatuation of the younger member of the pair for a dark-skinned visitor who had visited the fair, possibly a Mexican, leading them to run off in search of her rooming house. The two had been welcomed back to their compound by their fellow villagers, although they steadfastly refused to say exactly where they had been and what they had been doing. Their supervisor, Professor Pinckney, announced that the group would likely travel to Boston or Philadelphia at the close of the fair to participate in further scientific and public demonstration, pending the successful completion of financial and lodging arrangements.

It was enough to make her cry, the enactment of all of Chaia-ngasup's fears. More dislocation and exhibition, more distance from home. He was probably right. He would die in some strange cold city, an ocean and a continent away from his fields and his people.

She turned out the lamp and lay in the darkness, listening but not listening to the sounds of footsteps in the hallway, talkers in other rooms, until sleep finally deadened her brain.

The next morning she started the cycle again, visiting the café for breakfast, watching the passengers debark, walking around town, returning for the next train's arrival. She knew her presence was becoming talked about, and she knew also that it was only a matter of time before Newton or one of the boys arrived to pick up a guest, and then the questions would begin, and she would return home, if for no other reason than family pressure. One more day, maybe two, and that would be the end. Just as well. This whole adventure was starting to feel like a fool's errand.

And then she sat down for late lunch in the café to watch for the third train, which pulled into the station right on time. She watched the passengers straggle onto the landing: families returning home from the city, drummers with their cases of samples. She took a bite of her plain cheese sandwich and contemplated her future. And the last passenger off the train, stepping off just before the wheels began to turn, in a tan checkered suit with his valise in his hand, was Big Bill Langland.

Chapter 36

Charlotte had rehearsed what she would say and do if the confrontation ever came, but all those thoughts fled from her mind. In the absence of a plan there was only action. She got up from her table and walked to the door.

"Hold my spot, if you would," she told the waitress. "I'll be right back."

Langland stood on the platform, surveying the scene, and the sight of Charlotte crossing the street, walking directly toward him, soon caught his eye. He set his valise on the plank sidewalk and folded his arms as she approached. Charlotte stopped in the street and looked up at him.

"I should have known she'd send you," Big Bill said. "Where is the little bitch?"

"She didn't send me and has no idea you're here. You overestimate your importance, sir."

"Maybe so. But where is she? My man confirms that she bought a ticket to this God-forsaken burg."

"I sent her away. I couldn't have her here, or in Daybreak."

"Sent here where?"

"That's not for me to say."

"Hm."

Charlotte regarded him for a moment. "I think we owe each other a conversation. I have a table over there." She turned and walked away, not looking back.

She knew that Langland could hail a liveryman, or simply walk off in search of lodgings, or any of a dozen different things, but she gambled that he would take her departure as a challenge. And sure enough, by the time she reached the door of the café he was behind her. She walked to her table and sat down. Big Bill took the seat opposite from her.

"So converse then," he said.

Charlotte waited for a minute while the waitress arrived with coffee. She didn't know exactly what she wanted to say. "I had guessed you might send someone," she finally said. "But I'm not surprised you came yourself."

Big Bill interlaced his fingers and rested his hands on the table. "Some things can be delegated, and some cannot. This business is one of the latter. You seem like a reasonable woman. I expect you understand this."

He hunched his shoulders and leaned forward. Charlotte knew he was using his bulk to intimidate her, but refused to allow it to bother her.

"I wouldn't expect too much. We may have different ideas about what is reasonable."

"I often find that is the case. But I think of myself as a reasonable man as well. I have simple needs and ask for simple things. Like now, for instance. You couldn't have Rose here in your little town. I understand that completely. So you sent her away. All I want to know is where you sent her. One lone fact, and then I will leave you alone."

Charlotte cut her cheese sandwich into small squares. It had gotten cold, but she ate a couple of bites anyway. In small pieces, they went down easier somehow, and gave her time to think.

"I'm a simple person, too. And I'd like some information as well. I'd like to hear about how Charley Pettibone met his end. I learned the general story from Rose, but I don't think I understand the full event."

Big Bill waved his hand in annoyance. "What's there to understand? Your friend was a troublesome, annoying old man. End of story, as far as I'm concerned." He paused. "Besides, I didn't witness anything. And don't think you can trick me into saying something incriminating. What a man says in conversation ain't the same as testimony. I know the law."

"I'm sure you do. And I'm not interested in your legal affairs. That's between you and the law."

He gave her a sly look. "You're not going to preach to me, are you?"

"Hardly."

"Good. I've been preached to before, and it didn't take."

They measured each other across the table. Big Bill spoke first. "As I said, I'm a reasonable man. You want to know about your friend, I'll tell you. He came over to my place of business, yelling and hollering about his mistreatment. Now I'll admit, my saloon isn't exactly a tea room, but some things are just not allowed. And one of those is frightening off customers, which is exactly what he was doing. So I told Two-Eyes and Greasy to take care of him."

"Did you tell them to kill him?"

He frowned, but his gaze did not waver. "That's not an instruction you give in my line of work. If he'd a run off when they came out, he'd be alive today."

"Perhaps."

"No 'perhaps' to it. Dead people are bad for business. You can't imagine the amount of money I've had to pay to keep this quiet."

Charlotte pushed her plate away and signaled to the waitress. "I believe we've conversed enough."

"Agreed." Big Bill snapped a dollar coin onto the table. "That should make the waitress' day. So one last time: Where's the girl?"

"'The girl'? Can't you even bring yourself to say her name?"

"I'll call her whatever I damn well please, thank you very much. That girl has cost me a pretty penny, with her thieving habits and dope-fiend ways. I intend to extract my investment from the little bitch."

Charlotte lifted her handbag from the floor and placed it on the table so that it screened the view of the rest of the customers. "Mr. Langland, I want to show you something."

She took out the pistol box and opened the lid, then drew out the revolver and laid it on the table with its muzzle pointing directly at Big Bill's midsection. She pulled back the hammer and cocked it, leaving her hand draped over the trigger guard.

Big Bill didn't move. "What, you're going to shoot me?"

"I haven't made up my mind. But I want to make sure I have your undivided attention."

She paused to let the words settle. "I've handled firearms since my younger days, so let me assure you. If I do shoot you, it won't be by accident."

Big Bill sat very still, his hands folded as before, but his eyes focused on the barrel of the gun.

"It's too far to reach without risking I'd get a shot off," Charlotte said. "Even with the kick, and the pistol on its side, it would be hard for me to miss. So you might as well listen to what I have to say."

"I suppose so." Big Bill's voice was hoarse.

Now it was Charlotte's turn to lean forward. "This is Charley Pettibone's old service pistol. He carried it for twenty years while serving as deputy sheriff down here, but he rarely used it, and he often left it behind when he thought its presence might inflame matters. I'm guessing that's why he left it behind when he went to your whorehouse to collect his stolen money."

She felt her heart racing, and slowed herself down to keep from saying or doing anything rash. "You are right. Charley was a troublesome, annoying old man. But he was also a respected member of this community. He came up from nothing, he followed his conscience even when it didn't match what other people wanted him to do, and he didn't deserve the fate your men handed him. So if you wonder whether I'm feeling vengeful, the answer is yes, I am."

No one had noticed their intense conversation, at least not that Charlotte could tell. But she knew she needed to finish it soon.

"Charley was so well respected around here that when he showed up, criminals often surrendered to him without so much as an argument. That's because they knew he respected them, and he respected the law, and he wouldn't let them fall victim to the mob. Because I'm sorry to tell you, there are times around here when the mob would take the law into their own hands if given a chance. We were a hair's breadth away from a lynching last week."

Out of the corner of her eye she noticed that a man had walked past the windows of the café three times now, casually glancing in but not slowing down. She didn't recognize him, and his clothes marked him as an out-of-towner. The old timers' saying was right: Snakes travel in pairs.

She lowered her voice. "So you can imagine how bad for business it would be if I stood up right now and announced that you were the man who killed Charley Pettibone. I can't predict what would happen. Perhaps someone would run for the sheriff. Or perhaps the mob would assemble, and in twenty minutes you'd be swinging from the railroad bridge north of town. Charley wouldn't want that, because he believed in the equal application of the law. But Charley's not here. And you're left to deal with a vengeful old lady who can't decide whether to denounce you or just shoot you and be done with it."

Langland's expression was incredulous. "Are you trying to threaten me?"

"Looks that way. The northbound train arrives in ten minutes. I'm going to sit right here and watch. And if you aren't on it, I'm going to stand up at this table and holler that you're the man who killed Charley. And we'll see what happens."

He glowered at her in silence.

"And make sure your friend gets on with you, or else he'll be the one I point the finger at."

Big Bill's face reddened and his neck muscles tensed, the face of a man who was not accustomed to being talked to in such a way. Charlotte let her index finger drop down inside the trigger guard in case he did something sudden.

"Why are you sticking up for this girl? She's the one who betrayed your friend. She'll betray you, too, when it suits her. If you think she can be reformed, you're wasting your time. It's hopeless."

"So it's hopeless. I'm doing it anyway."

Langland looked at her in mystification. His glance drifted to the pistol.

"All right," he said. "But you can expect I'll be back."

"I doubt that. You have your watchers at the train station in St. Louis, and I'll have mine here. You're too good a businessman to chase a lost investment into uncertain territory—twice."

It was flattery, and they both knew it. But it was enough to give him an excuse to cast one more baleful look in her direction, tap his hat back onto his head, and walk out into the summer sunlight. He crossed the street and signaled to his companion, who was standing at the far corner, and together they walked into the depot.

Charlotte slowly lowered the hammer on the pistol with her thumb and placed it back into its box. She took some long, slow breaths and tried to calm the pounding of her heart. She didn't want to lift her coffee cup because she feared her hands would shake so much that she would spill the remainder, so she folded them in her lap and watched out the window.

She thought about what Big Bill was up to in the depot. Trying to bribe the station agent to tell him where Rose LaBelle had gone after arriving here, probably. Good luck with that.

A few minutes later, the northbound line from Belmont pulled in on time. No passengers debarked.

Charlotte waited. The wheels of the train began to turn, the couplings clanking one by one. She was about to stand up and walk to the door when the unmistakable form of Big Bill Langland came to the rear platform, his confederate beside him. Big Bill snipped the tips off two cigars, handing one to the man and keeping one for himself.

And as the train lurched forward, he lit his cigar and tipped his hat in her direction.

Chapter 37

The reply from Ohio was swift and brief, with careful logic and Biblical support in every sentence, explaining how forgiveness had to be preceded by repentance. It went on in great detail about how the love of God was infinite, but required a contrite heart and acts of restoration before it could begin to work in the human realm. There were innocent souls to be considered, whose well-being could be put in danger by proximity to a possibly unrepentant sinner, and of course the building of a faith community was a delicate matter, likely to be upset by the presence of one whose morals were subject to constant and deep question.

The judgmental, condescending tone of the letter was not lost on Charlotte, but she decided not to mention that in her next letter to Josephine conveying the news that there would be no return to Ohio for Margaret. They had all stopped using "Rose LaBelle" by unspoken agreement, as if Rose had simply disappeared and a new individual, Margaret Wightman, had appeared in the space she had formerly occupied. Just as pregnant, just as troubled, but with a new name that seemed to suggest a different set of prospects.

The man from the revenue bureau appeared after a month had passed, with a chartered railcar full of officers and a couple of reporters. But by then the Renicks had vacated. Some said they had crossed the line into Iron County, while others declared that they had returned to their origins east of town somewhere. In any event, the old silver mine was empty except for a few crocks and a boiler, which the revenue men dutifully smashed for the newspaper artist.

A few weeks later, she wrote to Ulysses S. Canterbury in St. Louis, letting him know that his chief antagonist had relocated in case he wished to return to his claim. Again, the reply was swift and brief, though far less certain. He appreciated the news about his former neighbors and would give thought to a return, but in the meantime he had to provide for his family and had found work in a factory on the north side, close enough to home that he didn't even have to spend money on streetcar fares on pleasant days. They had not visited the Fair. Negro Day had been canceled. So had his regimental reunion, in a dispute over whether they would be allowed to parade in full gear with shouldered arms, like a proper unit. Canterbury supposed he would have to decide about the property when tax time came, but until then he would work, keep his head down, and save his pennies. The missus sent special regards to her, and he would appreciate being remembered to Mr. and Mrs. Bridges.

Charlotte thought about writing him back, but she had said what she had to say. Reading his friendly but careful words, she realized a wall stood between them that could never be breached, no matter how much good will was expended upon it. She was a white woman, and he was a black man, two unalterable facts that reached out from the well of history and altered everything. They could look upon each other with respect; they could furnish help and support; but the barriers were too great for them to be friends. Perhaps future generations would find a way.

She walked up the hill to his homestead that afternoon. There wasn't much left in the cabin, just a cot and some cooking utensils, and Charlotte could tell that raccoons had found their way inside. At the corner of his diggings stood a heavy wooden box, secured with a pair of strap latches, and inside were all his rock-cutting tools, oiled and sharpened and neatly stacked. Charlotte reminded herself to ask one of the boys to come up with a wagon and collect them for safekeeping. And she would ask him nicely, and say please and thank you, and praise him for a job well done. She had not yet fully mended things with Sarah.

From Canterbury's she walked along the ridge, hoping to locate Dathan's grave, which she had not yet seen. And sure enough there it was, at the base of an outcrop of limestone atop the mountain, looking south toward the valley. She couldn't see Daybreak through the foliage but guessed that if she returned in winter the view would be fine indeed. So this was Dathan's lookout. Canterbury had marked the gravesite with one of his granite blocks, with "Dathan 1904" chiseled on the top. A good enough marker for anyone.

J.M. Bridges showed up on an October morning, before noon, which could only mean that he had left before dawn. Charlotte knew what that meant and started packing her kit before Bridges dismounted from his horse. By the time he reached the door she was ready.

"Josephine says she will need your help by nightfall or perhaps some later," he said as she opened the door.

Charlotte nodded. "Ride down and fetch Petey. I'll be ready to go by the time you return. We can take my wagon."

The trip was quiet at first, with all of them thinking about the tribulations ahead, but J.M.'s sociability soon appeared. "Margaret hasn't been a bit of trouble," he ventured.

"Is that right?" Josephine's letters had provided a more mixed account, but then Josephine tended to be more severe in general.

"Yes, ma'am. She's had her struggles, but who wouldn't?" Ever the optimist. "I think we're going to keep her around after this is all over. That is, if she wants to stay."

Charlotte hadn't felt it was her place to lobby for such a decision, but was glad to hear it. What else would become of Margaret if she didn't stay in Lucinda? A baby, a checkered past, and no family to take her in. The thought was too ugly to dwell on. "I'm happy she has worked out for you," she said.

"Yes, she's good with numbers and is learning things around the house. She's not the best cook, but all things in due time. And how's your family?"

"Well enough. We're getting back to normal from our adventure at the Fair. Adam's working on a new book for Mr. Kellogg, and Newton is thinking about running for office." It was a broken sort of normal, though, full of painful silences that stretched over deep wounds.

"What's the new book about?"

"Not sure. Something about an itinerant newspaper editor who comes to a town and exposes people's hypocrisies."

"That sounds fine. Plenty of those to go around."

Charlotte glanced over her shoulder at Petey in the back of the wagon, uncharacteristically quiet. She remembered the first time she attended a birth, always a frightening day, a day with no guarantee, a day marked by pain and mess. By the time they arrived in Lucinda, the shadows were lengthening across their path. It was likely to be a long night.

Josephine met her at the door. "Everything's all right so far," she said. "At least I think so."

Charlotte washed her hands at the kitchen sink, then walked into the bedroom, where Margaret lay propped up on a heap of pillows. Her face was drawn and frightened.

"Evening, honey," Charlotte said, placing her hand on her forehead. No fever, good sign. "Let's get this business over with as soon as we can, shall we?"

"No argument here," Margaret said through clenched teeth.

Charlotte checked to make sure J.M. was out of the room, then lifted the sheet to examine her body. She probed with two fingers. Everything felt normal.

The herbs she had brought to brew, in case the delivery needed hastening, seemed unnecessary. Why rush what would come in its own time? But Petey needed something to do, so Charlotte set her to the job. "And brew me some regular tea while you're at it," she said. "I could use the refreshment."

She moved to the chair beside the bed.

"Here's what to expect. You'll feel these contractions for another few hours. They'll grow more intense and painful. I'm sorry for that, but remember, it's only temporary. Your body is just adjusting to the task of giving birth, which puts a lot of strain on it. So it's understandable that it hurts. We'll stay with you the whole time. Don't be afraid."

So they waited, and as they waited they talked. For what else was there to do between contractions besides talk, and mop her face from time to time, and feel for changes? The conversation distracted Margaret, at least momentarily, so they kept it going with every topic they could think of. Josephine spoke of her desire for a family, a desire that had gone unfulfilled, and made the offer that J.M. had mentioned. But she put it in personal terms, telling her that although they had never had children of their own, she hoped that they could help Margaret raise her youngster so she could experience the pleasure of childrearing even from this remove. And naturally, when presented in those terms Margaret could only agree. For Josephine had made it sound as though she would be doing them a favor instead of the other way around.

And Charlotte spoke of childbirth, and of how she had no recollection of the pain. Something in the experience made the pain disappear after it was over with, so perhaps that would be a comfort to know. She spoke of how children changed one's perspective on the world, made it both smaller and yet somehow more threatening, made some things outsized in their importance while others disappeared. She talked about being a mother even when her children were adults, the instincts that never left. Although she didn't speak directly of their situation at the Fair, when she talked about how motherhood imparted an unexpected fierceness in her, the implications were clear.

And Petey spoke of her life ahead, how she hoped to go to college somewhere, and how opportunities for girls were opening up like never before. She had read of women who became scientists and doctors, leaders in life, women of consequence. At that she looked up, embarrassed. "Not that you are not women of consequence," she said. "Far from it."

"That's all right, girl," Josephine said. She reached out and gripped Petey's hand. "You follow that path. Even when it seems overgrown with briars, follow that path. Cut your way through it when you need to."

In time the pains grew stronger and more frequent. Charlotte knew that the critical moment had arrived. She brought Margaret to the side of the bed, her legs dangling, and knelt in front of her. "Put your hands on my shoulders," she said. "Push when I tell you."

Margaret's breath was hot on her face as they braced against each other. Then her fingers gripped deep into Charlotte's shoulders, and the grapple intensified.

The minutes passed, the labor continued. Then she felt the crowning head, and she managed to get her fingers underneath the chin, and then the shoulders, and the next thing she knew it was in her hands, slippery and limp, but with a heartbeat and all its parts intact, as far as she could tell by the lamplight. She cut the cord and handed the baby to Josephine, who stood by with a blanket.

Charlotte labored through the final cleanup, waiting for the sound they all were waiting for. And there it was, a baby's cry, strong and clear, no wheezing or whistling, just the ordinary cry of a baby who had entered the world in the ordinary way, unaware of wealth or status or legitimacy. Just a baby seeking air and nourishment like all others.

"It's a girl," Josephine said softly.

"All right, then," Charlotte said.

Josephine brought the baby, wiped clean and yawning, back to the bed. But Margaret had fallen exhausted onto the pillows, her eyes closed. Charlotte stood up and took the baby in her arms.

"Let her rest a while," she whispered.

Her back ached from the strain of the past few hours, and she too felt a profound exhaustion.

Charlotte walked outside into the starlit night, with Petey beside her. She pulled the blanket a little closer around the baby and listened to the sound of cicadas in the trees. Another child in the world, a fatherless, nameless being with nothing between it and the elements but this thin blanket and the loving care of strangers.

"Here," she said to Petey. "Take her a while."

Petey cradled the baby, a little nervous but unafraid. "Hello, baby," she whispered. "Grandma, I know they say she's not my sister, but I feel like her sister anyway. I hope that's all right."

"Of course it's all right."

In the distance the creek gurgled. Charlotte sat heavily on the steps, turned her face toward the darkness, and all at once began to cry, deep tears that seemed to come from her very center. And whether they were tears of relief, or apprehension, or fulfillment, or sadness, she could not say.

She released herself to the feeling, let the cry run its course, and after a minute the surge passed. She took her breath in long, aching draws. Danger and babies, and women to shield them. So it was and always had been. But why despair? So what if the world was full of harm and evil, and liars and graspers who stole and seized? A deeper wisdom ran beneath it all, the wisdom of love and persistence, which those men always failed to see. The doing of things you knew to be hopeless simply because they were right. And watching Petey coo and cradle this little lump of possibility, how could she feel anything but hope, despite the madness and cruelty of the world?

Charlotte stretched and yawned. In the distance she could hear the whistle of the northbound train, which would rumble past in another ten minutes or so. It would be morning soon.

The End

Questions for Book Club Discussion

1. How would you contrast the world of Daybreak with the world of St. Louis at this moment in history? What would you say are the most important characteristics of each region?

2. Charlotte Turner is the central character of the novel. How would you describe her? What are her dominant traits? How would you describe the relationship between Charlotte and her granddaughter Petey?

3. What is your perception (if any) of the St. Louis World's Fair of 1904? What significance do you think the Fair had for its time? How do you see it nowadays?

4. Charlotte is the dominant character in the Daybreak series of *Slant of Light, This Old World, The Language of Trees*, and now *Land of Joys*. How do you see her evolving as the series progresses?

5. What would you say are the main themes and motifs of the novel? Where do you see them beginning to take shape, and how do you see them developing as the novel progresses?

6. What symbolism do you see in the treatment of the natural landscape in this novel?

7. If there was something you could say to one of the characters in *Land of Joys*, who would it be, and what would you tell that person?

Acknowledgments

This book required a great deal of research, and for that reason I feel certain that I will forget some of my sources. For that I apologize. I do hope these acknowledgements will capture the most important ones.

For Ozarks history, the go-to source for anyone seeing a broad but thorough understanding of the region is Brooks Blevins' three-volume *A History of the Ozarks*, published by the University of Arkansas Press in 2018, 2019, and 2021. These books hold a valued place on my shelf, and I refer to them regularly. For knowledge about more specialized elements of Ozarks history, the list is long and rich. The grim story of lynching and expulsion of Black people in the Ozarks is covered in depth in Kimberly Harper's *White Man's Heaven* (Arkansas, 2010), and the social upheaval caused by the coming of modernity to the region is explored in David Benac's *Conflict in the Ozarks* (Truman State, 2010). The essays collected in *The Ozarks in Missouri History: Discoveries in an American Region*, edited by Lynn Morrow (Missouri, 2013), cast light on a wide range of Ozarks historical topics, and I found many of them helpful.

Before I began work on this book, my knowledge of the Louisiana Purchase Exposition (more commonly known as the St. Louis World's Fair) was limited to "Meet Me in St. Louis" and a few random articles. The more I learned, the more I realized that the Fair was a complicated and multi-layered experience that encapsulated many of the contradictory sides of turn-of-the-century America: its optimism, its faith in technology, its vulgarity, its entrenched racism, its boundless faith in "progress" however that term was defined at the moment. Two books were particularly helpful in my understanding of the Fair: James Gilbert's *Whose Fair?* (Chicago, 2009) and *Anthropology Goes to the Fair* by Nancy J. Parezo and Don D. Fowler (Nebraska, 2007). I hasten to remind the reader that my Fair is a fictional one, and although I have tried to keep the geographical and historical elements of the Fair as accurate as I needed to, I am more interested in what it represented for Americans of the time. When necessary for plot or character development, I have departed from the historical record. If you want to learn more about the actual Fair, I highly recommend becoming involved with the 1904 World's Fair Society (1904WorldsFairSociety.org), which is a wonderful group of Fair enthusiasts and historians who, unlike me, are scrupulous about maintaining accuracy in every detail.

The staff and the resources of the State Historical Society of Missouri have been particularly helpful to me in the creation of this book, and I wish to extend my thanks to them. I am perpetually refreshed by the scholarship presented at the annual Ozarks Studies Conference sponsored by Missouri State University-West Plains, and I'm likewise thrilled to see the resurgence of the Ozarks Studies Association, which had been dormant for a while but is now back and encouraging scholarship on a range of Ozarks topics.

Any writer who uses the Ozarks as a setting owes a debt to the tireless Phillip Howerton, who has raised the profile of Ozarks literature through his editing of anthologies such as *The Literature of the Ozarks* (Arkansas, 2019) and *Wild Muse: Ozarks Nature Poetry* (Cornerpost, 2022), his scrupulous editing and reissuing of classic early Ozarks writing, and his own writing and publishing. Phil has just about singlehandedly made Ozarks literature a part of the American canon. Here's a tip of the hat in the direction of West Plains.

My family, my loved ones, my friends, my writing partners, and most of all my readers help keep me going through the dry patches. I will never be able to express my gratitude adequately.

Special thanks are reserved for everyone at the Amphorae Publishing Group, who have been perpetually helpful as the publication of this novel series proceeds. In particular, Kristina Blank Makansi has edited every one of these books with patience and sensitivity, and they would not be the same without her.

About the Author

Steve Wiegenstein grew up in the eastern Missouri Ozarks and roams its backwoods and roads every chance he gets. The Black River and the Annapolis Branch Library were his two main haunts as a kid, and they remain his Mecca and Medina to this day. He is a longtime scholar of the 19th century Icarian movement in America, which provided the inspiration for the Daybreak series. He taught journalism, English, and communication for a number of colleges and universities during his career, but is now retired from teaching and writes full-time. He also writes and blogs about rural and Ozarks issues at stevewiegenstein.wordpress.com. The son of a rural librarian, he received the Missouri Author Award from the Missouri Library Association in 2022.